REQUIEM

WORLD FALLEN

SUSANNA STROM

The World Fallen Series

Pandemonium

Maelstrom

Bedlam

Cataclysm

Requiem

Visit my website at https://susannastrom.com/
https://www.facebook.com/susannastromauthor/
https://www.facebook.com/groups/1572291033136914

Developmental Editor: Christina Trevaskis
www.bookmatchmaker.com

Interior Designer: Jovana Shirley
Unforeseen Editing, www.unforeseenediting.com

Proofreader: Brittany Meyer-Strom
brittanym.edits@gmail.com

Cover Designer: Lori Jackson Designer
www.lorijacksondesign.com

Photography: Wander Aguiar Photography
www.wanderbookclub.com

Model: Kaz van der Waard

ISBN ebook: 978-1-7348292-8-0
ISBN paperback: 978-1-7348292-9-7

Published by Cougar Creek Publishing LLC

ONE

Georgia

"You sure about this?" Rachel cocked her head to one side and wrinkled her nose. "There's no going back once we do it."

I pointed to her spiky pixie cut. "Since when are you afraid of scissors?"

Rachel snorted. "We're not talking about me, Goldilocks." She tugged on a strand of hair that reached halfway down my back. "It's a big change. You really want to chop it off?"

"Do I *want* to chop it off?" I repeated, staring off into the distance.

The head of security for Marcus Havoc had a nose like a bloodhound when it came to sniffing out a lie. There was no point in offering a breezy assurance that I could care less about cutting off my hair.

I cared.

As long as I could remember, my long hair had been a familiar and comforting presence. When I was little, after every bath, I'd sit on a stool, chatting a mile a minute while my mom gently combed out the tangles. My hair would stream behind me when I chased my friends through the neighborhood. When I was tired, I'd twist a strand around my finger and make a little loop that I'd bounce my thumb against. When I wanted to retreat from the world, I'd lean forward and hide my face behind a veil of hair. I loved feeling it brush against my shoulders and its weight against my skin.

Did I want to lose my security blanket, something that tied me to my memories of childhood and home? No, but I would.

The pandemic that burned across the globe last summer had upended the world, robbing us all of family and friends, of our old familiar lives. In the big picture, cutting off my hair was no more than a blip on the radar. Time to pull up my big girl pants and do what needed to be done.

I sat up straight on the counter stool and met her eyes in the bathroom mirror. "I need to change up my appearance, and it's too much hair to hide under a wig. Just do it."

Still frowning, Rachel held up the stainless steel scissors. "Will Finn be okay with it?"

I blinked. "Finn? What does Finn have to do with anything?"

Rachel lifted one arched brow. "You telling me that you two aren't—" She made a suggestive hand gesture.

I rolled my eyes. "No, we're not. And even if we were, he wouldn't get a vote on whether or not I cut my hair."

"C'mon." Rachel leaned toward me, her eyes glittering. Marcus's bloodhound had caught a scent. "The way you two have been drooling over each other for the past month, you telling me you haven't boned yet?"

"Jesus." I made a face. "Did you forget that we're about to go to war with Allsop? This is no time to get distracted by—um—boning."

She shot me a pitying look. "If you plan to wait until the world is safe and secure to start something with Finn, your vadge is going to shrivel up from neglect."

I laughed. "My vadge and I thank you for your concern."

Rachel raised one slim shoulder. "I want my friends to be happy."

"How about you?" I countered. "Anybody making *you* happy?"

She flashed a satisfied smile. "Yep."

"Who?" I dragged the word out.

"Nobody you know." Her face took on a complacent expression, like the cat that got the cream. "Actually, *two* nobodies you know. Both very *fine* men." She waggled her brows. Clearly, she wasn't talking about their moral virtues.

Rachel had two guys? I shouldn't be surprised. The flu had killed every woman who came down with it, but a small percentage of the men survived the viral infection. Men outnumbered women in the post-pandemic world. Not everyone was wired for monogamy. Poly might become the new normal. Still, human nature being what it was, complications might arise, complications that could distract Rachel and jeopardize our mission.

"That could get messy."

"Nah. It's all good. Everybody is on board. In fact..." She grinned and her whole face lit up. "Sometimes the three of us—"

I held up a hand. "I don't need the details, but you go girl."

Rachel snapped the scissors open and shut. "So how short do you want it?"

While working undercover in Boise, spying on Allsop's organization, I'd been in the same room with Jonesy once or twice. Odds were he wouldn't remember me hovering in the background, posing as a member of the housekeeping staff at the downtown barracks. But I couldn't risk Allsop's hatchet man recognizing me by my most identifiable feature.

I suppressed a shiver.

"Maybe an inch past my chin. With bangs."

I sucked in a breath, steeling my nerves for the chop.

"You got it." Rachel ran her fingers through my thick hair. "What'd you do with all this when you were in the army?"

"Ponytail. Much better than those tight granny buns they used to make women soldiers wear."

"No kidding." Rachel shuddered. "I get a headache just thinking about wearing a bun." She snapped the scissors again. "Ready?"

I squeezed my eyes shut. "Yes." I was willing to cut off my hair, but I didn't want to witness the act.

Rachel kept up a steady stream of chatter while she lopped off my long locks. With each snip, my head grew lighter. Cool air touched my bare nape. The unaccustomed weight of bangs grazed my forehead. The scissors clattered against the counter.

"Open your eyes," Rachel ordered.

Leaning forward, I stared at my unfamiliar reflection. Still me, but different. My eyes looked bigger and my neck longer. I gulped, stunned into silence for a good five seconds.

"Shit. You hate it," Rachel said.

"No, I don't hate it. But it's going to take a minute to get used to it."

"And we're just getting started." She lined a dozen boxes of drugstore hair color across the counter, ranging from dark blond, to red, to black. "Pick a color."

I eyed the boxes. I was tempted to go red—my friend Nyx's burgundy red hair was gorgeous—but a less flashy shade was the order of the day. I pointed to a medium brown. "That one."

An hour later, after towel drying my short, newly dyed brown hair, Rachel and I hiked over to the small downtown Pendleton police station where Jonesy was being held.

By the time we reached the doors, my heart was hammering a mile a minute. Training kept my face a casual mask, but the thought of seeing Jonesy again made my throat go dry. We waved to the guard sitting behind the old reception desk, hung our coats on hooks, then walked down a corridor past the interrogation and observation rooms. Inside the janitor's closet at the end of the hall, one of Havoc's soldiers was pouring water into a commercial mop bucket.

"You know how to use the wringer?" he asked me.

"Yes."

I'd worked part-time at a mom-and-pop diner in high school and often had to swab the floors after closing. I pushed the big yellow bucket as we made our way up the hall toward the block of holding cells. Rachel unlocked the door, then handed me the key ring, which I clipped to my belt loop.

"Play it cool," she said in a low voice.

"I got it."

"Later." Rachel raised a hand in farewell, then she and the soldier retreated.

Dread prickled my scalp. Putting my palm on the door, I willed my hand not to shake. I slapped on my game face, the bored, slightly disgruntled expression of a woman who thought she was made for better things than mopping floors.

I shoved open the metal door, then held it in place with my shoulder as I wheeled the heavy bucket through. Inside the cellblock, I released the door. It slammed shut with a loud click that echoed off the walls and polished concrete floor.

My gaze swept over my surroundings, taking in the details of the spartan environment. Situational awareness was key to any mission.

To my left, four holding cells lined the corridor. To my right, a long wall topped with high windows ran opposite the cells. Through the metal bars covering the glass, sunlight flooded the cellblock and chased away the encroaching shadows.

Jonesy occupied the first cell, a bare-bones cubicle even before the pandemic crashed the infrastructure. Bolts screwed a narrow metal bed to the floor. The small sink hanging on the wall was useless, the faucets dry. The stainless steel toilet anchored to the floor had long since stopped functioning. A five-gallon bucket with a sturdy lid took its place.

Allsop's chief henchman sat on the thin mattress, his elbows resting on his knees. His head snapped up when I came through the door, and for the first time ever, I felt the force of Jonesy's scrutiny on me.

Locked securely behind metal bars, he posed absolutely no threat. My conscious mind knew that, but my limbic system—the part of my brain wired for fight or flight—shrieked a warning.

The fine hairs on the back of my neck jumped to attention. It took a lot to rattle me, but this man set my teeth on edge. Suppressing an instinctive shudder, I trundled the mop bucket past his cell.

"Why hello, pretty girl."

I stopped so abruptly that the water in the tub sloshed. As if pulled by a magnet, my body turned toward the prisoner. The keys on my hip jangled, drawing his eye. I resisted the urge to step back.

Get a hold of yourself.

"I'm not supposed to talk to you," I said.

The corners of his mouth turned up, and his eyes sparkled. In the blink of an eye, Jonesy's demeanor morphed from scary to harmless, like a chameleon slipping on a new mask.

"And why is that, do you suppose?" he asked.

I shrugged. "Above my pay grade."

Yesterday, Rachel and I stood in the police station's observation room, watching Jonesy through the one-way glass. A bald, broad-shouldered, bullnecked man, he'd sat at a table in the interrogation room, silently smirking while Marcus pelted him with questions about Allsop's operation.

You can't break me and you're a fool to try, that smirk promised.

Now, he positively beamed, a genial expression at odds with yesterday's defiance.

Asshole thinks he can play me.

Nobody expected Jonesy to whimper and cave during direct interrogation, but every prisoner would move if the right lever was applied. The trick was in finding the right lever.

I turned my back on Jonesy and pushed the bucket to the end of the cellblock. With a long-suffering sigh, I dunked the mop into the soapy water and began to swab the floor. Back and forth, stopping every once in a while to wring out the mophead, I worked my way toward Jonesy's cell.

"Any chance I could bum a smoke off you?" he asked.

Did the man seriously think I'd sashay over to his jail cell and hand him a cigarette, putting myself and my keys within reach?

I shook my head. "Cigarettes are like gold nowadays. Good luck bumming one off anybody."

He gave a satisfied chuckle. "So Havoc's people are running low on supplies?"

I froze, pretending to be struck dumb by the realization that I'd both disobeyed orders by talking to him and had accidentally revealed information to the enemy.

"Dammit." I thumped my forehead with the heel of my hand.

"That's all right, sweetheart." He winked. "It'll be our little secret."

I pressed my lips together, conspicuously silencing my wayward tongue. Jonesy and I shared a little secret. He'd manipulated me into spilling the beans about the scarcity of cigarettes.

All in all, not a bad start.

Without another word, I finished cleaning the floor and opened the door to the cellblock.

"See you around, pretty girl," Jonesy called.

Deliberately ignoring him, I locked the door behind me and blew out a deep breath.

"I'll take care of that." The guard pointed to the yellow bucket. "Somebody's waiting for you." He angled his head toward the main entrance.

Through the window, I spied Finn lounging on the sidewalk outside the station.

Hands shoved deep in the pockets of his jacket, he stood with his head tilted back, soaking up the weak December sunshine. His blond hair glowed golden in the light.

As if feeling my gaze on him, Finn turned his head toward me. His bright, piercing blue eyes met mine. He smiled and rocked back on his heels. My eyes honed in on his mouth. Good God, those lips. My stomach did a flip-flop at the memory of his mouth claiming mine.

His smile widened, a smile that held all the warmth of an August afternoon back home in Kansas. To look at him, with his boyish charm, you'd never know he kissed like a god.

My heart kicked against my chest. After my chilling encounter with Jonesy, I wanted to soak up that warmth.

Shaking the thoughts off, I slipped on my coat, walked outside, and bumped my shoulder against his. "Hey."

"This is new." Finn touched the tips of my short brown hair. His fingers grazed my neck, sending tingles zinging across my skin.

Only a small circle of trusted soldiers knew about my assignment inside the jail, Finn among them.

"Couldn't risk Jonesy recognizing me."

Finn's jaw tightened and his hand drifted to the scar that bisected his lip. "No. Don't want that."

Silence fell over us, a silence heavy with unspoken words. Finn had stated his objections when Marcus proposed the assignment, and I'd shot them all down. Two years in military intelligence left me the best candidate for the job. Finn knew it. He accepted it, but he didn't like it. Allsop's attack dog had beaten Finn within an inch of his life. Of course he hated the prospect of my getting close to the man.

"So what do you think?" I fluffed my hair, lightening the mood.

I was a pragmatic woman. Necessity dictated my actions. Whether or not Finn liked it shouldn't matter. Still, I held my breath waiting for his judgment.

He tipped his head to one side and pursed his lips, studying me.

"You fishing for compliments?" he asked.

I shuffled my feet. "Maybe."

"All right." He offered a crooked smile. "I like it. It suits you. But no matter what you do to your hair—hell, even if you shaved your head—you'd still be the prettiest woman I ever laid eyes on."

Pleasure warmed my blood and heated my face. I'd invited that over-the-top compliment, hadn't I? And I knew better.

"Thanks, Finn." I cleared my throat. "So… why are you hanging around outside the police station?"

"It's lunchtime. I thought we could walk over to the cafeteria together."

If I were ten years younger, I would have skipped with happiness. Instead, I fell into step next to him. "Sounds good."

We walked in silence for a few minutes. Finn glanced sideways at me, then turned his gaze straight ahead before looking my way again.

"Something on your mind?" I asked.

"Yeah." Finn stopped walking. He sucked in a breath and shoved a hand through his hair. "Havoc gave me permission to go home to the ranch for Christmas. I'd like you to come with me, to celebrate an old-fashioned Christmas at Valhalla."

"Christmas," I whispered.

Memory broadsided me and a pang of nostalgia bit deep. My family always made a big deal out of the holiday. Gingerbread houses. Caroling. Midnight service at the church. Thanks to Dad's determination to literally outshine the Guzmans across the street, our house groaned under the weight of colored lights. There wasn't a Christmas tradition we didn't embrace whole hog.

Now they were all gone. My Christmas plans involved a girls' poker night with Rachel, who promised to break out a bottle of tequila she'd been hoarding.

"Georgia?" Finn laid a hand on my shoulder, concern clouding his eyes.

Even through my heavy winter jacket, I felt the heat and weight of his palm. "Sorry. Thinking about Christmas made me homesick."

"Come to Valhalla with me," Finn urged, his voice husky.

My eyes shot to him.

"You'll have fun." He sounded more casual now. "Everybody would love to see you again, especially Nyx."

I smiled. Nyx and I had grown close during our undercover mission to secure a weapons cache in Prineville. I'd love to spend time with her and everybody else on the ranch. I'd love to spend more time with Finn, too.

And that was the problem. Friendship had come naturally to us. The cheerful, outgoing young rancher was easy to like. But behind the charm lay a spine of steel, a warm heart coupled with a warrior's soul.

Something more than friendship had sparked during our mission to Prineville. We'd posed as a badass biker and his old lady.

When we'd needed to distract a guard, we'd shared our one and only kiss. I'd been sitting on a counter. We heard the guard approaching, and Finn had stepped between my legs. His hand tangled in my hair. He hauled me close and ravaged my mouth with his. Surprise had frozen me in place for a few seconds, then I'd returned the kiss with a passion that matched his.

Playacting, I'd told myself. We were selling our roles for an audience. But even as I formed the thought, I'd known I was kidding myself.

I could love this man, but falling in love is a choice, a choice I couldn't afford to make. Not now.

"What do you think?" Finn's voice interrupted my reverie. "You in?"

An old-fashioned holiday celebration among friends presented a powerful temptation. But I had to make one thing crystal clear.

"I like you," I said. "I value our friendship—"

His brow wrinkled. "You friend-zoning me, Georgia?"

Finn was a straight shooter. I owed him an honest, unambiguous answer. It killed me to say my next words.

"No. I'm not friend-zoning you. At least not forever." I touched my bare nape. "We're at war, Finn. We have jobs to do. We need to keep our focus on defeating Allsop." I lifted both shoulders in a lame shrug. "Later, once things have settled down, then we can figure out what's going on between us. Till then, let's put a pin in it."

"I get what you're saying." He nodded slowly. "Business before pleasure. Duty before fun." He lowered his chin and his voice took on a gravelly rasp that made my heart thump. "But if the past six months have taught me anything, it's that you need to seize the moment, because the moment might be all you get. Cherish the people you love. Grab a hold of what gives you pleasure." He grinned. "Eat pie for breakfast."

"Pie for breakfast?" I raised a brow.

"Mrs. B. recommends it. She's supervising all the Christmas baking, by the way. So are you coming or not?"

I should keep my distance from this man. Really, I should. At least for the duration of the campaign against Allsop. But a real Christmas at the ranch? Days spent in the company of a brave and good man determined to find joy in life, even in the darkest of times? I didn't have the strength to resist.

"Yes. If Marcus gives the okay, I'll come. Thanks for thinking of me."

Finn's eyes sparkled. "You won't regret it. I promise."

From his mouth to God's ears.

TWO

Finn

Georgia combed her fingers through her short brown hair. The strands caught the afternoon sunlight, shimmering a pretty chestnut. The clean smell of lavender soap filled my nostrils, and I inhaled the scent. Sitting next to her in this confined space was messing with my head.

"I'm never going to get used to this cut," she said, pulling down the visor and peering into the mirror.

"Sure you will. It looks good."

Good? Who was I kidding? Try gorgeous. The sleek bob accentuated her pointed chin and high cheekbones. The dark color brought out the pink of her cheeks. It suited her.

She cleared her throat and looked out the pickup's passenger side window.

I smiled in satisfaction at my effect on her.

Georgia twisted sideways in the bucket seat, pulled another Red Vine from the package, and held it out to me. "Want one?"

I shook my head. "Sorry, Georgia. I'm team Twizzler."

She gasped in mock horror. "You mean to tell me that in the great red licorice debate, we're on opposite sides?"

Damn, why was she so adorable? "Looks like it. That a deal breaker?"

Eyes narrowed, she pondered the question, then her expression cleared. "Nah, not a deal breaker, but I'm not going to ask you to weigh in on Coke versus Pepsi."

"Now there's a truly divisive subject. We'd best keep our opinions to ourselves." I mimed pulling a zipper across my lips.

Snow had fallen overnight, but by the time we headed out of Pendleton in late morning, the temperature had risen to a few degrees above freezing. The streets were slushy rather than frozen, except for the occasional icy spots where shadows covered the roadway. I kept a close eye on the pavement as I drove. There was nobody to call for help if we skidded off into a ditch or crashed.

Georgia sat up straight and waved the Red Vine at me. "Query."

I grinned. She was initiating another round of the what-do-you-miss-from-the-old-world game.

"Christmas traditions," she continued. "What was your favorite?"

"You mean when I was a little kid? Presents, I'm sorry to say."

She nodded, shamefaced. "Yeah. Me, too. I was a greedy little rug rat."

My mood sobered then grew wistful. "But now, looking back, I'd say my favorite tradition was decorating sugar cookies."

"Decorating sugar cookies?" She shot me an incredulous look. Her brows drew together. "Somehow I never took you for the Martha Stewart type."

I preened, slapped a swashbuckling expression across my face, and lowered the timbre of my voice. "You mean because I'm such a tough, manly man?"

She snorted. "No, doofus. Because I can't imagine you have the fine motor skills for it."

"I'll show you fine motor skills." One hand on the steering wheel, I leaned over and dug a finger into her ribs.

Georgia shrieked and wriggled. "No. No tickling." She batted at my hand. "I hate being tickled."

I withdrew my finger. "You hate it, I won't do it."

She settled back in the seat, her chest heaving. "You promise?"

"I won't ever do anything that you don't want. Promise."

That statement hung in the air for a moment while Georgia chewed over my words. Her cheeks flushed. She gnawed on her bottom lip. Her reaction was cuter than heck. After a good minute she said, "Tell me about the cookies."

My fingers tightened on the wheel, and I stared straight ahead. Instead of the empty, two-lane country road I was driving over, I saw images of Christmas past, before the world went to hell.

"My mother would bake hundreds of cookies. All different kinds, but my favorite were the sugar cookies. She'd spread a plastic tablecloth over the coffee table in the living room and set out bowls of colored frostings and sprinkles. The tree was covered with lights and ornaments. Our stockings hung on the mantle. The house smelled like nutmeg and cinnamon and fir boughs. Mama would play Christmas music while we worked—Nat King Cole's *O Holy Night* was her favorite."

"That sounds nice," Georgia whispered.

I bobbed my head. "It was. We'd sit around the coffee table and decorate the cut-out cookies. Santas. Angels. Reindeer. Stars. Snowflakes. Mama's cookies were little works of art." I shook my head. "Bear was so serious. I can still see him bent over the table trying to spread the frosting just so."

"And you?" Georgia's eyes twinkled, as if she suspected I lacked my brother's dedication to perfection.

I sighed. "Globs of color. Tons of sprinkles. I did get into trouble when I was twelve for making anatomically correct reindeer."

Laughter erupted from Georgia's throat. "You gave Santa's reindeer hard-ons, didn't you?"

"Yep. Mama said we couldn't give horny reindeer cookies to the neighbors, so Bear and I ended up eating them all." I shrugged. "That's a win in my book." I turned to Georgia. "Your turn."

She bit into the Red Vine and chewed slowly. "My family celebrated the holiday in a big way, too. You name it, we did it. But my favorite tradition was something my mom and I did every Christmas Eve."

"What's that?"

She hesitated, as if reluctant to share. "Mom lit a fire in the fireplace, and we cuddled up on the sofa under a crocheted afghan. Then we read Hans Christian Andersen's 'The Little Match Girl' out loud."

Frowning, I swung my eyes her way. "I think I read that back in school, but it can't be the same story. The one I read was a tragedy. A poor little girl freezes to death in an alley."

"That's the one," Georgia said. "It's wintertime. She can't go home because her father will beat her for not selling any matches, so she curls up in an alley and lights the matches one by one." Georgia's voice caught.

I've seen different sides of Georgia. Sometimes she was lighthearted and playful. Sometimes all business and deadly. This was the first time I'd heard her emotionally raw and vulnerable.

I brought the truck to a stop, reached over, and took her hand. My eyes darted to her mouth. If I leaned over a few inches, my lips could be on hers.

She squeezed my fingers, then continued the story. "As long as each match burned, she saw the life she wanted but never had. A warm home. Good food. A beautiful Christmas tree. When each flame flickered out, she was alone in the dark again. One by one, she burned all the matches. Then she froze to death, and her grandma's ghost came and took her soul to heaven."

Georgia's chin trembled and she scrubbed at her eyes with her free hand.

I clamped my jaw shut to keep my mouth from falling open. Reading this sad story to your child every year… that had to be the damnedest Christmas tradition ever.

"Why?" I choked out. "Why would your mother want to make you cry on Christmas?"

"You don't get it." Georgia shook her head, rebutting my accusation. "I loved the story. I wanted to hear it."

"You're right. I don't get it."

Georgia inhaled a deep breath, then slowly blew it out. "I had everything the little match girl wanted. Food. A nice home. A loving family. I didn't do anything that made me deserve it more than she did. It was the luck of the draw. The story reminded me to be grateful for what I had and to share my good fortune by helping others."

"For a tough girl, you got a soft, gooey center," I said. Compassion and strength made an irresistible combination in my book. I knew better than to say that out loud, not when she was so determined to keep me at arm's length.

Georgia rolled her eyes. "And the truth is, sometimes I like to read a story that gives me all the feels and a good cry."

I never in my life went looking for a "good cry," but I guess we're all wired differently.

She let go of my hand.

"Tell me," she said, her voice suddenly too chipper. "*Die Hard*: Christmas movie, yes or no?"

We kept up an easy conversation for the next hour, stopping only when we pulled up to the gates of Valhalla. I put the truck in park, hopped out, and waved at the security camera mounted on the timber crossbeam. I unlocked the gate and we drove up to the house.

Somebody must have been watching the camera feed. Bear waited for us at the bottom of the porch steps, his arm around Nyx's waist. Ever stood in front of them, jumping up and down with so much gusto that her hair flew around her shoulders. Everybody else had piled out of the house and gathered on the porch, waving at Georgia and me as we approached. Everybody except Mrs. B.

My heart thunked. Had something happened to that sweet old lady? She was part and parcel of every event on the ranch and not likely to sit out my homecoming. I cut the engine, jumped out of the truck, and rushed around to open Georgia's door.

She waited patiently for me, her lips curved up in a tolerant smile. We'd tussled about this at first. A gentleman opens a door for a lady; that's what I was taught. Of course she could do it herself. It wasn't a question of competence. Only a fool would question Georgia's competence. I meant it as a sign of respect. I'd have changed my ways if she insisted. Instead, she called me a dinosaur, laughed, and told me I owed her one.

Georgia hopped down and we turned toward our friends. My brother whooped and pulled me into a bear hug. Nyx kissed my cheek. Ever launched herself at me like a heat-seeking missile. I dropped down into a crouch and pulled the little girl close.

"I knew you'd come home for Christmas," she cried, capturing my face between her palms. "I just knew it."

"You think I'd miss Christmas with my little sweet pea if I could help it?" I demanded. She smiled, revealing a missing canine tooth. I pointed at her mouth. "Did the tooth fairy visit while I was gone?"

Ever shot me a pitying look, and her voice dropped to a whisper. "Kyle and Sunny snuck into my room and left a mood ring under my pillow. I pretended to be asleep so they wouldn't know I saw them." She held up her hand. A bright-blue stone winked in the light.

"What does the blue color mean?" I asked.

She threw her arms around my neck. "It means I'm happy because you're home, silly."

I rose to my feet, Ever glued to my side.

She squinted at Georgia, frowning. "What happened to your hair?"

Georgia laughed, not at all put out by the little girl's blunt question. "I decided to try something new." No way she'd tell Ever that the change was part of a top secret assignment. "I like it."

"Me, too," I chimed in.

Sunny and Kyle—who'd found the orphaned girl back in Boise—rushed down the steps.

"Let Finn say hi to everybody, Ever." Kyle shook my hand in welcome.

Sunny hugged me then turned to Georgia, chatting excitedly.

Nyx pulled me aside. "Will Georgia be sleeping with you, or do I need to make up a bed in a guest room?"

"She'll be staying in a guest room. We're—um—we're not sleeping together."

Nyx arched a single eyebrow. "What's up with that? Everybody and their mom can see that you're into each other."

"We're friends. Good friends. That's all, at least for now."

"Leave the man in peace, sugar." Bear came to my defense.

I threw him a grateful nod.

He hooked an arm around Nyx's neck and continued. "After all, Finn's shy. It takes him a while to screw up his courage and talk to a woman."

Huh? Shy around women? Me? Never. Compared to my taciturn brother, I was smooth. Downright glib.

Nyx snorted and shot an elbow into his ribs. "Behave yourself, cowboy."

"Hey." Bear protested, rubbing his side. "Since when do you want me to behave myself, woman?"

Nyx grinned. "Almost never."

Slack-jawed, I watched the exchange. My brother was a man of few words. He never teased. Not until Nyx. Damn. She was good for him.

I touched Nyx's arm. "I can make up the bed in the guest room."

"Nope," she said firmly. "You're on vacation. I got it."

"Thanks, sis." I kissed her cheek.

Sahdev walked up, his hand extended. We shook.

"Where's Mrs. B.?" I asked.

"She slipped on some ice the day before yesterday and twisted her ankle," the doctor said. "It's a minor sprain, luckily, but I ordered her to stay off her feet for at least a week."

"You *ordered* Mrs. B. to stay off her feet?" I couldn't wrap my head around the notion of ordering Mrs. B. to do anything.

"She said as long as she can supervise the holiday preparations, she's willing to rest." Sahdev nodded toward the house. "She's ruling the roost from her throne by the fireplace."

"I'll check in with her in a minute." I thumped Ripper and Levi on the back in passing and hugged Kenzie and Hannah. Topher leaned against the post at the top of the stairs, still pale and scrawny after his brush with death. He straightened up when I climbed the steps and extended his hand. Ignoring it, I hugged the teenager, careful not to squeeze.

"I promised Havoc I'd report back on how you're doing," I said.

"I'm good." He frowned, his expression anxious. "Did he order me back to Pendleton?"

Topher had been one of the soldiers Havoc sent to fortify Valhalla during our mission to find the hidden weapons cache in Prineville. He'd formed a fast friendship with our boy genius, Levi. When Jonesy attacked the ranch, Topher took a bullet to the gut and barely survived his injuries. Far as I was concerned, he was family.

"No." I clapped a hand on his shoulder. "Havoc said it's your call whether you stay here or come back to Pendleton. Either way, you'll play a part in the fight against Allsop."

His eyes lit up with relief. "Then I guess I'm staying put."

I squeezed his shoulder. "And we're glad to have you."

I pushed through the front door. A fire crackled in the hearth. Hector, Ripper's German shepherd, dozed on a sheepskin rug in front of the fireplace. My footsteps roused him. He lifted his head, blinked at me, then settled back down. Mrs. B. sat in her rocking chair, her sprained ankle elevated on an ottoman. Her fluffy cat, Fitzwilliam, sprawled across her lap. True to form, the snooty puss ignored my approach.

Mrs. B. sat up and held out both hands, a welcoming smile on her bright-pink lips.

"Dear boy, welcome home."

My breath caught at the simple, heartfelt words. I took her hands, careful not to press on her arthritic knuckles. "Thank you, Mrs. B." Bending over, I dropped a kiss on her cheek.

"How long can you visit?"

"Nine days. Havoc said we can stay through New Year's."

"We?" She raised a brow. "You're not alone?"

"No, ma'am. Georgia came with me."

Her eyes danced. "What a lovely surprise. I'll wager you're pleased as punch to have such charming company."

No point in denying it. Few things got past the sharp-eyed woman.

I offered a conspiratorial wink. "I sure am, Mrs. B."

The front door flew open and everybody trooped inside.

Ever took my hand and tugged, dragging me across the room so we stood beside the Christmas tree laden with old family ornaments. "Bear said you guys used to buy a real Douglas fir from the Boy Scouts, but since there are no more tree lots, he found an artificial tree at a neighbor's house. It's pretty, isn't it?"

I nodded. "That it is, sweet pea."

She pulled me over to the fireplace. I came face-to-face with Christmas past and present. The same bearded, big-nosed Scandinavian gnomes that I'd grown up with—their eyes hidden beneath pointy red hats—were scattered across the shelf. More than a dozen stockings hung from the mantel, including the snowman ones my mama had needlepointed for Bear and me.

"Look." Ever pointed at a blue stocking with her name appliqued across the top. On the front, a yellow chicken sported a jaunty Santa cap. "Nyx sewed it for me."

I shot a smile at the artist who held my brother's heart. "Very nice."

Ever turned to Georgia and held out her free hand. "Christmas isn't till the day after tomorrow. We still have time to make a stocking for you, too."

Georgia crossed the room and took the little girl's hand. "I'd love that. Thank you, sweetie."

My fingers twitched with the urge to take Georgia's other hand.

Chatting excitedly, Ever pulled Georgia across the room and pointed out the decorations on the tree. Georgia tossed a smile at me over her shoulder before turning her attention to the tree, oohing and aahing over the blown glass ornaments.

A corner of Mrs. B.'s mouth lifted, and she crooked a finger, beckoning me to come close. I dropped down on my haunches next to her.

"You quite fancy Georgia, don't you?" she asked in a low voice.

"Yeah." I sighed. "I fancy her, all right."

"Well what do you intend to do about it? Time's a wasting, young man."

"She wants to wait till after the war is over and the world's more settled."

"Poppycock," Mrs. B. said. "I'm a firm believer in the old proverb, 'Eat, drink and be merry, for tomorrow we may die.'"

Exactly what I thought. Glad to see that we were on the same page.

"You got any idea how I can make her change her mind?"

She patted my arm. "From what I've seen, dear boy, you're more than capable of winning a woman's heart." Her faded blue eyes sparkled. "But if all else fails, find a reason to take off your shirt. Flex your muscles a bit. Get the girl's motor running."

Take off my shirt and flex my muscles? Last year, maybe, but now? Not likely.

She smiled impishly up at me. I had to say something. "Mrs. B., you're being a—" I paused, searching for the right word. "You're being a—"

"Cheeky little scamp?" she offered. "My late husband always said so."

Cheeky little scamp? Not the words I would have chosen, but they fit.

Ever dragged Georgia toward the fireplace and proudly showed off all the Christmas decorations. She nodded, complimenting each one. When they finished admiring the stockings, Georgia pointed to a long-handled copper pan with a perforated lid leaning against the stone wall.

"Is that an old-fashioned popcorn popper?" she asked.

"Nope." Ever picked up the pan and held it out to her. "Bear found this in the attic. It's a copper warming pan that the Rasmussens used in the olden days. Before we go to bed at night, a grown-up puts hot embers into the pan, then they move it back and forth under the covers. It makes our beds nice and toasty." Ever turned to me. "If you asked him, I bet Finn would warm up your bed for you."

Out of the mouths of babes. I glanced at Georgia. Give me half a chance and I'd warm her bed. Hell, I'd make it scorching hot.

I winked at Ever. "You bet, I will."

THREE

Georgia

"You have room for another one, Georgia?" Kenzie held up the platter of Swedish pancakes.

Leaning back in my chair, I groaned. Five. I'd put away five of the crepe-like pancakes, each one topped with a dollop of whipped cream and a spoonful of jarred lingonberries. I hadn't eaten this well in months. Fresh milk, eggs, and butter were rare treats in Pendleton. My friends were lucky to live on a ranch that provided such luxuries.

"No, thanks." I waved away the platter. "I'm stuffed to the gills."

Fourteen people sat around the long trestle table enjoying our first Christmas since the flu pandemic reconfigured the world. We were the lucky ones, the small fraction of the population who survived both the virus and the breakdown of society that followed. Only God knew if we'd survive the upcoming war.

For today, we'd set aside the loss, the grief, the worry about the future and celebrated what we still had. Bear powered up the generator. After months of relying on solar-powered lanterns, the electric bulbs looked unnaturally bright. Music—another reminder of the past—played in the background.

We stitched together everybody's favorite Christmas traditions to create a new normal. The Rasmussens always served Swedish pancakes with lingonberries for Christmas breakfast. Kenzie had made her Aunt Debbie's walnut-studded fudge. Last night, Sunny led the group in a Christmas carol singalong.

Sated and content, I touched the pink paper crown on my head. When we sat down to breakfast, we found cardboard tubes wrapped in brightly colored paper on each plate. Sunny, Hannah, and Ever had made Christmas crackers, a nod to Mrs. B.'s British heritage. Each tube held a paper crown and a joke.

Why does a bee have such sticky hair? Because he uses a honey comb. Ever had hooted with laughter when I read my joke. I suspected she had a hand in writing them.

"Levi," Ever piped up.

Levi raised a finger and finished swallowing a bite of what must have been his tenth pancake. "Yeah, kiddo?"

"How did your family celebrate Christmas?"

Levi wiped a smudge of berries from his chin. "Well, we didn't put up a tree or hang stockings, but every Christmas Eve we volunteered at a soup kitchen. On Christmas Day, we'd go to the movies, then out for Chinese food."

Wide-eyed, Ever turned to Bear. "Can we watch a movie today? For Levi?"

Finn leaned over and spoke in my ear. "We found a lot of DVDs while out scavenging. Every Saturday evening, Bear fires up the generator and we have a movie night."

His warm breath fanned my ear. Delicious shivers rushed over my skin, making it hard to concentrate on what he was saying. "Sounds fun."

"We watch a kid-friendly show first, then after Ever goes to bed, we watch a more adult film."

I shot him side-eye. "An adult film, huh?"

He rolled his eyes and continued without dignifying my comment. "We take turns picking. Ripper and Kenzie love sci-fi. Sunny and Hannah usually choose romantic comedies. Mrs. B. is all about the musicals."

"Query: What kind of movies do you usually choose?"

His face lit up. "Anything Marvel."

I grinned. "Superheroes. I can see that." Finn was a living, breathing hero. He had the muscles for the job. I could just picture him in a cape.

Bear looked around the table. "Everybody in favor of watching a movie later on, raise your hand." Every hand at the table shot up. "All right. It's a plan. We'll watch a movie. For Levi."

Levi fist-pumped the air, then dropped a kiss on his girlfriend's cheek.

After he finished his pancake, everyone traipsed out to the living room and squeezed together on the three leather sofas. I lingered, bringing up the rear.

At the entrance to the room, I squinted at the bright white lights that covered the tree. Ever played the role of Christmas elf, scampering back and forth to distribute the presents to everybody.

This might be one of the last years when presents were easy to come by. Survivors had picked the stores and houses clean and had stockpiled everything they found. Once we used up the leftovers from the old world, we'd be hard-pressed to replicate them. Thanh—the lieutenant in charge of Pendleton's distribution center—had allowed Finn and me to select gifts for our friends from the warehouse, among them an Etch A Sketch for Ever, baby books for Kenzie, red lipstick for Nyx, and a special surprise for Mrs. B.

As if searching for a homing beacon, my gaze traveled around the room until it landed on Finn. Every other seat was full, except for the spot next to him. We were friends. It shouldn't be a big deal to sit beside him, but being pressed up against this gorgeous cowboy was wreaking havoc on my sensibilities.

"You coming, Georgia?" Nyx asked. Bear had sat on the floor in front of her, leaning back between her legs. She slipped her arms around him.

"Yes." I walked over and plopped down beside Finn, as if I belonged there. Finn smiled at me and my stomach fluttered. Jesus. I had it bad.

Ever continued handing out gifts. I sat back on the sofa, smiling as people exclaimed over their presents. A grinning Ripper held up a small framed photo of Kenzie, a gift from Kyle and Sunny.

"It used to sit on my desk back home in Boise," Kyle explained. Kyle and Kenzie used to date, but any awkwardness between them was a thing of the past.

Ever skipped across the room and deposited a big box on my lap.

"It's from Mrs. B. and Hannah and Nyx and Sunny and Kenzie and me."

Surprised to receive a gift, I slipped the ribbon off the package and carefully removed the paper. Opening the box, I found a beautiful hand-stitched quilt inside, a riotous patchwork of colors and fabrics.

"We all worked on it. See?" Ever pointed to a corner of the quilt where my friends had embroidered their names.

I traced a finger over the letters that spelled out Cressida Birdwhistle. "This is amazing, Mrs. B." I said. "Thank you, thank you everybody. I love it."

"It will help keep you warm when you're back in Pendleton and remind you of all your friends at Valhalla," she said.

My stomach knotted. I didn't deserve such openhearted kindness from these good people. Not when I couldn't return it in kind. If I never saw them again, would they understand? Would they forgive me?

Clearing my throat, I hopped to my feet, picked up a small package from under the tree, and carried it over to Mrs. B. "This is for you. It's not much compared to the quilt, but I think you'll like it."

She clapped her hands together, and a look of childlike glee crossed her face. Tearing the paper from the gift, she gasped. She blinked rapidly then clutched the box to her chest.

"Finn told me that you like Jaffa cakes. I asked the people who run our warehouse to keep an eye open for them. One of our scavengers found a box."

Mrs. B. raised glistening eyes to mine, but didn't say a word.

"Mrs. B.?" I touched her shoulder.

She shook herself and laughed softly. "Going misty-eyed over Jaffa cakes. You must think I'm a silly old woman. It's just… well, they're my favorite, and I thought they were gone forever. Like so much of the old world."

Sunny rushed over to her side and gently hugged her.

Mrs. B. sat up straight and cleared her throat. "Shall we open the Jaffa cakes?"

"No." Several voices rang out as one.

"They're your favorite," Sunny said. "We wouldn't dream of eating them."

"I would," Ever grumbled.

Mrs. B. blew the girl a kiss. "I promise to save one for you."

"Okay." Good spirits restored, Ever continued passing out presents.

Once again, I squeezed in next to Finn on the crowded sofa, sitting so close that our thighs and shoulders pressed together. I resisted the urge to lean into his heat and not because the space was chilly. With a fire blazing in the hearth, the room was toasty warm. No, I was drawn to the man himself. His good humor, his strength, his ability to get the job done under the worst circumstances. I'd have Finn at my back in any fight.

Or at my front. Or under me.

Jeez, girl, get a grip.

My gaze traveled around the room, sliding over all the happy couples. Bear and Nyx. He leaned back against her, groaning with pleasure while she kneaded his shoulders. Seated on the floor next to his girl, a smiling Levi pushed a strand of hair behind Hannah's ear, then kissed her nose. They put their heads together, laughing as they shared a private joke. Sunny and Kyle cuddled together in the corner of a sofa. He'd slung his arm around her shoulders, and she'd tangled her fingers in his. Kenzie curled up on Ripper's lap, his big hand splayed across her barely-there baby bump. He whispered into her ear. She blushed and batted playfully at his chest.

Spontaneous, unselfconscious signs of affection everywhere. Between people who cared deeply for each other. People who chose not to wait for better times.

Loneliness pricked at me. Hyperawareness of Finn's big frame next to me shimmied up my spine. My chest tightened. I was a soldier with a mission, but the coming war would touch every one of us. My friends didn't hold back. They didn't play it safe because safety was an illusion.

But I couldn't afford to let my heart take over. Some of us faced greater peril than others.

Ever dropped a small box wrapped in sparkly silver paper onto my lap.

"It's from Finn." She placed a familiar red-wrapped present on Finn's lap. "And that's from Georgia." Eyes bright with curiosity, she planted herself in front of us, apparently planning to watch us open our gifts.

"Scram, sweet pea." Finn gestured her away.

Ever snorted a protest, then returned to her elf duties.

"You first." Finn gestured at my present.

Warm fuzzies fluttered in my chest. I tore open the paper and removed a bottle of expensive cologne from the box. My brow puckered.

"Oh, shit." Finn made a face. "Rachel told me perfume was an old lady gift, but I didn't listen."

"No." I touched his arm. "I love it. How did you know about the scent?"

"You don't remember?"

"Nope."

"A while back we were talking about our favorite smells. You said apple pie was number one, and orange blossom came in a close second. Don't think they make apple pie perfume—although if you ask me that would be a stroke of genius—but they do make an orange blossom one." He hesitated. "I figured you'd like it."

I took off the cap, sprayed a fine mist on my wrist, then inhaled the fresh, citrusy scent. "It's heavenly." I sighed. "I forgot that we talked about that."

Finn picked up my forearm. Strong fingers gently braceleted my wrist as he brought his nose to the spot. Warm breath tickled the sensitive skin.

"I remember everything you've ever said to me, Georgia." His thumb circled my pulse point.

Shivering, I swallowed. "Why don't you… why don't you open your present?"

He released my wrist, and I suddenly felt bereft.

Finn peeled back the red paper to reveal the latest—and most likely the final—Longmire mystery novel.

"Your favorite series, right? You said you hadn't read the last one." I scanned his face, searching for his reaction.

He grinned, thumbing through the pages. "Looks like you pay attention, too. It's perfect. Thank you." He leaned forward, as if he was going to kiss my cheek, then he stopped himself. Irrational disappointment speared me.

Ever finished distributing the gifts, then plopped down in the middle of the living room, surrounded by her own presents. She made quite a production out of opening and exclaiming over each one, hopping up to hug the givers.

Hannah and Levi pulled out the basket of DVDs and selected half a dozen for us to vote on for our Christmas Day movie.

Topher wandered into the kitchen for a piece of fudge. Ambling back into the living room, he paused in front of the laptop monitor. "Somebody's at the gate."

In a heartbeat, the atmosphere in the room morphed from festive to high alert. Kyle joined Topher in front of the monitor and leaned toward the screen. "I can't see the driver's face," he said. "They're still in the car."

Bear opened the small safe next to the front door and passed out weapons.

Ripper lifted the still-hobbling Mrs. B. up into his arms. "Ever, Hannah, you're going to a back bedroom with Mrs. B." He lowered his chin and fixed Kenzie with a steely glare. "You, too, Mac."

Defiance flashed in Kenzie's eyes. A pang of sympathy shot through me. Pregnant women weren't helpless, and she clearly resented being hustled out of harm's way.

"Mean it, Mac," Ripper growled. "Move your ass." He handed her her Sig P938 and nodded at Mrs. B. and Ever. "Counting on you to keep 'em safe."

I'd watched Ripper in action when he led our undercover mission in Prineville. He was hardwired to stand between danger and the people under his care. No way would he fail to protect his pregnant wife or the vulnerable members of his family.

Kenzie knew better than to argue with her man when bullets might fly. She nodded, the defiance fading from her gray eyes. She followed Ripper and the others up the hall. Within a minute, Ripper jogged back into the front room.

"Anything?" he asked.

"Car door's opening," Kyle said, his attention glued to the monitor. He huffed out a breath. "It's J.R. Dreyer. Havoc must have sent him."

The tension in the room ratcheted down. We all knew J.R. He was a former trucker who had driven the semi when we hauled the weapons cache to Pendleton.

"I'll get the gate." Finn grabbed his keys and jogged to his truck. A minute later, he appeared on the monitor, unlocking the gate and swinging it open. He spoke to J.R. for a few seconds, clapped the older man on the shoulder, then pulled his truck forward, locking the gate again once J.R.'s car was inside. The vehicles disappeared from the camera's view.

Anxiety ticked along my nerves. Finn and I weren't expected back until New Year's Day. Nyx and I exchanged glances, our brows raised. Something must have gone wrong, otherwise Marcus wouldn't have sent a man to Valhalla. We all stood, silently awaiting the news. Bear threw open the front door as Finn and J.R. climbed onto the porch.

J.R. stepped into the room.

"What happened?" Ripper demanded.

J.R. shoved a hand through his salt-and-pepper hair. "Allsop sent a white-flag delegation to Pendleton. He wants to parlay."

FOUR

Finn

"It looks like they're squeezed into a clown car." Georgia peered over her shoulder at the small economy sedan following behind us. "Every time we go over a bump, they bang their heads."

I glanced into the rearview mirror. The compact car might have been just fine for J.R.'s five-foot, seven-inch frame, but my brother stood more than six feet tall, and Ripper topped him by a good couple inches. With their height and broad shoulders, the ride had to be uncomfortable. Sardines anyone?

"Only about another hour to Pendleton," I said. "They'll be out of their misery soon enough."

"I'm sorry we had to cut our visit short," she said.

"Couldn't be helped."

Ever had cried when we left, declaring it wasn't fair that Georgia and I had to go back early. Sobbing, she'd stood on the porch, clinging to Sunny's waist. Ripper paused on his way to J.R.'s car and laid a hand on the girl's shoulder.

"Life ain't fair, kid. If you accept that, you'll have an easier time facing whatever comes."

Ever had hiccuped, her eyes narrowing. "Life should be fair."

Ripper shrugged. "Maybe, but don't hold your breath."

The biker never sugarcoated reality, not even to placate a child.

Havoc had ordered J.R. to stay behind at the ranch—an extra gun in case something went wrong—while Bear and Ripper followed us back to Pendleton for a meeting with the major. They could have ridden in comfort in one of the ranch trucks, but the economy sedan got better gas mileage. We were luckier than most. Valhalla's gravity flow fuel tank still held almost five hundred gallons of gasoline, but there was no point in squandering fuel for the sake of a luxurious ride.

Georgia gnawed anxiously on a Red Vine. "I wonder what Allsop is up to."

I snorted. "Nothing good."

When I was a kid, I remember our pastor describing the devil as a murderer and the father of all lies. By that reckoning, Allsop had to be close kin with Old Nick. The smarmy bastard had absolutely no regard for human life, and he lied as easily as he breathed. Allsop had tried to pass himself off as a new messiah, restoring order and stability to a world laid waste by the virus. Cross him, though, and he showed his true colors.

My fingers clenched on the steering wheel as images bubbled to the surface of my memory. Last summer, when Havoc had asked if I'd be willing to infiltrate Allsop's inner circle to spy on the bad guys, I'd said, "Hell, yes." I had no idea when I signed up for the mission that I'd be required to stand by, my face showing nothing but callous indifference, while Allsop brutalized terrified survivors.

Hardest thing I'd ever done. When Allsop's son, Brody—a spoiled and vicious little prick—set his sights on Sunny, I reached my breaking point. I helped Sunny and Kyle escape Boise. They got away. I didn't. A vengeful Allsop sicced Jonesy on me.

I tried not to dwell on what came next, to bury the memories, but they still snuck up and caught me unawares. I'd jolt awake in the middle of the night, Jonesy's gleeful, sadistic face swimming before my eyes.

Allsop had ordered my execution, but before the sentence could be carried out, my friends snuck back into Boise and rescued me. Snatched from the jaws of death, I had no right to bitch and moan about the suffering I'd endured.

I kept my mouth shut and cowboyed up, like my daddy used to say.

Of its own accord, my hand touched the puckered scar that split my lower lip. The scar was the most obvious remnant of the beatings, the one everybody could see, but it wasn't the worst. Not by a long shot.

Georgia looked my way, concern knitting her brows.

I dropped my hand and kept my eyes on the road, avoiding her gaze. Sitting beside this beautiful woman, I was suddenly glad for the shirt and jacket covering my chest and stomach.

Back before the pandemic—when I was cocky and untested by hardship—I used to peel off my shirt and flex my muscles, confident that I'd draw admiring glances from the women around me. Nature had smiled on me, and I knew it. If I peeled off my shirt now, would Georgia look at me with pity rather than lust?

Scowling, I shook my head. What kind of a shallow bastard worried about his looks when the world was poised on the brink of war? Besides, Georgia wouldn't care about my scars, other than to regret how I got them.

Would she?

"Hey, you all right?" Georgia touched my arm, her pretty face clouded with concern. My blood heated at her touch.

I blew out a breath. "Just thinking about Allsop and Jonesy."

"That's enough to make anybody frown. I wonder what Allsop wants."

"We'll find out soon enough."

Forty-five minutes later, we pulled off the freeway, were waved through the roadblock, then drove to Havoc's headquarters and parked in front of the building. Bear and Ripper climbed stiffly from the compact sedan.

"Fucking hate riding in a cage," Ripper muttered, stretching his arms backward till his shoulders popped.

Bear's lips quirked, like he wanted to say something, but thought better of it.

We approached the double doors leading into the library and city hall complex. I recognized the guards flanking the entrance.

"Havoc is expecting us," I said.

They nodded and we walked past them into the building and down a short corridor to the major's HQ.

Havoc had upgraded the place in the past few months, adding several wooden bookshelves and an area rug.

Havoc's big body occupied a leather executive chair behind a long conference table. His three lieutenants were all present. Justin, the chief of operations, sat to Havoc's right. Thanh, the supply chief, sat to his left. Rachel, the head of security, perched cross-legged on the table. Her normally pale face was flushed, and her spiky hair stood on end, like she'd been clutching at it with both hands. I'd never seen the normally self-possessed woman look more keyed up.

"Are you all right?" Georgia quietly asked her friend.

Rachel snorted and threw her hands in the air. Not a good sign.

"Pull up chairs," Havoc barked.

I took a seat opposite the major. Georgia sat across from Thanh, five feet from me, too far away for my taste.

I leaned forward, my elbows on the table. "What's going on, boss?"

"What's the fucker want?" Ripper demanded, cutting right to the chase.

Havoc offered a tight smile. "Yesterday evening—Christmas Eve, no less—a black SUV rolled up to a roadblock, waving a white flag. There were two men inside the vehicle. They said they were delivering a message from Allsop. Our guards searched the men and the SUV. Took their weapons. Radioed for Rachel and me."

"Havoc and I drove to the roadblock." Rachel picked up the story. "Allsop's men were superpolite, all shit-eating grins while they delivered the message from their boss."

No surprise there. Exaggerated good manners were a fundamental characteristic of Allsop's men. They'd smile and speak politely to you, right up until the moment they drew weapons and started shooting.

"Allsop wants two things," Havoc said. "First, he proposed a peace treaty dividing the Pacific Northwest into two spheres of influence."

Bear laughed. "Didn't he try something like that with Uncle Bobby in Prineville? Look how that turned out."

Havoc inclined his head, acknowledging Bear's words, then he continued. "Second—and hold your hats—he proposed a prisoner exchange. We give him Jonesy, he'll give us David, the leader of the Nampa Boys."

Originally a band of teenagers who helped feed and protect flu survivors, the Nampa Boys had evolved into an anti-Allsop resistance group operating west of Boise. Their leader, David, had a reputation for being cunning and ballsy beyond his years. The thought of him at Allsop's mercy...

Then it struck me.

"How the hell does Allsop know that we're holding Jonesy?"

"And that's the million-dollar question," Havoc said dryly.

FIVE

Georgia

"Allsop must have a spy in town. Somebody close enough to our operation to know about Jonesy." Rachel pointed a finger at her chest. "I vet all the newcomers. I allowed somebody to slip in under my nose. This is on me."

No wonder my friend looked ready to spit nails.

Allsop's number two man was a prize. Sequestered away from prying eyes, his presence was a closely guarded secret. Even the guards manning the jail knew him only as "the prisoner."

Havoc turned unperturbed eyes to his chief of security. "I have full confidence that you'll ferret out the spy."

"Damned straight I'll ferret out the spy." Rachel's jaw set with determination.

"I don't get it." Bear screwed up his face. "Why would Allsop let us know that he has a spy in our camp, a conduit for information? You'd think he'd keep that close to his vest."

"I get it." Finn leaned back in his chair. "I worked with Allsop day in and day out for months. I've seen how he operates. He loves mind games. He's trying to faze us, to undermine our confidence in Havoc and his team. Keep us busy chasing our tails."

"He's willing to risk exposing a valuable asset?" Ripper looked skeptical.

Finn shrugged. "Could be the spy has already left town. Or maybe he sent more than one. Maybe there's a whole nest of them in place."

Rachel growled.

"Everybody is dispensable to Allsop," Finn continued. "Even Jonesy. We can't know for sure what he's up to, but we can be damned certain he has an agenda."

Enough with the speculation. It was time to get down to specifics. I caught Havoc's eye. "How exactly does he propose that we proceed with a peace treaty and prisoner exchange?"

Havoc smiled his approval of the question, reached into a bowl on the table, grabbed a walnut, and tossed it to me. "You been to Meacham?"

I slammed the nut on the table, cracking open the shell. "Never heard of it."

"It's a tiny, hole-in-the-wall town about thirty miles from here," Finn said. "Just off the freeway, on the old Oregon Trail. Less than a hundred people lived there before the flu. It's probably uninhabited now."

"The Janissaries used to stop in Meacham when we went on a run to the eastern part of the state," Ripper said. "There was an old restaurant there that served great hamburgers and homemade pie. The prez loved it."

"So you know Meacham. That's good," Havoc said. "Can you sketch the layout of the town?"

Ripper raised a shoulder. "Sure. As I recall, there were a few buildings, roads, tall evergreens, hills."

Havoc snatched a walnut from the bowl and crushed it in his fist. "Allsop proposed that we meet at the old restaurant tomorrow at noon."

"You're not going, are you?" I asked. The proposed meeting could be nothing more than an attempt to draw Havoc out of the relative safety of Pendleton. We couldn't afford to lose the leader of the resistance.

Havoc flashed a smile. "Allsop's too smart to suggest that I leave Pendleton and show up at a place and time of his choosing. He knows I'd smell a trap. Nah. Each side is supposed to send a representative with authority to negotiate along with a five-person security team." He picked a piece of nutmeat from the shell and popped it into his mouth.

"I'm going to Meacham to represent Havoc," Justin said.

That made sense. Justin was a trusted lieutenant, smart, experienced, and loyal to the core.

"Ripper, since you know the area, I'd like you to come along as a member of the security team," Havoc said.

"I know the area, too." Bear spoke up. "I should go."

Finn shot his brother a look. "So should I."

What? No. No way should Finn get within a mile of Allsop's men.

Bear shook his head. "No. Allsop's men would likely recognize you. As far as they're concerned, you're a spy and a traitor. Why stir up a hornet's nest?"

"Why not?" Finn countered. "They want to mess with us—tell us they have a spy in our midst—we'll mess with them. Show them I'm alive and well. Rub their noses in it."

"Rattle the fuckers." Grim satisfaction crossed Ripper's face.

"Exactly what I was thinking," Havoc said. "I want Ripper and Finn on the security team for the meeting." His gaze swung to Bear. "Bear, you're not being left out. In case something goes wrong at the meeting, I'm concealing soldiers around the perimeter of the restaurant. I want you to join them. Of course, this means you and Ripper won't be turning around and heading back to the ranch immediately."

"No problem," Bear said. "We told our people we might be gone a few days."

"And me?" I asked. Havoc met my eyes.

"You'll team up with Bear in a camouflaged position outside the meeting spot."

Good enough. "Yes, sir."

Havoc inclined his head. "I've got preparations to make. We'll meet up again after dinner to go over our final plans." He turned to Thanh. "Thanh, find rooms for Ripper and Bear for tonight."

"Yes, sir."

Havoc stood, dismissing us. "Tomorrow we meet the enemy. Should be an interesting day."

SIX

Finn

We approached the entrance to the restaurant, Ripper and I marching a few paces ahead of Justin. Three of Havoc's best soldiers followed close behind the lieutenant. We surrounded him with a protective barricade, a wall of heavily armed muscle.

A wall of muscle. I bit back a smile. Well, wasn't that a highfalutin way to describe myself? I could picture Georgia rolling her eyes and snorting if she heard it. In case Allsop's men had eyes on us, I resisted the urge to glance at the spot fifty yards away where Georgia and Bear were hunkered down behind a bush at the base of a tree. Armed to the teeth, they were ready to jump in if the situation deteriorated.

My two favorite people in harm's way. If I got to choose, Georgia would have stayed safely back in Pendleton. I knew better than to suggest that. She would've fixed me with the stink eye and reminded me that she was a soldier. Shit. Had to trust that if things went sideways, they'd take care of themselves and each other.

That reminder of danger sobered me. Jogging up the steps onto the covered porch, I hardened my expression. By the time I got close to the massive elk head mounted over the door to the restaurant, I was strutting like a badass.

Strutting like a badass came naturally to Ripper. The biker exuded menace as he shoved open the door and stepped into the restaurant, his gaze sweeping the place for signs of trouble. I followed him inside. He held up a hand, stopping Justin and his guards in their tracks just outside the door. "Wait while we check the place out."

A long cafe counter topped with yellow Formica ran along one side of the restaurant. Somebody had pushed several tables off to the side, leaving one table and two chairs in the middle of the room. Six men stood next to the table, all wearing the Allsop uniform of jeans and a gray T-shirt, the same damned uniform that I'd worn for months.

Arms hanging loose at his side, one of the men stepped forward, his expression and body language as threatening as a golden retriever greeting his best friend. He looked to be in his midforties, of average height and build. A dimple dented his cheek when he flashed a smile. "I'm Steven, here representing Mr. Allsop."

I looked past him to a bristling bruiser with close-cropped red hair and beefy arms. My brain stuttered. My swagger faltered. I froze in place. An image flashed before my eyes. For a good ten seconds I gaped at the man who'd helped hold me down while Jonesy worked me over.

Pull your head out of your ass.

"Hey, Charlie." I kept my voice easy. "How's the shoulder?" I'd dislocated it when the asshole came at me the last time.

He spat on the wooden floor and turned to his compatriots. "Fellas, you've heard of Finn Rasmussen. The boss has a hefty bounty on his head."

Ripper shifted his weight, his hand sliding toward his shoulder holster.

"Now, now." Steven glanced over his shoulder at his men. "None of that. Mr. Allsop sent us here to make peace, not to settle old scores. We're all friends here."

Scowling, Charlie subsided.

"Need to check the back rooms," Ripper growled.

Steven raised both hands, appearing as harmless as a flea. "Be my guest."

The spot between my shoulder blades itched when I stepped past the cluster of men. Outnumbered six to two, it felt like an exercise in foolishness to turn our backs on Allsop's men. Still, I followed Ripper's lead. The experienced soldier wouldn't do anything stupid. And Allsop was up to something. Wasn't likely he called us here just to take out a handful of Havoc's soldiers.

I checked the bathrooms and the storeroom while Ripper prowled through the kitchen and pantry.

"Clear." Ripper emerged from behind the counter. "Call 'em in."

I stepped over to the entrance and signaled our men to enter. Justin led the way, looking every bit a badass himself. Before the pandemic, he'd taught high school biology and had served with the Oregon National Guard. Intelligent and capable, he carried himself with an easy confidence. His eyes swept the room before settling on Steven, whose dimples were showing again.

"Justin Mrachek, representing Major Marcus Havoc," he said, extending a hand to Steven. The men shook hands.

Steven waved toward the small table. "Shall we get started?"

The two official delegates sat opposite each other, their security teams fanned out behind them. Justin folded his hands on the table, cool and collected, waiting for Allsop's man to get the ball rolling.

"Mr. Allsop asked me to convey his regrets over that little brouhaha in Prineville."

Brouhaha? That was a fancy-ass word for what went down when Allsop's men turned on their prospective ally and tried to steal his stockpile of weapons. Uncle Bobby had already decided to join forces with Havoc rather than Allsop, but the wannabe dictator's men had no idea of that when they made their move. They got their hands on the key to his treasure, and they struck.

Allsop thought a simple apology could sweep that betrayal under the rug?

Justin cocked a brow and waited for Steven to proceed.

After a long moment, Steven cleared his throat and started again. "Mr. Allsop hopes we can put all that unpleasantness behind us and move forward toward a mutually beneficial relationship."

The man spoke with all the sincerity of a carnival barker. My fingers twitched with the urge to smack him.

"And how does Allsop suggest that we achieve this mutually beneficial relationship?" Justin asked.

Steven's smile widened. "By acknowledging that both Mr. Allsop and Major Havoc have established hegemony over portions of the Pacific Northwest. There's no need for us to waste men or materials making incursions into each other's spheres of influence.

No need to quibble over the lines of demarcation between their spheres. Both sides have enough to do meeting the needs of their citizens, reestablishing law and order, and overseeing public health. We don't need to fritter away precious resources making war against each other."

"So what—specifically—does Allsop propose?" Justin asked.

"May I?" Steven pointed toward an inside pocket in his jacket.

"Slowly," I warned.

Steven nodded. With two fingers, he pulled a paper map of the western United States from his pocket. He opened it and laid it across the table.

"Mr. Allsop proposes that we formalize the borders between our sides. He's willing to pull out of Oregon and Washington entirely, ceding the states to Major Havoc's control. Mr. Allsop will center his power in Idaho, Montana and Wyoming, and perhaps eventually Utah and Colorado."

"Huh." Justin scratched his chin. "You're saying he's willing to abandon his claims to territories inside Oregon and Washington?"

"Yes, he is."

Bullshit. No way the power-hungry man I knew would sacrifice the footholds he'd made in the states.

Justin's blank expression revealed none of my skepticism. "Now that's an interesting proposal. Tell me, when does Allsop plan to pull out of Oregon and Washington?"

Steven spread his hands. "It's the middle of winter, and many of the roads are icy. It's no time to evacuate hundreds of men. We'll pull out of the states in the spring, after the thaw. Assuming we reach an agreement, of course."

How did the bastard keep a straight face when he spun such a far-fetched story? Nobody moved an army during winter? Tell that to Napoleon. Or Hitler.

"Now that's an interesting offer," Justin said noncommittally.

"Moreover, Mr. Allsop proposes a mutual defense pact," Steven said. "With Logan Voss consolidating power in central California, we all need to look to the future."

I shot Ripper a look. He jerked his head once. He hadn't heard anything about a Logan Voss coming to power in California either. Maybe it was true. Maybe it was a bald-faced lie. I had no clue. If Havoc had sent spies to investigate conditions outside of the Pacific Northwest, he hadn't shared the information with me.

"Logan Voss," Justin repeated.

"Can you believe it?" Steven made a face. "The nerd who created that new dating app last year. Word is he had a doomsday shelter built under his mansion. He and a group of his tech buddies rode out the virus in comfort. Now *he's* taking over the state." He rolled his eyes, clearly outraged by the prospect of a California nerd rising to power.

Or maybe the tale of Logan Voss was nothing more than a pile of horseshit meant to throw Havoc off his game. I didn't have enough information to distinguish the truth from a lie.

"Allsop's message mentioned a prisoner exchange," Justin said.

Steven folded his arms over his chest, an infuriating smile on his face. "The Nampa Boys are little more than pests. Still, we were pleased to take David, their so-called leader, into custody."

The Nampa Boys had supervised the overnight evacuation of a couple hundred civilians from the Boise suburbs to safety in Pendleton. David led a guerrilla campaign against Allsop's forces. Pests? So-called leader? Hardly.

"You have proof that you're holding David?" Justin asked.

Steven sighed, as if insulted by the question. He pointed to an inner pocket on his jacket again. Justin nodded. Allsop's man pulled out a Polaroid photograph and set it on the table.

Justin and I leaned forward to get a better look. A dark-haired young man glowered at the camera. His left eye was swollen shut, and a purple contusion covered his right cheek. His mouth hung open, his jaw bruised. Staring at his split and swollen lip, I balled my fists to keep from touching my own scar.

Justin had met with David when he helped to infiltrate Boise and rescue me. I knew the teenager only by reputation. I glanced at Justin and he nodded, confirming that it was a photo of David.

Jesus Christ. I knew exactly what that poor kid was going through, if he was still alive. A photo wasn't proof of life.

I cut my gaze to Charlie. A satisfied grin twisted his lips, and his eyes gleamed, as if he was remembering the happiest day of his life. I took a step forward. He lifted his chin, daring me to keep coming. Summoning every bit of my self-restraint, I halted and sucked in a deep breath. Later. I filled my expression with promise. We'll settle things later.

"Mr. Allsop proposes exchanging David for Jonesy." Steven's words hung in the air, unembellished by any explanation of how he knew we were holding Allsop's number two man.

Acknowledging that we'd taken Jonesy prisoner had been a subject of debate last night. Rachel took a hard line and argued against admitting it, even if that meant abandoning David to Allsop's tender mercies. David knew what he was risking when he took up arms against Allsop, she said. He'd be furious if we sacrificed Jonesy in order to save his life. Moreover, maybe they didn't know for sure that we were holding Jonesy. Maybe Allsop was taking a shot in the dark after his number two failed to report in.

How likely was that? Rachel's guilt might be steering her toward a serious case of denial.

My brain saw the sense behind her insistence that we not turn over Jonesy, but my heart rejected it. Abandoning an ally felt all kinds of wrong. How about staging a rescue, like they did for me? I'd asked. Ultimately, Havoc decided that Justin would listen to Allsop's offer, but make no comment one way or the other about Jonesy's status. Any rescue attempt would be a matter for another day.

"Why do you think that we've taken Jonesy prisoner?" Justin asked, his voice and expression bland.

Steven leaned back in his chair and sneered. "So that's how you're going to play it, huh? We come to you in good faith, and you won't even admit that you're holding our man?"

Justin shrugged. "I don't know what you're talking about."

Tongue in cheek, Steven nodded. "Uh-huh." He tapped the image of David. "David dies and it's on you."

Justin leaned forward. "No. If David dies, it's on *you*. And you'll pay."

The two men locked eyes. The threat of violence hung heavy in the air, so thick that it clogged my throat. Time slowed to a snail's pace. My gaze moved from one man to the next, alert to any twitch, any sign that somebody was about to draw his weapon.

Steven slid the photograph toward Justin. "How about you take this with you to show Havoc? Remind him what's at stake."

"I will." Justin slipped the picture into a pocket.

"The question of the hostages aside, you'll convey Mr. Allsop's offer for a peace settlement to the major?"

"I will," Justin repeated.

Steven rose to his feet and stuck out his hand. "Shall we meet here again in a few weeks? Say the third Saturday in January, at noon?"

Justin took the proffered hand and gave one brisk shake before relinquishing it. His fingers flexed as he withdrew. I imagined him fighting the impulse to wipe his hand clean on his jeans, but his was the kind of impurity a man couldn't scrub or wash off, a pollution of the soul.

We closed in around Justin, re-creating the wall of muscle as we retreated. Ripper and I backed up to the door, keeping our eyes on Steven's team. Once outside, we jogged to our minivan, slid the doors open, and jumped inside. Ripper drove and I rode shotgun, both literally and figuratively. Five minutes after we pulled away, the rest of our team would follow, rendezvousing on the side of the freeway heading back to Pendleton. My mind wouldn't rest easy until I saw that Bear and Georgia had made a clean getaway.

We rode in silence to the prearranged meeting spot, each consumed by our own thoughts. Ripper pulled onto the freeway shoulder and put the van in park, the engine idling in case we needed to pull away fast.

"What do you all think?" Justin broke the silence. "What is that bastard up to?"

That was the million-dollar question.

SEVEN

Georgia

We stood in the parking lot of the two-story motel that Finn and I—and the rest of Marcus Havoc's top people—called home. After our meeting with Marcus and his lieutenants yesterday evening, Bear and Ripper had spent the night at the motel. Now they were getting ready to return to Valhalla.

We'd said our goodbyes to Bear and Ripper inside the motel, yet the four of us lingered in the parking lot, our breaths frosting the air.

I squinted into bright morning sunshine that carried no hint of warmth. The cloudless blue sky felt like a cheat, as if nature was trying to pull a fast one. Bitter cold bit the tip of my nose. I stomped my boots against the asphalt and jammed my gloved hands deep into my jacket's pockets.

Beside me, Finn wore a down parka, the hood pulled up to cover his head. Bet my hands would warm up real fast if I pushed them up inside that coat, if I slid my palms against his heated muscular chest.

During the mission in Prineville—when I'd played the part of a biker's old lady—I'd ridden on the back of Finn's Harley. I'd leaned against his broad back, slid my arms around his waist, anchored myself against him. I was simply doing what was required to stay on the bike, or so I told myself. But in truth, every time I locked my legs around his hips or felt his abdominal muscles tense beneath my fingers, pleasure jangled along my nerves.

At the thought of sliding my hands over his skin once again, heat suffused my whole body. Gritting my teeth, I kicked the image out of my head. For chrissakes, I was standing five feet from his brother and Ripper. Now was not the time to moon over Finn. I schooled my face and prayed they didn't notice me ogling him.

"You sure you won't follow us to the ranch?" Bear asked. "You weren't due back in Pendleton until the first. You've got days of vacation time left."

Finn shook his head, regret stamped across his face. "Nah, it wouldn't feel right to be away from Pendleton, not knowing that Allsop's stirring up trouble. Besides, I can justify burning gasoline for one trip to Valhalla, but not two."

Ripper clapped Finn on the shoulder. "You take care. We'll see you soon, brother." He turned toward J.R.'s punishingly small sedan, and his lip curled.

"You could borrow a more comfortable ride from the car pool," I suggested.

Bear made a face. "J.R. loves this thing. I promised him I'd bring his 'baby' back to him in one piece. He'd probably have a heart attack if he saw us driving up in a different car."

Laughing, I slipped my arms around Bear and hugged him tight. "If you can't ride in comfort, at least drive safe. And give Nyx a kiss from me."

The corners of his eyes crinkled, eyes the same deep blue shade as his brother's. "Will do. Just as soon as I'm done kissing her myself."

"Bye, Ripper." I lifted a hand in farewell. I'd gotten over my initial unease around the big, intimidating biker, but I still wouldn't feel comfortable throwing my arms around him. Nothing about the man invited casual physical contact.

"Bye, sweetheart." He wrapped an arm around my shoulder and dropped a kiss on the top of my head. I blinked back my surprise, deeply touched. I must have crossed some invisible line. Ripper had accepted me as one of his people.

Finn and Bear hugged, pounding each other on the back, then Bear and Ripper climbed into the small car. Even with the front seats scooted all the way back, their knees bent at sharp angles, and their long legs almost banged against the dashboard. I didn't envy them the long ride home. With a final wave, they drove away.

Turning to Finn, I rubbed my cold nose. "Do you think Mrs. B. could crotchet nose cozies?"

Finn barked out a laugh. "I don't see why not. Let's ask next time we see her."

"It's a plan." I cocked my thumb toward my room. "How about some hot cocoa? I have a box in my room."

"With marshmallows? Because I've got to have my marshmallows."

"You think I'm a heathen? Of course with marshmallows."

Smiling, he gestured for me to lead the way.

I bit back a rueful sigh. When I'd fantasized about inviting Finn to my bedroom, the circumstances had been entirely different.

My room was on the second floor, an end unit, next to Rachel's and three doors down from Finn's. I unlocked the door then pulled aside the curtain that covered the big window overlooking the second-floor walkway. Weak sunlight spilled across the room's interior.

It had been a challenge to personalize a bare-bones room from a discount motel chain, to make it feel homey, but I'd managed to tweak it to my satisfaction. The generic landscape paintings hanging on the walls were the first to go, replaced with Dante Gabriel Rossetti art prints I'd found in a shop downtown. Other items came from the warehouse of supplies supervised by Thanh. Sage-green area rugs gave a much needed shot of color to the space. My favorite paperbacks lined the shelves of a small bookcase. I'd replaced the scratchy poly-cotton sheets with a set of luxury bamboo ones that made me feel like I was sleeping on a cloud. Nice new pillows, too. The quilt my friends at Valhalla had given me for Christmas now covered my bed.

My room lacked electricity and running water, but all in all, I was more than happy with my private sanctuary.

I was suddenly acutely aware of Finn standing next to my bed.

We'd slept side by side several times. During our undercover assignment in Prineville, we'd shared a room. Despite the pretense that we were a couple, we didn't know each other well at first. Like the cowboy gentleman he was, Finn offered to sleep on the floor. I refused. We were adults, professionals doing a job. Besides, the king-sized bed was plenty big for two.

Not a problem, I'd airily assured him.

I was fooling myself. Within days, I'd lie awake in the dark, listening to him inhale and exhale. Waking early, I'd study his profile. The straight nose. The angled planes of his face. The indentation on his chin that begged to be touched. Sometimes, one corner of his mouth tugged up in his sleep. I longed to shake him awake, to ask him what made him smile. But, of course, I didn't. We were working a mission.

"I like how you've fixed up the place."

I shook myself out of my reverie. "What?"

"I said, I like how you've fixed up the place." Finn's gaze moved over the room. "It looks cozy. Maybe you could help me spruce up my room?"

"I'd be happy to."

Finn crossed the room and stood in front of my dresser.

When Marcus and I made our way north from our base in California, I'd carried a backpack holding a few precious souvenirs from home. Those souvenirs now occupied a place of honor in my room. Framed photos were scattered across the dresser. My parents. My childhood pet, a St. Bernard named Bonnie. A picture of me and my best friend at ten years old, wearing our Little League uniforms. A red, blue and yellow plush Jayhawk from my alma mater and the university where both my parents had taught. A small seashell-covered box from a family trip to Florida. In the evenings, battery-powered candles cast a golden glow over the photos and knickknacks.

Finn picked up the photo of me in my softball uniform. "Look at you," he said under his breath. "So stinking cute."

Pleasure wound through my chest.

He set down the photo of me and lifted the silver-framed picture of the St. Bernard. "Whew. That's one big dog."

Three steps brought me to his side. "That's my girl Bonnie. A gentle giant." I touched her image with a reverent finger. "I loved her so much."

"I bet she loved you, too. Who could help it?" Finn bumped his shoulder against mine then carefully set down the photo.

My heart stuttered. Flustered, I pointed toward the small table. "Light the alcohol camping stove, will you?"

"Sure thing." He tossed a knowing smile, seeing right through my discomfiture.

I poured bottled water into a pan then dumped hot cocoa mix into two mugs. A minute later, we stirred boiling water into our mugs then sat cross-legged facing each other on the bed while we sipped our cocoa.

"Bear was right," Finn said. "Technically we're still on vacation."

I shot him an outraged look. "I'm not going to sit around for the next five days just because we're supposed to be on vacation. There's plenty of work to keep us busy."

"I agree," Finn assured me. "But I was thinking that we could take today off and do something fun to make up for missing out on our vacation."

"What do you have in mind?" I asked, intrigued by the prospect of a fun day with Finn.

He waggled his brows. "You'll have to wait and see."

Wait and see, huh? My curiosity piqued. My thoughts wandered to places they shouldn't go. I took a long sip of cocoa, then balanced the mug on my knee.

Finn reached out and brushed his thumb over my upper lip, wiping away a smudge of melted marshmallow. "I swear, I can't take you anywhere."

I couldn't breathe for a good ten seconds.

Studying the gooey smear, he shook his head, as if disappointed by my messiness. His tongue darted out from his mouth. He licked the marshmallow from his thumb, closing his eyes while he savored the taste.

My heart skipped a beat. My lips parted. How could… how could such a simple act hold so much intimacy? I gaped, frozen in place.

Finn's eyes slid open and a knowing smile curved his lips.

He touched my mouth again, his fingertip tracing its outline. "Looks like I got it all."

I swayed, my weight shifting toward him, as if drawn by a lodestone, a force too enticing to be denied. Then my spine snapped straight.

I can't. No matter how much I want to, I can't. Not until my assignment is over. Not until it's safe.

Finn watched me struggle with myself. His forehead puckered. He touched my knee. "Are you all right?" His voice dropped to a low rumble. "Is there anything I can do to help?"

"I'm fine." My good cheer sounded fake even to my own ears. "And I'm ready for a grand adventure, just like you promised."

Emotion streaked across his handsome face. Frustration, perhaps. Or disappointment. His features smoothed out so quickly that I couldn't be exactly sure what I'd seen.

"We'll need a couple flashlights." Tearing his eyes from me, he drained the last of his cocoa and stood.

I pointed toward the desk. "My solar-powered flashlight is charged."

"Mine, too. I'll grab it on our way down."

I finished my cocoa and carried the mugs over to the sink. "Will we be taking your truck?"

"Nope. Where we're going is an easy walk from here."

"Now you've got me more than a little curious," I said.

"Good." He flashed a grin. "I like to discombobulate you."

"You do, huh?" I playfully smacked his arm.

"Ouch," he deadpanned. He flashed a smirk that made my insides dance.

Bundled up against the brisk weather, we headed out on foot. We walked northeast along Dorion Avenue, then turned right onto South Main Street. We passed a bronze statue of a local celebrity, a famous—or infamous depending on your point of view—brothel madam.

"Hi, Stella." Finn tipped an imaginary hat at the statue. Two minutes later, he signaled a halt in front of a building in the historic part of town. "You figured it out yet?" he asked.

I craned my neck, looking up and down the street.

"Not a clue."

Finn fished a key out of his pocket and tilted his head toward a red door under a striped awning. "We keep the place locked up because we don't want kids poking around in there, but Justin gave me the key."

I walked up to the door and touched the gilt letters emblazoned across the window: Pendleton Underground Tours.

"My parents brought Bear and me here the first time when I was about eight. I've been back three or four times since." Finn unlocked the door.

I pictured Finn as a towhead eight-year-old, bouncing with excitement as he peppered his parents with questions. He must have been a cutie, a cutie who grew into the tall, muscular, square-jawed cowboy I followed into the building.

Some light filtered into the room from the windows, but any illumination faded the farther we got from the street. We clicked on our flashlights.

"Thanh's people have emptied out most everything from the stores in town." He swept the flashlight beam toward the empty shelves in the gift shop then directed the light high on the walls.

I jumped back, my heart kicking. Mounted animal heads stared straight ahead into the gloom.

"They left behind the taxidermy," he said.

I pressed my palm against my thundering heart. "No kidding."

Finn laid a hand on my shoulder. "You don't jump at things in the dark, do you?"

"Not usually, but disembodied heads will do it every time."

He chuckled. "Like I was saying. The stores have been emptied, but some places were left as is, including the underground. There's history down there, both good and bad."

"So we're going down?"

"Only if you want to."

Yeah, I wanted to go down. On Finn. Dammit. Cut it out.

Intrigued, I nodded. "I do."

He led me back outside and around the corner of the building to a short flight of stairs leading down to a basement door. Metal railing surrounded the stairwell, each post topped with a sharp point.

"Romeo spikes," Finn said.

My brows shot up. "What?"

"Back in the late 1800s, this was the red-light district of town." He pointed at a second-story balcony hanging over the sidewalk. "Prostitutes would toss buttons and call out to get men's attention. The Romeo spikes kept cowboys from climbing on the railing to get to the women."

I touched one of the pointy stakes. "Very clever."

"Yep." He jogged down the stairs and unlocked the door. Once inside, Finn held out a hand. "We'll need to stay close and watch our footing in the dark."

Under the circumstances, it made sense to hold hands. I twined my fingers through his. Callouses born from hard work on the ranch dotted his palm.

What would it feel like to have those big, calloused hands grazing over my skin?

Finn gave a gentle squeeze, clicked on his flashlight, then swept the beam over the room.

I jerked back and clutched at Finn's hand.

"I probably should have warned you about the mannequins," he said.

"You think?" I gasped.

Almost a dozen men sat at round, baize-covered tables, to all appearances playing cards and drinking booze. They wore cowboy hats and old-timey clothes. In the unsteady beam of light, their shadows jumped, giving the scene a disquieting illusion of movement. If they were real, the place would have echoed with raucous laughter and clinking glasses. Instead, silence reigned. They were dummies, of course, incapable of producing a peep, but stumbling on them in the dark gave me a shock.

"This is the Shamrock Card Room," Finn said. "You want to keep going?"

"Of course." The mannequins had startled me, but now that I knew what to expect, nothing would keep me from exploring the underground world. We walked through a Chinese laundry and an ice cream parlor, eventually making our way to a Prohibition era speakeasy.

"They had a bell they could ring if the cops were coming to raid the place," Finn said. "If the bell rang, everybody grabbed their moonshine and bolted."

We climbed the "thirty-one steps to heaven," a stairway leading to an old brothel. After checking out the brothel, we followed more steps down into what looked like a jail.

Finn nodded at a cell. "Mama took a photo of Bear and me standing right there, grabbing hold of the bars. She liked the picture so much that she framed it."

"I'd love to see that. Do you still have it?"

"Maybe." His expression turned pensive, then sad. "She used to keep it on her dresser. I'll ask Bear and Nyx if they have it. Could be the Wilcox Brigade tossed it out."

"Bastards." I squeezed Finn's hand. I'd heard all about the white supremacist group that had taken Valhalla and killed Finn and Bear's parents.

"Yeah, bastards. But if there's any justice, they're all rotting in hell."

We climbed a short flight of stairs and stepped out into a parking lot, blinking as our eyes adjusted to the light. Finn locked the door leading from the underground and pocketed the keys.

Without giving it a moment's thought, I reached out and slid my palm into his again, as if walking hand in hand with Finn was the most natural, most inevitable thing in the world. And dammit, it sure felt like it was.

Finn didn't glance at our joined hands as we started to walk back toward the motel. He didn't gloat, didn't say a word, but his fingers closed around mine, and a small, satisfied smile played on his lips.

My chest tightened. Shit. This was wrong. I was giving a good man a false impression. I stopped in my tracks and tugged my hand from his.

Finn pivoted to face me. He shoved his hands into his pockets. His expression took on an unaccustomed seriousness. "I wish I knew what's going on in your head. If there's a problem, you can tell me, you know."

God, why did he have to be so understanding? That just made it harder to shut things down between us.

"The only problem is the timing," I said. "I meant it when I said that I want to wait until after we've dealt with Allsop."

"Why?" Finn raised his shoulders. "Bear and Nyx didn't wait till things were safe. Neither did Kyle and Sunny, or Ripper and Kenzie. They were willing to risk falling in love. Why aren't you?"

Truth and honesty were the foundation for any worthwhile relationship. I couldn't give them to Finn. Not now. And if things went wrong, not ever.

"I'm sorry," I whispered, my throat thick. Regret burned in my belly, and I tasted acid.

Finn stepped close, so close that I felt his breath on my face. He touched the corner of my eye, where a tear threatened to spill. "I want you. We're good together. If the only problem is the timing, I'll wait it out."

The lump in my throat threatened to choke me. I swallowed it back. "I hope so."

Finn bent his elbow and offered me his arm, not his hand. "I'm getting hungry. How about we head over to the cafeteria for some lunch?"

"Sounds perfect." I tucked my hand in the crook of his arm and fell into step next to him. We passed by a liquor store, its front windows covered with plywood. On the plywood, somebody had spray-painted the words *Carpe Diem.* Across the street, on the front of an insurance building, the same words in bold red. I pointed them out to Finn. "That's new, isn't it?"

"You're right," Finn said. "I walked by here last week and didn't see it." He rubbed his jaw. "Now that I think about it, I saw *Carpe Diem* tagged on the side of a building when we drove out of town yesterday. I was too preoccupied with the meeting with Allsop's men to mention it, but it was definitely new."

"Carpe Diem," I mused. "Seize the day. I wonder who's going around town painting that on buildings. And why?"

"Let's find Rachel and see if she knows about it," Finn said. "It's probably nothing. Just kids messing around, but you never know."

"Yeah, it's probably just kids," I echoed, but an uneasy shiver raised goose bumps across my back.

EIGHT

Finn

Rachel hunched over the pile of papers scattered across her desk, one hand clutching at her hair. Her lips moved silently, furiously, like she was arguing with an invisible companion. I knocked on her door again, this time louder.

Rachel looked up from the papers and waved Georgia and me into the room.

She gestured at the mess on her desk. "This sucks. I miss my laptop."

"You're going over all the intake forms?" Georgia sat down on one of the two chairs facing Rachel's desk.

"Yeah." Rachel leaned back in her chair and swung her feet up onto the desk, a red sneaker pushing aside a file folder. "There's a little more than a thousand people in Pendleton, and I have an intake form on every one of them." She swept her hand at the pile. "Allsop's spy is somewhere in there."

"Unless they snuck into town," I offered helpfully, dropping down onto the chair next to Georgia.

Rachel shot me a dirty look. "Past the roadblocks and guards? Not likely. But even if somebody did manage to sneak in, we check everybody's names against the records before we assign lodging and a job." She scowled at the papers. "Carbon paper. Can you believe it? We're back to using freaking carbon paper and a manual typewriter to make copies of our records." She shook her head in disgust. "Anyway, I've got an intake form on the spy. I know it. I just have to figure out who it is."

"We've had two big influxes of people recently," I said. "The fifty soldiers and dozen townsfolk who came in from Prineville with Uncle Bobby and the two hundred civilians the Nampa Boys smuggled out of Idaho."

"Uncle Bobby vouched for all his people," Rachel said. "Doesn't mean one of them couldn't have been recruited by Allsop, but they're not at the top of my list."

"The folks from Idaho?" I guessed.

Rachel bobbed her head. "They're anonymous survivors. The Nampa Boys brought them supplies and tried to protect them, but the Boys didn't know them personally. It would have been easy for Allsop to plant a spy in their midst when he was making his power grab in Boise."

That made sense. "I worked for the man for months. Learned a lot about his operation and plans. If he sent a spy to keep an eye on the Nampa Boys, I never heard a word about it." I shrugged. "But Allsop plays it close to the vest. He wouldn't blab about a spy. The only man likely to know about it is Jonesy."

"And we're back to Jonesy." Rachel threw her hands in the air. "Havoc is treating him like an enemy combatant. It's the end of the world, and he still wants to respect Article 13 of the Geneva Convention."

"Havoc's a pragmatic idealist. That's what he told Ripper."

Rachel flashed her teeth in a humorless smile. "I've never been much of an idealist. I'm more of a get-er-done kind of woman. I just wish Havoc would let me have a real go at Jonesy, you know what I mean?"

"Yeah. I know what you mean." Memory rooted me in place. Georgia laid a hand on top of mine.

"Oh, fuck." Rachel dropped her head. "I'm sorry, Finn. Me and my damned mouth. I wasn't thinking."

"It's all right." I offered my friend what I hoped was a reassuring smile. "We all wish Jonesy would tell what he knows."

"He will." Georgia's voice was firm. "Marcus has a plan, remember?"

Remember? I wasn't likely to forget any plan that required Georgia to wheedle her way into the confidence of the most callous bastard I've ever encountered.

I swung my eyes toward Georgia. "No need to remind me of Havoc's plan." We stared at each other. Tension lay heavy between us. I clenched my jaw. I'd spoken my piece, and Georgia wouldn't take kindly to any words of protest about the scheme, but damn, I hated her assignment.

Georgia withdrew her hand and settled back in her chair. She turned to Rachel. "If we can do anything to help with your investigation, just let us know."

"Technically we're still on vacation, so we've got the time," I added.

"I will. Thank you," Rachel said. "Is that why you guys stopped by?"

"No." Georgia frowned. "We hate to pile on—"

Rachel groaned, covering her eyes with her hands. "What now?"

"Finn and I've noticed new graffiti around town," Georgia continued. "*Carpe Diem.*"

Rachel blinked. "Graffiti? You're worried about graffiti?"

"It's probably nothing to be concerned about," I said. "*Carpe Diem.* Seize the day. It doesn't sound like much of a rallying cry for dissidents. But Sahdev told me that the crazy religious cult they dealt with had spray-painted Back 2 Eden all over Portland before they burned down the city." I lifted a shoulder. "Like I said, it's probably nothing, but we wanted to bring it to your attention, just in case."

"Great. Just great." Rachel briefly closed her eyes, a woman feeling the pressure of her responsibilities. "You said you're still technically on vacation. How about if I put you two in charge of getting to the bottom of this *Carpe Diem* graffiti? Take it off my plate so I can keep my focus on ferreting out the spy?"

Georgia and I exchanged a glance. I doubted that the investigation would produce anything earth-shattering, but somebody should look into it. And I'd welcome any job that kept me at Georgia's side.

"I'm willing to play sleuth," I said.

Georgia nodded. "Me, too."

NINE

Georgia

"Where do you want to start?" Finn asked as we emerged back into the weak early afternoon sunshine. "Should we take my truck and drive around town, see how much more *Carpe Diem* graffiti we can spot?"

I thought about it. It would be a good idea to have some sense of how big the potential problem was. It was one thing if there was only a handful of tags, something entirely different if the number had exploded over the past days.

"I'd rather not spend too much time looking for the graffiti." I glanced at my watch. 12:22. "It's going to be dark by five o'clock. How about if we cruise up and down the main streets in town and check out how much graffiti is out there"

"And then?"

"Let's go to the warehouse and talk to Thanh. He could tell us if anybody has asked for red spray paint."

Side by side, we jogged up the street to the motel parking lot and jumped in Finn's truck.

Settling in next to Finn, I bit my lip, suppressing a smile. We were on assignment from Rachel. With an untroubled conscience, I could spend the entire day in the company of a man who drew me like no other. No need to wonder if I should be keeping my distance, not when we were going about the chief of security's business.

I glanced at his profile, admiring the surprisingly dark lashes under thick, tawny eyebrows. The high cheekbones. The strong, determined chin. The firm mouth. I balled my fists, fighting the need to reach out and trace a finger over his lips. Memories of our one-and-only kiss stirred my blood.

Damn my conscience. Would it really be so wrong to give in to my feelings?

I won't ever do anything to you that you don't want. That's a promise.

Finn's words. Finn's guarantee that he'd respect my boundaries. But if I launched myself across the center console and threw myself on him, he'd reciprocate. If I let down my guard, if I opened the door to a relationship, the man would be all over me. And it would be glorious. At that thought, my nipples pebbled. I sighed.

Finn's gaze cut my way. "You okay?"

Not trusting my voice to keep steady, I nodded, but couldn't drag my eyes away from his.

His forehead furrowed and his eyes bore into me. A slow, knowing smile crawled across his face. "It's all right to want me, Georgia. In fact, I'd call it a damned fine thing."

I sputtered and only honesty—a deep need not to lie to him or to myself—kept me from denying his assertion, from telling him to get over himself. "Wanting you doesn't change anything."

"No?" He threw the truck into reverse. "Keep telling yourself that, darlin'."

There was nothing I could say to that, was there?

After twenty minutes of driving up and down the main streets of Pendleton we discovered five more *Carpe Diem* signs. Including the one Finn had spotted on the outskirts of town and the two we saw earlier today, that brought our total to eight.

"Somebody's been busy," Finn observed.

"Yeah, but it's still relatively small scale. The town isn't blanketed with them."

"To the warehouse?"

"Yes."

Finn steered the truck toward the city's warehouse and distribution center, located in a church next door to the town's only medical clinic. We found Thanh, a former pharmacist, sorting through the prescriptions his "gophers" had brought in that day.

Scavengers—the folks he sent to go-fer supplies—had finished searching and clearing out all of the houses and stores in Pendleton and now were going farther afield, searching other towns for survivors and supplies. They'd returned last night from a run to Condon and Fossil.

Thanh looked up when we entered the Sunday-school room that he'd transformed into the town's pharmacy. He raised a hand in greeting and set his clipboard on the table.

"Do you have a minute?" I asked.

"For you guys? Always." The corners of his dark eyes crinkled with pleasure when he smiled at Finn and me. "What's up?"

"We're looking into some new graffiti that's been showing up around town," Finn said. "*Carpe Diem.* In red paint."

"Has anybody come in asking for red spray paint?" I got right to the point.

His brows drew together while he thought about it. "Not that I'm aware of, but I'm just one cog in the machine."

Thanh was being modest. The man was an organizational genius. Little went on at the warehouse that he wasn't on top of. He was so devoted to the job that he'd turned one of the church offices into his quarters, choosing to live and sleep where he worked.

I rolled my eyes. "Who are you trying to kid?"

"Yeah, you're no cog, man," Finn added. "You're the beating heart of the operation."

Thanh inclined his head, acknowledging the well-deserved praise. "Let's head over to the building materials and check out the paint supplies."

We followed him to the daylight basement, now filled with row after row of metal shelving holding everything people might need to maintain and repair houses and other structures. Thanh had imposed order on the collection of materials. Bags of concrete mix, raised off the floor on wooden pallets, lined the closest wall. Glancing to my left, I saw insulation and roofing materials, and stacks of plywood and lumber. Whiteboards on the end of each row of shelves listed their contents.

A young man with light-brown hair and a wispy goatee sat at a table under a window, sorting nuts and bolts into plastic containers. He looked up when we bustled into the room.

"Christian, this is Georgia and Finn. They work with Major Havoc."

Christian jumped to his feet. "Nice to meet you."

"Christian is assigned full time to the building supply room," Thanh explained. He turned to the young man. "Has anybody come in recently looking for red spray paint?"

Christian shook his head. "Not that I know of. Other than Lydia Barton. She came in yesterday and asked for paint for a chicken coop she was building."

"Let's go check the paint section." Thanh led the way.

In the middle of the room, an entire row of shelving units held cans of paint and paint thinner. The spray paint alone filled one metal unit. Thanh picked up a clipboard and scanned the list.

"It says here that Lydia Barton picked up three cans of red spray paint." Thanh looked at the top shelf. He moved the front row of cans aside then counted the cans behind the ones in front. He checked the clipboard again, then glanced at Christian. "Eleven cans of red spray paint are missing."

Christian flushed. "I'm not in the basement all the time," he stammered. "I go on breaks and to lunch. And I help unload trucks when the gophers come back from a run. Anybody could have come in and taken the spray paint when I was out of the room."

I caught Finn and Thanh's eyes and jerked my head, trying to convey that I wanted to take the lead. Experience told me we needed to keep our mouths shut and to let Christian keep talking. Silence made people uncomfortable, and they yammered away to fill it. Especially people with something to hide.

"I mean, missing spray paint isn't that big of a deal," he continued, his eyes wide. "It's not like somebody was stealing food or medicine. Nobody needs spray paint in order to survive. And besides, if it happened when I was busy someplace else, it's not my fault."

After that second proclamation of innocence, he lapsed into silence again.

"You done?' Finn asked.

Christian stilled, his expression stricken, as if he'd figured out that his long-winded denials only made him look guilty.

"Did you take the red paint?" Thanh asked gently.

"Of course not," Christian protested.

"Do you know who took it?" Thanh said.

Christian shook his head in a vigorous and utterly unconvincing denial. Before Thanh could persist with his questioning, I spoke up.

"Thank you for your time, Christian. We really appreciate your help with our investigation. If we think of anything we forgot to ask, how late will you be working today?"

"I get off at seven."

"Seven," I repeated. "And if you think of anything else that might be of assistance, ask Thanh to let us know." Smiling broadly, I extended my hand to the flustered young man.

He grasped at the lifeline I threw him. "I sure will." He pumped my hand up and down, the tension easing from his face. "Good luck with your investigation."

"Thanks. And like you said, missing spray paint isn't a huge deal. We just need to know if there's a problem with the warehouse system, with the way we keep track of our supplies and who takes what."

I'd apologize to Thanh later for suggesting that he was slacking off.

Christian bobbed his head in enthusiastic agreement. "I get it. We can't afford to lose supplies. I'll keep my eyes open for any problems."

"I appreciate that." I turned to a confused looking Thanh. "Thank you so much for your help. Finn and I will be on our way now."

"Then we're done here?" Thanh asked slowly.

"For now," I said brightly. "We'll let you get back to work."

I marched up the stairs and out of the building, a silent Finn at my side. Once we climbed back into the truck, his silence broke.

"That squirrelly guy looks guilty as all get-out. What are you up to?"

I smiled. "What are you doing at seven?"

He shrugged, catching on. "I don't know. What *am* I doing at seven?"

TEN

Finn

When I was a kid, I was obsessed with James Bond movies. I fantasized about being a secret agent when I grew up. Suave and sophisticated, I'd give 007 a run for his money. With brains and brawn, I'd thwart the nefarious schemes of evildoers and save the day. Then, after my feats of derring-do, I'd ride off into the sunset with a pretty woman by my side.

Twenty years later, reality proved nothing like fantasy. Oh, I was finally a spy—twice over including my time in Boise—but the role bore no resemblance to my childhood imaginings. Who dreams about crouching down under a window in three inches of snow, freezing their keister off in the dark while listening to a bunch of ass clowns inside a house get drunk?

A pretty woman by my side, that was the only part my fantasy got right. Georgia squatted next to me in the snow, blowing onto her gloved hands to fight the cold.

What would my folks say if they could see me skulking under somebody's window like a Peeping Tom, like some kind of perv? I huffed out a breath. Suave and sophisticated, my ass. Spying was a dirty business.

Glancing at my shivering companion, I rubbed the tip of my cold nose. The scarf that Hannah had knitted me for Christmas was wrapped around my neck. I slipped it off and draped it around Georgia, then pulled the wool scarf up to cover the bottom half of her face.

She wrinkled her brow in protest and started to give it back to me, but I lifted a hand. "Humor a cowboy, will you?"

A beat, then Georgia nodded. "Thank you, Finn."

We'd followed Christian home when he finished work at seven. He lived only a few blocks from the warehouse, in a small bungalow with a detached garage. Once he entered the house, we jimmied the lock on a side door and slipped into the one-car garage. Sure enough, half a dozen cans of red spray paint were lined up on the work bench.

Christian was our culprit. Whether he was a one-man operation, a loner going out at night to paint his motto across town, or whether he worked with like-minded friends, that was yet to be seen.

"His living room curtains are open," Georgia had said. "Let's watch him for a while."

We'd circled the house then duck-walked into position under the living room window. The big rhododendron bush we crouched behind should keep any neighbors from spotting us. Peeking inside, I'd spied Christian and two other young men. An old-fashioned kerosene lantern illuminated the messy room. Looked like one of the men had taken a bat to the big-screen television hanging useless over the fireplace. Empty and half-empty cans of food littered the tables and floors, some of the contents spilling out onto the rug. Shit. Why hadn't they just rolled out a red carpet for vermin?

In giant letters, somebody had spray-painted *Carpe Diem* across one wall.

His friends sprawled at opposite ends of a sofa, clearly feeling no pain. One of them chucked a can of beer to the other. It sailed right over the guy's head and hit a ceramic lamp on the end table, shattering it into pieces. Without electricity to power it, the lamp wasn't much of a loss, but it made a real mess. The knuckleheads laughed like hyenas, then leaned over and high-fived each other.

Close to a dozen empty beer cans and an unopened six-pack sat next to the kerosene lantern on the coffee table. I frowned. Where did they get so much beer? Was Christian pilfering booze from the warehouse in addition to spray paint? What else had he made off with?

Christian perched on the edge of a beat-up recliner, waving his hands excitedly while he spoke. I held my breath, straining to hear his words, but all I could make out for sure was "Thanh" and "Havoc."

His friends didn't share one lick of his nervousness. One of them hopped up, slapped Christian on the back, and pressed a beer into his hands.

I leaned over and whispered in Georgia's ear. "You want to stick around?"

"Yeah, for a while." Her breath billowed white in the frigid air. "Let's see if they head out. If we catch them in the act, it's case closed."

"You sure you're not too cold?" I asked.

"I'm from Kansas," she scoffed. "This is nothing."

Maybe so, but she wasn't in Kansas anymore, and her body had acclimated to a less frozen environment.

I shifted my weight from one foot to the other, the chill biting into my bones. I'd follow Georgia's lead, but this was starting to feel like a colossal waste of time. If Christian and his friends were tagging buildings at night, so what? We could deal with that. Rachel could summon them to headquarters and order them to cut it out, to stop wasting paint. Thanh could give Christian a stern talking-to, fire him from the warehouse if need be. Somebody had to talk to him, to get to the bottom of the tagging, but *Carpe Diem* wasn't exactly a call to arms for political dissidents. It was more a rallying cry for folks looking to party.

Fifteen minutes later, squatting in the cold was starting to make my knees cramp. Georgia and I pressed our backs against the siding, popping up every now and then to peek through the window. Raucous laughter from inside the house occasionally punctuated the quiet. I was about to suggest that we call it a night, when the front door swung open. Georgia and I flattened ourselves against the snow.

Giggling, Christian and one of his friends trudged across the driveway. They lurched down the sidewalk, their way lit by the kerosene lantern clutched in Christian's hand. At least they had the sense to don parkas, so the drunk fools wouldn't freeze.

"Let's follow them," Georgia breathed.

"All right."

Three sheets to the wind, Christian and his buddy ignored us as we trailed a block behind them. If they chanced to look back over their shoulders, they'd see a young couple walking hand in hand, out for an evening stroll. With the hoods of our jackets pulled up covering our heads, Christian wasn't likely to recognize us from the warehouse.

They walked the few blocks back to the warehouse, then halted. Christian plopped down onto a curb and set the hurricane lantern in front of him on the street. His friend followed suit and they fell into an animated conversation.

Heads lowered, Georgia and I walked past the pair.

"Hey," Christian's buddy called out to us. He held up his can of beer. "You guys looking to have some fun?"

"Not tonight, thanks," I said, averting my face.

At the end of the block, Georgia and I turned right. She squeezed my hand, bringing me to a stop, then she slipped both arms around my waist. "Let's keep an eye on them for a few minutes," she said, smiling broadly up at me.

I wrapped my arms around her, too. We hugged each other in the moonlight, to all appearances a young couple in love. Over her shoulder, I watched the two men laugh and nudge each other. Christian's friend pulled a can of beer from the pocket of his parka and passed it to his companion.

"Nothing but drinking and talking," I said.

We lingered for another five minutes, our arms locked around each other. The cold had brought a rosy glow to her pretty cheeks, and the moonlight sparkled in her eyes. Even if it was an act, it felt damned good to hold Georgia. It felt right. My chest grew tight. Why was the woman so bound and determined to make us wait? Christian and his friends got one thing right. In an uncertain world, we should seize the day and make the most of whatever time we have.

Georgia shivered and my protective instincts rose to the fore. "C'mon," I urged. "Let's get out of the cold."

Georgia sniffed, then reached for a pocket of her jacket. She pulled out a tissue and dabbed her nose. "My nose is really starting to run."

"That settles it. Back to the truck." I took her hand and tugged. We walked briskly the two blocks to where I'd parked. We climbed inside and I started the engine, letting it idle while the heater took the chill out of the air.

Georgia held a hand out to the heat vent, sighing with pleasure when the warm air blew over her fingers. "Of all the amenities, I think I miss central heating the most," she said. "How about you?"

"It's hot showers for me." I smiled, remembering how good it felt to stand under a showerhead while water so hot I could barely stand it pummeled my skin. Man oh man, a shower right now would be great. A shower with Georgia—all warm and slippery and wet—would be better.

"Running water." Georgia nodded. "That's a contender, too."

"Yep," I agreed. "And the internet." Once we got started on what we missed from the old world, we could keep going forever.

"We took so much for granted, didn't we?" she said.

"That we did." I studied Georgia's face. She was in a contemplative mood. Would this be a good time to suggest that we throw caution to the wind and grab a hold of what we still had? Each other.

She pulled the seat belt across her chest and clicked it into place. "Let's get back to the motel. I want to snuggle down under my new quilt."

"Will you make me some more hot cocoa?" I asked.

"You bet. But you have to BYOQ."

My eyebrows shot up. "Huh?"

"Bring your own quilt," she explained.

Damn. "No problem. I got one for Christmas, too."

I threw the truck into gear, drove back to the motel, and parked. As we slammed the doors shut, I spotted Rachel trotting across the street from the headquarters. She raised a hand. We waited for her to catch up with us.

"You're working late," Georgia observed.

"No rest for the wicked. Or the incompetent." Stress and self-recrimination pinched Rachel's face. "Havoc kicked me out of the office and sent me home to get some sleep."

"Finn and I are about to drink some hot cocoa and warm up under our new quilts," Georgia said. "You want to join us? I make a mean cup of instant hot chocolate."

Say no. Say no.

"Interrupt your slumber party?" The snark and good humor returned to Rachel's face. "I wouldn't dream of it."

"Come on." Georgia slipped her arm through Rachel's. "It'll be good for you to spend some time relaxing with friends."

"Somehow I don't think Finn's plans involve getting *me* under a blanket." Rachel swung her gaze to me. "I'm right, aren't I, cowboy?"

"Behave," I growled.

Rachel rolled her eyes. "Never."

I chuckled, then stiffened, my spidey senses tingling.

What was that?

Georgia frowned. "Do you smell something?"

"I smell smoke." Rachel pivoted around, scanning the area.

Nothing looked amiss, but I caught a faint whiff of smoke in the air. We ran out into the street, looking around in all directions.

"There." Georgia caught my arm and pointed to the north, to the direction we'd come from just twenty minutes ago. Orange flames licked at the horizon, highlighting the column of black smoke that shot up into the night sky.

"Holy fuck," Rachel gasped. "The warehouse. The clinic."

ELEVEN

Georgia

Across the street from the motel, the guards stationed outside the city hall had alerted to the fire, too. Shouting, they pointed at the flames, and one of them ran inside. Good. The guard would tell Marcus about the conflagration.

Finn grabbed the fire extinguisher mounted on the wall near the base of the motel's cement stairs, then dashed to his pickup. "Let's go," he cried.

Rachel and I threw ourselves into the truck. Finn peeled out of the parking lot, his tires slipping on the icy street. We raced north, crossed the Umatilla River, then skidded to a stop in front of the warehouse.

"Oh, thank fuck," Rachel moaned.

The fire hadn't touched the church that warehoused our supplies.

I pressed a hand against my chest, almost choking on my gratitude. God. What would we do if our stockpile of supplies was reduced to ash? What would become of Havoc's band of survivors if we lost all of our food, clothes, medicine, and everything else we needed to survive?

My relief was short lived.

"The clinic," Finn choked out. "Had to be Christian and his damned kerosene lamp."

Fire engulfed the small clinic located next door to the warehouse. Flames danced along the roof, and the interior glowed a brilliant golden-orange. Finn snatched up the fire extinguisher and bounded toward the medical facility, Rachel and I hard on his heels.

Pounding heat kept us at bay, and we halted in the parking lot. Finn wouldn't be able to hear me over the crackle and roar of the blaze. I grabbed his elbow and pointed at the fire extinguisher, shaking my head. The extinguisher was no match for the inferno. He nodded, acknowledging the bitter truth.

He touched my cheek, a fleeting gesture. Sorrow and resolve flickered across his face. Finn's mouth swooped down, and his lips crushed mine, a quick, hard kiss that stole my breath. My pulse leapt.

Then he whirled and bolted toward the entrance to the clinic. The heat scorching through my veins turned to an icy spike of fear.

"No," I shrieked, staggering after him. Rushing into the fire was suicide. And for what? To try to save Christian and his friend? Finn was worth a hundred Christians. A thousand. He was worth everything.

Rachel caught me around the waist and held me fast. Feet pounded behind us. Marcus and four of his soldiers ran to our sides. I struggled desperately to escape Rachel's arms.

"Make her let me go," I begged.

An unspoken message passed between the major and his chief of security. Havoc's expression hardened. He jabbed a finger at Rachel and me.

"Stay." His lips shaped the word. He barked an order to one of his soldiers. Without a backward glance, the big man raced into the inferno.

TWELVE

Finn

I hurtled across the parking lot, each step bringing me closer to the firestorm. Regret bit deep. This was my fault. I shouldn't have left Christian to wander drunk through the town carrying a goddamned kerosene lamp in his hand. I should've stayed close till he made it back home safe and sound.

If I had—shit, if I had—our clinic wouldn't be burning to the ground. I wouldn't have had to see the look on Georgia's face when she understood what I was going to do. I wouldn't have to risk a fiery death that would cheat Georgia and me out of all our tomorrows.

Burying my nose in my elbow, I crashed through the open door. Blistering heat and acrid smoke came at me from all sides. My eyes stung. I coughed and retched. Gritting my teeth, I stumbled across the lobby. My foot struck something. I dropped to my knees, patting the floor. My fingers found a man's leg. I slid my hands up across his chest to his arms. Bracing myself, I tried to haul him to his feet.

He didn't budge. *C'mon.* Hard-earned muscle covered my six-foot, two-inch frame. Christian was short and slight. I should be able to carry him out of there with no trouble. Grunting, I pulled again.

The man groaned and turned his head. Despite the heat, my blood chilled.

Not Christian.

Rocco. Rocco de Campo. My friend. The obstetric nurse who helped run the clinic. Just the sort of guy who'd rush into a fire to see if he could help. A burly, tattooed beast of a man, he stood at least six foot four.

No way would I leave Rocco to burn. Gritting my teeth, I grabbed him under his arms and heaved. He slid an inch toward the door. I held my breath and pulled with all my might. His body slid another two inches.

A burning timber crashed to the floor not ten feet away. If Christian and his friend were in the back of the building, they were goners. If I didn't get us out of there soon, Rocco and I were goners, too.

God. If you've a mind to help, I sure could use it.

I blinked hard against the smoke. Setting my jaw, I braced my feet and tugged on Rocco's dead-weight. His eyes fluttered open and he stirred.

Someone dropped onto their knees next to me. Marcus Havoc seized Rocco's limp arms and pulled him into a seated position. I crawled to one side of the big man, jamming my shoulder under his arm. Havoc positioned himself under Rocco's other arm. Havoc raised three fingers in the air, then one by one he folded each finger down.

Three. Two. One. At zero, Havoc and I pushed to our feet, balancing Rocco's bulk between us. We half-dragged him through the door and out into the parking lot. A loud rumble. Sparks flew as beams in the lobby collapsed behind us.

A small crowd had gathered. Somebody kicked snow out of the way and spread a blanket on the ground. Havoc and I gently lowered Rocco onto the blanket.

Georgia wrenched herself out of Rachel's grip and staggered toward me. I held out an arm and pulled her to my side.

She patted my chest and arms and face, the movements desperate and jerky, like she was trying to assure herself that I was really standing there and that I was okay.

"You're all right?" Her voice broke on the question.

"I'm fine, angel. It's Rocco we need to worry about."

"I'm okay." Rocco coughed. "How about the other guys?"

Shit. Christian and his friend *had* been in the clinic.

"What other guys?" Havoc asked.

"We'll fill you in later," I said.

Wearing nothing but pajamas and slippers, Sara rushed toward us. Her eyes went wide and she stumbled, her hand flying to her mouth. Shock and dismay crossed her pretty features. She worked hand in glove with Rocco, running the clinic. He was a good friend and constant support to the young doctor. And Havoc, well I didn't know precisely what Havoc and Sara were to each other, but there was something going on.

Sara touched Havoc's arm, then dropped to her knees next to Rocco, her professional mask slipping firmly into place. "I need to check his circulation, airway, and breathing."

"And we need to get him off the wet ground," Havoc said.

Behind us, the roof to the clinic collapsed, sending showers of sparks into the air.

"What should we do about the fire, sir?" one of the soldiers asked Havoc.

"The clinic is gone, but at least the building is isolated. Most important thing is that we don't let the fire spread. Watch for burning embers blowing onto nearby structures." Hands on his hips, Havoc surveyed the area. "There's snow on the ground." He glanced at the cloudy sky. "And more on its way. That's good."

My mind raced. We were too far from the river to quickly organize an effective bucket brigade. "I could get a bunch of buckets from the warehouse and drive my truck down to the Umatilla," I suggested. "Then haul water back here. You could assign soldiers with buckets of water to patrol the area to make sure the fire doesn't spread."

Rachel pointed a finger and leveled me with a stern glare. "You aren't doing anything until Sara checks you for smoke inhalation." She turned to Havoc. "I'll fetch the water."

Havoc nodded. "Do it."

Georgia squeezed my arm, discouraging any objections on my part. I knew when I was beat. I fished in my pocket for the keys to my truck and tossed them to Rachel.

"With me." She jerked her head to a couple of soldiers.

They took off at a run, passing Thanh, who was pushing an ambulance gurney across the parking lot. Havoc and two of his soldiers lifted a protesting Rocco onto the stretcher.

"Now what?" Georgia asked. "Where do we take Rocco?"

Sara frowned. "Ideally, I'd do a series of blood tests and a chest X-ray. I'd examine his airway for signs of damage. But without the right equipment, electricity, and a lab, I can't do any of that." She shook her head, frustration creasing her forehead. "Let's take him home. I'll stay with him and monitor him."

Sara and Rocco lived in opposite sides of a duplex a couple of blocks from the clinic. It was as good a place as any to take the big man.

"I'll get an oxygen tank from the warehouse and bring it over," Thanh offered.

"Good idea," Sara said.

A small sedan careened into the parking lot. Justin Mrachek and a woman I didn't recognize climbed out. She held back while Justin rushed over to our side. He gaped at Rocco on the stretcher. "What the hell happened? You all right, man?"

"I'm fine," Rocco rasped.

Havoc quickly filled his chief of operations in on the details.

"We think we know who started the fire," Georgia said. "Finn and I were looking into some new graffiti that's been showing up around town. We found the tagger and followed him back to his place. He looked harmless, a party hearty at the end of the world type."

"We left him wandering the streets drunk with a kerosene lamp." My voice was heavy with self-blame. "It was a stupid mistake."

"Hold on." Rocco raised one weak hand, stopping the soldiers from pushing the stretcher away. "I went on a walk after dinner. Saw lights moving in the clinic." Rocco coughed and cleared his throat. "Found two guys messing with the tank of laughing gas. They were slaphappy. Clumsy. One of them dropped a kerosene lamp. Curtains caught on fire. Flames spread. They thought it was funny." He blinked, his eyes heavy. "Kept giggling and pointing at the fire… I tried to get them out… but the flames were between them and me."

"That's enough talking." Sara laid a hand on Rocco's arm and turned to Havoc. "You can interview him tomorrow."

Havoc nodded and jerked his chin at his men. They started to push the gurney across the parking lot. Sara turned to follow them. Havoc caught her hand. "I'll check in on you as soon as I'm finished here."

"Okay."

Havoc crossed his arms over his chest. His gaze skated from Justin, to Thanh, to Georgia, to me. A muscle in his jaw twitched. "I'm calling a meeting. Tomorrow. Nine a.m. Things in Pendleton are going to change."

THIRTEEN

Georgia

We were uncharacteristically solemn as we took our seats across from Marcus in the conference room of his headquarters. Even Rachel was unusually subdued. She'd foregone her usual cross-legged perch atop the table and was seated in a leather executive chair to Marcus's right.

Rocco, Finn, and Marcus had emerged relatively unscathed from their brush with fire, at least as far as Sara could tell. None of them experienced chest pain, an irregular heart rate, or had trouble breathing. Rocco was confined to his bed—a precaution he much lamented—his head and shoulders propped up on a mountain of pillows to help him breathe easier.

We'd lucked out, but you couldn't tell that from the expression on Marcus's face.

He leaned forward in his chair. "I've been so focused on preparing for the war with Allsop that I've been remiss performing my other duties. I put off setting up essential services. That ends today. The buck stops here."

None of us dared to interrupt him.

He hopped to his feet, strode over to a whiteboard, and picked up a black marker. "So what did we learn from last night's fiasco?"

"We need a fire department," Justin said. "The city's hydrants are dry, but a pumper truck can carry a thousand gallons of water, enough to put out a small fire. We need to keep the trucks' reservoirs filled and train a fire brigade." His mouth set in a hard line, and he slapped his chest. "I'm the chief of operations. If anybody was remiss, it was me. I was so focused on sanitation—body disposal—that I didn't plan for fires."

"Guys, we don't have time for a guiltier-than-thou circle jerk." Rachel swept her hand, gesturing at everyone seated around the table. "We've all let things slide. Shit, I let a spy to slip into town right under my nose. I'm as guilty as anybody else. The question is, what do we do to set things right?"

"Exactly." Havoc tapped the whiteboard with the pen, then wrote #1 Fire Department on the board.

A thoughtful expression crossed Rachel's face. "You know, if we don't have a working fire brigade, maybe Allsop doesn't either. Finn? Do you know?"

"When I was working for him, he didn't. Public safety was never a priority for Allsop."

Havoc frowned. "What are you getting at, Rachel?"

"We could disrupt Allsop's operations by sending teams into Boise to set fires. Maybe burn down his soldiers' barracks, or their hospital, or their supply warehouses."

Finn held up a hand. "I'm all for disrupting Allsop's operations, but setting fires in Boise? Burning warehouses? Think of the collateral damage. The risk to civilians. Think of the waste of valuable supplies." He shook his head. "There's gotta be a better way."

Rachel sighed. "I respect the hell out of you, Finn, but your moral compass is blinding you to how things work in the real world. You can't—"

"Hold on," Finn interrupted. "Are you accusing me of being a clueless Boy Scout?"

"No." Rachel hesitated. "If we don't defeat Allsop, everybody in the Pacific Northwest will suffer. That's a certainty. When faced with a certainty we can't be afraid to act because some innocent people *might* get hurt."

"So you're saying the end justifies the means?" he asked.

"I'm saying we need to look at the big picture."

Havoc thumped his fist on the table, silencing the debate. "Rachel, Finn, I hear you. We'll circle back to this discussion another time, but now I want to stay on task. What else do we need besides a fire brigade?"

"We need a new medical clinic," I said. "It was nice to have the clinic next door to the warehouse, but there are plenty of places in town where Sara and Rocco could relocate. Preferably something within walking distance of their duplex."

"How about you and Finn work with Sara to choose a new location?" Marcus asked.

I glanced at Finn, who bobbed his head. "Of course. We'd be happy to."

Despite the serious nature of the discussion, my heart fluttered. Last night had proved to me how much I cared about Finn. When he rushed into the fire—shit—I thought my heart would stop.

Marcus wrote #2 Medical Clinic on the whiteboard. "What else?"

"The *Carpe Diem* people," Rachel said. "We can't afford to have people wandering around town at night, drunk as skunks, and starting fires."

"What do you propose we do about that?" Marcus asked.

"Well, first, beef up security at the warehouse so that the workers can't help themselves to the booze or any other scarce commodity. Maybe we'll have to search workers before they leave the building."

#3 Warehouse Security, Marcus added to the list.

"People might object to being patted down when they leave their work," Thanh said. "It implies that we don't trust them. That we're not a team working together for the common good."

"That's something to consider," Havoc conceded.

"Right now, we've told people that if they do something truly egregious—like murder or rape—they're done, execution or exile at Havoc's discretion," Justin said. "But for lesser offenses, if they steal, if they make mischief, if they vandalize property, we have no formal mechanism for maintaining law and order."

"I don't like the idea of summary execution," Marcus said. "Thank God we haven't had to resort to such extreme measures."

The prospect of summary execution didn't appear to trouble Rachel. "We haven't had to resort to it *yet*. Sometimes people need to die in order to keep everybody else safe."

Marcus rubbed his chin. "You know, up till now we haven't had much trouble with people acting out. After living through the pandemic, most folks were grateful to find other survivors, to have a safe place to live, to have access to food and water and medical care."

"Maybe we've been living through a sort of honeymoon period, when everybody was happy and grateful and on their best behavior," Finn said. "That had to change. Folks can't live together—form any kind of society—without conflict arising."

#4 Law and Order, Marcus wrote on the whiteboard.

"What does law and order mean?" I asked. "Are we going to create a police force? Are we going to send out patrols?"

"Will they be armed?" Rachel picked up the thread. "Will they be authorized to use deadly force?"

"What laws will we enforce? Will we follow laws from the old world? Or create new laws for the new world? And what happens to people who violate them? Will we have trials? Judges? Juries? Prison?" I continued.

"Whatever we do, we can't follow the eye-for-an-eye system of justice Uncle Bobby tried in Prineville," Finn said. "That blew up in his face big-time."

"Fuck." Marcus clutched at his head. "You guys are making my head spin." He turned to Rachel. "You have intake records on everybody in town. Look them over. Do we have any former judges, lawyers, or cops in town? Form a committee. Bring me a recommendation about how to maintain law and order."

Rachel rolled her eyes. "You mean in my copious spare time? When I'm not busy tracking down Allsop's spy?"

Havoc flashed a smile. "Nobody said it would be easy to rebuild society."

"You might want to invite Uncle Bobby to join the committee," Finn suggested.

Rachel shot him the stink eye. "You offering to run the committee?"

"No, but I'll help any way I can."

A simple statement that encapsulated everything you needed to know about Finn. He never shirked his duty. An image of last night's fire flashed across my memory, and I shuddered. Finn would risk his life to do what he thought was right. He always stepped up, and he did it with good humor and an easy smile.

Before I thought better of it, I reached under the table and slipped my hand into his. Caught off guard, Finn flexed his fingers before he wrapped them firmly around mine. He kept his eyes on Rachel—giving nothing away about our holding hands under the table like a couple of teenagers—but one corner of his mouth tipped up.

"Two men died in the fire last night," Thanh said. "We need to figure out what's going on with the *Carpe Diem* people. Was it just Christian and his roommates, or are more people indulging in this eat-drink-and-be-merry behavior?"

"I had the third roommate brought in for questioning last night." Marcus dropped onto his leather chair. "After he sobered up, we talked. He said a couple of weeks ago, Christian started stealing from the warehouse. Candy bars at first, then booze. The flu had killed almost everybody, he said. Death could take you without warning. They decided that they might as well have some fun while they're still alive."

"*Carpe diem*," I said.

Marcus nodded. "They had no political agenda. It was just a hedonistic fling."

"Thanh asked the right question," Rachel said. "Did they party alone, or were other people involved? If there are a bunch of people getting wasted, roaming the streets at night, being careless, starting fires, it could turn into a public safety issue."

"Yeah." Marcus scrubbed a hand over his jaw. "The roommate said they'd been meeting up with other like-minded people, but he didn't recall many of their names."

"We've got enough shit to deal with," Rachel said. "How about if we impose a temporary curfew, order people to stay home at night, just until we get a better handle on things?"

"Do we really want to go there?" I asked. "A curfew? Restricting people's right to go out at night?"

"Allsop ordered a curfew in Boise and Bend," Finn said. "Are we taking our lead from the bad guys?"

Rachel scrunched up her face. "We're nothing like Allsop. We're just trying to keep people safe while we stabilize the situation."

"I've heard that line before." Finn's fingers tightened around my hand. "In Boise. 'Trust me. It's for your own good.' That's on the business card of every would-be tyrant."

Marcus raised one hand, silencing the debate. "Nobody wants to take away anyone's rights. I swore to protect and defend the constitution, and I mean to keep that oath. A temporary curfew—to protect life and property—seems like a good idea to me."

"A slippery slope, my friend," Finn muttered.

Clearly, the months he'd spent watching Allsop's operation in Boise had colored Finn's perspective. It had colored mine, too. It was inevitable. Experience altered your view of the world.

"Your objections are noted." Marcus reached into his ever-present bowl of walnuts, took out a nut, and tapped it against the tabletop. He looked around at his circle of friends, his gaze moving from one person to the next. "We're all doing the best we can under trying circumstances. We have the same goal. We're going to defeat Allsop and build a stable and just society. But like I told Rachel, nobody said it was going to be easy."

One by one, we nodded. An odd sinking sensation filled my chest. This was the first time I'd sensed any potential rift between us. We were the good guys. We'd work it out, but the fissure was disquieting. At least Finn and I were on the same page.

We stood and filed silently toward the door.

"Georgia," Marcus called.

I turned back to him. "Yes, sir?"

"I'm sending you to meet with Jonesy again today. Report to Rachel at 11:30 for a briefing."

"I'll be there."

At the mention of Jonesy's name, Finn's jaw clenched. My assignment in the jail pushed all his buttons. I sighed.

Just wait.

"Hello again, pretty girl," Jonesy crooned.

My expression deliberately blank, I carried a plastic tray holding his lunch toward his cell. "Stand… stand back," I faltered.

An obliging smile crossed his face. Jonesy raised both hands in the air and stepped to the back of his cell.

Crouching down, I slid the tray under the pass-through, then retreated several feet. I moved quickly, as if Jonesy were a venomous snake who might bite if I got too close. I deliberately backed into the wooden stool that sat opposite the cell, knocking it over with a clatter that made me jump.

"Shit," I hissed.

"Such language from a young lady." Jonesy clicked his tongue in disapproval.

Ignoring him, I righted the stool then perched on the round seat. I balanced my heels on the footrest and folded my hands on my lap, tilting my face down toward the cement floor. I was here to supervise his lunch, not chat; that's what my body language proclaimed.

"What do we have here?" Jonesy might have been speaking to himself.

I watched through lowered lashes as he lifted the plate of food to his nose and delicately sniffed.

"Tomato soup and what is this? Canned lunch meat?" he asked.

"It's good," I said, then bit my lips, a frown line forming between my brows. I dropped my gaze to the floor again, and my shoulders slumped.

I just couldn't resist breaking the rules, could I?

"Well if you say so—" Once again, I studied him from beneath my lashes. He tore off a small piece of the meat and brought it to his mouth. Tilting his head to one side, he chewed, his expression thoughtful. A wide smile broke out across his face. "You're absolutely right. It's delicious."

I dipped my head, twisting my fingers together.

He ate two bites of the meat, then lifted the plastic bowl of soup to his mouth and took a swallow. "There was a big hullabaloo in town last night, wasn't there?"

I jerked in surprise and my gaze darted to his face before returning to my lap.

I'm not supposed to talk about that. My actions conveyed that sentiment as clearly as if I'd spoken the words.

"I smelled smoke."

I shifted uncomfortably on the stool and chewed on my thumbnail. Jonesy gave a self-satisfied chuckle. I yanked my thumb from my mouth, scowled at the ragged nail, at this incriminating evidence of my nerves, then jammed my hand into the pocket of my jacket.

"Did somebody set a fire in Havoc's happy little town?"

He was taking a shot in the dark. There was absolutely no way that Jonesy could know that the fire he smelled was anything other than an accident.

The man, he just knows things. It's uncanny. One of Allsop's soldiers had whispered that to another over lunch back in Boise, when Jonesy strutted past the cafeteria, conspicuously going about his boss's business. There was a sense among the soldiers that nobody could pull one over on Allsop's chief henchman. That reputation served him well.

I didn't believe in precognition or sixth sense, or whatever you wanted to call psychic powers. It didn't fit with my rational view of the world. Jonesy was no telepath. Still, I firmly believed that some people were more observant than others, that they possessed finely honed powers of perception.

Jonesy, I suspected, was such a man.

I gnawed on my thumbnail again, and my brows drew together.

"The fire." Jonesy's voice was gentle and persuasive. "Did somebody set the fire?"

I withdrew my thumb from my mouth and met his eyes. "You need to keep quiet and eat your lunch, or else we're both going to get into trouble."

I was playing a long game here. I couldn't appear eager or overly cooperative. I had to dole out my concessions one by one over time.

He plastered a pleasant smile on his face. "That's all right, pretty girl. I wouldn't want to get you into trouble. Not for all the world."

I nodded my thanks.

"Could you at least tell me your name? Unless you want me to keep calling you pretty girl."

I hesitated, indecision etched across my face. I swallowed. "My name's… my name's Carrie, short for Carolyn."

My mother's name. Maybe some of her strength would wear off on me if I used it.

"Carrie," he repeated slowly, as if savoring the syllables. "Thank you for telling me your name, Carrie."

"Please," I said, my voice beseeching. "Just finish your lunch, okay?"

He examined my face for a long moment. I felt like I was under a microscope. I allowed my composure to crack and my anxiety to bleed through.

“Have it your way, sweetheart.” His low voice reeked with sincerity. If I didn’t know better, the soothing tone might lull me into lowering my guard. But I knew better. This man had tortured Finn. I’d never fall for his blandishments.

I nodded. “Thank you.”

I pretended not to see the self-satisfied smirk that crossed his face.

FOURTEEN

Finn

"This is bullshit," Reno erupted. He sprang up from his seat with such force that the chair rocked. Spitting mad, his eyes flashed and his face contorted with rage. He jabbed a finger at the conference table where Marcus Havoc, his lieutenants, Uncle Bobby, and I sat facing rows and rows of survivors in the jam-packed gymnasium.

The fire and loss of the clinic rattled people who were already traumatized by the flu pandemic. The curfew and plans for a police force provoked mixed reactions in town. Some people shrugged and accepted it as a necessary safety precaution. Others resented being ordered to stay home from 8 p.m. till 6 a.m. Feelings ran so high in certain quarters that Havoc called a town meeting to address their concerns. Nearly everybody in town had shown up.

Reno's mouth twisted. "A curfew? No fucking way."

Nothing like a pissed-off biker to set folks on edge. On a good day, the sight of Reno's leather Janissary cut still sent some people scurrying. This wasn't a good day. The people sitting around him looked scared out of their wits.

"Sit down, baby. Please." Olivia, Reno's girlfriend, tugged on his arm.

I'd met Reno and Olivia during our undercover mission to secure Uncle Bobby's weapons cache. Reno was one of Uncle Bobby's most trusted men and had accompanied him to Pendleton when the older man decided to throw his lot in with Havoc.

Reno shook off Olivia's hand, ignoring the pretty, young woman.

Havoc stood. Lowering his chin, he fixed the younger man with a steely glare. "Rein it in, Reno."

Reno choked out a laugh. "You expect me to bend over and take it up the ass when you try to make me a prisoner in my own house?"

"Calm down, son." Uncle Bobby raised both hands in a placating gesture.

"Sorry, Uncle Bobby, but I can't calm down when somebody is trying to steal my freedom."

"Nobody is trying to steal your freedom," Havoc said. "Don't get your panties in a twist."

Reno's face flushed red. "You son of a bitch."

He launched over the table, lunging for Havoc, who shoved him away. Two soldiers rushed forward and grabbed Reno. He freed one arm and took a swing at one of the men. The soldier's head snapped back when Reno's fist made contact with his chin. Three other soldiers piled on, driving Reno to the floor.

Olivia leapt to her feet and pressed her hands to her mouth. From her position in the second row, Georgia hurried to Olivia's side and threw a comforting arm around her shoulders.

Most of the folks in the audience had jumped out of their seats to get a better eye on the commotion. People craned their necks and gawked at the ruckus. An excited murmur swept over the crowd.

Havoc pounded a gavel on the table.

"That's enough," he roared. The crowd fell silent.

The soldiers hauled Reno to his feet.

"Assaulting your commanding officer is a serious crime," Havoc said.

Reno spat blood on the floor. "I didn't sign up to be one of your soldiers, Havoc. You aren't my commanding officer."

"No? But you chose to live in Pendleton under my protection and authority."

"Well maybe that wasn't such a good idea," Reno said.

"Maybe it wasn't. You just earned yourself thirty days in lockup." Havoc turned to me. "Finn, take two men and escort Reno to the jail."

"Yes, sir." I hopped to, rounding the table and accepting the pair of handcuffs one of the soldiers held out. "Wrists," I said to Reno. Rolling his eyes, he held out his arms. I slapped the cuffs on him, then grabbed his elbow and shoved him toward the door. "Let's go."

Flanked by two soldiers, I marched the surly biker from the gymnasium. We held our tongues as we walked toward the jail, our boots crunching over the ice on the sidewalks. The sun rode low in the winter sky, and a powder-fine snow sifted to the ground.

Outside of the jail's front door, Reno paused and tilted his face up. He stuck out his tongue, tasting the snow.

"Move it." I pushed Reno inside the jail's lobby. A guard looked up from behind the reception desk. "Dumbass took a swing at Havoc," I explained.

Shaking his head, the guard handed me the keys to the cellblock. "Death wish or poor impulse control?"

"Who knows. Maybe both." I unlocked the door to the cellblock and gestured for Reno to go in. The soldiers followed us inside. "All the way to the end." I pointed at the fourth cell, the one farthest from Jonesy.

"Yes, sir." Sarcasm laced Reno's voice. With a defiant expression on his face, he strutted past Allsop's top lieutenant.

Jonesy grasped the bars of his cell, watching the four of us pass with avid eyes. "Why if it isn't Finn Rasmussen," he called. "Alive and well. Who would have thunk it?"

His familiar, melodious voice raised my hackles. Despite all my fine resolutions to ignore him, I stopped in my tracks and turned my gaze toward the man who'd tried to break me.

"Why if it isn't Allsop's attack dog. Locked in a cell. Helpless. Who would have thunk it?"

He laughed, delight shining in his eyes. "Life is full of surprises, isn't it? The wheel of fortune turns. Sometimes you're at the top. Sometimes at the bottom. Then fate smiles, your fortune reverses, and you're back on top."

"I wouldn't count on that if I was you," I snorted.

He shrugged. "Who knows?"

I tore my gaze from Jonesy and signaled for Reno to keep walking. At the end of the cement corridor, I undid his handcuffs, pushed him inside the cell, and locked the door.

"I got it from here," I told the two soldiers. "You can go."

They nodded and left.

Planting my hands on my hips, I shook my head at Reno, who'd stretched out on his cot. "I don't know what you were thinking, man. I get that you object to the curfew, but trying to punch out Havoc might have been counterproductive. You know, especially for a man who claims to value his freedom. Look where it got you. Thirty days inside."

"Fuck you," Reno said easily.

I scratched my head. "One of us is fucked, but it ain't me."

Reno jumped to his feet and rushed at me. His hand shot out between the bars. I stepped back, out of his reach. "You don't think you're fucked? You're gonna wake up one day and find that Havoc has the final say in everything. If you want to kiss his ass forever, be my guest, but I'm nobody's yes-man."

"Gentlemen, keep it down. I'm trying to sleep," Jonesy called.

Reno and I locked eyes. My friend winked at me. I stifled a grin.

Reno was in play.

FIFTEEN

Georgia

"Let me carry that." I tried to snatch the box of office supplies from Rocco's hands.

Elbowing me away, he swung it out of reach. As if it were a barbell, he raised and lowered the box. He fixed his gaze pointedly on his massive arms. His rock-hard biceps bulged. His triceps protruded, and the corded muscles underneath the colorful tattoos that covered his forearms jumped.

"Seriously? Do I look like I need help?" he asked, his eyebrows shooting up.

"Yeah, seriously." I reached for the box again. "Sara ordered you to rest."

He dismissed the doctor's concerns with a loud harrumph.

"You could have died in the fire or later from smoke inhalation," I reminded him. "I thought we might lose you."

And lose Finn, I didn't add. Rocco already felt guilty that he hadn't saved Christian and his friend. When he'd realized that Finn and Marcus had risked their lives to rescue him, the big man had blanched and gone silent. I couldn't pile on.

Rocco dropped the box on the reception desk and held out his arms. "Come here."

Rocco was the living, breathing embodiment of a gentle giant. I stepped close and laid my cheek against his chest. Strong arms enfolded me and he patted my back. A sense of safety surrounded me, the same all's-right-in-the-world feeling I'd experienced when I was a little girl and my dad swooped me up in one of his bear hugs. I wallowed in the hug for a good minute before pulling away.

"Are you going to rest while I haul in the boxes?" I wasn't above a little emotional manipulation. I sniffed and put a quaver in my voice.

Rocco chucked me under the chin. "Not a chance."

The clinic would reopen tomorrow. I'd borrowed Finn's pickup. Thanh's people had loaded the truck bed with supplies for the new medical facility, a former day care center one block over from the church. I'd backed the truck up to the door, and Rocco and I were hauling in the boxes.

It was originally supposed to be a group effort, but Sara was called away to set a broken arm. Thanh was out of town on a supply run. Marcus summoned Finn and Justin to an emergency meeting. Rachel—no doubt—was up to her eyeballs in her search for Allsop's spy. We hadn't expected her to show up anyway.

"How about I get some people from the warehouse to help?" I suggested.

"It's been almost two weeks since the fire. I'm operating at one hundred percent, so how about you and I buckle down and finish?" Rocco countered.

I give up.

I grabbed the two-wheel dolly and got to work. Thanh's people had already brought over three examination tables, file cabinets, and several rolling chairs from a hospital in town. We hauled in everything else Sara and Rocco would need to run the operation. When we finished emptying the truck, Rocco lit the alcohol stove and boiled water for tea.

"Look what I got." Rocco held up a package of chocolate sandwich cookies, a hot commodity in today's world.

"Oh, nice." I held out both hands, waggling my fingers. Laughing, Rocco dropped a cookie onto each of my outstretched hands. We carried our mugs of tea to the waiting room and sprawled on a comfy, overstuffed sofa.

Workers had installed a small wood-burning stove in the corner of the waiting room. It radiated a welcome heat.

"So, what's going on with you and Finn?"

I took a sip of tea, buying time while I thought about my answer. "Have you been talking to Rachel?"

He snorted. "Sweetie, Rachel isn't the only one who's noticed the way you two look at each other. Now, spill. Tell Uncle Rocco all your secrets."

Instead of evasion, I opted for the simple truth. "I'm crazy about him. And it appears that he's crazy about me."

"And…?" Rocco drawled.

I shrugged. "I told him that I wanted to wait to start anything, you know, until the world is safer and more stable. Until we've defeated Allsop."

A furrow creased Rocco's brow. "Now that's just plain stupid."

I choked on my tea. "What? You're calling me stupid?" I was more startled than offended.

"If you plan to wait until the world is safe and everything is tied up with a nice bow, then yeah, I'm calling you stupid. There's no such thing as safe." He set his mug on the round coffee table and took my hands, his expression uncharacteristically serious. "Listen. Two years ago, my husband was killed. Ian had walked up the street to pick up coffee and donuts. He was in a crosswalk. The signal was with him, he should have been fine, but somebody was in a hurry. They ran a red light." Rocco paused, pain clouding his eyes.

"Rocco," I choked out.

"It was a stupid accident nobody could've seen coming. Ian walked out into a sunny, beautiful day, and he never came back." He shook his head. "You never know. You never know how much time you have with the people you love."

My throat ached at the realization that my friend had been carrying this pain. "Rocco… shit… I'm so sorry."

"Don't throw away a single minute of your time together. Don't try to play it safe. That's what I'm saying. I'd give anything for one more day with Ian."

I squeezed his fingers. "Thanks for telling me about Ian. I can see that it stirred up some painful memories for you."

"The memories—both good and bad—they're never far away." He released my hands and tapped a finger against his chest. "I carry Ian here, all the time, every day. And I'm happy knowing that we didn't squander a single minute waiting for things to be perfect."

Of course Rocco was right. No matter how much we'd like to believe so, nobody was guaranteed that their happily ever after would last forever. The best we could do was to move forward in faith, hoping that we had more tomorrows with the people we loved. It's what Bear and Nyx had done. And Ripper and Kenzie. And Kyle and Sunny.

But none of them were working for Marcus Havoc.

Shit.

"What's going on in that head of yours?" Rocco asked gently.

I sighed. "I'm thinking about some advice I got from a very smart friend."

"Good." Rocco stood and picked up our empty mugs. "I'm going to hang some pictures and put out books and toys in the pediatric exam room. You want to help?"

I nodded. "Sounds fun."

An hour later, I was finishing arranging a shelf full of picture books when I heard the clinic door open. We'd attached one of those old-fashioned shopkeepers bells on the door, the kind that rang whenever the door opened or closed.

"Hello?" Finn called.

"We're in the back," I said.

Finn stuck his head in the room. "Sara stopped by headquarters on her way from setting the broken arm. She should be here within an hour. Justin's coming soon. And guess who he's bringing with him?"

My mind flashed back to the night of the fire, when Justin showed up at the scene with an unfamiliar woman in tow. "A date," I guessed.

Finn's face fell. "How did you know?"

I shrugged. "Call it female intuition. What do you know about her?"

"A couple of weeks ago, Justin put up a sign-up sheet at city hall, asking for people with experience in education to help set up a school. Lorelei was a kindergarten teacher before the pandemic. She signed up and the rest—as they say—is history."

"Good for them." Rocco shot me a smug look. "Nobody should be alone if they can help it."

Finn's eyes pivoted to me. "Couldn't agree more, brother. And get this—Lorelei is bringing lasagna."

I groaned. Memories of melted cheese, tender noodles, and spicy tomato sauce rose up to torment me. I hadn't had lasagna since the power grid collapsed.

"How did she manage to make lasagna?" I asked.

"Justin said she'll explain over the meal."

"Can't wait." I turned to Finn. "Query: Favorite Italian food?"

"That's easy. Pepperoni pizza. How about you?"

"I used to get pasta puttanesca at my favorite Italian restaurant," I said. "Spaghetti with Kalamata olives and capers and anchovies and red pepper flakes." I moaned, remembering. "It was so good."

"I ate a marinated eel dish in Naples that I'll never forget." A dreamy expression crossed Rocco's face.

"I bet," I said under my breath. Eel were little more than water snakes. I've pushed back all my life against expectations of what a girl should or shouldn't like or do. But I could never shake my aversion to snakes. Like the girliest of girls—a walking-talking stereotype—my toes would curl, and I'd fight not to shriek every time I saw one.

Marinated eel? Blech. I made a face.

"Have you tasted eel?" he demanded.

I squirmed. "No."

"So your reaction is based on nothing more than squeamishness and prejudice," he said.

Well, yeah. I'd never been an especially adventurous eater. I'd tried escargot at a French restaurant once while on a date. My teeth bounced off them, like I was chewing on a rubber spatula. They tasted like butter and garlic. Snails were my biggest culinary escapade.

"Have you tried Rocky Mountain oysters?" Finn asked Rocco. "Otherwise known as cowboy caviar? Swinging beef?"

Why did I have such a bad feeling about this?

"Never heard of it," Rocco said.

"Deep-fried bull testicles." Finn rubbed his stomach. "Yum."

I shuddered. If given the choice, I'd take marinated eel over deep-fried bull testicles any day. I held up a hand. "That's it. You are *never* kissing me with that mouth."

Finn's eyelids slid to half-mast, and a cocky grin curved his lips. "As I recall, I already have."

Rocco hooted and crossed his arms over his chest, grinning with delight.

I stepped right into that one, didn't I?

"And it wasn't so bad, was it?" Finn persisted.

Don't hold back. Don't play it safe. That's what Rocco had urged me. I swallowed, then threw caution away. "No. It wasn't bad at all. In fact, it was quite nice."

Hope, or maybe it was triumph, flashed across Finn's face, then his eyes narrowed. "Hold on. Did you say *nice?*"

Nice, a tepid endorsement at best. There was nothing nice, or sweet, or gentle, about the sizzling kiss Finn had laid on me that night in Prineville. Every detail of it was branded in my memory. The way Finn's fingers tightened in my hair when his mouth crashed against mine. The way his tongue teased my lips apart. The way surprise had locked limbs in place before I melted against him, my body soft and yielding, my core liquefying. My heart had battered my chest. My breath had caught in my lungs.

I'd relived that kiss a thousand times when I lay in bed at night, my restless fingers seeking relief from the clawing desire the memory stirred.

Nice. No, nice didn't do it justice. I shrugged at Finn, biting my lower lip.

The shopkeepers bell rang. The entry door banged shut. "We're here," Justin called from the lobby. "Come meet Lorelei."

Saved by the bell. Literally.

"Lasagna." Rocco rubbed his hands together then headed for the front of the clinic.

I started to follow him. Finn caught my arm and lowered his mouth to my ear. "Later on we're going to talk about that nice kiss crack you made."

"That a promise?" I asked.

"It is." His warm breath tickled my ear, and goose bumps erupted across my shoulders. He bumped his shoulder against mine—our old, familiar gesture—then wheeled around. After a few seconds, I followed, my eyes fixed on his broad back and tight ass as he swaggered up the hall.

A short, curvy woman with honey-brown hair spilling over her shoulders and big gray eyes stood next to Justin in the lobby. She held a pink, insulated casserole carrier in her arms. A wide, friendly smile lit up her face.

"Hi, everybody," she said. "I'm Lorelei."

"This is Rocco, Georgia, and Finn." Justin introduced us to his friend.

Lorelei held up the casserole carrier. "It's early for dinner, but we'll probably want to eat this while it's still hot."

At the prospect of warm lasagna, we sprang into action. Rocco fetched plates and forks from the newly furbished break room. Finn pulled the large, round coffee table into the middle of the room.

"Do you mind if we sit around the coffee table to eat?" I asked Lorelei. "With a fire in the stove, this is the coziest room in the clinic."

"I'm a kindergarten teacher." Lorelei laughed. "I spend a good part of my day sitting on the floor with my students." She stopped talking and her face fell. "I mean, I used to, before the pandemic."

Justin threw a comforting arm around her shoulders and squeezed.

"From what Justin told us, you might be working with students again soon," Finn said.

"That's right." Lorelei glanced up at the tall lieutenant, and her expression brightened. "We plan to start a school next month. Justin is too busy to teach full time, but there are a half dozen certified K through 12 teachers in town. And several people—including Rocco—have offered to share their expertise. We're looking for more volunteers." She glanced at Finn. "How about you? What do you know?"

"I studied agricultural animal breeding," he said. "Anatomy. Biochemistry. Genetics."

Lorelei's eyes sparkled. "I'm adding you to the list of guest instructors."

Finn scratched his head. "I plan to go back to my family's ranch once we settle things with Allsop, but as long as I'm in town, sure. I can talk to the kids about animal breeding."

Valhalla was Finn's home, and I wasn't surprised that he planned to return to the ranch. I'd committed to Marcus's cause early on in the pandemic, accompanying the major from California to Pendleton. For the duration of the fight against Allsop, I'd stick by his side. But afterwards? Assuming my mission went well. Assuming Finn and I built something real, would I be happy living on a ranch at "the ass end of nowhere," as Bear liked to say? With Finn and Bear and Nyx and all my other friends?

Certainty flooded me. Yes. Yes, I would. In fact, it sounded like a little slice of heaven on earth.

"How about you?" Lorelei swung her eyes my way. "What can you teach?"

Not would you be willing to teach, but what can you teach. Lorelei didn't hesitate to ask for what she wanted. Good for her.

"I have a bachelor's degree in American history," I said.

"Perfect." She clasped her hands together. "We can use you."

Justin took the casserole carrier from Lorelei and set it in the middle of the coffee table. "Now that you've drafted my friends to your cause, how about we eat?"

Lorelei unzipped the insulated carrier and pulled out a foil-covered baking dish. She peeled back the foil, and steam curled above the golden melted cheese. The succulent aroma of tomato sauce and herbs wafted into the room. As one, we all groaned.

I turned to Finn, whose knee was pressed against mine, and gave him a thumbs-up.

Lorelei scooped a mound of lasagna onto Justin's plate. Mine came next. I clasped my hands on my lap to stop myself from digging in before everybody was served. As soon as good manners allowed, I sank my fork into the lasagna. At the first bite, flavor exploded in my mouth.

I polished off half my plate before I paused, pointing at the baking dish. "How did you do this? Without electricity?"

"Freeze dried mozzarella and beef crumbles, and a solar oven," Lorelei said.

"A solar oven? It's the middle of winter."

"Doesn't matter." Lorelei waved her fork. "People have used solar ovens during expeditions to Mt. Everest. It's the amount of sunshine, not the outdoor temperature that matters."

"Really?" I was surprised.

"Yep. Although you can only use a solar oven on sunny days during peak daylight hours. That's why we're eating before the sun goes down."

"Well, kudos to the chef." Finn wiped his mouth with a napkin. "This is a treat."

Lorelei beamed. Justin leaned over and kissed her on the temple. It was too bad Rachel wasn't here to witness our friend's happiness. The little matchmaker would be dancing with glee.

The shopkeepers bell rang again, and Sara bustled into the clinic. Tucking her gloves into her coat pocket, she followed her nose into the waiting room. "Something smells delicious."

Rocco scooted over to make room for the doctor and filled a plate for her.

Sara took a bite and sighed with pleasure. "I wish Marcus and Rachel were here to enjoy this."

"I can drop the leftovers off at HQ on my way home," Lorelei offered. "It's not out of my way."

"I'm sure they'd love that," Sara said.

"You're a sweetheart," Justin murmured, tucking a strand of hair behind Lorelei's ear. My eyes widened at the sight of the no-nonsense chief of operations doting on a woman. A rosy-pink blush blossomed across Lorelei's cheeks, and she dropped her eyes to her plate.

Good lord. I wouldn't have suspected that the friendly and assertive woman was a blusher. Justin and Lorelei were adorable together.

Sara paused, her fork halfway to her mouth. "Before I forget, you know that meeting that Marcus had called for 8:30 tonight? It's been postponed until tomorrow morning."

Finn's gaze cut sideways to me. "Guess we have the entire evening off."

"I guess we do." I smiled, my pulse beating faster. It looked like we were going to have our little talk about his *nice kiss* tonight.

SIXTEEN

Finn

My brother, Bear, was always the strong and silent type, the solemn, laconic cowboy. But me? Mama used to accuse me of trying to talk her ear off. She said I was full to the brim with stuff and nonsense, the exact opposite of my sensible brother. I'd calmed down a mite since my chatty childhood, learned when to say my piece and when to keep quiet. Still, in my whole life, I'd never once been tongue-tied around a woman.

Not until tonight. Not until Georgia.

After dinner, we all spent a couple of hours setting the clinic to rights. Lorelei left early to carry the leftover lasagna over to city hall for Havoc and Rachel's supper. Georgia, Justin, and I stayed until Sara kicked us out a little before eight.

Now Georgia and I walked side by side back toward the motel, our breaths making clouds in the frigid night air, our boots scuffing against the icy sidewalk. A deep freeze might have gripped the city, but unless I misread the signs, Georgia was warming up to the idea of a relationship.

And I had no clue what to say or do to help her find her way across the line between maybe and yes. I'd promised her that we would never do anything she didn't want to do. As a man of honor, that meant I couldn't push her over that line. She had to cross it on her own.

The banter that had always come so easily eluded me now. When it mattered the most.

Georgia's boot caught on an uneven spot in the sidewalk and she started to slip. I grabbed her elbow to steady her, and we both slid, clutching at each other's forearms.

"Oopsy-daisy," I said.

Georgia swung disbelieving eyes my way. "Did you just say oopsy-daisy?"

I made a face. The expletives I sometimes uttered had all but disappeared once I started spending time with Ever. Crude language in front of my little sweet pea earned a raised brow and judgmental scowl from Mrs. B. I'd learned to curb my tongue, but sometimes the goofiest words came out of my mouth now.

"I guess I did," I confessed.

Georgia laughed, a happy, carefree sound. "I like it. I can tell you've been spending time with Ever."

We found our footing and continued on our way, holding hands now in case we slipped again.

"You miss them, don't you, Ever and everybody back at Valhalla?" Georgia asked.

No need to think about my answer. "I do, but going home for Christmas helped, even if the visit was cut short. Seeing everybody reminded me of what I'm fighting for."

"You're a lucky man."

Don't I know it. I've got my brother and our family ranch. Good friends. A woman I adored. I was one of the luckiest cusses in the world.

"Do you think—" I started, then hesitated. *Come on, Rasmussen. Out with it.* "Could you see yourself settling down at Valhalla? After the war, I mean."

Georgia chewed on her lips for a moment then she bobbed her head. "Yes. I think I could be happy there."

"With me." Nothing to be gained by pussyfooting around the question. "Could you see yourself settling down at Valhalla with me?"

She stopped walking, turned to me, and laid both hands on my chest. "Maybe." Something in my expression must have alarmed her. She shook her head. "I'm not trying to dodge your question.

Honestly, I don't know the answer. I *think* you and I might be good together. I *think* we might be endgame, but until we give it a shot, we won't know."

A pragmatic answer from a pragmatic woman.

Bear told me that he had to break down Nyx's walls, breach her defenses, and show her that despite her reservations, she really wanted him. That approach wouldn't work with Georgia. She had to unlock her gates and welcome me in.

I smiled down at her. "All right. That sounds fair. We'll give it a shot and see how it goes."

For a long time, I'd wanted to have the right to reach out spontaneously and touch Georgia. Simple acts of affection. To smooth her hair from her brow. To lay my hand on her thigh when we sat next to each other. To slide my arm around her waist and pull her close. I'd held back, of course. But now, her willingness to try emboldened me.

I brushed my knuckles over her upturned cheek. Her skin was petal smooth and cool beneath my touch. Moonlight reflected in her beautiful eyes.

"I'm not ready to sleep with you," she said.

Disappointment tightened my chest, but I pushed it away. "That's your call, angel." This was no hookup, no one and done. We'd go as slowly as Georgia needed.

"But I do want to spend more time together. Would you like to come back to my room with me?"

"Would I?" I grinned. "More than anything. Especially if you fix me a cup of hot cocoa. Like my grandpa used to say, it's cold enough to freeze the balls off a brass monkey."

Her pretty face screwed up. "First Rocky Mountain oysters and now brass monkeys. What's with you and testicles?"

In this weather, my balls had pulled up tight to my body. Truth be told, they were the last thing on my mind. At least until I warmed up. "Just a coincidence," I said firmly.

"If you say so." She took my hand and we shuffled our way back to the motel.

The wall-mounted electric heaters inside the motel rooms were as dead as door-nails. Thanh's people had found a crate of rubber hot-water bottles in the back of a pharmacy chain's warehouse, an old-fashioned remedy against the cold that worked just fine nowadays. Every resident of Pendleton was given a hot-water bottle when they were assigned quarters. I stopped in my room to pick up my bottle and my Christmas quilt, then I followed Georgia to her room.

She switched on a solar lantern and lit the alcohol stove. We dumped the cold water from our bottles into a pan—recycling the water was the only way to go—and Georgia put the pan on the stove. When the water was hot enough, she filled our bottles then boiled clean water for the cocoa.

We sat cheek by jowl against the headboard, cocooned under a double layer of quilts, holding hot-water bottles and sipping hot cocoa. Shivering, Georgia laid her head on my shoulder.

"Here." I shoved my bottle onto her lap.

"Nope. Keep it." The stubborn woman pushed it back. "It takes a couple of minutes under the blankets to warm up, but I'll be fine."

I didn't argue. Instead, I slung an arm around her shoulders and pulled her close.

Georgia was right. After a few minutes, the combination of thick blankets, shared body heat, and two hot-water bottles created an island of warmth in the chilly room.

"We're lucky to be in Pendleton," she said, thanking fate out loud for the second time this evening. "Not everybody who survived the flu is going to make it through the winter. But we have everything we need to get by. Maybe not in comfort, but we'll survive."

The subtle scent of Georgia's orange blossom perfume tickled my nostrils. Satisfaction coursed through me. I'd given her something she loved, something that gave her pleasure. Twisting my head, I nuzzled her neck, drawing in the sweet scent. My tongue darted out and I tasted the perfume. It possessed a bitter bite, similar to orange peel. Sweet and sharp at the same time, like Georgia herself.

"Nice," I murmured. Her body relaxed against mine. I was very aware of her soft breast pressed against my side, of her long, lean thigh touching mine.

"Right now, I wouldn't trade places with anybody in the world," she said.

I nodded. "Me, neither."

Georgia wove her fingers through mine. "Do you think we'll ever manage to get back everything we lost?" she asked. "Electricity? Running water? The internet? Even television?"

"The whole shebang?" I lifted my shoulders. "Humans created all those things once. No reason we couldn't do it again, especially since we wouldn't be starting from scratch. The knowledge for how to bring it all back is still there. I don't know if it will happen in our lifetimes, though. We all might be scrambling to survive for a while."

"You could be right." She let out a long sigh. "Query." She spoke in a small voice, a voice barely above a whisper. "If you had a magic wand and you could bring back only one thing from the old world, what would it be?"

"That's easy," I said. "My parents."

Her fingers tightened around mine. "Yeah. Me, too."

This was the first time while playing the what-do-you-miss game that our answers aligned perfectly.

"My folks would have liked you," I said. "A smart, kind, capable woman who's not afraid to get her hands dirty and to do what needs to be done."

"And my parents would have loved you," she said. "You're a good man, you know. Brave. Honorable. And after what you did in Boise—risking your life to help that woman escape from Allsop—you're a straight-up hero."

My throat felt thick. I swallowed hard. "Thanks, Georgia."

"And one hell of a pool player." Her voice took on an upbeat tone, like she was trying to lighten the mood. "I loved watching you in action in Uncle Bobby's fancy billiard room."

I mimicked her lighthearted tone. "I do pride myself on my mastery of the cue stick."

She rolled her eyes. "Actually, I was talking about how good you looked bending over a pool table."

"My ass and I thank you kindly, ma'am." I touched the brim of an imaginary cowboy hat. "We aim to please."

I took her empty mug from her and set it next to mine on the nightstand, then pulled the quilts up over our shoulders. She tucked her head under my chin and splayed her fingers across my chest.

"Comfortable?" I asked.

"Mm-hmm."

Cuddling with Georgia under a pile of blankets felt damned fine. If I had my druthers, we wouldn't take things this slow, but good things were worth waiting for, weren't they? I rubbed my hand down her back, and Georgia arched against me, as boneless and content as one of the barn cats I used to pull onto my lap and stroke.

When my fingers kneaded the muscles at the base of her neck, she moaned in pleasure.

"I could hold you like this all night," I said, ignoring the hard-on that was straining at my jeans. I shifted my weight and tugged at the denim, easing the pressure.

"You can stay if you like," she said.

My hand stilled, but my imagination ran riot. Sharing a bed with Georgia. Her warm body tucked up next to mine. Her soft inhalations and exhalations punctuating the night. It'd be both heaven and hell to a man who had to keep his hands to himself.

"I'd like that," I said. "But before we settle down for the night, I need to run a file over to headquarters. Havoc will want to see it before our meeting tomorrow morning."

"Okay." She yawned, then forced her eyes to open wide. "I can come with you."

"No need. Stay comfortable. I won't be gone more than twenty minutes."

"You sure?" She yawned again.

"Yep. You can keep the bed warm for me."

"It's a deal," she said, her eyes heavy. "I swear, I don't usually crash this early. I feel like my grandma after the early bird special."

"A big meal and a warm bed will do it to you every time. Why don't you close your eyes and doze until I get back?"

"You don't have to twist my arm."

I pressed a kiss against her tousled brown hair—brown, I was still getting used to that—and slipped out from under the quilts. Georgia slid down and stretched out on the mattress, her head burrowed into a pillow. I tucked the blankets around her, then stood by the side of the bed, watching her. A half-smile curved her lips, as if she was thinking happy thoughts.

My heart thumped. Lucky. I was so damned lucky.

Stop mooning and get your ass in gear.

I picked up her room key from the top of the dresser, clicked off the solar lantern, and locked the door on my way out. I retrieved the file from my room and jogged down the stairs and across the motel's parking lot. Light from lanterns glowed dimly inside the city hall-library complex across the street. As always, a pair of armed guards flanked the entry to the headquarters.

Tucking the file under one arm, I pulled up my hood and shoved both hands into my pockets. I crossed Dorion Avenue and trotted across the library parking lot as quickly as the icy surface would allow.

Boom.

A single explosion shattered the night. I staggered, dazed and thunderstruck. Our headquarters lit up. The windows blew out, glass shards raining down on the parking lot. Behind the gaping maws, brilliant orange flames roiled through the interior of the building.

A bomb. I was too far away to feel the percussive shock wave, but the boom and the fireball left no doubt about what happened.

Fuck. Marcus. Rachel.

Shaking off my astonishment, I bolted toward the building.

SEVENTEEN

Georgia

Boom.

I startled awake, torn from sleep by the violent blast. It took a moment to orient myself. I blinked into the darkness. Something flickered in my peripheral vision. Turning my head toward the window, I saw an orange glow behind the curtains. I threw off the covers, lurched toward the window, and drew back the fabric.

My breath froze in my lungs. Icy fear skittered up my spine. My knees wobbled and I grabbed at the windowsill. Holy shit. Our headquarters was on fire. Somebody had planted a bomb, and our headquarters was on fire.

"Finn," I whispered.

Finn had left me safe and snug in my bed while he brought a file to Marcus. At the headquarters. Unbidden, hideous images flashed before my eyes. I saw Finn, ripped apart by the force of the blast. Finn, writhing in agony as he burned. I hunched over, gasping.

Get a grip.

My training asserted itself, overriding my panic. Squaring my shoulders, I summoned all my willpower. I wrapped my fear up tight and shoved it to the darkest corner of my mind. With cool detachment, I studied the scene.

The large city hall and public library complex stood intact—more or less—the roof and exterior walls untouched. I'd heard only one explosion. Whoever planted the bomb hadn't intended to destroy the building. The fire burned bright in the central part of the structure, close to the conference room where Marcus met with his lieutenants and other top people, where a meeting had originally been scheduled for tonight.

Bombs had blast radius issues. Shock waves dissipated quickly. My best bet? Someone planted C-4 packed with shrapnel in the conference room. Not to bring down the building, but to kill Marcus and his top people, to cripple the leadership of Pendleton.

Who? That was a question for later.

As I watched, two fire engines pulled into the parking lot, pumper trucks that carried water. The fire brigade sprang into action. Thank God we'd revamped the fire department since the big meeting with Marcus. Soldiers carrying fire extinguishers ran into the building.

Time to move.

Shrugging into my coat, I strode from my room and ran toward the stairs leading to the parking lot. The metal handrail slid against my ungloved hand, glacial cold, but no more cold than the lump that had lodged in my stomach.

Where was Finn?

I stumbled across the street and ran past the fire engines, my gaze scanning the crowd for any sign of my man. A wild-eyed Rachel stood a dozen yards from the entrance to the building, waving her hands. I ran toward her. She clutched my upper arms, her face twisted in helpless rage.

"Fucker planted a bomb," she spat out.

"How bad is it?" I asked.

"Nobody was in the conference room when it detonated, thank fuck."

"Have you seen Finn?" I choked out.

"Yeah, he's inside with Marcus and Justin, fighting the fire."

Relief was a punch to my gut. I sagged, the breath hitching in my lungs.

Rachel pulled me close and lowered her mouth to my ear. "Finn's all right. Not a scratch on him. I promise."

I gave a jerky nod, then corralled my wayward thoughts. Later. I'd deal with the emotional fallout later. This was the time to focus, to stay razor-sharp.

"Come on." I pointed to the far side of the parking lot, away from the noisy commotion.

We pushed our way through the looky-loos the explosion and fire attracted. It was past curfew, but Marcus's people were far too busy dealing with the fiery aftermath of the bomb to hand out citations.

People huddled in small groups, clutching at each other. Firelight danced across shocked faces, faces that showed a range of emotions: sadness, fear, anger, stunned incredulity.

Pendleton was supposed to be a safe haven, a place where good people gathered to rebuild the world. And now, within the span of ten days, our medical clinic had burned to the ground and a bomb had been detonated in the top brass's headquarters.

What would happen if people lost faith in Marcus Havoc? If they questioned his ability to protect and lead them? Discontent was already stirring among people who resented the curfew. Who would stop Allsop if Pendleton fractured?

I dragged Rachel down next to me on a wooden bench under an ornamental tree on the edge of the parking lot.

I waved my hand at the fire. "We have to figure out who did this and stop them before we lose everything we're trying to build here."

"No shit." Rachel shoved a hand through her hair.

"Who wants Marcus dead?"

"Allsop is number one on my list," she said. "If he can get rid of Havoc and his top people—decapitate the resistance—there'll be nobody to stop him."

"So you think his spy planted the bomb?"

"Yeah, probably." Rachel made a face "Although we shouldn't write off the possibility of a disgruntled citizen, somebody pissed off by the curfew and new restrictions."

No. We couldn't afford to dismiss any possibility.

"How many people came into the building this evening?"

Rachel shook her head. "I was in my office going over files all evening, except when Havoc and I ate dinner together." Her shoulders slumped. "And it's Tuesday. The book club meets at the library between five and seven every Tuesday."

Book club, an attempt to give the citizens of Pendleton a touch of normalcy. In a world without television or the internet, the book club was a hot ticket. I'd sat in on several meetings. The name book club was deceiving. It was more a freewheeling social group where people talked about books and reminisced about old television shows and movies. Sometimes somebody read a short story out loud, or a group of people acted out a scene from a play.

"At least fifty people usually show up for book club, right?" I asked.

Rachel nodded glumly. "A lot of people in and out, and the sentries don't take names. Obviously it's another place where we need to tighten up security. Assuming the library survives and we still hold book club. Shit." She pounded a fist on the bench, her frustration palpable.

I laid a hand on my friend's arm. "This isn't the end of the world. Nobody died. Tomorrow morning, we'll assess the damage to the building and its contents. If we have to, we can relocate our headquarters. We can move the books. And we'll find the person responsible for the bomb."

"Yeah, we will." Rachel rose to her feet. "I'll go talk to the sentries. Maybe one of them will remember something suspicious from this evening."

I stood and followed her. The crowd parted as one of the two fire engines pulled out of the lot, probably heading back to the river to refill their tanks. The flames had died down, although smoke still clogged the air.

Finn and Marcus stumbled out of the building. My heart lurched. Blood ran down the side of Finn's face. He staggered, leaning against the major. My feet flew across the parking lot, and I dropped to my knees as Marcus gently lowered Finn to the asphalt.

"I'm okay." Finn waved a dismissive hand. The blood trickling down his soot-covered face gave the lie to that assertion. "Just dazed. Give me a minute and I'll be fine."

I turned my eyes to Marcus, who nodded. "It's a scalp wound—a bleeder—but probably nothing serious. The cut isn't deep. His skull isn't deformed. Get Sara or Rocco to look at him." He stood. "I need to get back inside." Marcus jabbed a finger at Finn. "You're done for the night. After you get the all clear from the doc, go home and rest."

"He will," I said firmly.

Marcus whirled and ran back into the building.

"Rocco and Sara must be somewhere around here," Rachel said. "I'll go find them." She disappeared into the crowd.

Finn and I locked eyes. "You really have to stop running into burning buildings." I tried to keep my tone light, but failed miserably. My voice cracked. "My heart can't take it."

The truth of the words slammed into me. This man—this brave and easy-going man—owned my heart.

What was it that Rocco had said? Safety was a lie. Don't throw away a single moment of your time together.

The war against Allsop. I pressed my lips into a straight line. What of it? Would I allow my fears for tomorrow to rob me of today's joys? At least Finn and I would have had some time together. He'd never be haunted by thoughts of what might have been if only I hadn't been so cautious.

"Georgia?" Finn caught my chin between strong fingers. His eyes scanned my face, his expression uncharacteristically serious. "What are you saying?"

I sucked in a breath. "I'm saying screw it. I'm done playing it safe."

His eyes narrowed and he tilted his head to one side. "That mean what I think it means?"

"If you think it means that I'm planning to have my wicked way with you, you'd be right."

A slow smile creased his handsome face, and his gaze focused on my mouth. "Gotta admit, that sounds promising. Just so long as you understand that it cuts both ways. I aim to have my wicked way with you, too, angel."

Behind me, someone cleared his throat.

I turned my head and looked over my shoulder. Rocco hovered a few feet away, a first aid duffel in his hand. Rachel stood by his side, a smug, self-satisfied smile on her face.

"You're obviously feeling better," she said to Finn.

"I told you, it's nothing serious," he said, unfazed by their ill-timed arrival.

Rocco dropped down on his haunches next to Finn and pulled on a pair of latex gloves. With gentle fingers, he examined the gash on Finn's scalp. "Let's check you out and make sure it's nothing serious."

I stood up and stepped back, giving Rocco room to work. Rachel shot her elbow into my side. I sidled away. She pursued me. “Finn aims to have his wicked way with you? Seriously? I’m gone for five minutes, and I miss all the good stuff.”

Watching Rocco clean Finn’s wound and wrap gauze around his head, I considered Rachel’s words. Despite everything—the uncertainties and dangers still hanging over our heads—all the good stuff wasn’t over. Tension leeched from my body, replaced by gratitude.

I was going to grab onto happiness and hold it close, for a little while at least.

EIGHTEEN

Finn

Everything I know about courage, duty, and honor I learned at my parents' knees. *Cowboy up* was more than a folksy slogan, it was a guiding principle. Bear and I were expected to work hard, to keep our word, to do what was necessary without whining, and to handle life's obstacles with grit and grace.

My folks had little sympathy for self-inflicted injuries. I poked a hornets' nest with a stick once and stumbled to the house howling with pain. Mama put me in a cold bath then daubed baking soda paste over all the stings. I sniffled and felt sorry for myself, till Mama told me I was a darned fool who had no one to blame but myself. Tough love was the order of the day.

After the explosion and fire last night, when he asked how I felt, I made the mistake of telling Rocco that my head hurt and my vision was a little blurry. Just like that, I became the first overnight patient at the new medical clinic. Rocco abandoned the comfort of his own bed to bunk out at the clinic so he could keep an eye on me.

Talk about overkill. I knocked my noggin plenty of times growing up and lived to tell the tale. When you run into a burning building you accept that it's a risky proposition—that you might get hurt—and if you walk away with a scratch, you don't expect folks to make a fuss over it.

Georgia wanted to spend the night sleeping in a chair in my room at the clinic. I put the kibosh on that, telling her I wanted her rested and ready for tonight. I said it in front of Rocco, too. He grinned like a skunk and told her to go home and get some sleep.

I woke up in a former day care classroom that had been decorated like something out of Old MacDonald. Farm murals covered the walls. Black-and-white Holstein cattle grazed in a grassy meadow. A big Brahma rooster strutted across a yard. It was like old home week for a country boy like me. I sat up in bed and swung my legs to the floor. The wooziness was gone and the pain in my head had simmered down to an inconsequential ache.

Rocco rapped on the door then stuck his head inside. "Thought I heard you stirring. How are you feeling this morning?"

"Right as rain." I scrubbed my hands over my gritty face. "But I'd trade my left nut for a shower."

He set an insulated travel mug on a table. "I'll bet." The big man's eyes twinkled. "You've got big plans for tonight, don't you?"

I grinned, but kept my mouth shut. A man doesn't crow about his sex life. I'd been chatty last night after smacking my head, but in the cold light of day my manners made a comeback.

Rocco rolled a stool over to my bedside and sat down. He tested my pupils and checked the wound. "Looks good. How're the headache and dizziness?"

"Gone and gone."

He held out the travel mug. "It's only instant coffee," he said apologetically.

"Instant is fine by me. Thank you." I gratefully accepted the mug.

"Stay put. I'll be back in a few minutes." He trotted from the room.

I sipped my coffee, sighing with pleasure when the caffeine kicked in. We'd used up all the gourmet beans that Ripper and Kenzie loved, but we still had quite a few cans of grocery store coffee tucked away at Valhalla. They wouldn't last forever, though. Levi and Topher talked about growing coffee plants in the greenhouse, but I had my doubts about the viability of that scheme. Mrs. B.'s beloved tea wouldn't last forever, either. Sooner or later we'd have to face mornings without caffeine. In the big picture that was the least of our worries, but man-oh-man, I dreaded the day.

Rocco pushed open the door, a steaming pot of water in his hands, a clean pair of sweats and a towel under his arm. He set the hot water on a table and handed me a bar of soap and a washcloth.

"I thought you might want to clean up before you take off."

"You're a good friend," I said.

I dunked my head in the warm water then washed away all the soot and sweat that covered my body. Dressed in clean sweats, I padded out to the waiting room. Rocco handed me a bottle of ibuprofen and sent me on my way.

I showed up at the tail end of the meeting with Havoc and his lieutenants.

By the grace of God and thanks to the speedy arrival of the fire brigade, the city hall and library complex was salvageable.

Havoc checked his watch. "Olivia is visiting Reno in the jail now." He looked at me. "You need to show up in fifteen minutes. Then Georgia will make her appearance ten minutes after that. You know what to do?"

"Yes, sir." I nodded.

"We'll head over now," Georgia said.

Bundled up against the cold, Georgia and I started to walk toward the police station where Jonesy and Reno were being held. An awkward silence hung between us. Was it our plans for tonight that had us holding our tongues and casting sideways glances at each other? If so, I couldn't allow that to stand.

I stopped walking and turned to face Georgia. "You having second thoughts about tonight?"

She shook her head, her face glowing pink from the cold. "No. Not even a little bit. Are you?"

"Hell, no." I tugged off a glove, then slid a fingertip across her silky smooth skin, tracing a line from her delicate cheekbone to her full mouth. Was her skin as soft and supple all over? I was going to find out tonight, wasn't I?

Her lips curved up in a saucy smile. "You promised to have your wicked way with me, and I'm holding you to that promise, Finn Rasmussen."

"Yes, ma'am. You can count on it. A cowboy always keeps his word."

I snaked an arm around her waist and pulled her close against my chest. Layers of down from our heavy coats separated us, but I swore I could feel her heart hammering against mine. I lowered my head till my mouth hovered over hers. We panted, our frosty breaths mingling. With the tip of my tongue, I traced the seam of her lips. Georgia moaned. Her lips parted. I dove in, my mouth staking a claim to hers.

Across the street, somebody whooped. "Get a room."

Laughing, we pulled apart.

"We're going to be good together, aren't we?" Georgia asked.

How could we not? "We're going to be great together, sweet girl. The best."

"Till tonight." Georgia rose up on her toes and planted a quick kiss on my mouth.

"Till tonight."

Hand in hand, the awkwardness between us a thing of the past, we walked the rest of the way to the jail. Through the window, I spied Olivia pacing back and forth in the lobby, wringing her hands. The pretend estrangement from the man she loved was clearly hard on the young woman.

Georgia and I stepped into the lobby and greeted the soldier behind the reception desk before turning to Olivia. Georgia placed a comforting hand on the young woman's back. "How are you, sweetheart?"

"This is harder than I expected," Olivia faltered. "I know it's all an act. Reno doesn't really believe what he's saying, but he's looking me in the eye telling me he'd rather lose me than change his mind."

"You know that man loves you," I said. "He nearly lost his mind when you got hurt back in Prineville. Nothing in God's green earth would make him leave you. Like you said, it's all an act."

"You're right. I know you're right." Olivia squared her shoulders. "It'll all be worthwhile if Reno can get Jonesy to confide in him."

Georgia shot Olivia a quick glance then looked down at her feet. "It'll all be worthwhile in the end."

"You're up next?" Olivia asked me.

"Yep, then Georgia."

"Good luck." Olivia touched my arm, hugged Georgia, then waved goodbye.

I took a moment to adjust my frame of mind and slip into my role. Sucking in deep breaths, I slapped on my game face.

I'm pissed and I'm looking for a fight.

Scowling, I unlocked the door to the cellblock and stomped inside. Behind the bars of the first cell, Jonesy slowly rose to his feet. An expression of pure delight crossed his face.

"Finn Rasmussen," he called. "Nice to see you again, son. You look good."

I hadn't planned to acknowledge him. I'd planned to walk past his cell without a word, without a glance, like he was an inconsequential bug who didn't matter one bit. Apparently, my limbs didn't get the message. My legs refused to cooperate. I halted then turned to face the bastard who'd beaten me bloody, who'd broken my ribs, who'd made himself a part of my nightmares.

I forced a smile. "You look better than the last time I saw you, Jonesy. You know, after my brother kicked your ass."

Jonesy threw his hands in the air, a gesture that almost made me jump. Dammit. "All water under the bridge." He pointed at my chest. "How are you healing, son? The burns giving you any trouble?"

God. The man sounded solicitous, almost like he cared. Like he wasn't the one who pressed the tip of a lit cigarette against my skin. While I gritted my teeth and tried not to cry out or puke. While he beamed down at me, his eyes bright with glee, looking for all the world like he was having fun. There were few things in life scarier than a man who was downright chipper when he was inflicting pain.

"You are one sad, sorry, fuck," I spat out.

He laughed, refusing to take offense. "You shouldn't take things so personally. It's bad for your blood pressure."

I had a ten minute head start on Georgia, and I was burning time. I tore my gaze away from Jonesy and marched to the fourth cell, the one that held Reno. My friend's eyes held a reassuring sympathy, a kindness I appreciated, but had to ignore. We had parts to play.

I pointed an accusatory finger at the young Janissary. "You know anything about the bomb? Did you and your buddies plan to kill Havoc?"

Out of the corner of my eye, I saw Jonesy shuffle to the end of his cell, an expression of eager interest on his face.

"What bomb?" Reno asked.

I curled my lip and painted a scornful expression across my face. "Don't play stupid. You had to hear it go off last night. It's only by the grace of God that nobody got hurt and we were able to contain the damage."

"I got no fucking clue what you're talking about," Reno said.

"No?" I rolled my eyes. "You didn't hear any explosion, and you sure as hell don't know who planted the bomb. Is that what you're telling me?"

Reno shrugged. "That's exactly what I'm telling you. Although I would be surprised if Havoc's high-handed laws didn't push people into taking matters into their own hands."

"So now you approve of assassination as a means of political change?"

"Desperate times call for desperate measures, my friend," Reno quoted.

I planted my hands on my hips and shook my head. "We were friends once, weren't we? What happened to you?"

"I'm a Janissary, first and last." Reno wrapped his hands around the bars of his cell. "No self-respecting member of a motorcycle club would trade his freedom for security."

I pointed at the prison bars. "How's that going for you? You're not so free now, are you?"

"I took a swing at a wannabe tyrant. I can live with the consequences of standing up for my beliefs."

"And Olivia? Is it fair to ask her to live with the consequences?"

It was a low blow, and his face reflected both surprise and pain. I narrowed then widened my eyes. *C'mon, man. Stick with the script.*

Reno lifted his chin, his expression now defiant. "Do I look pussy whipped? Olivia will straighten up and fly right or I'll cut her loose."

The heavy door to the cellblock swung open, and Georgia pushed a rolling cart inside.

I scowled at the woman who held my heart. "Are you stupid? Can't you see I'm not finished in here?"

She stood stock-still. Her mouth fell open, then she pressed her lips in a straight line, shock and helpless anger registering on her pretty face. "It's… it's lunchtime for the prisoners."

"So fucking what? Is your time so valuable that you can't wait till I'm done?"

I could scarcely believe the words coming out of my mouth. My mama would have smacked me upside the head if I ever spoke to a woman so disrespectfully.

Georgia blinked rapidly, like she was trying to hold back tears. "I'm sorry. I'm supposed to give them lunch at 11."

My stomach cramped, but I persisted. "You think your schedule is more important than mine?"

She shook her head, her cheeks coloring.

I pointed a finger at her, shaking it for emphasis. "Roll the cart back through the door. Park your ass outside, and cool your heels till I'm finished in here."

Shoulders hunched like a beat dog, Georgia scuttled from the room.

I swallowed. My face ached from the strain of maintaining my surly expression.

Jonesy gave a low whistle. "Well, I guess you showed her."

"Shut up." I didn't spare him a glance, turning my attention back to Reno instead. "Havoc wants to talk to you himself. You can expect to be hauled to the interrogation room this afternoon."

"Can't wait." Reno looked bored and unimpressed by the threat.

"We're done here." I strode for the door. "I'll leave you men to your shitty-ass lunch."

"Give my regards to your brother," Jonesy called. "I'm looking forward to seeing him again real soon."

Unlike the first time I walked past his cell, this time I managed to ignore him and keep moving. The threat against Bear was an attempt to rattle me, nothing more. No way would Jonesy ever get free and go after my people. Nobody I cared about would ever come face-to-face with the monster, find themselves subject to his tender mercies, the way I had. Thank God for that.

I locked the door behind me then leaned against it for a moment while I caught my breath. My eyes searched for Georgia, seeking confirmation that despite my mean-spirited playacting, we were all right.

Georgia stood at the reception desk talking to the guard. She whirled around then frowned at whatever she saw on my face. She stepped toward me. I met her half-way and hauled her into my arms.

"I'm sorry," I said.

She laid a hand on my face, shaking her head back and forth. "No. There's nothing to be sorry about." She pointed toward the cellblock. "The part you played in there, that's not the real you. I know it. Don't apologize for doing what you had to do."

"So we're good?"

"Of course we're good." A mischievous expression crossed her face. "Remember what you said when we were walking over here? We're not just good, we're great. The best."

I grinned. "Yeah, but I was talking about sex."

Georgia bit her lips, holding back a laugh. Her eyes danced. Color touched her cheeks. Damn, if she wasn't the prettiest thing I'd ever seen.

She patted my chest. "I need to get in there and give Jonesy and Reno their lunch."

"I think I'll walk back to headquarters and see if there's anything I can do to help with the cleanup," I said.

She nodded. "I'll see you tonight, then?"

"Yeah." My eyes hooded and my imagination ran wild. I leaned forward and caught her ear-lobe between my teeth. "I'll see you tonight, Georgia. Every inch of you."

NINETEEN

Georgia

"He's got no business talking to you like that," Jonesy said.

I slid his lunch tray under the pass-through and into his cell, then lifted my shoulders in an exaggerated shrug.

"It hurt my heart." Jonesy laid a hand on his chest. "The way he talked down to you. You were just doing your job. You don't deserve that."

It took a supreme effort of will not to roll my eyes and snort with derision. Jonesy's heart was a puny, shriveled, ice-bound thing. I tried and failed to imagine what might actually hurt the organ. Certainly not concern for anybody's well-being. A bullet, maybe, although I suspected that Jonesy might be as hard to kill as a cockroach.

I lifted my gaze to his face, a fleeting glance from a woman too timid to maintain eye contact. "Thanks."

Jonesy beamed. "You're welcome."

"Rasmussen is a prick," Reno called from his cell. "The kind of man who kisses up to people in power, but treats everybody else like shit."

"That certainly was my experience of the man," Jonesy agreed.

I stopped in my tracks, as if summoning the courage to speak. "Sometimes… sometimes eating shit is the only way to survive."

"What did you say, sweetheart?" Jonesy asked.

"I said, sometimes a person has no choice but to eat shit. Not if they want to get by."

Jonesy clucked his tongue. "Sounds like you might be growing disenchanted with life in Pendleton."

"Of course not," I said quickly, my eyes widening with panic. "I'm grateful to Major Havoc and his people. I have a bed, a job, food, and medicine. I'm luckier than most people. Please don't tell anybody that I complained."

Finn needn't have worried that I took his harsh words to heart. Some perverse part of me truly enjoyed a good mind-fuck.

"I'd never make trouble for you," Jonesy said.

If I didn't know better, I'd swear I heard sincerity in his voice. I bobbed my head, grateful for his assurance. "Thanks. I'm okay. No place is perfect. I'll get by."

"A smart woman like you? You have options. You can make a good life wherever you go," Jonesy said, baiting his hook at last.

I carried a tray and a water bottle to Reno's cell. His back to Jonesy, he winked at me. Operation Win Jonesy's Confidence was coming along nicely.

I pushed the cart toward the heavy cellblock door.

"Carrie," Jonesy called. "I sure would appreciate a cigarette, if you could get your hands on one."

I paused and glanced at Allsop's minion. "I'll see what I can do."

He wasn't quick enough to hide the look of triumph that flashed across his face at my concession.

I found Rachel at her desk, poring over her files.

She lifted her head when I entered, and the distracted expression cleared from her face. "How did it go with Jonesy?"

I mimed casting a fishing rod, then reeling in the line.

Rachel sat back in her chair and swung her red sneakers up onto her desk. She waved me into the seat opposite her. "We can use a win about now, and pulling one over on Jonesy is sweet," she said.

"Amen, sister," I agreed. "I didn't see Marcus or Finn when I came in. Where are they?"

"They're bringing a couple of generators over from the warehouse so we can set up electric fans to air the place out," she said.

The explosion and fire were bad news—no way to sugarcoat that—but the aftermath could have been much worse. The library and city hall had been constructed with fire-retardant materials. The dry wall, ceiling tiles, and carpet in the conference room where the C-4 detonated didn't burn. They were scorched and would need to be replaced, but the fire didn't spread to consume the building.

The C-4 produced a blast of high heat for only a short period of time. In the absence of fuel, the resulting fire could have been easier to contain. Except somebody forgot to close the fire door. Real wood bookcases lined one wall. Paper maps were tacked up everywhere, and a synthetic rug had been brought in to cozy-up the place. And the first soldier on the scene sprayed his fire extinguisher across the top of the fire, not at the base, and succeeded only in fanning the flames.

"It's a good thing the fire didn't spread to the library," I said. "Can you imagine explaining to Mrs. B. that the books were gone?"

"Yeah." Rachel shook her head at the thought of confronting the feisty, retired librarian.

"What can I do to help?" I asked.

Rachel shoved a pile of papers across her desk. "I've interviewed the sentries and all of the soldiers who were on the scene last night. You can help me go over the notes."

"You got it." A few hours helping Rachel was exactly what I needed right now while the clock counted down to evening.

Rachel cocked her head to one side and narrowed her eyes. "What's going on?" she asked slowly. "Why do you have that goofy expression on your face?"

I raised my shoulders in an exaggerated shrug.

She sat bolt upright. "Oh my God. That's right. Your vadge is coming out of retirement tonight, isn't it?"

A soldier walking by the open door swung his head and peered inside. His eyebrows lifted.

"Shut up," I hissed. I'm a grown-ass woman. I'm not shy, but I saw no reason to trumpet my plans to everybody within earshot.

She flopped back in her chair. "You need anything? Condoms? Lube? Toys?"

I made a face. "Much as I love you, I don't want to borrow your lube."

"Ew, no. Thanh has a closet full of sex stuff. Brand new. You can ask him if you need anything."

Like I said, I'm not shy, but somehow I couldn't see myself approaching the polite young lieutenant and asking to paw through his selection of "sex stuff." Besides, I already had lube for those times when a girl has to take matters into her own hands. And I snagged more than a year's worth of birth control pills early on in the pandemic.

"Thanks, but I'm all set."

"All right, but if you need anything I got your back."

I opened a file and buried my nose in an intake report.

At a quarter past five, Finn stuck his head in the office. When his gaze fell on me, his expression warmed, as if seeing me made his day. He smiled and the corners of his eyes crinkled. My heart turned over in my chest.

"I've been looking for you," he said. "I'm going to help Marcus and Justin pick up another load of sheet rock. We should be finished here by 6:30. You want to meet back at your place at 7?"

"Sounds perfect. See you then."

He hovered in the doorway for a moment. Finn respected boundaries. That was one of the things I admired about him. Was he wondering if I'd welcome physical affection in front of my friend? Was I ready to out us as a couple? I crooked a finger, giving him the go-ahead.

That was all the encouragement he needed. Three steps brought him to my side.

He manacled my upper arms, pulled me from the chair, then slid one arm around my waist. Strong fingers caught my chin. He angled my head back and brushed his mouth over mine. What started as a gentle kiss, a tentative meeting of lips, shifted into something else entirely. There was nothing hesitant or timid about that kiss. He nipped my lower lip, and when I gasped, his tongue swept into my mouth. After a mere handful of seconds, he withdrew, as if he'd made his point, staked his claim, planted his flag.

Veni, vidi, vici. I came, I saw, I conquered.

Why did that old quote from Julius Caesar come to mind?

My jaw dropped and I drew in air. With one finger under my chin, Finn pressed my mouth shut. His eyes glittered.

Rachel made a small sound, and my eyes turned her way. She watched us with rapt attention, pure delight reflected on her face.

Finn's gaze never left my mine. "Tonight."

One word stripped me of my ability to speak. I nodded mutely.

He whirled and retreated from the room, taking all the air with him. I sunk down onto my chair.

"Details, woman." Rachel's voice pierced my stupor. "I'm going to want details."

My ability to concentrate was shot. A few minutes after Finn's departure, I took off. I'd intended to swing by the cafeteria and eat a light dinner, but butterflies cavorted in my stomach. No way could I manage a meal.

Rachel had opened a desk drawer and tossed me a granola bar. "You're going to need your strength," she'd said helpfully.

I walked to the motel, nibbling on the granola bar. Back in my room, I brushed my teeth and washed my face. Despite the cold, I stripped out of my jeans and sweater and spritzed orange blossom cologne over my body. Teeth chattering, I examined my paltry rack of clothes. More jeans and sweaters. An old favorite sweatshirt from the University of Kansas. Absolutely nothing that was even remotely sexy or seductive. At night, I slept in merino wool long johns—

thermal underwear intended for winter sports enthusiasts—not exactly a come-hither look. Sighing, I slipped into a pair of bright-red long johns, a red knit cap, and thick socks. I shrugged on my heavy cotton bathrobe.

I wandered through my room, smoothing the quilt, fluffing the pillows on the bed, and lighting the battery-powered candles. On impulse and feeling a little ridiculous, I flipped the photos of my parents and my best friend down on their faces. I didn't want to feel their eyes on me tonight. Reluctant to muss the bedding, I sat on the armchair in the corner of the room. I drew my knees to my chest and huddled under my robe, pressing the palm of my hand against my cold nose. I was too antsy to doze, but I closed my eyes and let my thoughts meander.

Finn Rasmussen. My friend and soon to be my lover. I saw him in my mind's eye, and my lips curved in a small smile. Finn had good genes. Tall, broad-shouldered, with a wide chest tapering down to a narrow waist, he was far too masculine to be beautiful. But damn, that's the word that came to mind when I pictured him. Heavy lashes framed deep-set eyes of a startling blue. Chiseled cheekbones, a square jaw, a firm, generous mouth. He was gorgeous.

A simple smile from Finn could lay waste to the world. Such a man might be tempted to coast by on his looks alone, cocky and complacent. But not Finn. Never Finn.

My entire body stiffened and my nerves pulled tight. God. I hoped I wasn't making a mistake. I hoped he'd understand what I had to do.

A soft rapping sound shattered my reverie. I hopped out of the chair and opened the door. Finn stood outside, clutching a branch of winter-blooming camellias in his gloved hands. Ruffled red petals surrounded bright-gold stamen. I recognized the distinctive flower. Camellias thrive in Kansas, and my mom grew them in our garden in Lawrence.

He held out the branch. I touched one delicate petal. "I love camellias. Thank you."

"I saw a bush blooming in a yard and thought you might like them." He stood outside the door, an expectant expression on his face. After a moment, he raised a brow. "You going to invite me in?"

A flush heated my cheeks. Why was I acting like such a goober? I stepped back and waved him into the room. He took off his gloves and coat and laid them across the small table. I poured water into an empty wine bottle and stuck the camellia branch in the makeshift vase.

We faced each other in silence. He eyed me and his forehead puckered. "You having second thoughts?"

"No," I said quickly, then gave a slight shake of my head. "I feel awkward as hell, and I don't know why."

He stepped forward and slid both palms around my nape. Strong fingers massaged the back of my neck, the spot where tension had knotted my muscles. "We've got nothing to prove and no time-table."

"You're right." I dropped my forehead against his shoulder, allowing his skilled fingers to ease my stiff muscles. "Umm… That's nice."

"Did I ever tell you how much I admire your intelligence and your competence?"

I tilted back my head and searched his face. As far as compliments from a man went, that was a first. "Really?"

"Yeah, really. Listening to you and Havoc talk about C-4 and shock waves and blast radiuses—" He shook his head. "I love that you're so damned smart. Smart and sweet. The combination is a real turn-on."

My conscience pinged and I mentally castigated myself. Here I was just thinking about how damned hot Finn was. Of course, that wasn't the only thing I admired about the man, but my mind had gone there first.

"Thank you." I sank my teeth into my lower lip, a motion Finn watched with avid eyes. I'd meet his confession with one of my own. "Do you want to know what I love about you?"

He brushed his thumb over my bottom lip, as if entranced, then lifted his eyes to meet mine. "Yeah, I do."

"You probably don't remember the first time we met."

Finn rocked back on his heels, surprise etched across his face. Why did I bring that up? Clearly it wasn't a memory he wanted to revisit.

A few hours before his scheduled execution, Marcus, Justin, Kyle, and I had infiltrated the Boise prison where Allsop was holding Finn. We'd found him drugged and battered. Against all odds our rescue was a success. We fought our way out of the prison and escaped back to Pendleton.

"I don't remember much about that night," he said slowly. "I'd passed out from the drugs and the pain. I recall coming to in the backseat of the car, and you were there. You smiled at me. Gave me water and told me I was safe. I remember…" He paused, his expression wistful. "I remember the moonlight streaming in through the car window. The light touched your hair and made it glow like a golden halo. I thought for a second that I had died and you were an angel, a beautiful angel, welcoming me to heaven."

I had no idea he remembered that moment, or what it had meant to him. An angel. Me. "Finn." My voice broke on his name. I clutched at his chest.

"You were going to tell me what you love about me," he reminded me.

"Yes." I nodded, swallowing hard. "The first time I saw you—beaten within an inch of your life—I knew that you were an extraordinary man. You could have escaped from Boise earlier, but you went back to try to rescue Allsop's housekeeper."

"Anybody would have done the same thing."

"No. That's not true. After the pandemic, a lot of people were too scared and traumatized to think about anything but their own survival. But you…" I laid a hand over his heart. "You're guided by your heart, by your sense of right and wrong. I love… I love the way you take care of people. Ever. Mrs. B. Me. You watch out for everybody, and you do it with a laugh and a joke, like it's no big deal. But it is."

Finn shoved a hand through his hair. "You make me sound like a saint. Trust me, Georgia, I'm no saint."

"And I'm no angel."

He arched a brow. "Neither saint nor angel. Where does that leave us?"

We were far too serious. It was time to turn the tide of this conversation. I stepped closer and pressed against him. "I don't know. If you're not a saint, and I'm not an angel, maybe we should get together and try to raise a little hell."

"Maybe we should." His eyes hooded. He slid both hands around my ass and yanked, pinning my belly to his groin.

Levering up on my toes, I nuzzled the base of his throat, slowly drawing in his scent. Soap. Musk. A hint of clean, masculine sweat. I parted my lips, tasting the tantalizing aroma. I dragged my teeth along a tendon in his neck, stopping when my mouth grazed the stubble on his jaw. I nuzzled again, seeking the spot where his heartbeat tap-tap-tapped against his skin.

Beneath my lips, his pulse sped up. His cock twitched. His breath hitched. *I* did that to him; *I* made his heart race and his breathing unsteady. *I* made him hard. Feminine power surged through my veins, and my own breath caught in my throat.

Finn's fingers tunneled through my hair, and he yanked my head back. His nostrils flared. Before my eyes, the man I'd described in heroic terms—a saint, practically a knight in shining armor—devolved into mere mortal. A man who hungered. For me.

His fist squeezed in my hair. I gasped at the slight sting.

He lifted heavy eyes to mine. "You good?" Finn's powerful body froze in place, awaiting my response.

I nodded, the gesture only increasing his taut grip on my hair. He held me immobile. Rather than feeling constrained, I gloried in it, in the unyielding control that slicked my sex and made my panties wet.

He tugged my head to one side, exposing my throat. Lowering his mouth, he nipped at my neck, his teeth sketching a chain from my breastbone to my ear. His mouth found a sensitive point beneath my jaw and latched on. Goose bumps erupted across my shoulders. I shuddered, trembling against his hard body. He gave a low moan of male satisfaction, a rumble I felt to my bones.

I felt weak, enervated. My head lolled, my neck unable to support its weight. Only Finn's fist clenched in my hair kept my head upright. Heat spiraled through me, zinging from my nipples to my sex.

Jesus. What was happening to me?

"Finn." I fought for breath.

He stilled then lifted his head. His eyes scanned my face, searching for… something. Hesitation, perhaps. A sign that I was changing my mind. Or maybe encouragement.

I could give him that. I smiled, my lips trembling. "Don't stop."

His expression cleared, any doubt cast aside. He tugged on the collar of my thick terrycloth robe. "This damn thing's in the way." His fingers worked the belt, loosening the knot that held it in place. He shoved the robe down my arms until it puddled on the floor at our feet. His gaze swept over my red long johns and the red knit hat, over my polka-dotted socks. His lips quirked.

I raised one finger in warning. "If the words Santa Claus cross your lips, we're going to have a problem."

He shook his head. "No ma'am. I was going to say… um… *hawt*." He drawled the word.

I batted at his chest. "These things keep me warm at night, and in the middle of winter, warm trumps *hawt*." I drew out the word the same way he did.

He brushed his knuckles over my cheek. "You got me to keep you warm at night now, angel."

Angel. His angel. The endearment held meaning, forever bound us to a moment of time only the two of us shared. My insides melted to a warm puddle of goo.

Finn was so damned sweet. "What am I going to do with you?" I asked.

He chuckled. "I got lots of ideas."

I couldn't get close enough. Rising up on my tiptoes, I arched my body against his. "So show me."

Without warning, Finn bent forward and threw me across his shoulder. He swept the quilt and blankets aside and deposited me on the sheets. I bounced and the air whooshed from my lungs. His eyes locked on mine, Finn stripped off his gray sweatshirt and sweatpants, and toed off his shoes.

He palmed a cock that was already erect, thick and long, a dream come true. I stared at it wide-eyed with appreciation, then tore my eyes away from the mouth-watering sight. My gaze meandered up his body, over the glorious V-line that angled down from his hip bones to his cock. Over his well-defined abs, a chiseled six-pack I longed to explore with my fingers and my tongue. Over his muscular chest.

His chest. Angry red, raised circles marred the smooth golden skin.

I gasped. My gaze flew to his face. "Oh, Finn," I choked out. Jesus Christ. The bastards had burned him, burned this good, kind man. They'd hurt him when he was helpless to fight back. And he'd never said a thing to us afterward. He'd just covered up his scars and went about his life uncomplaining.

Murderous rage flooded my veins.

Under my horrified scrutiny, the lust slid from Finn's face. His confidence dissolved. His shoulders hunched and he stood stock-still.

Oh my God. Did he think that I was turned off by his scars? That he was anything less than perfect in my eyes? No. No. No.

I rolled up onto my knees and reached for him. He shuffled forward, stopping when his legs hit the side of the mattress. With one fingertip, I gently touched the edge of the worst scar, a round red welt under his left nipple. I raised my eyes to his face.

He looked away, as if embarrassed. Or ashamed.

Everything inside me stilled, my muscles locked, my breath froze in my throat. Certainty sank talons deep into my flesh.

Finn was ashamed of his scars.

"The burns itched something fierce while they healed. I made that big one worse by scratching at it. It was dumb luck they didn't get infected. Sara—" He paused and swallowed. "Sara says the scars will fade over time, but right now my chest and stomach are a mess. Every time I look in the mirror, I'm reminded of my failure. I was weak. I got caught. I couldn't save myself."

"You put yourself in harm's way in order to help other people," I reminded him. "You saved Sunny. Hildy escaped because of you. Yeah, you were caught, but that was bad luck, not failure or weakness."

"Marcus told me the same thing. Maybe someday I'll believe it."

My throat ached from tears I refused to shed. "Do the burns still hurt?"

His head slowly moved from side to side. "Not really."

"Good. I don't want it to hurt when I touch you."

Rising up onto my knees, I pressed soft lips against the mark, then glanced up at his face. He watched me with flat eyes and a face devoid of emotion, his expression so inscrutable that I couldn't tell if he welcomed my touch. I kissed another scar, then another.

"My beautiful man," I murmured against his skin.

His hands caught my shoulders and gently pushed me away, creating distance between us. "You don't care about the burn marks?"

"Hell, yes, I care about the burn marks." My voice shook with fury. "I want to gut everybody who hurt you."

"Jonesy. It was Jonesy."

Jonesy, the sadistic sociopath. "I'm not surprised it was him," I said. "He's going to pay for his crimes someday."

He touched my cheek, his expression softening. "You're a fierce woman, Georgia Abbott."

"I'll do anything to protect the people I care about." I meant it, and I hoped he'd remember my words later. "But you asked about the burn marks. If you want to know if it matters to me that you have scars on your chest, the answer is no. Scars are just—" I shrugged. "They're a part of life. They're a reminder that you survived something. We'll all go to our graves dinged up."

"How about you?" he asked. "Do you have any scars?"

"I do." When I was little, a surgeon had removed an oddly shaped birthmark from my right butt cheek. To this day, a red blotch marked the spot.

"Where?"

I tossed my head. "A smart man like you should be able to figure that out on your own."

"Challenge accepted." Finn planted one knee on the bed and pushed me backward till I sprawled across the sheets. He pulled off my polka-dotted socks and tossed them over his shoulder. My thermal shirt came next, flying across the room to join my fluffy socks. Exposed to the chilly air, my nipples bunched.

I shivered, either from the cold or from the heated expression that crossed Finn's face. He slid both hands up my thighs, tucked his thumbs in the elastic waistband of my thermal pants, and peeled them down my legs. Naked, I lifted up on my elbows while his gaze raked over me.

"Well?" I demanded. "See anything?"

He grinned. "I see plenty, but no scar."

With a sigh, I folded my hands under my head and settled back, allowing him to examine my body. Cool fingers glided up my legs, skimmed over my belly and breasts, then trailed down my arms.

"Roll over," he ordered, his voice thick.

I made a show of it, stretching languidly and arching my back—like a cat lolling in front of a hearth—before I obediently turned onto my stomach.

"Ah-ha." His finger followed the outline of my surgical scar. "Where did this come from?"

"I was born with a big brown birthmark on my ass. The doctors thought it might turn into skin cancer someday, so when I was six, they removed it."

He palpated the spot. "I'm glad they caught it in time."

"Me, too."

When I've been pissed off in the past, I may have told a man or two to kiss my ass. Finn was the first man to actually do it. His lips took the place of his questing fingers as he pressed his mouth against my scar. He kissed a line to the twin indentations in my lower back—the dimples of Venus I think they're called—before his mouth followed a leisurely path up my spine, nipping at each vertebrae.

Holding his weight on his elbows, the big cowboy stretched out on top of me. He brushed away my hair, exposing my neck. His tongue traced the shell of my ear, then he blew against my wet skin. Shivers racked my body and I trembled beneath him.

"Easy, angel," he whispered. "We're just getting started."

TWENTY

Finn

Beneath me, Georgia quivered like a live wire. Her fingers grabbed a hold of the sheet and held tight, as if it was the only thing tethering her to the bed, as if she'd splinter and fly apart if she let go.

The woman had nothing to worry about, not with a 210-pound cowboy lying on top of her, pinning her to the bed.

My arms shook, too. I held myself above her so our skin touched, but she didn't carry my weight. I wasn't afraid that I'd squash her, not exactly. There was nothing frail or delicate about Georgia. She was a strong woman, all toned muscles and supple limbs. I've watched her spar with Havoc. She could pack a punch and sweep an opponent right off his feet.

Strong, smart, and sweet, the perfect trifecta. She was an exceptional woman, and I was a lucky man.

From her reactions—her little moans and the way she wriggled—I was learning that Georgia craved intense sensation, sensation that skirted close to the edge of pain. Her hair pulled tight. Her skin caught between my teeth. I kissed the hollow behind her ear then nipped my way down to where her neck curved into her shoulder. I bit down, not hard enough to bruise, but enough to demonstrate that I paid attention. That I knew what she liked. And that I'd give it to her.

Her back arched. Her hands scrabbled against the bedding. I slid one palm under her body. My fingers found her nipple. I pinched the taut nub. Georgia moaned. Her hips undulated against the mattress. I pinched harder. She gasped and threw her head back.

I lowered my mouth to her ear. "You good?"

"God, yes."

I sat up and flipped her over onto her back. I straddled her hips, my cock lying heavy against her stomach. Breathless, her cheeks flushed a pretty pink, Georgia looked up at me. Her eyes glinted and her lips curved up in a saucy smile. She wrapped her fingers around my cock. Her thumb brushed over the head, smearing the slippery pre-cum that seeped from the tip.

I was the one who groaned now. The first time I climaxed with Georgia it wouldn't be shooting ropes of cum across her belly and breasts. Although—shit—a visual of that act flashed through my mind and almost undid my fine resolve. Before I could think better of it, I seized her wrist.

"Let go," I ordered.

She chewed on her lower lip, clearly considering her options.

I got no dog in this race, no deep need to make her obey. I wasn't wired that way. Still, Georgia's response to hair pulling, to being constrained, suggested that maybe she was. Maybe she was a strong woman who sometimes liked to yield. If that was the case, I'd give her what she needed.

I lowered my chin. "Do as you're told, Georgia."

Her eyes widened, but her fingers let go of my shaft. I lifted her hand to my mouth and kissed her palm, rewarding her for her compliance. I nodded my approval then pressed both of her hands against the bed.

"Don't move, angel. Not till I'm done playing."

She jerked her head in assent, curiosity dancing in her eyes.

I flattened my palms against her stomach, gazing down at the beautiful woman laid out before me like a banquet of sumptuous delights.

I intended to feast.

My hands shaped the curves of her ivory breasts. I plucked at rosy pink nipples that hardened under my touch. She shuddered and arched her back, her lips parting as she gasped for breath. Leaning over, I teased a nipple with my tongue. Georgia writhed. Her hands clenched into tight fists.

Good God, the woman was responsive to the slightest touch.

I fell forward, catching my weight on my elbows. Nuzzling her throat, I inhaled a whiff of orange blossoms. It pleased me no end that she wore my scent. I sketched a chain of kisses up her neck, along her chin, then my mouth laid claim to hers. Heat speared throughout my body. My dick throbbed, demanding satisfaction.

Down boy. I sat back on my heels once again, palming my cock.

A fine sheen of sweat covered Georgia's breasts, and her rapid pulse tapped against the thin skin on the side of her neck. Through half-closed lids, her eyes glittered with challenge.

I glanced down. Georgia's hand had snaked between her legs, her fingers circling her clit. Defying me, was she? This willful insubordination could not stand. I wrapped my fingers around her wrist and pulled her hand away.

"I told you not to move till I was done playing." Her lower lip jutted out in a pretty pout. I licked her juices from her fingertips then pressed her hand to the mattress once again. "Be good."

"I'll be good, as long as you make it worth my while."

I chuckled. "That another challenge? If it is, you should know that a Rasmussen always rises to a challenge."

Her lips kicked up. "So show me."

I jumped onto my feet, bent over, and hauled her ass to the edge of the mattress. Dropping to my knees, I nudged her thighs apart, then draped her legs over my shoulders. I blew a long, slow breath against the blond curls that covered her sex, then inhaled, tasting the scent of her arousal. My fingers teased apart her lips. With a broad, flat tongue, I slowly licked over her sex. Georgia whimpered. I did it again then circled her clit with the tip of my tongue. I found my rhythm and settled in. She tilted her hips, grinding against me while I ate her out.

I slid a finger into her pussy, then groaned. Lifting my head, I met Georgia's eyes. "You're so freaking hot and tight, angel. You're going to feel good around my cock."

She whimpered again. "Please, Finn. Fuck me. Now."

I'd planned to make her come before I took her, but when she begged me to fuck her, my brain shut down and my body took over. I crawled up between her legs. My mouth descended on hers. I eased the tip of my cock into position.

"Yes," Georgia moaned. She gyrated her hips, and my shaft slid against her wet heat.

With one explosive thrust, I drove my cock into her molten core. Georgia clenched her muscles around my dick. I gripped her ass and jerked her close, tilting her pelvis so I could go deep.

My good intentions were well and truly shot to shit. Instead of taking my time, lingering over our first lovemaking, I pounded into Georgia, fast and hard.

Her desperation matched my own. Sweat slicked her shoulders and breasts. She clawed at my back, leaving marks I'd gloat over tomorrow. When her teeth fastened on my shoulder and her back arched off the mattress, my balls drew up tight. Her pussy spasmed around me, and she cried out my name, going limp in my arms. Shuddering, I came, pleasure rocketing throughout my body. I rolled onto my side, drawing Georgia close.

We were hot and sweaty now, but the cold room would chill us soon enough. I pulled the blankets and quilt up to our chins. Georgia snuggled against me, her head tucked under my chin. She yawned.

"Query," she mumbled.

I braced myself for a what-do-you-miss-from-the-old-world question. "Yeah?"

Her fingertip traced a circle around my nipple. "Next time we go, would you mind if I'm on top?"

TWENTY-ONE

Georgia

"I hear you slept with Finn last night." Marcus swung his booted feet up onto the conference table, assuming his favorite position.

I shot an evil glare at Rachel. The blabbermouth. She folded her hands on her lap. The smile she flashed showed not one shred of repentance.

"Really?" I said. "We've got nothing better to talk about than my sex life?"

Marcus lifted one heavily muscled shoulder. "If you and Finn are starting something, good for you. I wish you well. What I need to know is how it impacts your work for me."

"It doesn't," I said quickly, apparently too quickly for Havoc's satisfaction.

"Huh." He snatched a walnut from a bowl, crushed the shell, and started to pick out the meat. "What does Finn know?"

"He knows that I'm working undercover, trying to insinuate myself into Jonesy's good graces, but nothing more than that."

Marcus swung his feet down, reached across the table, and laid his hand on my arm. "Listen up. It's not too late to change your mind and give up the undercover work, especially if it keeps your relationship with Finn from going south."

This was my friend speaking, not the man leading the resistance against Allsop. I couldn't allow sentiment to get in the way of achieving our goal.

"No. I'm already in play. Jonesy thinks he's been softening me up. It's got to be me."

His piercing eyes scrutinized my face, weighing my words. Whatever he saw in my expression must have satisfied him. "All right. The plan stands. For now."

"We want you to bring Jonesy his lunch today." Rachel spoke up. "It'll be just the two of you. Finn's taking Reno to be questioned by Havoc. At least that's the story."

"While Reno's out of his cell being *interrogated*." Marcus made air quotes around the word. "Give this to Jonesy." He lobbed a small, foil-wrapped packet my way.

"What is it?" I asked.

The two-way radio squawked, the third time a call interrupted my morning meeting with Marcus and Rachel.

"Dammit." Marcus heaved a deep sigh and picked up the radio. "Havoc." He listened intently. "No. Let 'em go. You know the drill. Personal items, a full tank of gas, and a week's worth of food. Uh-huh… Uh-huh… Havoc out." Frowning, he tossed the radio onto the table in our new conference room in the city hall.

"More people taking off?" Rachel guessed.

"Yeah. This group said they're going to try their luck in California. That makes fourteen souls leaving town in the past few days."

"People are running scared after the bomb and fires," I said.

"That's part of it." Lines of discontent slashed across his forehead. "Some folks have lost confidence in me. They don't think that I can protect them. Others don't like the curfew and new regulations."

"I say good riddance," Rachel said. "Who needs cowards and whiners? Fuck 'em."

Havoc looked skeptical.

"A smart man told me once that nobody said it was going to be easy to rebuild society." I threw Havoc's words back at him.

Marcus offered a wry half smile. "I suppose dissension was inevitable once we got past the honeymoon period."

"Dissension, sure, but the bomb. I didn't see that coming." Rachel wore guilt like a hair shirt. "I've interviewed everybody the sentries recall entering the building that night, but no joy."

"We've tightened up security, restricted access to headquarters," I reminded her.

She threw her hands in the air. "And folks are bitching that they have to sign in and be patted down to use the library."

Justin opened the door and stuck his head into the room. "Can I talk to you for a few minutes, Havoc?"

"Of course." Marcus jumped up and followed Justin into the corridor.

"So—" Rachel turned to me, a salacious grin splitting her face. "How was it? Did the cowboy ride you hard and put you away wet?"

I groaned at her abuse of the old idiom. "I love you, girlfriend, but you're not getting details."

"What?" She looked indignant. "Why not?"

I've never been one to kiss and tell. "It's private. And I don't think Finn would appreciate my gossiping about his sexual prowess, magnificent though it is."

At the word magnificent, her eyes lit up. "I won't blab. I promise."

"Yeah." I rolled my eyes. "You're the soul of discretion when it comes to sex." Trying to distract her, I pointed toward the hallway, where Marcus and Justin carried on a muted conversation. "Have you met Justin's new girlfriend? Lorelei?"

"Met her and declared my undying love," Rachel said. "She brought Havoc and me lasagna for dinner. Warm, cheesy lasagna, can you believe it?"

"She said she was a kindergarten teacher before the pandemic."

"That's right." Rachel nodded. "She's helping Justin set up a school. They seem good together. Justin looks happier than I've ever seen him."

"He deserves it."

"Yep." Rachel rubbed her hands together with satisfaction. "And now Justin's found Lorelei and you've hooked up with Finn, I need to find somebody for Thanh and Rocco."

"Good God. You're incorrigible."

"I want my friends to be happy," she said primly.

Havoc strode back into the room. "I'm needed at the warehouse. Unless you have some questions, I think we're done here."

I held up the foil packet he'd tossed me. "You said to give this to Jonesy?"

"That's right. It's a cigarette and one match."

A cigarette. He'd be thrilled, more for what the cigarette signified than any nicotine hit. A chink in my armor, a sign that I was falling sway to Jonesy's blandishments.

Our plan was moving forward nicely.

"I'll sneak it to him with his lunch," I said.

"Report back to Rachel this afternoon," he called over his shoulder.

"Will do."

Rachel stood and gathered up her papers. "You sure you don't want to come back to my office and fill me in on all the dirty details?"

"I'm sure."

She sniffed. "Killjoy."

"Snoop." I blew her a kiss.

At the exit to the building, I signed out. The new protocol required everyone—even Havoc's top people—to sign in and out when they entered headquarters. I crossed the parking lot, keeping my eyes peeled for Finn. He spent the morning helping to reinforce a sentry house on the west side of town, but had to be finished in time for his meeting with Reno.

I spotted Lorelei, instead, and waved her over.

"Everybody is still raving about your lasagna," I said.

Pleasure flushed her cheeks. "I'm glad you liked it. It was nice to finally meet you all."

I pointed to the thermal jug that swung from her hand. "What did you make this time?"

"Justin and I have a meeting with the school planning committee. I'm bringing homemade soup." She made a face. "That's a lie. It's not exactly homemade soup. It's more like canned vegetables and rice and chicken bouillon. Nothing to write home about."

"Nowadays that will pass for an epicurean treat. I'm sick to death of granola bars and ramen."

Lorelei touched my arm. "Let's all get together soon for another real meal, okay?"

"I'd like that."

Lorelei glanced at the old-fashioned, windup watch on her wrist. "Yikes. I'm two minutes late. See ya!" She skipped backward, waved, then whirled and scampered toward the building.

I checked my own watch. I was supposed to report to the police station in half an hour. I had just enough time to drop by the cafeteria and find something to eat before heading over to the jail with Jonesy's lunch. With any luck, I'd run into Finn at the cafeteria.

Finn. Images from our first night together unspooled in my memory. We'd fallen asleep, our limbs entwined, then woke up a couple hours later, ready for another round. Desire stirred to life again, just as dawn was lightening the sky. After our third time, I collapsed and fell into a deep sleep.

The man was insatiable, with the refractory period of an eighteen year old. Lucky me.

Distracted by memory, I didn't pay attention to the icy sidewalk. My foot slipped. My arms flailed.

"Whoa. Got you." Finn came up from behind and caught me, setting me upright on my feet.

We wobbled. I clutched at his chest. He slid both arms around my waist and pulled me close. He bent over and playfully brushed the tip of his cold nose over mine. I giggled, feeling very young and giddy.

"Good morning," I said. Finn had been gone when the windup alarm clock startled me awake at nine. I'd stretched in bed, stiff and achy from our exertions, and feeling irrationally happy, all of my worries about the future pushed to the back of my mind.

"Good morning," Finn echoed. A slow, knowing smile crossed his face. "I had a great time last night."

I returned his smile. "Me, too."

Finn pulled off a glove and dragged his bare knuckles across my lips and my cheek. "Your skin is so soft. I can't resist touching it."

"Well that's convenient, because I like being touched by you." I turned my head and kissed his fingers. "I like all the things you do with your hands."

Heat flared in his expression. "Is that right?"

Biting my lower lip, I nodded. "Mm-hmm."

Finn craned his neck, his eyes scanning our surroundings. He blew out a breath, disappointment flooding his features. "Too bad there's people around. Otherwise I'd push you up against that tree and show you exactly what I can do with my hands."

I rose up on my toes and pressed a quick kiss against his lips. "Rain check?"

"Count on it." His mouth descended on mine, a claiming kiss that left me breathless and swaying in his arms.

Not the time or the place to get carried away. I shook myself, refocusing on the task at hand. "I need to pick up Jonesy's lunch at the cafeteria then take it over to the police station."

"I'm heading there myself." Finn put his glove back on and took my hand. "Let's go together."

Hand in hand, we walked to the cafeteria. At the counter, a worker handed me Jonesy's lunch, a peanut butter and jelly sandwich and a cup of applesauce. Finn and I split another PB&J sandwich to eat on our way to the police station.

"I asked Olivia to meet me there," Finn said. "I'm sure it's hard on her to have Reno locked up. They can have some time together before I take him back to his cell."

"You're a thoughtful sweetheart of a man," I said, meaning every word.

He rolled his eyes. "A thoughtful sweetheart of a man? Couldn't you call me something that sounds at least a little bit hot?"

I stopped walking and tugged on his hand. "There's nothing hotter than a thoughtful sweetheart of a man."

He grinned down at me, his expression unguarded and openhearted.

My conscience pinged. My stomach knotted and acid burned my throat.

Dear God, please let him forgive me.

TWENTY-TWO

Finn

We stomped the snow off our boots and tromped into the lobby of the small downtown police station. Olivia stood at the reception desk, visiting with one of the soldiers standing guard at the facility. She turned around when we entered, a big smile on her pretty face.

Georgia hugged Olivia then gently touched the side of her head, the shaved spot where the hair was starting to grow back. "How are you feeling, sweetheart? Any more headaches?"

Olivia had suffered a subdermal hematoma—a brain bleed—after falling down a flight of stone stairs at Uncle Bobby's castle in Prineville. Georgia and I had rushed back to Valhalla to fetch Sahdev. Thank God, the emergency surgery Sahdev performed saved the plucky young woman's life.

"The headaches are gone," Olivia said. "The only thing bothering me now is trying to sleep in an empty bed. I miss Reno. I can't wait for this assignment to be over."

Olivia's distress hit Georgia hard. The skin pulled tight over her face, and she looked positively stricken.

"I'm so sorry," Georgia said. "If you need anything—somebody to talk to or to spend time with—come to me." She glanced over her shoulder and met my eyes, her expression beseeching, like she was asking me a favor. "And if you can't find me, come to Rachel or Finn."

"You bet," I said firmly. "If you need anything while Reno isn't around, all you have to do is ask."

"Thanks, guys. I appreciate it."

"I'm going to go get Reno," I said. "Give me a few minutes alone with him in the interrogation room, then he's all yours for half an hour."

Olivia bounced on her toes, her excitement palpable, her happiness contagious. I couldn't help but smile.

I unlocked the heavy door leading to the cellblock. As soon as I stepped inside, my gaze fell on Jonesy. My mood sobered. He sat on his cot, but when he saw me, he stood and ambled over to the door of his cell.

"Hey, Finn. You look mighty pleased with yourself today. You get laid last night? You find a woman who doesn't mind the scars?"

Shit. How did the bastard know the scars bothered me? And how the hell did he know that I'd had sex last night?

Hardening my expression so I wouldn't give anything else away, I strode past his cell, stopping outside of Reno's. I unlocked the door. "Hands out," I barked. "And don't think about trying something. The place is crawling with armed guards."

I zip tied his hands together and marched him out of the cellblock. Olivia threw herself on him. Reno lifted his bound hands over her head and pulled her against his chest.

"I'm all right, baby girl," he murmured, brushing his lips over her hair. "Tell me how you're doing."

"I'm okay." The tears slipping down Olivia's cheeks gave the lie to that assertion.

I cut the zip ties, freeing his hands.

Reno cupped Olivia's face between his palms. "I need a few minutes with Finn, then I'm all yours."

"All right," she said softly.

He dropped a quick kiss on her lips. "I love you."

"Love you, too."

I felt like a heel for dragging him away from her, but it had to be done. "Follow me." I led the way up the hall to the interrogation room.

"Any progress with Jonesy?" I got right down to business. The sooner we were finished, the more time Reno would have with Olivia.

"I've griped plenty about Havoc and life in Pendleton, and Jonesy has lent a sympathetic ear," he said. "He's trying to tell me that things are better in Boise under Allsop, but I still have my doubts." He flashed a smile.

Yeah. Jonesy would smell a rat if Reno caved too quickly.

"He spill anything useful?" I asked.

"Not yet, but this is a long con. I'll get there."

I admired Reno's confidence. It reminded me of Ripper's, an unshakable conviction that he'd figure out what needed to be done and find a way to do it. Before I met the two Janissaries, I never would have guessed that I'd genuinely like and respect members of a motorcycle club. But I did. Shoot, next to my brother, Ripper was the man I most respected in all the world. And Reno was a fine fellow. I'd fight at his side any day.

"Anything else you need to report?" I asked.

"Nope."

I shook his hand. "I'll get Olivia for you. You've got the place to yourself for half an hour."

He angled his head at the observation room on the other side of the mirrored glass. "And nobody's in there?"

"Not a soul. Like I said, you've got the place to yourself. Nobody is watching or listening."

"Good."

I clapped him on the shoulder, stepped into the hall, and crooked a finger, silently beckoning Olivia. She hugged Georgia then skipped up the corridor to the interrogation room. She kissed my cheek and slipped into the room, shutting out the world while she spent precious time with her man.

I found Georgia in the lobby, arranging Jonesy's lunch on a plastic tray. She unwrapped a foil packet and removed a cigarette and wooden match, then rolled the items up in a paper napkin. Her mood had altered, become more serious, her expression showing none of her usual good humor. She looked both petulant and sulky, a woman who held a grudge against the world. Even her posture was different. She stood stiffly, her shoulders slumped, her movements jerky and ungraceful. She was slipping into character for her role, I realized with a start. Inhabiting a different body and a different spirit.

I'd best leave her alone.

I nodded to Georgia and took a seat across from the reception desk. For a good minute, she stood stock-still outside the door to the cellblock. She blew out a deep breath and slipped the key into the lock. Without a backward glance, she disappeared into Jonesy's orbit.

I fought the urge to chase after her, to extract her from the monster's clutches. But Georgia was no victim. She faced Jonesy of her own free will. It wasn't my place to run roughshod over her choices. And locked inside his cell, no way in hell could Jonesy hurt her. Georgia was just fine.

So why was my heart thumping so hard it threatened to rattle my ribs loose?

TWENTY-THREE

Georgia

"Georgia, honey, is that you?"

I stopped walking and whirled around.

Two men shuffled toward me, the pair a study in contrasts. Short and tall. Plump and rail thin. Bearded and clean-shaven. The chubby, bearded man turned to his much taller companion, a thin fellow with iron-gray hair and thick spectacles. "I told you it was her, Anton."

"And you were right, Bobby." Anton offered me a warm smile.

"Uncle Bobby." I held out a hand, which he ignored, sweeping me instead into a big hug.

From his hometown of Prineville, Oregon, Uncle Bobby Banyon had built the country's most successful chain of outdoor recreational stores. In the early days of the pandemic, he'd set aside a massive stockpile of weapons, bullet-making supplies, camping equipment, and freeze-dried foods. He flirted with the notion of allying with the powerful Elliot Allsop, who was scheming to get his hands on Banyon's supplies. I was part of the team Marcus Havoc sent to Prineville to secure Banyon's weapons cache. With the help of Anton Milewski—a retired high school history teacher who'd suffered under Allsop's harsh regime—we persuaded Banyon to throw in with Havoc and the good guys in Pendleton.

"This is new." Anton pointed at my head.

Smiling, I ran my fingers through hair that still felt alien. Most mornings, I did a double take when I looked into the mirror and spied short brown hair instead of long blond locks.

"I wanted to try something different," I said airily, minimizing the change. "If I decide that I don't like it, I can always grow it out."

"You look lovely, my dear." Uncle Bobby squeezed my hands. He glanced to his side. "Doesn't she, Anton?"

"She does indeed," Anton agreed, but he narrowed his eyes. I swear I could see wheels turning in his head as the shrewd older man studied me. A teacher with a lifelong passion for military history and spycraft, he'd become one of Havoc's advisors. A couple of times, I'd found Marcus and Anton bent over a chessboard, deep in conversation. Anton knew nothing about my assignment, but the drastic change in my appearance definitely roused his suspicions.

"Thank you," I said. "Why are you gentleman out and about this cold morning?"

Anton held up a hardbound book. "We're going to the library. I just finished this fascinating book about British special agents—women—who were sent to occupied France to spy on the Nazis during World War II." He turned the book so I could see the title. "You might enjoy it, Georgia."

Maybe I was reading too much into Anton's smile. "I'll keep it in mind. Thank you."

"If you're going to the city hall, we can walk together," Uncle Bobby suggested.

"I'm heading downtown."

Uncle Bobby's face fell. "Too bad, but it was nice to see you again, honey, even if it's only for a minute."

"It was good to see you, too. Bye." I waved, then continued on my way to the police station. I'd stopped by the cafeteria and had picked up Jonesy's lunch: another peanut butter and jelly sandwich and a cup of fruit cocktail. Most days now, I brought Jonesy his lunch.

By all appearances, I'd warmed up to the bastard. I smiled shyly when he called me his "sweet, sweet Carrie." I passed him an occasional cigarette and match, sidling so close to his cell that, if he had a mind to, he could reach out and grab me.

He consoled me when I complained that the women at the warehouse were mean to me. I was given a pair of nasty, cheap-ass jeans, while the girl who came in before me got a brand new pair of expensive ones from Nordstrom. I got the dollar store shampoo while the other girl got the fancy stuff from a salon. And did Jonesy see my shoes? Guess it paid to kiss up to the bitches behind the counter, didn't it?

Jonesy frowned and made supportive noises when I regaled him with my tales of woe.

Reno chipped in, too, airing his own complaints. After being a big shot in Prineville—one of Uncle Bobby's top dogs—it sucked to find himself a peon in Pendleton. The fuckers assigned him to garbage collection. Him. Could you believe it?

Shaking his head in disgust, Jonesy commiserated with the aggrieved biker. He slyly suggested that Reno would have fared better if he'd sided with Allsop. Allsop knew how to treat loyal men.

The con was going well.

When he let down his guard, Jonesy's eyes gleamed with satisfaction. Day by day, he was reeling Reno and me in. We were falling under his sway, helpless against his phony sympathy and subtle persuasive powers. Jonesy held entirely too high an opinion of himself. That was fine by me. Arrogance and ego had led more than one man to his ruin.

The con was wearing on me.

As I approached the police station, the door swung open. Finn and Olivia stepped outside. Finn's face lit up when he saw me. He stepped forward and pulled me into his arms.

"Hey, you." He touched my cheek. "I'm glad I bumped into you."

"Me, too. You finish another 'interrogation' with Reno?" I guessed.

"Yep. I can't do it too often, not without making Jonesy suspicious, but every once in a while is fine."

Olivia's face glowed with happiness. "Finn lets me know every time he comes to talk to him. Seeing Reno for even half an hour means the world to me."

My smile faltered. There was no help for it, but the situation truly sucked.

I focused my eyes on the sidewalk for a handful of seconds while I composed my features. By the time I lifted my gaze to Finn's face, my smile had returned. Hiding my feelings. God. This was a skill I never wanted to master.

Finn dropped a kiss on my temple. "The sooner you go in, the sooner you'll get done."

I threw myself against his chest and buried my face in his coat.

"Angel—" Strong arms enclosed me, and I gave myself to the count of ten to feel sorry for myself, then I straightened up.

"You're right. I need to get this done. See you tonight, babe."

TWENTY-FOUR

Finn

Preoccupied was an understatement. Georgia was downright absent, like her mind had hightailed it for the hills, leaving her body behind. I touched her arm. "Georgia, Lorelei asked if you liked the apple pie."

Georgia turned her head toward me and blinked. She sat up straight on the blue love seat and shook herself. The vacant expression cleared away. She pasted an unconvincing smile on her face before turning to Lorelei. "The pie was amazing. Did you use the solar oven again?"

I slid an arm across her shoulders and pulled her close, anchoring her to the here and now.

"I'm glad you liked it. It's not bad for a pie made from dried apple slices, right?" Lorelei exchanged a glance with Justin, who smiled proudly at his girlfriend. "It was too cloudy today to use the solar oven, but the people running the cafeteria were baking bread in the wood-burning stoves. They let me put the pie in with the loaves."

"First the lasagna, and now apple pie. You've moved to the top of my list of favorite people." Sitting cross-legged on the floor,

Rachel rubbed her stomach. For a tiny woman, Rachel sure could pack away the grub.

Nobody in Pendleton was going hungry yet. We'd cleared out every store and pantry for a hundred miles around, but our supplies wouldn't last forever. Allsop's solution to any potential shortage was to cut off food and water to everybody over sixty-five. He acted like Mrs. B. and Anton Milewski were nothing more than useless mouths to feed, drains on society. And that was the difference between our side and his. Everybody mattered to us. Nobody mattered to Allsop, except himself and maybe the flunkies who kept him in power.

Thank God he no longer had that vicious prick Jonesy at his beck and call.

"We need to look to the future," I said to Justin. "Oregon and Washington were always big fruit-producing states. We can't let the orchards go to rack and ruin."

Justin ducked his chin in agreement. "Havoc and I have been talking about that. As soon as we settle our business with Allsop, we can shift our focus to food production and rebuilding."

"That day can't come soon enough, brother." I leaned back against the sofa cushion and swung my feet up onto the coffee table. Georgia elbowed me and tipped her head at my boots, frowning. My gaze followed hers. I'd absentmindedly planted my boots smack in the middle of Lorelei's coffee table. I lowered my feet to the floor and shot Lorelei an apologetic look. "Guess I made myself at home. Sorry about that."

From her perch on Justin's lap, Lorelei smiled and waved a hand around the living room of the small one-bedroom apartment she'd been assigned. Compared to the old motel rooms the rest of us occupied, it was positively commodious, but the five of us crowded the space. "Not a problem. *Mi casa es su casa.*"

"That's kind of you, but still, I was raised better."

Lorelei picked up Justin's hand and twined her fingers through his. "Justin said you grew up on a ranch."

"Yep. A cattle ranch in the central part of the state. Three thousand acres of God's country. How about you? Where did you grow up?"

"Meridian, Idaho, just west of Boise," Lorelei said. "I was teaching kindergarten there when the flu struck."

"You're one of the people the Nampa Boys helped to evacuate?" Georgia asked.

"That's right."

"That must have been harrowing. Sneaking out of town in the middle of the night, right under Allsop's nose."

Lorelei expression sobered. "It was scary, but all's well that ends well."

"It didn't end well for David," Justin muttered.

At the mention of the teenage leader of the Nampa Boys, Lorelei's eyes filled with tears.

"Shit, sweetheart. I'm sorry." Justin squeezed Lorelei's shoulders. "I shouldn't have reminded you of David."

"Don't apologize." Lorelei wiped at her eyes. "Whether you mention him or not, I think about David every day. I think about everybody who's living at the mercy of Allsop."

"Hey, Lorelei." I leaned forward and caught her eye. "After the war, I hope you and Justin can visit the ranch. I'd love to show you Valhalla."

"We'd like that," Justin said.

"After the war." Lorelei sighed. "It always comes down to that, doesn't it? Sometimes it feels like everything is on hold, that nothing we do is real, that our lives won't start again until the war is over."

"I don't know," Georgia said. "It all feels too real to me."

"Yeah," Rachel agreed. "The *Carpe Diem* guys stealing from the warehouse. The fires. The bomb. It feels real to me, too. Things sure have gone to shit in the past few weeks."

"Folks are scared right now," I said. "Half of them want Havoc to do whatever is necessary to keep them safe. Half of them think their rights are being stomped on."

"We're only doing what's necessary." Justin leaned back against the cushion. "The curfew, the extra patrols, the searches, it won't last forever."

"The bomb at headquarters was a wake-up call," Rachel said. "If somebody planted explosives and started a fire at the warehouse, we'd be screwed. We can't take any chances with the town's supplies. We've doubled the guards at the warehouse. Nobody gets in or out without being searched. If people don't like it—if they can't see why it's necessary—fuck 'em."

"We all have to make whatever sacrifices are necessary to stop Allsop," Georgia said. "That's the most important thing. Then life can get back to normal, or whatever passes for normal nowadays."

Silence fell on the room.

"How about we play a few rounds of gin rummy?" Lorelei suggested after a minute. Bless her heart, she was trying to be a good hostess and lighten the mood. The least we could do was to play along.

"Good idea." I sat up. "Unless I'm mistaken, Rachel still owes me $50,000 from the last time we played."

"Right," Rachel drawled. "As soon as the banks are open, I'll pay you first thing."

Lorelei fetched a deck of cards. We sat on the floor around the coffee table for an hour, playing rummy. By the time we called it a night, Rachel owed me another $100,000.

Georgia and I started back to the motel. The sky had cleared and there was a full moon, so we kept our flashlights in our pockets and walked with only the moon to light our way.

"You were quiet earlier tonight. Something on your mind?" I asked.

Georgia slid her arm through mine and leaned against me. "You've been happy the past couple of weeks, haven't you?"

What an odd, out-of-the-blue sort of question. I stopped walking and turned to face her. Moonlight had washed all color away from the world, rendering everything in shades of black and gray and silver. She lifted a bone-pale face to mine.

"What do you mean?" I touched her chilled cheek.

Her fingers clutched at my coat. "Since things changed between us, since we slept together, you've been happy, haven't you?"

Where was this coming from? If my woman needed reassurance, I'd give it to her. "Every minute I've spent with you has made me happy. From the first time we spoke in the back of that car, until right here, right now."

She pressed her lips together, and tears glittered in her eyes. "I'm glad. After the pandemic changed everything, I didn't expect to feel this kind of happiness again. You gave that to me, Finn Rasmussen. I'll always be grateful."

A cold finger touched my heart, an irrational feeling that she was saying goodbye. But that made absolutely no sense.

"Angel." I cupped her face between my palms. "You're stuck with me. I'm not going anywhere. We've got years and years of happy ahead of us. I promise."

That promise pulled a smile from Georgia's lips. "From your mouth to God's ears."

"Come on." I grabbed her hand. "Let's get back to our room, and we'll see how happy we can make each other."

We scuttled over the slippery sidewalks, climbed the motel stairs, and burst through the door into her room. Georgia locked the door and leaned against it, a shadowy form in the dark room.

"You want me to switch on a candle?" I asked.

Instead of replying, Georgia seized the collar of my coat and jerked me toward her. Off balance, I pressed my hands against the door, trapping her between my arms. She stood up on her tiptoes. Her mouth molded against mine, greedy and insistent.

More than happy to meet her demands, I caught her lower lip between my teeth and sucked it into my mouth. Our tongues dueled, parrying and thrusting. Georgia squirmed beneath me, panting. She toed off her boots, shoved her leggings and panties down her thighs, then kicked them off. I unzipped her coat and pushed her sweater up out of the way. My fingers undid the hook on the front of her bra. The lace cups fell to her side, and her breasts filled my hands. I squeezed the luscious mounds and brushed my thumbs across her nipples.

Georgia gasped and tore her mouth from mine. Desperate hands yanked my coat open and jerked my shirt up, baring my stomach and chest. She writhed against me.

I tunneled fingers through her hair and clenched my fist, holding her head still while I growled into her ear. "Tell me what you want."

She stilled, her ragged breaths the only sounds I heard. "You. Now. Please." She moaned, grinding against me.

My eager hands worked the buttons on my jeans. I shoved the denim down my hips. My cock sprang free. With a grunt, I hoisted her up.

"Wrap your legs around my waist." She complied. I slammed my cock deep into her wet heat. "The bed?" I asked.

Her head sliced left then right, a blur of movement in the gloom. "No. Fuck me here."

Well, shit. What man could deny that request? I wrapped one hand around the back of her head. Wouldn't want it to bang against the door when I pounded into her.

Georgia dug her heels into the small of my back, pulling me close, urging me on. I slid out and she moaned a protest. The head of my cock throbbed against her slick slit.

Not yet. I sucked in a breath, savoring this moment where time stood still, teetering between anticipation and ecstasy. My pulse clanged inside my head, the sound almost drowning out her small, needy whimpers.

"Finn," she begged, undulating her hips in an invitation as old as time.

My restraint broke. I plowed into her sweet heat. The walls of her pussy clenched around my shaft, squeezing me tight. Her teeth grazed my jaw then latched onto my neck. She sucked so hard against my skin that I'm sure blood vessels exploded under the pressure.

"Damn it, woman," I growled. "Did you just give me a hickey?"

My vision adjusted to the darkness. Georgia laughed and challenge sparkled in her eyes. Her shoulders shook, and she lifted her chin. "Give me one, too. A big one."

"Yes, ma'am." My hands trembled. What had she done to me? I was as eager and fired up as a horny first-timer.

I tugged her head to one side, baring the long line of her neck. I licked my lips, then kissed the pulse point in the soft hollow on the side of her throat. Beneath my mouth, her heartbeat thudded, a vital, living thing. Yeah. This was the spot.

Gently biting down, I shaped my lips into a circle. I sucked, slowly increasing the pressure till I was sure a telltale bruise had formed. All the while my hips rocked against hers, and my cock pummeled her pussy.

Georgia moaned and thrashed. Her sharp fingernails clawed my shoulders, the bite of pain only urging me on. My balls drew up.

"You close?" I demanded.

"So close," she panted.

I drew back my head until our faces were mere inches apart. Our chests rose and fell. We gasped for air, our breaths mingling. Tightening my fist in her hair, I compelled her to meet my eyes. I slammed my cock home. "Come for me, angel."

As if waiting for my command, she threw her head back and spasmed around me. With a groan, I came, shooting hot jets of cum deep within her core. Pure pleasure overwhelmed me and drained the strength from my limbs. Bracing my arms against the door, I dropped my forehead against hers.

The chill air touched our overheated skin, and Georgia shivered. Holding her up on my hips, I shuffled over to the bed, my jeans still around my thighs. I peeled off Georgia's sweater and coat then deposited her on the sheets. Shucking my own clothes, I kicked off my boots, and crawled onto the bed next to her, pulling the blankets up to our chins.

She rolled onto her side and threw a leg over my thighs.

I pulled her against my chest, one hand cupping her head. Georgia yawned.

"Sleepy?" I asked.

"Somebody wore me out," she said with a low laugh. She slid her hand across my chest and splayed her fingers over my heart. Cocking her head to one side, she held her breath. "I can feel your heart beating."

"It beats for you," I said lightly, as if I was teasing. I stilled. Teasing or not, the words held truth, a truth I'd never expressed. I sucked in a deep breath then blew it out, seeking the courage to lay my cards on the table. "I love you, Georgia."

The hand lying over my heart trembled. Georgia sighed and my chest constricted. Shit. I'd put her on the spot.

"It's all right—" I started.

"Shhh." She pressed a finger to my lips, silencing me. She drew in her own deep breath. I waited for her to speak, anticipation jangling my nerves. Tilting her face up to mine, her fingers touched my cheek, her expression solemn. "I love you too, Finn. Never forget that."

Relief was a gut punch. Turning my head, I kissed the center of her palm. "Then everything's all right in my world."

"I love you," she repeated, peppering my chest with kisses. She captured a nipple between her teeth and tugged.

I hissed. My cock stirred to life. "You want to go again?"

Her lips curved. Her eyes sparkled. "I'm game. How about you?"

"Always." I rolled on top of her, bracing my weight on my forearms.

Georgia tilted her pelvis, dragging her slick heat over my shaft. My mind splintered. Cognition fled.

I nudged the tip of my cock against her dripping entrance. Her fingernails dug into my ass. With a moan, I slid home.

Something tickled in the back of my mind, a nagging, insistent voice. What was it Georgia had said? *I love you too, Finn. Never forget that.*

What the hell did that mean?

TWENTY-FIVE

Georgia

I jerked awake, my chest heaving, my pulse hammering. Cold sweat beaded my forehead. I gasped for air, my fight-or-flight response kicking into high gear. If I didn't know better, I'd swear that thirty seconds ago I'd been running for my life, instead of startling into wakefulness from a deep sleep.

Sharpening my senses, I glanced around the dark room. From a crack between the curtains, a thin ribbon of moonlight slanted across the bed. Shadows hugged the walls and congealed in the corners of my familiar room. I blew out a slow breath. I was lying in bed next to Finn, exactly where I wanted to be.

For now.

Only the soft ticking of the windup alarm clock and Finn's deep, rhythmic breathing punctuated the quiet.

Not a single thing was amiss. No reason for me to wake up paralyzed with fear.

Everything was fine.

Yeah, right.

Careful not to disturb Finn, I slid my hand out from under the quilt, picked up the clock, and brought it close to my face. The pale glow on the luminous clock hands showed 2:42. Hours to go before I had to get up.

Was there anything in the world more precious than time spent with the people you loved?

Rolling onto my side, I stretched a hand out toward Finn, then closed my fingers into a tight fist. My throat ached. I swallowed. I couldn't risk waking him. Instead of indulging my need for touch, I looked my fill.

Finn slept on his back. Despite the cold, his arm had snaked out from under the covers and was thrown over his head. Moonlight sliced across his handsome face, highlighting his high cheekbones and his firm lips. Beneath his closed lids, his eyes darted back and forth, observing whatever unfolded in his dream world.

From his relaxed expression and steady breathing, Finn was lost in a pleasant fantasy. Had his mind flashed back to his happy childhood on the ranch, to life before the pandemic and the threat of war? Or might he be dreaming about us, about the future we hoped to build once this sorry mess with Allsop was over?

I had no clue, but it was good to see him sleeping peacefully, his dreams unencumbered by nightmares.

"I love you," I whispered, my voice barely perceptible. A rush of tears flooded my eyes. "Please don't be mad at me."

TWENTY-SIX

Finn

Half-awake, I slid my hand across the sheet, reaching for Georgia. Every night, we fell asleep wrapped around each other. I'd sling an arm around her shoulders and hold her against my chest. She'd lay her hand on my stomach. Our legs tangled up like a pretzel. But during the night, we'd overheat and draw apart, each seeking our own side of the bed. As morning got close, we always found each other again.

Except this morning when my hand sought Georgia, she wasn't there. I patted the sheet. My eyes flew open and scanned the dark, silent room.

Where the heck was she?

I sat up. Alarm prickled the back of my neck. I squashed the irrational sense of dread and swung my legs out of bed.

"Georgia?"

Nothing.

Maybe… I padded over to the window and drew back the curtain, looking for a light glowing inside one of the port-a-potties in the parking lot. Again, nothing. I checked my watch. 6:52 a.m. The alarm was set for 7:30. As far as I knew, Georgia had no reason to be up and about earlier.

So where was she?

I clicked on a lantern and searched the room for a note. If she'd forgotten to tell me about an early meeting with Marcus or breakfast plans with Rachel, she'd have left some kind of explanation. She wouldn't want me to worry.

Nothing.

On the off chance I'd accidentally brushed against a slip of paper and sent it drifting to the floor, I dropped down on my knees and checked under the bed and table.

My gut told me that something was definitely wrong. I threw on my clothes and jogged across the street to headquarters.

I signed in quickly then would have rushed past the sentries, but one of them held up a hand. "Marcus and Rachel are waiting for you in the conference room."

What the hell was going on? I broke into a run, dashing past the burned-out shell of our original meeting room. At the end of the hallway, I threw open the door to the new conference room. Havoc and Rachel sat behind the long table, their faces uncharacteristically serious.

Havoc tipped his head at a chair opposite them. "Sit down, Finn."

Whatever was going on, it was bad. My limbs locked. I shuffled stiffly over to the chair.

"Where is she?" No pussyfooting around. I got straight to the point.

"You aren't going to like it—" Rachel started.

"I already don't like it," I said. "Just tell me where Georgia is."

Marcus dropped his chin and fixed unwavering eyes on me. "Georgia is on her way to Boise with Reno and Jonesy."

My head reared back as if he'd slapped me. I couldn't have heard him right. He couldn't be saying that Georgia was going to Boise. To Allsop. With Jonesy, the sickest, most merciless bastard I'd ever encountered.

Jonesy was my boogeyman, the demon who haunted my nightmares. I'd thought that the worst thing in the world would be to find myself in his clutches once again. Shit. Not even close. Far worse to think of Georgia at his mercy.

I gaped, struck dumb for a good ten seconds. Then the dam broke and the words tumbled out. I jumped to my feet.

"What the fuck is wrong with you?" I snapped.

Havoc lifted a hand, ordering me to keep quiet, to listen.

I was beyond complying with any order, beyond the ability to hold my tongue.

"What the hell were you thinking?"

"Listen to me, son," Havoc said.

"No." I shook my head, rejecting any attempt at rational explanation. No way could he justify putting Georgia's life at risk like this. Havoc had sent her into the belly of the beast, delivered her into the hands of a sadist. "No."

Havoc's expression hardened. "Listen up. If you want to know what's going on, you'll sit down and shut up. Now."

Havoc was my friend, but I wasn't dealing with my friend right now. I was nose to nose with the commander. If I refused to obey, he'd call the sentries and have me removed, let me cool my heels in jail until I was ready to listen to his explanation. Fat lot of good that would do me. Or Georgia.

I jerked my head in a reluctant assent, then dropped down onto the chair.

Marcus leaned forward and steepled his hands. "It didn't take long to figure out that Jonesy was never going to break and give us reliable information on Allsop's operation and plans."

"That's why you sent Georgia and Reno in undercover," I said. "To gain his confidence, to get him to talk."

"True, but that wasn't the extent of our plan. The endgame always was for Georgia and Reno to help Jonesy escape to Boise, to plant our agents in the heart of Allsop's operation."

"Always?" Disbelief made my voice crack. "Georgia knew she was leaving me?"

"Finn." Rachel tapped the table to get my attention. "You have to understand that Havoc ordered Georgia *not* to tell you about her assignment. She had no choice but to keep it a secret from you."

Like it or not, I understood what she was saying. I hadn't served in the military. Following orders—the chain of command—wasn't ingrained in me the way it was in Georgia.

"What did you order her to do?" I asked, already suspecting the truth.

"Georgia and Reno passed themselves off as disenchanted with life in Pendleton," Havoc said. "They allowed Jonesy to slowly win them over to his side."

I snorted. "Jonesy always thinks he's the smartest man in the room. Of course he believes in his powers of persuasion."

"They agreed to help him escape. Georgia had keys to the jail cells," Rachel continued. "She supposedly got her hands on a car and drugged the guards."

"And now she and Reno are on their way to Boise. New recruits in Allsop's army," Havoc added.

"Jesus." I hunched forward, feeling sick to my stomach. "What's their mission in Boise? To gather intel about Allsop's preparations for the war?"

"That's part of it." Havoc leaned back in his chair.

"Wait a minute." A horrible thought occurred to me. "You didn't send Georgia to Boise as part of a hit squad, did you?"

I wouldn't cry a single tear if somebody killed Allsop, but the notion of Georgia acting as an assassin didn't sit right with me. I knew her. Murdering a man in cold blood would haunt her. Necessity be damned. Murder would cast a pall over the rest of her life. She didn't deserve that.

"If Allsop were assassinated, somebody—probably Jonesy—would step in and assume command. A better way to disrupt his operation is to sow discord in the ranks," Havoc said. "Georgia and Reno will flatter Jonesy's ego. Persuade him to attempt a coup, to depose Allsop. Jonesy takes out Allsop. Reno and Georgia—Jonesy's faithful disciples—are positioned to take out Jonesy."

Shit. Georgia might be part of a hit squad after all. My stomach twisted in knots.

Something occurred to me. "This isn't the first time Georgia was sent to Boise as a spy. She worked in the housekeeping staff at the downtown barracks. Somebody might recognize her."

"Georgia Abbott, a woman with long blond hair worked at the downtown barracks," Rachel said. "Jonesy knows her as Carrie Malone, a woman with short, brown hair. It's unlikely she'll run into anybody who would recognize her."

Unlikely wasn't impossible, was it? "I don't like it," I said.

Havoc shrugged. "Georgia is a trained soldier who's worked in military intelligence. She thinks fast on her feet. She was the best person for the job."

"We have another agent in Boise who will report back on their progress," Rachel said.

So much could go wrong with the mission, and I wouldn't be there to fight at Georgia's side. God damn it. I shoved both hands through my hair and rocked back and forth in the chair. Helpless fury burned in my gut.

"I have an assignment for you," Havoc said.

Was this some bullshit assignment to distract me from the danger Georgia was in? I turned suspicious eyes to him. "What is it?"

"Jonesy knows the exact location of Valhalla."

Oh, shit. Blood roared through my head. I'd been so preoccupied with my fears for Georgia that I hadn't considered the very real danger Jonesy posed to the ranch and my family.

"Kyle killed Allsop's son. Allsop wants Kyle's head on a spike," I sputtered. "Jonesy wants payback against everybody on the ranch who helped to capture him."

"We got this." Rachel raised a hand. "We won't leave Valhalla a sitting duck."

"What's the plan?" I asked, my gaze moving from one to the other.

"You'll drive a passenger van to Valhalla this morning," Havoc said. "I'm sending eight soldiers and additional weapons to help defend the ranch against any attack. They'll stay, you won't. Spend the night, then tomorrow morning, I want you to evacuate Valhalla's vulnerable to safety inside of Pendleton. Mrs. B. and Ever, for sure, and anybody else who wants to flee. I imagine Ripper will insist that Kenzie comes with you."

Whisk his pregnant wife away to safety? Yeah, even if she protested, Ripper would insist on it.

My mind raced. With the very real prospect of Allsop's forces launching an assault against my home, a big part of me wanted to stay on the ranch to fight. But I understood the need to get my little sweet pea and the others to safety.

Unless Allsop sent a large force to Valhalla—which he could scarcely afford—eight soldiers and the inhabitants of the ranch should be enough to make a stand. And I needed to be in Pendleton, to hear firsthand any reports of Georgia and Reno's mission. To be ready to spring into action if something went wrong.

I lifted my chin. "When do I leave?"

Havoc looked at his watch. "In twenty minutes. Just enough time for you to grab some breakfast and pack an overnight bag." He stood—dismissing me—and extended a hand.

Jaw set, I stared at his hand for several seconds before reaching out and shaking it. "I can't even pretend to like your plan," I said.

Havoc inclined his head. "I understand."

"But I'll do my part."

"I know you will. You always do."

Rachel scuttled around the table and hugged me, a surprising gesture from the unsentimental woman. "Georgia will be fine," she said in a low voice. "She's smart and she's tough. Have faith that she can pull this off."

I had all the faith in the world in Georgia's abilities, but I knew what Jonesy was capable of. If the mission went south… shit… if the mission went south, I'd take matters into my own hands. I'd never abandon Georgia to Jonesy's tender mercies.

TWENTY-SEVEN

Jonesy

Three Hours Ago

A key rattled in the lock, and the heavy door slowly swung open. I sat on the edge of my bunk, hands folded on my lap, my features composed into a guileless mask. I looked as gentle as a lamb. I bit back a smile. *As gentle as a lamb.*

The notion put me in mind of another dumbass idiom: Like a lamb to the slaughter. Except old Jonesy was nobody's fool. If anybody was gonna be slaughtered today, it wouldn't be me. I smothered a laugh, tickled pink by my own wit.

Carrie slunk inside, her eyes nearly popping from her skull. She spun her head from side to side in a ridiculous show of caution, as if Havoc's soldiers might be hiding *inside* the damned cellblock. Fucking amateur.

The stupid bitch got on my last nerve, always whining about her petty grievances. Crappy jeans, cheap shampoo. Boo-fucking-hoo.

All the while I had to smile and make nice. How many times had I thought about reaching out and snapping her neck when she wandered close to my cell? I stifled a sigh.

Patience is a virtue.

If patience was a virtue, I was a saint.

"Carrie, sweetheart," I crooned. "I knew I could count on you."

She simpered, scampered to the end of the cellblock, and unlocked Reno's cell. He took the key from her and strode toward me.

"Ready, boss?"

Was I ready? No. I planned to stand here with my dick in my hands while the two of them escaped. Seriously. The dumb fuck annoyed me as much as the whiny bitch.

The door slid open. I stepped forward and stuck out my hand. "Pleased to finally shake your hand, son."

"Thank you, sir."

My fingers closed around his. I briefly considered yanking him down and stomping on his head. The notion of his brains squishing out under my boot nearly brought a smile to my face.

Another suppressed sigh. I *was* a saint, resisting my natural instincts for the greater good. I had to get back to Boise, and I needed Reno and Carrie to escape this shithole town. I bet Mr. Allsop would be pleased that I showed up with the biker and the pretty girl in tow.

Reno was a Janissary. Janissaries were tough bastards, good fighters. Mr. Allsop would see Reno as a promising recruit. Moreover, he'd been one of Robert Banyon's top men. No doubt he possessed valuable information about Banyon's weapons cache and what the old fart was up to in Pendleton.

And Carrie. Annoying or not, it would be a waste to kill her. Young, pretty, fertile women were a valuable commodity. Not as scarce as hen's teeth, but a definite minority of the population.

After she spilled everything she knew about Havoc and Pendleton, Mr. Allsop could decide the best way to put her to use. There were plenty of jobs to be filled. Or he might choose to give her to one of his top men, a reward for services rendered.

I bit back another smile. As a prize, Carrie left a lot to be desired.

I tilted my head and glanced at the girl who stood behind Reno, wringing her hands. She was attractive enough, with a shapely figure and the plump, bee-stung lips I liked. She could learn to keep her mouth shut, I supposed. It might be fun to train her to stop with the constant caterwauling. Or equally fun to give her something real to complain about. Maybe I'd ask Mr. Allsop to give her to me.

We'd see.

Reno fell into step behind me as we marched toward the door to the cellblock. Motorcycle clubs were regimented. Everybody knew their place in the pecking order. No need to teach the man proper deference toward his superiors. I liked that.

"The guards?" I paused and turned to Carrie.

"I brought the guards a thermos of hot cocoa that I'd spiked with a sedative. I hung around and chatted with them until they both collapsed."

Good. No danger of stepping into the lobby and facing the business end of the guards' pistols.

"The escape vehicle?"

She hesitated. "I know you asked for the black Allsop Corporation SUV, but they must have hidden it away somewhere. It wasn't parked with all the other vehicles in the carpool garage. I had to take another car."

Well, fuck. So much for my fantasy of showing up in Boise behind the wheel of the boss's stolen SUV. Now I'd have to talk my way through a roadblock driving some unremarkable communal car, hardly the triumphant return I deserved.

She failed me.

I gentled my voice. "Where did you park the car, sweetheart?"

"Out front."

"All righty, then." I led the way into the lobby. The two guards were slumped over the reception desk, out cold.

"Get their guns," I barked.

Reno snatched up the weapons. He kept one gun and handed me the other. I glanced with longing at the unconscious guards. Too bad I couldn't plug them—deprive Havoc of two loyal soldiers—but the sound of gunfire might draw attention.

"We gotta go." Reno shifted his weight from foot to foot, looking nervous.

Well, duh. I tore my gaze from the guards and shoved through the swinging front door. Swiveling my head from left to right, I scanned the street for any sign of danger. Nada. From the looks of the sky, the blue light, dawn was no more than fifteen minutes away.

"Give me the keys." I held out my hand. Carrie passed them over.

We trotted down the walkway to a nondescript four-door sedan. I climbed into the driver's seat with Reno riding shotgun. Carrie crawled into the back.

Turning the key, I glanced at the fuel gauge. Half-full, barely enough to get us the two hundred twenty miles to Boise. Was it so hard to steal a car with a full tank of gas? I looked over my shoulder at the girl who had disappointed me once again.

"You remembered to put *some* gas in the tank. Thank you." I damned with faint praise.

"All I could find was one five-gallon can full of gas, I… I did my best." Her voice faltered, as if she sensed my frustration.

Not good. I couldn't afford to get slipshod, not when I'd worked so hard to master the happy face. I pasted on the semblance of a smile. My eyes crinkled with counterfeit pleasure. My voice oozed sincerity.

"I know you did your very best, honey. I appreciate you," nice Jonesy, the gentle lamb, told the stupid cunt.

God damn, this part was fun.

Carrie bobbed her head. "Thank you, Mr. Jonesy."

"None of this mister nonsense," I said. "We're friends. Call me plain ole Jonesy."

"Thanks, plain ole Jonesy."

Irritation knotted my shoulders, but I slapped my knee and laughed like her quip was the funniest thing I ever heard. Yeah, I'd enjoy teaching the girl to mind her tongue.

I pulled onto the street and cut my eyes toward the biker. "How are we going to get past the roadblocks?"

"We'll cross the river and head north." Reno pointed out a turn. "I know of a private drive that eventually leads to a county road that bypasses the roadblocks. We'll head east until it's safe to drop back to the freeway."

"All right."

I smacked both hands against the steering wheel. Exhilaration coursed through my body, and I wriggled. Free. Of course I was free. Nobody—not even the big, bad Marcus Havoc—could keep me down for long. Fate wouldn't allow me to languish in some pissant jail cell. I had a destiny to fulfill.

TWENTY-EIGHT

Georgia

"Keep your mouth shut and let me do the talking." Jonesy eased the sedan up to a roadblock off of Highway 26. He lowered the driver's window.

Two men wearing jeans and gray T-shirts under their open jackets—the signature uniform of Allsop's men—swaggered toward the car. Their hands rested on the butts of their weapons, like they were ready for trouble, or maybe they were trying to look intimidating.

What they weren't ready for, apparently, was the reappearance of Allsop's second-in-command. They froze in place, stunned incredulity sketched across their faces. One man turned away, barking excitedly into a two-way radio. The other cautiously approached the window, his eyes round.

"It's good to see you again, sir." He swallowed and his prominent Adam's apple jumped. "Mr. Allsop will be pleased to have you back."

Jonesy ignored the pleasantries. "Is the boss at the big house?"

The man whirled around, poked his companion in the ribs, and hissed, "Is Mr. Allsop at his estate?"

The second man lowered the radio and jerked his head in the affirmative. "Mr. Allsop asks you to meet him at the house, sir."

Jonesy's arrival sparked both deference and terror in Allsop's men. I'd no doubt that his reputation as a Big Bad was well deserved. One look at the burns on Finn's chest confirmed that. His two-month absence hadn't diminished his power to inspire fear. These men were scared shitless, a good reminder for Reno and me to stay vigilant.

Jonesy pointed straight ahead at the cars angled across the roadway blocking his path. "You want to get those cars out of my way?" he asked, his voice deceptively mild.

Both men hopped to it, waving their arms and shouting at the drivers to move the damned vehicles. Without another word to the men, Jonesy drove through the roadblock and toward downtown.

"Wow. You really are a big deal, aren't you?" I put just the right note of wonder into my voice.

Reno glanced at me from over his shoulder. "Looks like we hitched our wagon to a star."

A self-satisfied smile lifted Jonesy's lips. "Mr. Allsop appreciates what I bring to the table."

"I'm sure he does." Reno leaned forward, craning his neck while he peered at the streets. "Where are we heading, boss?"

"To the east side of town," Jonesy replied.

While spying for Marcus Havoc, Finn had worked his way into Allsop's inner circle. He'd lived at the estate, a trusted member of Allsop's personal guard. The sprawling mansion clung to the side of a rocky ridge that overlooked the city. The house held a war room and an armory, both of which Kyle and Sunny had raided before fleeing Boise. The information they found led directly to our mission to Prineville to secure Uncle Bobby's weapons cache.

Fifteen minutes later, Jonesy turned onto a long, curving driveway. We made our way past once-magnificent trees and shrubs—some dead from neglect or lack of water—and pulled up in front of a stucco, Mediterranean-style mansion. At least a dozen men lined the front walk and flanked the double-door entry. Jonesy cut the engine then leaned back, silently watching the assembled men.

"Aren't we going to get out?" I asked after a moment.

"Shut up." He spoke through clenched teeth.

I allowed the irritation to wash right over me. Georgia would smack down anybody who spoke to her like that, but Jonesy wasn't speaking to Georgia. He was talking to Carrie, a sulky, disaffected menial worker. Carrie would pout or grovel.

"I'm sorry," I whispered, opting for the grovel.

The front door flung open and a smartly dressed older man stepped outside. Tall, going gray at the temples, with an athletic build and immaculately styled hair, he looked like a slightly over the hill television star. He wore an expensive-looking suit and tie. Nobody wore a suit and tie anymore, not since the pandemic left us all scrambling for survival. Elliot Allsop, apparently, didn't get the note. From his elegant appearance, I would have guessed that he was on his way to preside over a meeting of the board.

He walked to the end of the sidewalk, then halted. His arms hung loose at his side, his feet set in a wide stance. He fixed his eyes on Jonesy, his expression blank. I recognized a power pose when I saw one.

Jonesy lifted his chin. After a beat, he raised one hand and gave a little wave.

"Everybody out," he said cheerfully.

As soon as Reno stepped out of the car, two men leapt forward. They patted him down and appropriated the gun he'd taken from the guard back at the police station. I raised both arms, anticipating a similar search. They didn't disappoint, patting me down with brisk efficiency. Reno and I hung back while Jonesy shuffled toward Allsop.

"It sure is good to see you again, sir." Jonesy smiled and bent his head, friendly and deferential. If he had a forelock, I bet he'd be tugging on it.

Allsop inclined his head graciously at his subordinate. "After I discovered you'd been taken prisoner by Marcus Havoc, I despaired of your return."

"My place is at your side, sir." He glanced over his shoulder at Reno and me. "My new associates helped me escape from Pendleton."

Allsop raised one well-manicured brow. His gaze swept over Reno and me, lingering over Reno's Janissary vest, before flicking my way. I felt the force of his judgment. He dismissed me as inconsequential, honing in instead on the big bad biker. Fine by me. Less interest meant less scrutiny, and less scrutiny suited me just fine.

Allsop stepped forward and offered Reno his hand. "It appears I owe you a debt of gratitude—" His eyes cut toward the patches on my friend's vest. "Reno."

"No need for thanks." Reno shook Allsop's hand. "I was fed up with Havoc and his bullshit regulations. Jonesy convinced me that I might fit in better in Boise."

"I always have room in my operation for good men. I'll meet with Jonesy first, then we'll speak." He pointed at two of his guards. "Escort Reno and the young lady to the kitchen. Tell Winnie to give them something to eat. Doubtless they're sick of the swill they've been eating in Pendleton. Stay with them until I summon them to my study."

"Yes, sir." The men gestured for Reno and me to follow them into the house.

We walked through the foyer and down a short hallway to the kitchen. Bright overhead lights illuminated a spacious room filled with gleaming stainless steel appliances. A refrigerator, a stove, a microwave, a coffee maker. The delicious aroma of bread baking in the oven filled the air. I blinked. Like Allsop's suit, working appliances were another shock to my post-pandemic expectations.

"Two for lunch, Winnie," one of the men said.

Reno and I took seats at the granite-topped counter. A smiling woman wearing a white apron and gray dress bustled over to greet us. "Coffee?"

"Yes, please," I said. Reno nodded his agreement.

"Does Caesar salad with chicken sound good?" she offered. "Fresh rolls will be out of the oven in just a minute."

"Sounds perfect." Salad and warm bread. Heaven.

Reno and I sipped our coffee in silence while Winnie assembled our salads. With the guards keeping an eye on us from a few feet away, we couldn't speak privately. We didn't need to talk. We knew what to expect. Allsop would be leery of anyone coming from Pendleton. He'd keep us close and under watch until he decided if he could trust us. Most likely, we'd be assigned jobs within the house.

The kitchen was the heart of the house, with guards in and out throughout the day. Who knew what the kitchen staff might overhear when they prepared and served meals? Time to impress Winnie and the guards with my kitchen knowledge.

I pointed at an espresso machine on the counter. With its curved lines, it looked like a space-age metal sculpture. "I used to work at a bakery and coffee shop that had that same espresso machine. It's from the Netherlands, right?"

"Yes. That's the one." Winnie looked surprised. "You worked at a bakery?"

"Yep." When I was in college, I worked part-time serving coffee at a bakery. I never touched dough or went near the ovens, but I *did* work in a bakery. And I could follow a recipe. "I can make a fabulous napoleon." That much was true too. My mom taught me how, but there was no need to explain the particulars, not when I was trying to make an impression.

"Mr. Allsop's last cook was an accomplished pastry chef, but my skills are only so-so," Winnie said.

Mr. Allsop's last cook was Hildy. Finn was captured while helping her escape. And now I was trying to ingratiate myself to the same men who imprisoned and tortured Finn.

Nope. Don't think about it.

I kept the smile on my face and nodded encouragingly at Winnie. "If you need help in the kitchen, I'd love to apply."

"I'll speak to Mr. Allsop." She placed plates of salad in front of Reno and me, then took the rolls from the oven.

We finished our salads and were sipping our second cups of coffee when another guard summoned Reno for a meeting with Allsop.

"Not me?" I asked, frowning.

"No. Just the Janissary." The guard signaled for Reno to follow him.

Reno laid a hand on my shoulder. His gaze lingered on the two guards who would be staying with me. "I know these men will take good care of you while I'm meeting with Mr. Allsop." His voice held bite, a definite note of menace.

The scary Janissary was telling the guards that I was under his protection. Never mind that I was perfectly capable of defending myself. For our ruse to work, I couldn't reveal that.

"Okay, Reno. See you soon."

He squeezed my shoulder, ambled from the room, and disappeared from sight.

I held my breath. Separated, alone with the enemy, if things were about to go sideways, now was the time. If Allsop was determined to avoid any risk, if Jonesy saw no advantage to keeping us alive, they'd make their move soon.

Of course, both Reno and I carried knives hidden in our boots, so we wouldn't go down without a fight.

I cocked my head, listening for sounds of a scuffle or a weapon discharging. Nothing. So far so good. Reno and I were in play.

I held up my coffee cup. "How about topping me off?"

TWENTY-NINE

Finn

"Finn."

The familiar voice stopped me in my tracks. My heart sank. I wheeled around and pasted a thin smile on my face, shifting the duffel bag to my left hand. With my free arm, I reached out and hugged Olivia.

"Good morning, sweetheart."

She clutched at my arm. "Do you know what's going on? A soldier knocked on my door ten minutes ago and said Marcus and Rachel want to see me. Did something happen to Reno?"

Shit. She had no idea that Reno was in Boise with Georgia and Jonesy. Sympathy twisted my stomach into knots. "You need to talk to Havoc."

"You know something," she cried. Her fingers dug into my arm. "Please, if you know what's going on, tell me."

Olivia had caught up with me on the edge of the city hall's parking lot. Turning my head, I spied a white van idling near the entrance to the building. The reinforcements Havoc was sending to Valhalla were ready and waiting for me. I was beyond eager to get on the road. Still, Olivia's distress tugged at my heart. Not so long ago, she lay at death's door, and Reno had been half-mad with fear.

Now it was her turn to tremble at the prospect of losing him. Life wasn't fair, was it?

Something in my expression alarmed her, made her take a step back and her face turn pale. Her hand fluttered to her throat. "Finn?"

I dropped the duffel and hauled her into my arms. "Reno is alive. He and Georgia are on a top secret mission. Havoc and Rachel will tell you what they can."

"A secret mission?" I saw the wheels turning behind her eyes. "Please tell me they're not with Jonesy."

Olivia was one hundred percent trustworthy and committed to Reno and the cause, but the details weren't mine to share. I picked up my bag and slung an arm around her shoulders.

"I'll walk you over to the building." I nodded to the soldiers in the van and held up a finger, letting them know I'd be another minute.

Olivia signed in with the sentries then glanced at my bag. "Are you going someplace?"

"Valhalla."

Understanding filled her eyes. Valhalla was at risk because Jonesy was free. She rose up on her toes and kissed my cheek. "You take care of yourself."

"I'll see you soon, sweetheart."

Olivia drew in a deep breath, clearly preparing herself for her meeting with Havoc. "Bye." She waved and walked into the building.

I jogged over to the waiting van, climbed into the driver's seat, and twisted around. One by one I met the eyes of the eight soldiers seated behind me, six men and two women. "I appreciate what you're doing, that you're willing to defend my family's ranch."

A young man with a buzz cut—Wade, if I remembered correctly—spoke up. "I'm from Baker City. I've seen Allsop's people in action. I'll make a stand against them any time, any place."

The others nodded their agreement.

"I'm grateful that you're willing to make a stand for Valhalla," I said.

Wade pulled a CD out of a pocket. "How about some music for the trip?"

I glanced at the dash. Luckily, the van had an old-fashioned CD player. "Hand it over."

Wade had come prepared with a pile of CDs. Country and pop music rocked the van during the drive to the ranch. In the middle of the afternoon, I pulled up to the gates to Valhalla. I carried a key, but only a fool would unlock the gate and drive up to the house in an unfamiliar vehicle.

"Gimme a minute." I climbed out of the van and positioned myself in front of the security camera that Levi and Topher had installed over the gate. I waved into the lens.

Somebody was supposed to watch the security feed twenty-four-seven, but I knew from experience the mind-numbing drudgery of keeping an eye on the screen. Folks got distracted or took a break. There was no guarantee that somebody would see me standing there, but I had to try to catch their attention. Still, we'd approach with caution.

After a few minutes, I opened the gate, drove the van inside, then locked up again. I steered slowly up the long driveway and parked in front of the house.

Strangers should definitely not mill around the yard. "Wait till I call for you." I hopped out and stood at the bottom of the porch steps, where anybody in the house could get an eye on me.

The front door opened. Bear and Ripper raced down the steps. "What the fuck are you doing here?" Ripper demanded. As always, the biker got right to the point.

"Jonesy's back in Boise. Valhalla needs to prepare for an attack." I signaled for the soldiers to climb out of the van. "Havoc sent reinforcements and weapons."

Bear shook his head, his brow furrowed. "You've got some explaining to do, little brother."

Nyx and Kenzie stepped onto the porch. "What's going on?" Kenzie asked.

"We got company, darlin'." Ripper angled his head at the group of soldiers. "Looks like they'll be here a while."

Ever peeked out through the open doorway, Sunny at her side.

"Finn." The little girl flew across the porch and flung herself at me. "Are you staying?" she asked, her eyes wide and hopeful.

"Just for the night, sweet pea. I gotta head back to Pendleton tomorrow morning, but guess what?"

"What?"

I crouched down and laid a hand on top of her shiny hair. "You're coming to Pendleton with me. You and Mrs. B. and whoever else wants to visit the city."

"Fitzwilliam, too?" she whispered, like we were sharing a secret.

Mrs. B. wouldn't go anywhere without her fancy cat. "Of course, Fitzwilliam too."

"I'm going to go tell Mrs. B." Ever dashed back into the house.

"We need to talk," Ripper growled.

"I'm calling a family meeting." Bear rang the old cast-iron dinner bell that hung from a porch rafter. Anybody within earshot would come running. "Nyx, could you and Kenzie give our guests a tour of the place? Start with the old bunkhouse. It has a wood-burning stove and it sleeps six. The men can sleep there, and the two women can share the vacant guest room inside the house."

I suspected that he wanted to meet without any outsiders present.

"All right," Nyx said slowly. She didn't look happy about being excluded from the meeting.

"We'll fill you in on what's up after you've seen to our guests," Bear added.

Kyle and Sahdev jogged toward the porch from the big barn. In the distance, Levi and Topher hotfooted it from the direction of the winter pasture.

Kenzie and Nyx stepped inside then reappeared a moment later, wearing jackets.

"Follow us, please." Kenzie climbed down the steps, pulling on a pair of gloves.

Ripper's arm snaked out, and he hauled her to his side. He whispered something in her ear. She flashed him a dazzling smile full of so much warmth that my heart thumped.

No doubt about it. Ripper would do anything to keep her safe. If only I could have done the same thing for Georgia. My stomach churned. I pushed away my fears. Later. I'd worry about Georgia later.

The soldiers retrieved their sleeping bags and packs from the back of the van. The two women dropped theirs on the front porch then Havoc's soldiers followed Nyx and Kenzie across the yard in the direction of the bunkhouse.

"What happened?" Kyle came to a stop at the bottom of the steps.

"Who are all those people?" Sahdev frowned, watching Nyx and Kenzie lead the group of strangers across the yard.

"Meeting. Inside. Now." Bear marched into the house.

Kyle and Sahdev turned to me, confusion marking their faces.

"I'll explain everything inside," I said. They followed me into the house.

A roaring fire blazed in the stone fireplace. Hector and Fitzwilliam dozed on the sheepskin rug near the hearth. The fluffy cat occupied the middle of the rug—like it was his God-given right to hog the center stage—while the German shepherd clung to the periphery.

Mrs. B. sat in her favorite rocking chair; Ever perched on the ottoman.

"Ever, please go play in your room while the adults talk," Sunny said. Unlike Kyle, she'd probably overheard enough of the conversation to suspect that this discussion was not suited for a child's ears.

"Really?" Ever made puppy dog eyes and turned to me for support.

"You heard Sunny." I put on a stern expression and pointed toward the hallway. "Time to skedaddle."

Crossing her arms over her chest, Ever flounced from the room.

"And no eavesdropping from the hall," Kyle called after her.

"Harrumph," Ever shouted, followed by the sound of heavy footsteps retreating down the hall, every stomp a protest.

"What's going on, dear boy?" Mrs. B. twisted her hands together on her lap.

I stood with my back to the fireplace, facing my circle of friends. Hannah had emerged from the kitchen, and she joined Levi and Topher on one of the three leather sofas. Kyle, Sunny, and Sahdev sat together. Ripper and Bear stood. Hector roused himself and ambled to my side. I dropped a hand on the dog's head.

"I can't go into all the details," I said. "But you need to know that Jonesy escaped from Pendleton early this morning. No doubt he hightailed it back to Boise and Allsop."

Sunny gasped and clutched Kyle's hand. She turned frightened eyes to her man. "Jonesy knows where we live, and he wants your head on a spike."

"Everybody at Valhalla is on his shit list," Ripper rumbled. "Not just Kyle."

"Marcus Havoc sent you to warn us to expect an attack?" Sahdev asked.

"To warn you and to bring soldiers and weapons to help defend the place," I said.

"Soldiers and more weapons are good." Levi linked eyes with Ripper. "And we still have my Grandpa Kurt's stash."

Levi had told me about his grandpa, an old-school survivalist who'd retreated to the countryside and stockpiled food and weapons against Armageddon. The flu took him, but my friends had found his hidden hoard, which was now stored in Valhalla's basement.

"Two AK-47s, Israeli Tavors for distance shooting, sniper rifles, shotguns, M67 fragmentation grenades, not to mention all the handguns." Ripper smiled grimly. "We got a few surprises up our sleeves. Allsop's people won't have a clue what they're walking into."

"Don't forget my favorite." Kyle said. "A compound hunting bow with a fifty-pound draw."

Fragmentation grenades? Sniper rifles? Did Bear know exactly what we were keeping in our basement? I lifted my brows and glanced at my brother. He nodded. Yeah, he knew.

"I'll be heading back to Pendleton tomorrow morning," I said. "Havoc suggested that I bring Mrs. B. and Ever with me. Keep them out of harm's way until we've dealt with Allsop. Anybody else who wants to come is welcome, too."

"Mac will be going." From Ripper's tone, the subject was not up for debate. No surprise there.

Levi turned to his girlfriend. Despite her shooting lessons, Hannah was still uneasy around guns. "What about you? Do you want to stay or go?"

"I'm staying." Hannah stuck out her jaw. "We don't know for sure that Jonesy will come back. I don't want to be separated from you on a maybe."

"It's more than a maybe." Kyle looked toward her. "I killed Allsop's son and he wants me dead. It's only a matter of time before he sends more soldiers to Valhalla."

"I don't care if it's risky," Hannah said. "I was separated from Levi once. I won't let it happen again."

Sunny turned to Kyle. "Don't bother asking. I'm not leaving, either."

"But Ever—" Kyle protested.

Sunny raised a palm so quickly that her charm bracelet jangled. "Stop. Listen to me. Mrs. B. and Kenzie will look after Ever. I'm staying here with you."

Kyle looked unhappy, but he didn't argue. I felt his frustration. Both Sunny and Georgia would put themselves in harm's way to do what they thought was right. That's how they're wired.

"Don't worry about Ever." Mrs. B. sat up straight, her expression resolute. "Sunny is correct. Kenzie and I can watch over her. We'll keep her busy and happy until it's safe for us all to come home."

"Folks are setting up a school in Pendleton," I said, thinking of Justin and Lorelei's committee. "It might do Ever good to spend some time with other kids."

"Yes." Mrs. B. gave a clipped nod. "Spending time with other children will do Ever a world of good." She held out a hand. "Sunny, will you help me pack?"

"Of course." Sunny hopped up and assisted the older woman from her chair.

Mrs. B. paused next to Ripper and laid a frail hand on his arm. "Good luck telling Kenzie that you're banishing her to Pendleton."

Ripper gently patted her gnarled hand. "Don't you worry. Mac will see reason."

Mrs. B.'s lips quirked and a you've-got-to-be-kidding-me expression crossed her face. "Indeed."

Sunny and Mrs. B. had barely disappeared from sight when the front door opened. Nyx, Kenzie, and the eight soldiers walked into the front room.

Hannah jumped to her feet and waved at the strangers. "I just took a batch of snickerdoodles from the oven. Do you guys want to come to the kitchen and have some cookies?"

Wade glanced at me, one eyebrow arched. I tilted my head, giving him the go-ahead. We needed a few minutes to talk to Nyx and Kenzie in private.

"Well, all right, fellas." Wade rubbed his hands together. "Let's go have some cookies."

The soldiers followed Hannah to the kitchen.

"What the hell is going on?" Nyx demanded, stepping close to Bear.

Ripper held out an arm and tugged Kenzie to his side.

"Jonesy escaped," I told them. "We can expect another attack on the ranch. That's why Havoc sent reinforcements."

Kenzie frowned. "Wait. Jonesy had to be under lock and key. How did he manage to escape?"

I'd dreaded the moment where somebody asked the obvious question. Georgia and Reno's role in the escape—their mission in Boise—that information wasn't mine to share. And knowing Georgia was in danger would just twist them up with worry when there wasn't a damned thing they could do about it.

"The how doesn't matter. What matters is that Valhalla is exposed, and we need to take steps to keep everybody safe."

"We'll have to step up security," Nyx mused. "And figure out the best way to stretch our stores to feed eight more people."

"It won't be eight more mouths to feed," I said, glancing at Ripper.

"It'll be five," Ripper said. "Mrs. B., Ever, and Mac will be going back to Pendleton with Finn."

Kenzie pulled away from Ripper, stunned confusion stamped on her pretty face. "What did you say?"

Ripper lifted his chin, bracing for a fight. "You heard me. I won't have you and the baby in harm's way. You'll go to Pendleton and stay safe, just until we sort out this mess with Allsop."

"That could take months," she sputtered. "You think I'll agree to be separated from you for *months*?" Kenzie straightened her spine and planted her hands on her hips. The position highlighted her small baby bump. Calling attention to the baby definitely wouldn't help her cause.

"Darlin'—" Ripper started.

"Don't you darlin' me, Mr. Solis." Kenzie wasn't about to be placated. "Do you remember what you said to me when you stopped my wretched wedding to Pastor Bill? I do. I'll never forget the words. 'Whatever happens, whatever comes, we're sticking together.' You made a promise." Kenzie paused and swallowed, choking back emotion. "And you remember what Miles used to say, don't you? 'Ripper always keeps his promises.'"

Kyle dropped his face into his hands. He'd told me about Miles, Kenzie's cousin and Ripper's next door neighbor. Miles had sheltered her in the early days of the pandemic. The virus killed Miles, or rather, Kyle shot him when he succumbed to the homicidal flu mania. Miles's death still haunted them all.

"I remember." Ripper brushed his knuckles over her cheek. "Don't want to be separated from you, either, but we have to do what's best for the baby."

"I'm not stupid. I don't want to put the baby in danger, but I can't—" Kenzie's face crumpled. She waved a hand. "Shit. Pregnancy hormones make me emotional." She sucked in a breath then continued. "I can't be separated from you for months. Find a better way, Ripper. Please."

"I got a better way." The words fell out of my mouth before I had time to think. Everybody's eyes turned toward me. I hadn't been able to keep Georgia safely at my side, but I could help Kenzie and Ripper stay together. I looked to Ripper. "Come to Pendleton with Kenzie. We're getting ready for the war against Allsop. There's plenty for you to do there to help. And don't think you'd be abandoning Valhalla. You'll be leaving sixteen people behind to defend the ranch."

"Finn's right." Bear spoke up. "You should go to Pendleton with Kenzie. You may be the best soldier in our group, but with the reinforcements Havoc sent, we can keep Valhalla safe."

Kyle lifted his head. "I agree. Go with Kenzie. We got this, brother."

"Studies have shown that maternal stress during pregnancy can affect the fetus." Sahdev piled on. "You've seen her swollen feet. Kenzie is already experiencing edema, and her blood pressure is higher than I like. In my professional opinion, you need to do everything in your power to minimize her stress."

"Fuck." Ripper shoved both hands through his hair. Running from a fight ran counter to everything I knew about the man, but his devotion to Kenzie was undeniable.

"C'mon Ripper. This is a no-brainer," Nyx urged.

Kenzie bit her lips, waiting for his reply.

"All right." Ripper squared his shoulders. "Looks like we're going to Pendleton, darlin'." Kenzie threw herself against his chest. He held her close, but over her head his eyes met Bear's. "Before we leave tomorrow morning, I want to go over plans for repelling any attack on the ranch."

"Sounds good." Bear nodded.

Cookies in hand, the eight soldiers wandered into the front room.

"No more slacking off. Somebody needs to watch the feed from the security cameras twenty-four-seven," Ripper continued. "We need to establish a defensive perimeter with manned outposts. We have binoculars and night-vision goggles that we can keep charged with a solar-powered USB battery pack."

"You have a large property and a limited number of people to defend it," a broad-shouldered, dark-haired man said. "We should leverage personnel by putting sentries in an elevated position. I saw a tall silo and a windmill when we drove up. They may or may not work, depending on what else is available."

"Who are you?" Ripper asked.

"Sean Darragh. Before the pandemic, I was a Marine, but you know what they say: 'Once a Marine, always a Marine.'"

"Oorah." Ripper inclined his head respectfully. "An elevated outpost is a good idea, Sean. We could build a platform on the windmill, but it would be exposed to the elements and colder than a witch's tit. The silo's not ideal either. It's metal with a rounded roof. But there's an exterior hay door off the loft in the big barn. Anybody positioned there would have a clear line of sight over a big swath of the property. No need to build a platform. And the position is concealed and sheltered from the elements."

"That would work," Sean said. "We brought det cord and ignitors. We could place manually triggered booby traps around the property. If somebody crosses the perimeter, all a sentry has to do is press a button and *boom*." Sean's hands simulated an explosion.

"Now you're talking." Levi pumped a fist into the air.

Sean cocked a brow at the overeager teenager.

"Levi is our resident expert on booby traps," Ripper explained. "Punji stake traps. Rock snares. Feather spear traps. Swinging logs embedded with spikes. Cartridge traps. You name it, Levi can build it."

"That's a handy set of skills," Sean said.

"Trip wires." Levi's eyes sparkled with excitement. "We have fishing line and eyelet screws and magnetic window alarms in Grandpa's stash. I can set up trip wires at likely spots around the perimeter. If somebody kicks the wire—breaks the connection—an alarm goes off that's loud enough to wake the dead."

"This is Levi's dream come true." Bear shook his head. "He's been wanting to booby trap the place since he moved in."

"We could position mortars to cover a target zone on an approach to the house," Sean said.

Eyes wide, Levi snapped his head toward the Marine. From his expression, you'd think Levi was a kid who saw Santa Claus for the first time.

Sean lifted a shoulder. "Yeah, we brought mortars."

"If you don't mind, I'd rather we didn't blow up any outbuildings," Bear interjected.

I caught my brother's eye and jerked my chin toward the kitchen. Bear gave a tight nod and followed me to a kitchen that still smelled like fresh cookies. I helped myself to a snickerdoodle and leaned against a counter. Bear followed suit.

"Sorry I didn't give you a heads-up before I suggested that Ripper come back to Pendleton with me."

"No apology necessary. It was a good move." Bear took a bite from his cookie.

"I wish I could be here to defend the homestead." I scrubbed a hand over my face, suddenly very weary.

"Something is eating at you. What's going on, Finn?'

It was nearly impossible to hide anything from my big brother. "Havoc let Jonesy escape on purpose. All part of his plan to install a pair of spies in Allsop's camp."

I paused, shaking my head, desperate to reject the ugly reality, to rewrite history, to keep Georgia safe and out of Jonesy's hands. A fool's errand.

"Finn?" Bear laid a hand on my shoulder.

"Georgia—" I swallowed the bile rising in my throat, then started again. "Georgia is one of the spies. Havoc sent her and Reno to Boise. That news isn't for general consumption. The fewer people who know, the better, but… shit..."

"I know you're close. I'm sorry."

"We're more than close. I love her. We're together."

Bear pulled me into a hug, clapping me hard on the back.

I stepped back and lifted up my shirt, exposing my stomach and chest, the one secret I'd managed to keep from my brother.

"What the fuck?" Bear gasped, looking queasy. He reached out and gently touched a raised red burn mark.

"Jonesy. Burned me with cigarettes. And now Georgia's in the hands of the same sadistic bastard. It's killing me."

"Say the word and we'll sneak into Boise and find her. Shoot anybody who gets in our way. Haul her out, kicking and screaming if we have to." A reckless, foolhardy proposition, but from the defiant set of his jaw, Bear meant every word.

The offer touched me deep. "Thank you, brother. That means the world to me, but Georgia would never forgive me if I got in the way of her mission. I gotta trust that she knows what she's doing, and that she can handle herself."

"If it was Nyx, I'd be out of my head," Bear said.

"I am, but there isn't a damned thing I can do about it right now."

"Except pray and hope for the best." Bear looked grim.

Prayer and happy thoughts? Since when had that been enough?

THIRTY

Georgia

"Keep your eyes down," Winnie cautioned. "And don't speak unless you're spoken to."

"Yes, ma'am." The sterling silver coffee service was heavy, and carrying it downstairs from the kitchen a chore. I balanced the tray on my hip, grinding my teeth into a smile while Winnie droned on.

"Pour Mr. Allsop's coffee first, then Mr. Jonesy's. Mr. Allsop takes both cream and sugar. Jonesy takes his coffee black. Then circle the table and offer coffee to the rest of the men."

"Yes, ma'am." My smile wobbled under the strain of holding the tray steady.

A thermos of coffee and a stack of mugs would make more sense, but for Elliot Allsop, ostentatious luxury trumped practicality.

I struggled under the weight of a heavy antique tray holding a silver pot full of coffee, a sugar bowl, and a cream pitcher. Winnie carried a similar silver tray holding half a dozen delicate porcelain cups and saucers.

Winnie offered a reassuring smile. "You'll do fine, Carrie."

For Pete's sake, get on with it.

Winnie nodded at the guard stationed outside of Allsop's war room. He pushed the door open then flashed me a sympathetic grin when Winnie and I entered the room. I returned the young man's friendly look—it couldn't hurt to make nice with a guard—and gratefully set the tray on a side table.

Allsop, Jonesy, and four other men sat around a conference table. Allsop wore an impeccable blue suit and red tie, the rest sported standard-issue gray T-shirts and jeans.

"Coffee, gentleman?" Allsop gestured for Winnie to proceed.

While Winnie placed a cup and saucer in front of each man, I glanced quickly around the room. Maps of Oregon, Washington, and Idaho hung on one wall, several whiteboards on another. Two tall file cabinets were tucked into a corner, and a scattering of folders covered another conference table. It was all very old-school, dependent on pen and paper rather than computers, similar to our setup in Pendleton.

If Allsop had learned his lesson after Kyle and Sunny raided the place, he'd keep a guard stationed outside the door twenty-four-seven.

"Carrie." Winnie signaled for me to start.

I carried the coffee service to the table and filled Allsop's cup, adding a spoonful of sugar and a splash of cream.

"How are you settling in, Carrie?" he asked solicitously.

"Very well, thank you, sir."

I allowed my hands to shake when I poured Jonesy's coffee. Big bad Jonesy scared me, that tremor conveyed.

He touched the back of my arm with the same hand he used to torture Finn. I suppressed a genuine shiver and fought not to jerk my arm away. "You're doing fine, honey. Just fine."

I gave a jerky nod, grateful for the praise, but intimidated. He liked that. He leaned back in his chair and raised the cup to his lips, his eyes crinkling with pleasure.

I finished serving the coffee then folded my hands in front of my stomach, awaiting instructions. From under lowered lashes, I studied the men sitting around the table, committing their faces to memory.

Allsop waved a hand. "You may go. Leave the coffee until later."

"Yes, sir," Winnie murmured. I followed her from the room.

"See?" Smiling, she squeezed my arm. "That wasn't so hard, was it?"

"No, it wasn't. First-time jitters got the best of me, but I'll be fine next time."

"Good."

We walked back to the kitchen. Winnie glanced at her watch. "We won't start preparing lunch for almost an hour. Why don't you take a half-hour break? Rest in your room, or go enjoy the view from the balcony."

"I will. Thanks, Winnie."

Winnie slept in the housekeeper's room down the hall from the kitchen. A small storage room next to her bedroom had been converted into sleeping quarters for me. It held a cot, a small dresser, and a wooden chair, nothing more. The windowless cubical afforded me privacy—for which I was grateful—but it was an uninviting space.

I poured myself a cup of coffee, threw on a jacket, and wandered out onto a wide stone balcony. I stood at the railing, sipping blissfully hot coffee and admiring the view of downtown Boise in the distance.

"How's it going?"

I startled, spilled a few drops of coffee, then whirled around to face Reno. We hadn't been alone together since we arrived two days ago. It felt damned good to see a familiar face.

"Winnie is keeping me busy preparing and serving meals," I said. "I saw the war room this morning. I'd love to rifle through the files, but if Allsop keeps a guard at the door, I doubt I'll get a chance. I might check late at night on the pretext of offering the guard a drink or a snack."

"Sounds like a plan."

"How about you?" I asked.

"Jonesy's keeping me busy, too. Don't think he's entirely sure what to do with me, or if he can trust me yet. He had me out with a team yesterday, searching buildings on the west side of town. They're looking for the new headquarters for the Nampa Boys."

The Nampa Boys would have relocated their base of operations after Allsop captured David.

"Any word on David?"

"Yeah. Overheard a soldier mention him. He's alive, thank fuck. Looks like they're still keeping prisoners in the old state pen, the same place they held Sunny and Finn."

I knew the prison. Mere hours before his scheduled execution, Marcus, Justin, Kyle, and I had broken Finn out of the place.

"How are you handling the mission?" I asked. "Personally."

"I hate the way I snuck out of town without saying a word to Olivia. If things go wrong, I'll never have a chance to tell her that I'm sorry I left without saying goodbye."

Man, did I understand where Reno was coming from. "That woman loves you and she knows that you love her. No matter what, you two are good."

He shoved a hand through his shoulder-length hair. "Hope to hell you're right. Keeping the mission secret from Olivia—shit—that was one of the hardest things I've ever done. She trusts me and I lied to her."

"I get it. I totally get it. We chose to risk our lives, and we didn't say a word to the people who care most about us."

"Because Havoc ordered us not to." Reno's expression turned rueful. "Part of me wishes I'd said 'screw it' and told her anyway. She can keep a secret."

"I'm sure she can, but it would have killed her to act like nothing was wrong when she knew you were marching into the lion's den."

"You're right." Reno heaved a deep sigh then pointed at my coffee cup. "You mind sharing?"

"Help yourself." I passed him the mug.

He took a sip then groaned with pleasure. "Real coffee, not that instant stuff. I've missed it."

He passed back the mug. I drank a swallow. "I miss Finn," I confessed.

His sharp gaze cut my way. "You two together?"

Ever since we fled Pendleton, I'd carried a knot of anxiety in my stomach. Talking to Reno, some of that tension loosened. Intelligent and capable, his steady presence was a comfort, a balm over my jangled nerves.

I smiled. "We're together."

"Good for you." He accepted the mug and took another sip. "I saw the sparks flying at Uncle Bobby's. Surprised it took you so long."

"I struggled with it. The timing isn't ideal, but you know how love is. Sometimes you can't fight it."

Discussing my love life with a biker. Not something I ever would have imagined myself doing, but life was full of surprises, and Reno was a damned fine man.

"When it's right, it's right. Olivia is the best thing that ever happened to me. You and me—" He pointed at my chest, then at his own. "We're gonna complete our mission, and get back safe to the people we love."

"To do that, we need to start buttering up Jonesy," I said.

"Already have, though I'm trying not to be too obvious about it."

"I suspect that Jonesy's ego is so inflated that he takes any praise as his rightful due."

"Bet you're right, but still, we can't overplay our hand."

I nodded in agreement. "I should get back inside. Winnie and I are making minestrone for lunch."

"We'll talk soon." Reno took a final swallow of coffee then handed back the empty mug. "Thanks for sharing."

Reno sauntered back inside. "Stay safe," I whispered at his retreating back. He needed to return safely to Olivia as much as I needed to return safely to Finn. We all deserved our happy ever afters.

I shivered.

How often do people get what they deserve?

THIRTY-ONE

Finn

"Yuck. The porta-potty stinks." Ever slammed the motel door shut, wrinkled up her face, then collapsed dramatically across the bed.

"The outhouse back home is no garden of roses either, dearest." Mrs. B. looked up from tucking Ever's clothes into a drawer.

"Next time hold your breath, sweet pea," I suggested. "That's what I do."

Mrs. B. and Ever were settling into my room at the motel. I decided to stay in Georgia's room, surrounded by things that reminded me of her, things she had selected to personalize her place. I smiled every time I saw that photo of her wearing her Little League uniform. Last night, I'd buried my nose in her pillow. I swore I caught a whiff of her orange blossom cologne.

Ripper and Kenzie took the vacant end unit to the right of my old room. Justin occupied the room to the left. Ever and Mrs. B. would be surrounded by friendly faces.

Somebody rapped against the door. Ever hopped up and flung it open. Kenzie stood on the covered walkway.

"Hey, kiddo," Kenzie said. "Ripper is meeting with Marcus. While he's busy, I thought I'd go for a walk. Would you like to come with me? We can put a leash on Fitzwilliam and take him out for some exercise."

"Yes." Ever jumped up and down. "It's okay, isn't it, Mrs. B.?"

"Of course." Mrs. B. adored Ever, but I suspected that she was ready for a break from the chatty child. "Let's find Fitzwilliam's leash. And it's nippy outside. He should bundle up."

I grew up with barn cats who roamed free. Fitzwilliam was a fancy indoor cat who wasn't allowed outside on his own. Nyx had sewn a powder-blue, fleece-lined sweatshirt for Fitzwilliam to wear when they took him on walks around the ranch in chilly weather.

I would've bet good money that a cat would fight wearing a sweatshirt and a leash—consider it an affront to his dignity—but Fitzwilliam took to it like a fish to water. Head held high, his tail swishing back and forth, he'd prance around like he didn't have a care in the world. Had to be one of the darnedest sights I'd ever seen.

Ever tugged the sweatshirt on over Fitzwilliam's head and clicked the rhinestone-studded leash to his collar. With a wave, she skipped after Kenzie.

Mrs. B. sighed and dropped into a chair. "I am absolutely knackered."

"You do look tuckered out," I said. "How about I leave so you can put your feet up and get some rest?"

"Wait, please Finn." Mrs. B. pointed to the chair on the opposite side of the small table. I obliged her and sat. "When you visited at Christmas, I saw sparks flying between you and Georgia. You intended to make your feelings clear."

"Yes, ma'am." No point in denying it.

"Yet since we arrived in Pendleton yesterday, we haven't seen her. In fact, you're staying in Georgia's room so Ever and I can have yours."

I nodded. "I know I can trust you to keep a confidence. Georgia is out of town on an assignment for Major Havoc. We've told people that she's visiting the ranch."

Mrs. B. frowned. "I don't like the sound of that."

"Me, neither, ma'am, but it is what it is."

She studied my face, her faded blue eyes seemingly seeing right through my stiff upper lip. "Are you all right, dear boy?"

The question took me aback. *I* was fine and dandy, safely ensconced in Pendleton, while the woman I loved… damn… *while the woman I loved…* I hunched over, like somebody had punched me in the gut.

"I'm so sorry," Mrs. B. murmured.

I swallowed, unsure how to respond to her sympathy.

She reached across the table and patted my hand. "Georgia is a bright and competent young woman. She'll be home very soon. I know it."

"From your mouth to God's ears." Georgia had said that a few days ago, and the old saying sure fit now.

Mrs. B. wobbled to her feet, bracing her hands on the table. "I'm going to follow your advice and have a lie down."

"I'll let myself out." I stood, then on impulse, I bent over and kissed her cheek. "You're a smart lady and a good friend, Mrs. B."

She waved a hand. "Off with you, young man, before you turn my head with your compliments."

I pulled on my jacket and walked outside into the crisp morning air. Resolve filled my chest. I needed to step up and do my share to keep Ever busy and entertained. Take her on walks around town. Go to the library. Play board games. I could ask Rachel if there were any kids in town around Ever's age and arrange playdates. That's what folks called them, wasn't it? Playdates?

And school. Justin and Lorelei were setting up a school. I glanced at my watch. I was supposed to meet up with Ripper and show him around town, but that wasn't for a couple of hours. Justin was busy meeting with Havoc and Ripper, but Lorelei might be home. I had time to go talk to her about their progress with the school.

Lorelei's apartment was a little more than a mile away. No need to waste gasoline driving over there, and like Fitzwilliam, I could use the exercise. I'd hoof it to her place.

A few blocks from the motel, I crossed paths with Uncle Bobby and Anton. The sight of the two gents gave me another idea.

"Uncle Bobby, I heard that you and Anton hold a weekly poker night at your place."

"We do, and you'd be more than welcome to come." Uncle Bobby beamed and clapped me on the shoulder.

"Thank you for the invite, but poker isn't my game. A good friend of mine just came to town, and she enjoys playing. I wonder if you'd be willing to invite her over for poker night?"

Enjoys playing? Can't believe I said that with a straight face. Mrs. B. was a shark, and I was angling to set her loose on my unsuspecting friends. Guess they'd figure it out soon enough. And she was such charming company that I doubted they'd hold it against me.

"We'd be happy to invite your friend," Uncle Bobby said. "We play every Thursday at 7 p.m."

"You'll like Mrs. B.," I said. "She's a retired librarian and sharp as a whip."

"A retired librarian? Maybe she'd like to come to book club with us, too," Anton suggested.

"I bet she would." Mrs. B. was a walking encyclopedia. She'd probably hit it off with the former history teacher.

We parted ways. Satisfaction coursed through me. This was turning into a productive day. I was setting good things in motion for both Mrs. B. and Ever.

I rounded a corner. Lorelei's apartment building came into view. She lived in a ground floor unit. Her front door was open, and she stood in the doorway. I raised a hand to wave and catch her attention, then stilled.

Lorelei wasn't alone. She was deep in conversation with a middle-aged man I didn't recognize. He was no stranger to Lorelei, apparently. A stranger wouldn't be gripping her upper arms, his blond head bent close to hers while they talked. She jerked her head, nodding at something he said. If she looked scared, I would have intervened, but she looked more pissed off than frightened.

Who was this guy? What the hell was going on?

THIRTY-TWO

Georgia

"Something smells mighty good."

The hairs on the back of my neck bristled, the instinctive, involuntary reaction of prey to the appearance of a predator.

Dammit. I'm not prey.

If anything, I was the predator, stalking my victim, watching from the shadows, biding my time until I brought down my quarry. So why did Jonesy's silky voice trigger an atavistic shiver?

The kitchen timer dinged. I opened the oven door and peeked inside. The scones looked perfect, golden brown and studded with ruby-red cranberries. I grabbed a pair of potholders, pulled the cookie sheet from the oven, then turned to Jonesy.

"Thanks. If you'd like a scone, it'll be a few minutes till they're ready. They need to cool down before I glaze them."

Jonesy lowered himself onto a counter stool, planted his elbows on the granite, and folded his hands together. "Good things are worth waiting for, honey." His lips tipped up and he winked.

Jesus. Did he think I'd buy that unconvincing facsimile of a smile?

I lowered my eyes then simpered up at him through my lashes.

"I've been meaning to tell you how grateful I am that you brought me to Boise," I said. "My old job sucked, but I like working at Mr. Allsop's house."

"My pleasure." He inclined his head and his mouth stretched into a benevolent smile.

Would Carrie remind him that he wouldn't have escaped Pendleton without her help? Maybe, but I saw no advantage in rubbing him the wrong way, not when we were entering the kissing-up-to-Jonesy stage of the mission.

I drizzled glaze over the scones, plated one for Jonesy, then presented it to him with a flourish.

He took a large bite. "Yum."

"Scones were my mom's specialty. I used to help her bake them every Sunday."

The most convincing lie—the cover story that holds up best to scrutiny—falls into the gray area between truth and falsehood. When Havoc and I crafted my backstory, we stuck as closely as possible to the truth. I *knew* I'd be giving Jonesy pieces of my real life. I *did* bake scones with my mom every Sunday. Telling him so wasn't a big deal, but as soon as the words slipped out, they felt wrong, like I was giving away something that mattered.

His eyes sharpened, but his tone was easy. "Where did you grow up, Carrie?"

Here we go. "Lawrence, Kansas. A university town in the eastern part of the state."

"I've been to Lawrence. Pretty place." He tilted his head. "If I remember right, there was a big massacre there during the Civil War."

"That's right. Quantrill's Raid in 1863. If you grow up in Lawrence, you know all about it."

Lawrence was founded by abolitionists and was a hotbed of antislavery sentiment. In the middle of the Civil War, a group of Confederate guerillas attacked the city, burning down two hundred houses and killing one hundred and fifty men and boys. What did it say about Jonesy that the first thing that came to his mind when I mentioned Lawrence was the massacre?

"Lawrence, Kansas," he drawled. "You miss it?"

It felt like Jonesy was deliberately poking a wound, stirring up feelings of loss.

"Sure. I miss my parents and my friends back home." I busied myself wiping down the counter. "I miss watching the Jayhawks play basketball. The Haskell Indian Nations University is...was... in Lawrence. We lived close to it. I miss sitting on the porch in the evening and listening to the students drumming and singing. I miss chasing fireflies and seeing cardinals. I miss a lot of things."

"Anything you don't miss?"

I snorted. "Yeah. Tornado watches and humidity."

He laughed. "We don't have to worry about those in Boise."

"No, we don't," I agreed, sharing a smile with the monster. "How about you? Where did you grow up?"

"I was an army brat and grew up all over the place."

"Any brothers or sisters?" I couldn't help the question. It was hard to imagine Jonesy as part of a family.

"I was a middle child. Had a younger brother and an older sister."

I blinked. Conventional wisdom said middle children were natural peacemakers and people pleasers. So much for conventional wisdom.

"Did any of your family survive the pandemic?" I asked, fully expecting him to say no.

"My sister's dipshit son survived. Twenty-three years old and not the sharpest tool in the shed, but he does what he's told. He knew I worked for Mr. Allsop, and he showed up in Boise a few months ago. I sent him to Bend to work with the team that runs the city."

Interesting. During our mission in Prineville, Finn, Bear, Ripper, and Reno had met with members of Allsop's Bend team. There was no way to come right out and ask his nephew's name, not without triggering Jonesy's curiosity, but I'd tell Reno about him.

"Dipshit or not, it must be nice to have some family alive."

Jonesy lifted a shoulder.

Reno and two other men ambled into the kitchen. Reno still wore his leather biker vest, but underneath it he had on the Allsop uniform of gray tee and jeans. Looked like Allsop enjoyed showing off his personal Janissary.

"Take a scone, fellas," Jonesy suggested.

The men helped themselves then shuffled their feet and exchanged glances, as if they didn't know what to make of an affable Jonesy.

"This is good. Thanks, Carrie." Reno held up his pastry.

"Mr. Allsop may be out of town, but that doesn't mean we can take the day off. I'll meet you boys out front in five minutes." Jonesy cocked his head toward the door. The men took off. Leaning back against the stool, he dusted crumbs off his fingers.

I held up the coffee pot. Jonesy dipped his chin. I filled a cup for him. "Black, right?"

"You remember how I like it." A simple statement of fact that made my fine hair jump to attention again.

Shit. I really couldn't let Allsop's henchman rattle me like this. Of course, Carrie would feel cowed and intimidated by Jonesy. If some of my genuine anxiety bled through my performance, it would only make my act more believable.

"You're—" I started.

Jonesy's ears perked up.

"You're good with your men. A natural leader."

He preened, his chin jutting into the air. "I know how to read people."

I set the coffee cup down in front of him. "What you're really good at is helping people see the truth about a situation. Cutting through the bullshit. That's a real talent."

"I appreciate that, honey." He studied me over the rim of his coffee cup.

"It's what you did for Reno and me," I persisted. "We were going nowhere fast in Pendleton. We were always going to be stuck doing drudge work and making do with third-rate crap. You made us see that. You made us think about what we really wanted and the best way to get it."

He promised us the moon if we turned traitor and helped him escape.

"I'm glad you see it that way."

I swept a hand around the kitchen. "And look at me now. I'm living in a fancy house." I gestured at my gray dress and frilly white apron. "I get to wear nice clothes and eat a warm scone for breakfast. Boise is so much better than Pendleton." I frowned, remembering that a sense of grievance was Carrie's defining characteristic. "Although I would like a bigger bedroom. Mine is little more than a closet."

"Play your cards right, and you'll be sitting pretty for the rest of your life." He dabbed his mouth with a napkin and stood.

"Yes, sir. I plan to." I changed the subject. "What are you and Reno doing today?"

"Kicking down doors. Ferreting out the last of the Nampa Boys."

A chill iced my spine. I'd heard all about the Nampa Boys. Brave. Defiant. A little cocky. What had become of the band of insurgents once Allsop captured their leader?

My lips twitched into a smile. I forced a chipper tone into my voice. "Good luck to you."

Jonesy tapped the side of his head. "You don't need luck when you got smarts."

I laughed. "Then you're in great shape."

He tilted his head. "I do like you." He sounded surprised. I wasn't. A little flattery went a long way with Jonesy.

"I like you, too."

Jonesy strutted from the room. I slid another tray of scones into the oven and set the timer, then went to check on Winnie, who was in bed with a migraine. She'd stumbled to her room half-blind an hour ago. I found her lying in the dark, snoring softly. Good. The pain pills must have worked.

I tiptoed back to the kitchen and cleaned up while the second batch of scones baked. Winnie and I usually worked together around the house. With her out of commission, I could go about solo. I rolled the vacuum cleaner down the hall then bumped it down the stairway to the daylight basement.

The same young man who'd flashed a grin when Winnie and I brought coffee to the war room stood sentry again outside the closed door.

"Hi." I put a little extra swing in my hips and offered him my brightest smile. "Mr. Allsop and Jonesy are out of the house. I thought this would be a good time to vacuum downstairs."

"No problem." His eyes lit up and he returned my smile. "But orders are I keep the door open and my eyes on you while you're in the war room or the armory."

"That makes sense." I dropped my voice into a conspiratorial whisper. "If I was up to no good, you wouldn't want to leave me alone down here."

Instead of laughing—like I expected—his mood sobered. "Don't even joke about that. Jonesy runs a tight ship, and he's got absolutely no sense of humor when it comes to security."

"Thanks for the warning." I laid a hand on his arm. "I'm new here, and I don't want my big mouth to get me into trouble. I'm Carrie, by the way. What's your name?"

He lifted his chin, his good humor restored. "I'm Andrew. If you need help or have any questions, come to me."

"I will. Thank you, Andrew."

Under his watchful eye, I vacuumed the hallway. He unlocked the door to the armory. While Andrew watched, I ran the vacuum over the carpet. With my back to him, I studied the weapons mounted on the tactical walls. A dozen AK-47s and twice that number of handguns. The cabinets held ammo, according to Kyle, who'd made off with a couple of AKs when he raided the place.

"All done." I rolled the vacuum past Andrew and waited outside the door to the war room. "I baked scones this morning. Make sure you get one before they're gone."

Was it too much to hope that the young sentry would skedaddle upstairs for a scone, leaving me alone downstairs for a few minutes?

Yes, apparently it was.

"Save one for me, will you? I'll stop by the kitchen for it after shift change." He unlocked the door to the war room and stood aside for me to enter.

"You bet."

Andrew leaned against the doorframe and watched me work. The whiteboards stood blank and empty, with only a few indecipherable black smudges that the eraser had missed. I glanced longingly at the folders strewn across the table.

If I "accidentally" rammed the vacuum into a table support, maybe a folder would fall off and scatter its contents. No one would blame me if I dropped to my knees and stuffed the papers back into the folder, would they? I suppressed a snort. I was too well-trained to attempt such a clumsy and obvious move.

My gaze fell on a paper shredder tucked into the corner next to a file cabinet. A tantalizing stack of papers four or five deep had jammed the shredder blades. The machine had chewed up less than an inch of the papers before the blades clogged. If any of Allsop's men had noticed, they would have pulled the papers out and tried again. They must not have noticed.

Andrew couldn't see the machine from the door. Could I rip the papers out and stuff them into my dress without attracting his attention?

I switched off the vacuum and turned it over.

"There a problem?" Andrew called.

"The roller is stuck. I must have sucked up something that got tangled in the brush. It'll just take a minute to fix it."

"Let me know if you need help."

"I will." I waited for a count of ten. "Are there any tweezers or pliers downstairs? I need to get a hold of this string and tug."

Clearly conflicted, Andrew glanced over his shoulder into the hall. "Gimme a minute." He disappeared.

I tore the papers from the shredder, folded them in quarters, and shoved them into my bra. I righted the vacuum just as Andrew ran into the room carrying a pair of needle-nose pliers.

"Wouldn't you know it." I laughed. "As soon as I asked for the pliers the string pulled free." I patted the pocket on my apron, pretending I'd stuck the string in there. If Andrew was a suspicious sort, he'd ask to see it. I held my breath, my eyes wide and innocent.

He spread his hands. "No harm done."

I finished cleaning then carried the vacuum upstairs. A peek into her dark room revealed that Winnie was still asleep. I slipped into my small room. The door didn't lock. I had no guarantee of privacy, no idea if Jonesy had our rooms searched, no safe place to hide the papers. To buy some time, I stuck the wooden chair under the door knob. I could claim I was changing clothes if anybody tried to enter.

I pulled the papers from my bra, unfolded them, and spread them across the cot.

Inventory Report: Gasoline stockpile, Bend, Oregon, 1 September through 1 December

I scanned the figures, memorizing the number of gallons of gasoline kept in reserve on September first and the number on December first. Despite several small additions, the supply of available gas had declined significantly. Allsop's forces were running low on gasoline, invaluable information.

Next door, a mattress creaked. Winnie moaned. I had to hurry. I glanced around my spartan cubical. The cot, dresser, and wooden chair offered no good places to conceal the papers. A five-year-old could find them if I hid them under the mattress or in a pillowcase. My sock drawer? The first place even a novice thief would look, and the men who worked for Jonesy weren't novices.

I grabbed a nail file from the top of my dresser, knelt down, and unscrewed the cover plate from a wall outlet. I stuffed the folded-up papers into the receptacle box and screwed the cover back in place. Not ideal, not by a long shot, but the best I could manage at short notice.

I moved the wooden chair away from the door and padded to the kitchen. I plated the rest of the scones—setting aside one for Andrew—and started washing the cookie sheets. Winnie staggered up the hallway, her face pinched and pale. Wincing, she held up a hand to protect her eyes from the bright lights. I rushed over to the wall and switched off the overhead lights.

"You should go back to bed," I urged, genuinely concerned for the kind woman.

She shook her head then grimaced at the movement. "Mr. Jonesy will want his lunch."

"Jonesy will be gone most of the day. And Mr. Allsop is out of town, remember? If any of the soldiers ask for lunch, I can warm up some leftover minestrone or make them a sandwich."

She wavered, clearly torn. "What about dinner?"

"How about if I check on you later this afternoon? If you feel better, you can get up and fix dinner. If not, I can manage."

"All right." Her voice was weak. "Could you vacuum and dust the main floor? And change the sheets in the guards' quarters?"

"I'm on it. Go lie down, please."

"Thank you, Carrie." Her lips trembled as she attempted a smile, then she shuffled back to her room.

Winnie had told me that Allsop's bedroom and study were locked, and if we needed to gather up laundry or change his sheets or clean the rooms, we had to ask a guard to let us in and to supervise us while we worked. With Andrew standing sentry in the basement and soldiers wandering in and out of the house all day, snooping was a no-go.

I spent the day cleaning.

A little after 4 p.m., I stood in front of the open refrigerator door, studying the contents. Winnie wasn't up. It appeared that I'd have to fix dinner for the men.

The mansion's front door slammed shut. Footsteps tromped up the hallway toward the kitchen. Shutting the fridge, I turned around.

With his hand clamped around the kid's shoulder, Jonesy marched a boy into the kitchen. The boy looked to be around twelve. Brown eyes glared angrily from his narrow, dirty face. The Idaho

Steelheads jersey he wore hung loose on his frame. He needed a bath and a meal.

I glanced at Reno, who stood behind Jonesy. The indifferent, hard-ass mask he wore might fool most people, but from the tic in his jaw, I could tell that my friend didn't like this one bit.

"Sit down, son," Jonesy said with deceptive mildness, nodding at the counter stool. "Carrie, honey, can you get the boy a scone and some milk? The poor mite is half-starved."

The *poor mite* had to be a Nampa Boy. I hoped the kid was too savvy to fall for Jonesy's phony nice-guy act. I jerked my head in the affirmative and scuttled toward a cupboard to fetch a plate and glass. I poured milk into the glass, plated a pastry, and slid the food toward the boy.

"Eat up, kiddo. If you want a second one, let me know." God knew when he'd be getting his next decent meal.

He ate the scone in three bites then shoved the plate at me. I handed him a second one. He guzzled the glass of milk before downing it, too.

"Now that you've been fed, how about we have a nice little chat?" Jonesy said.

The kid burped, a long, rolling belch that left a potent miasma floating in the air. His lips curved up in a cheeky grin. "How about you go fuck yourself, old man?"

Nobody talked to Jonesy like that. I braced, fully expecting him to give the kid a beatdown. And what would Reno and I do then? Stand by or break cover and intervene?

Instead of striking out, Jonesy returned the smile, his eyes sparkling with delight. He whistled and shook a disbelieving head. "You got a pair on you, don't you, boy?"

The kid crossed his arms over his chest and slouched against the back of the stool, a blasé expression on his face. He looked much older than his years.

"Hey," I said. The boy swung his head toward me. I gentled my voice. "What's your name?"

He narrowed his eyes, considering my question. No doubt, I was one of the bad guys as far as he was concerned. Only a bad guy would work for Allsop. Finally, he shrugged. "Ethan. What's yours, sweetheart?"

Sweetheart? Good lord, the kid was flirting with me?

"Boss," Reno spoke up. "In my experience, sometimes a man needs to sit and stew for a while before he gets smart and does the right thing. How about we tuck Ethan away, give time for his imagination to run wild, before you have your little chat?"

Jonesy pursed his lips.

Do it. I willed Jonesy to heed Reno's advice, to stop this train from derailing.

Finally, Jonesy spread his hands, a magnanimous gesture. "All righty. I'll give him time to contemplate the error of his ways. Reno, you and the men put Ethan in lockdown with his buddy."

His buddy had to be David. We suspected that David was being held at the Women's Ward of the old penitentiary—where Allsop had locked up Sunny—but now Reno would know for sure.

"Yes, sir." Reno stepped forward and grabbed Ethan's arm. He hauled him from the stool and frog-marched the boy from the room, leaving me alone with Jonesy.

Jonesy sauntered around the granite island and made his way toward me. Warning klaxons went off in my head.

I pressed my lips together, fighting the irrational urge to turn tail and run. I hadn't done anything to earn his ire. He couldn't possibly know that I'd swiped the papers from the shredder, could he? Not unless there were security cameras watching my every move. In the war room.

In my bedroom.

Shit, what a horrifying thought. Any cameras would have to be well-hidden because I didn't see them. I was trained to see them.

Jonesy moved forward, as intractable, as unrelenting as an incoming wave.

I took a faltering step backward, scanning the kitchen for a weapon. The knife block sat on a counter a dozen feet away. The heavy pots and pans were tucked away in cupboards, well out of reach. Snatching up and flinging a toaster at an armed man would be ridiculous.

Jonesy carried a gun in a shoulder holster. He wouldn't expect me to make a play for the weapon, not his "sweet, sweet Carrie."

He backed me into the refrigerator, his thick-set chest pressing against me. I inhaled and readied myself to move.

Cigarette-scented breath swept over my face. Jonesy lifted a hand and tapped me on the nose.

"Bop," he said.

What the hell?

He lowered his chin. Menace glittered in his eyes, but his voice sounded amiable, almost cheery. "Don't you ever do that again, pretty girl."

"Don't do what?" Dammit, my voice shook. Carrie's voice would shake, but I couldn't even pretend that the quiver was part of an act.

He tilted his head to one side and pressed his lips together in a disappointed, disbelieving smile. "You know what," he chided.

My head sliced back and forth. I really didn't.

Jonesy leaned close. He sighed and his warm exhalation washed over my cheeks.

I held my breath, not wanting any part of this man inside of me.

He tapped my nose again. "Offering the boy a second scone. Asking his name. Don't you ever interfere with an interrogation again. You feel me?"

THIRTY-THREE

Finn

"Cool," Ever breathed, tracing the edge of a pink flower decal with her finger.

Ever, Kenzie, Ripper, and I paused in the parking lot of the new medical clinic.

"That's Daisy. It used to be Sunny's van," I said. "She gave it to her friend Rocco when she moved to the ranch."

"She gave Daisy away?" Ever looked dumbstruck, as if she couldn't fathom handing over such a prize. "For free?"

"Yep. She didn't need a van anymore, and Rocco wanted it."

"Who wouldn't." Genuine sincerity filled Ever's voice.

Ripper coughed into his hand, a backhanded answer to Ever's question. Ripper wouldn't be trading in his Harley for a boxy, underpowered van anytime soon.

I leaned into the story. "Once upon a time, Sunny put fake black eyelashes on over Daisy's headlights."

"Cool," Ever repeated, her eyes wide with wonder. If Ever got her hands on some car lashes, no doubt the girl would slap them on every vehicle at the ranch. I guess there's an upside to the end of internet shopping.

"Wanna get Mac inside out of the rain." Ripper nudged Kenzie, hustling her toward the door.

"C'mon, sweet pea." I tapped Ever's arm. "Let's go sit by the woodstove and dry out. I bet Rocco has some cocoa we can fix."

We stepped inside the clinic, and a wave of heat washed over us. Not so long ago, a warm room in the middle of winter was no big deal. Now? Shoot. A warm room was a rare treat.

Rocco rushed from around the reception desk and enfolded Kenzie in his big arms. "How are you doing, sweetheart?"

"I'm good." She laughed, returning his hug. "How are you?"

"I'm great. Happy to have you here. We have three pregnant women in town now. By next summer we'll be up to our eyeballs in babies."

"About that," Ripper said. "Mac has fluid retention and high blood pressure. Sahdev wants you and Sara to keep an eye on her as long as we're in town."

Rocco clapped the biker's shoulder. "Don't you worry. We'll take real good care of her."

"I like your van," Ever piped in.

"Me too. It sure was nice of Sunny to give Daisy to me."

Rocco escorted Kenzie and Ripper to an examination room. Ever and I helped ourselves to mugs of hot cocoa then sat down close to the fire. Half an hour later, Ripper and Kenzie walked back into the waiting room.

Kenzie held out a hand to Ever. "Come on, kiddo. Ripper and Finn are meeting up with Marcus and Justin across town. How about you and I walk over to the library?"

"Yes." Ever eagerly hopped to her feet and took Kenzie's hand. The children's section of the library had quickly become Ever's favorite place in town.

Ripper wrapped a hand around Kenzie's nape, pulled her close, and dropped a kiss on her forehead. "See you this afternoon, Mrs. Solis."

She tossed back her head and offered a saucy smile, her eyes brimming with love. "I'm counting on it, Mr. Solis."

My chest squeezed tight, and I had to look away. Just like that, my thoughts turned to Georgia. I always figured that sooner or later I'd fall in love and settle down, the way my parents and grandparents did. I took for granted the notion that someday I'd build a family.

Then the damned flu struck. War loomed. The future was never more uncertain.

Georgia was doing her part, fighting for everybody's right to a happy ever after. I was proud of her. I truly was, but fear for my woman lodged deep in my heart.

"God, keep her safe," I muttered.

"How come Ripper calls you Mrs. Solis?" Ever asked as they headed out the door.

We parted ways with Kenzie and Ever. Ripper and I headed east toward a former health club that Havoc had turned into a training center for his citizen soldiers.

Walls of windows flooded the place with natural light. Without electricity, the treadmills were dead in the water, but stationary bikes allowed for aerobic exercise. The free weights were popular with folks determined to build up their strength. We'd moved equipment out of the way and spread mats over the floor, creating a space for hand-to-hand combat training.

"Havoc told me that I'm more valuable as a trainer than in the field." Ripper made a face. "How's that for a kick in the pants?"

"Nobody and I mean *nobody* questions your value in the field." I'd watched the man in action. Flashy acts of derring-do were not his style. Ripper operated with quiet, deadly efficiency. Nothing rattled him. When a situation went south, I'd seen him take aim and drop men before they could twitch.

Ripper grunted.

"Havoc's trying to turn office managers and stockbrokers into soldiers. As a former Ranger, you're one of a handful of professional warriors in our ranks. Do you think there's anybody better suited to turn civilians into soldiers than you?"

"I'm not really complaining." Ripper shot me a rueful grin. "But the 'more valuable' comment bites."

"What are you working on today?" I asked. In the one and only bar fight I found myself in, I handled myself reasonably well, but I never was a brawler. Everybody back at the ranch—well, almost everybody—had been training with Ripper for months.

"Close combat fighting with knives." Ripper's eyes gleamed. "Gotta be ready if a weapon malfunctions."

"Knives, huh?" I'd carried a stockman pocket knife for years. Most ranchers did, but before I trained with Ripper, I'd never considered using one as a weapon.

"Yeah. We'll work on body position. How to conduct an attack. Leading with the dominant foot. Offensive and defensive drills. The goal is to create muscle memory through repetition."

I nodded. The same lessons I'd learned during my training sessions back on the ranch.

"You need me to help?" I was no expert, but I was miles ahead of raw recruits.

"Havoc, Justin, and I can handle it." He tilted his head. "You got somewhere to be?"

The memory of Lorelei's conversation with the strange man kept eating at me. "Something's going on with Justin's girlfriend."

"What do you mean?"

"I saw her having a real intense, up-close conversation with another man."

"So?" Ripper rolled his eyes. "This ain't the Victorian age. No need to swoon if an unchaperoned woman talks to the opposite sex."

"I know that. There was just something about their body language and the way they were talking—" I groped for an explanation that would make me sound like less of a gossipy busybody. "It didn't look like a friendly chat. Lorelei looked uncomfortable. I'm wondering if somebody she knew back in Idaho is giving her a hard time. Maybe a jealous ex. Or maybe somebody who doesn't like that she's seeing Justin."

Ripper lifted a shoulder. "So check it out. Ask her what's going on."

I waved my hand. "Never mind. Listen, I'm going to head over to Lorelei's place. I want to talk to her about Ever and the plans for a school."

We fell into silence, the only sound our boots scuffing over the wet sidewalk.

Ripper turned back to me. "Havoc told me about Georgia and Reno's mission. You okay, brother? Could that be what put you on edge?"

I sighed. "I'm as okay as I can be. The thought of Georgia up close with Allsop and Jonesy—" I shuddered. "I won't know a moment's peace until she's safely back home."

Ripper stopped walking and laid a hand on my shoulder. "Georgia is smart. She's trained. If she wasn't up to the job, Havoc wouldn't have sent her."

"I know, but no matter how smart and well-trained she is, she can't anticipate every variable. The situation can still go fubar."

"True enough, but if it does, we won't leave Georgia and Reno high and dry."

"No man—or woman—left behind, right brother?" I cracked a weak smile.

"That's right." He squeezed my shoulder. "Don't get so worked up worrying about Georgia that you look for trouble where it doesn't exist."

We continued on our way. At the gym, I lingered long enough to say hello to Marcus and Justin, then took off for Lorelei's place. Fifteen minutes later, I rapped on her door.

Lorelei answered my knock. Her forehead furrowed. "If we had a meeting today, I totally forgot about it."

"Nah, you didn't forget anything. I wanted to talk to you and took a chance that you'd be home."

"If you'd come twenty minutes later, you would have missed me, but I have time to talk now." She gestured for me to enter. "Come on in."

I scraped my boots on the welcome mat and dropped onto her love seat. "Thanks for taking the time to see me."

"Of course." She sat down on the chair opposite me and tucked a yellow afghan over her lap. "What's up?"

"I assume Justin told you that some of the people from the ranch are staying in town for a while?"

"Yes." She plucked at a thread on the afghan.

"I was wondering how your plans for setting up a school are coming along. We have a nine-year-old girl named Ever who's looking forward to getting back into class."

"It'll be at least a month before the school opens up," Lorelei said. "But if Ever would like to get some tutoring from me, I'd be happy to work with her."

"That's real nice of you. I bet she'd like that."

"I'm used to spending my days with a bunch of noisy kindergartners. I miss the chatter and hubbub. I'd love to spend some time with Ever."

"If you miss chatter and hubbub, you and Ever are a match made in heaven."

"Perfect." A smile danced across her pretty face. "I can't wait."

"Now that that's settled, tell me, how are things going with Justin? He treating you right?"

Her smile faltered. "He's the best man I know. I'm crazy about him." The strained expression flitting across her face was at odds with her words.

I leaned forward. "Are you all right, Lorelei?"

She shook herself and coughed out an unconvincing laugh. "I'm fine. I had a nightmare last night that left me on edge, but I'm good. Really."

"You have friends in town, you know. If you ever need to talk, come looking for me or Rachel."

"I'm fine." She pulled on a loose thread on the afghan. I pretended not to notice. "Justin tells me that Georgia went to spend some time at the ranch."

"That's right."

A visit to the ranch, that was our cover story to explain Georgia's absence. I was glad to hear that Justin kept Georgia's assignment a secret, even from his girlfriend. The fewer people who knew, the better.

"You two looked happy when you were here for dinner the other night." Her voice sounded wistful.

"We are. Guess you and I are both lucky in love." I watched closely for her reaction.

Lorelei's chin trembled. I swore she wanted to say something. Instead, she cleared her throat and rose to her feet. "I… I have my meeting to get to. It was nice of you to stop by, Finn. Why don't you bring Ever over tomorrow so we can get to know each other?"

I stood. "I guess I'll be on my way." I walked to the door then looked over my shoulder, my hand on the knob. "You sure you're okay?"

"Yes. I'm right as rain." She pressed her lips together, waved goodbye, and closed the door firmly behind me. The lock clicked.

What the hell was up with her?

THIRTY-FOUR

Georgia

"A governorship is out of the question."

Allsop's smooth, overly mannered voice grated on my nerves, and I wasn't the one he was talking to. I paused next to the swinging door leading to the dining room, the tray with the silver coffee service in my hands. Holding my breath, I brazenly eavesdropped.

"I value your loyalty, Jonesy. You'll always have a place in my organization," Allsop continued. "You'll be well compensated for your service, but I don't see you playing an administrative role. No."

A pause.

I imagined Allsop dabbing his mouth with a linen napkin or straightening an immaculate cuff.

"You'll stay where your talents are best employed, as my chief of security. We each have our role to play in the new world, and you function best as a… as a blunt instrument."

A blunt instrument? Burn.

I jumped back as the door flew open. I slapped my best innocent expression across my face. Jonesy stomped past me, his face contorted with barely suppressed rage. I smiled to myself. Looked like it was time for Reno and me to pick up the pace of our butter-up-Jonesy campaign.

I bumped the door open with my shoulder and carried the silver tray to the head of the table. "More coffee, sir?"

He inclined his head. I felt his eyes on me when I set the tray on the table, refilled his cup, and stirred in cream and sugar. He placed a hand over mine.

Startled, I looked down at his long, tapered fingers, at his buffed and shaped nails, at his flawless cuticles. His manicure was more on point than mine.

An ache shot through me, a longing for Finn's strong, work-calloused hands.

Why was Allsop touching me?

I shook myself out of my stunned reverie.

"Do you want anything else, sir?" As soon as the words slipped out of my mouth, I winced.

Shit. I'd created a perfect opening for him to suggest some kind of lusty lord of the manor and winsome chambermaid dalliance. Time to correct the course, to make my lack of interest clear.

I slid my hand out from under his and stood up straight. "Maybe another croissant?"

He tapped his fingers on the polished wood. "You're on good terms with Jonesy, are you not?"

The conversation had taken an unexpected turn. "Sir?"

"You and Jonesy. You get along well, yes?"

"We get along fine, sir."

"You enjoy living here, in the big house, with all of its amenities?"

The wheels turned in my mind, and I guessed where Allsop was going. I nodded enthusiastically. "I love living here, Mr. Allsop. I feel like one of the luckiest girls alive."

He smiled. "And I'm pleased with the conscientious manner with which you perform your duties."

Good grief. His stilted, unnatural language reminded me of one of Dad's colleagues in the history department, a pontificating blowhard whose students made fun of him behind his back.

"Thank you, Mr. Allsop."

"I can imagine you living and working here—in comfort—for a good many years."

"I'd like that."

"Of course, I expect absolute loyalty and obedience. And if I occasionally ask you for… special acts of service… I would expect you to comply."

Special acts of service? Crap. Were we back to my horny lord of the manor and helpless chambermaid fantasies? "Sir?"

"If you were to overhear any grumblings among my men, if Jonesy complained about his position, for example, you'd keep me abreast of the situation, wouldn't you? I could count on you to be my eyes and ears among the staff?"

Allsop wanted me to spy for him? Hell, yes. If anything I said or did made Jonesy suspicious, I could claim to be acting under Allsop's orders.

"Yes, sir. I'd be happy to keep an eye on the men for you."

"Very good." Allsop brushed a crumb off his sleeve then took another sip of coffee. "You may go, Carrie."

I picked up the tray and scurried to the kitchen.

Through the glass panels of the french doors, I spied Jonesy on the rain-splattered balcony. Hands locked around the railing, he stared out over the Boise skyline. Clouds blanketed the distant buildings, the day as gloomy and forbidding as his mood.

Anger rolled off him in waves. Approaching a pissed-off Jonesy was as smart as kicking a rattlesnake, but I couldn't afford to play it safe.

I slipped outside and padded across the balcony. Cold drizzle pelted me. Dark wet splotches bloomed on my dress and apron.

I laid a tentative hand on Jonesy's back. He whirled around, his eyes blazing. I staggered backward and pressed a hand to my throat.

"I'm sorry," I sputtered. "I was just going to ask if you want me to bring you a coat."

Before my eyes, his affect altered. The muscles and tendons beneath his skin shifted, erasing the angry mask and reshaping his features into an affable expression. His gaze softened and his lips curved into a genial smile. It was like watching a wizard conjure up a new face.

Creepy as fuck. A chill ran down my spine, and my shoulders shook.

"Carrie, honey, what were you thinking? You'll catch your death of cold out here." He *tsk-tsked* and ushered me back inside. He snatched up a kitchen towel and wiped at my wet face, arms, and chest. When his hands lingered over my breasts, I sidestepped him, laughing.

"You're wetter than I am, Jonesy." I reached into a drawer, pulled out a dry towel, and handed it to him.

"Thank you. I do appreciate how you always take good care of me." He scrubbed the towel over his dripping face and his soaked gray tee and jeans, the outfit that marked him as one of Allsop's henchmen, a worker bee and not a suit-clad prince.

With nice Jonesy in ascendance, I rolled the dice. "I heard what Mr. Allsop said to you, and it made me mad. It's not fair that he won't reward you with a governorship. You deserve it. You deserve to be in charge. Reno feels the same way."

Jonesy tilted his head. "You like to listen in at doors, Carrie?"

"Not on purpose." Crap. I thought he'd take the bait. "Sometimes I can't help but overhear things."

"Is that right?" His eyes narrowed. "You think maybe you could try to overhear things for me, on purpose?"

"Huh?" I played stupid.

"Could you keep your eyes peeled and your ears open for any information that might be of use to me?" He spoke slowly, with exaggerated care, as if he was addressing a dimwitted child. "Especially anything you overhear about Mr. Allsop's plans for after the war."

"You want me to spy on Mr. Allsop for you?" My mouth fell open.

"Spying is an ugly word." Jonesy frowned and waved a disdainful hand. "Don't think of it as spying. Think of it as helping a friend."

"A friend," I repeated, painting a thoughtful expression across my face.

"That's right. A good friend who—like you said—deserves to be in charge."

I bit my lower lip then lifted my eyes to the man who watched me with barely concealed impatience. I thrust out my hand, like we were sealing a deal. "I'm Team Jonesy. Reno is Team Jonesy, too. You can count on us."

"Good." We shook hands then he chucked me under the chin. "We're going to go far together, pretty girl. You'll see. One day soon you'll be sitting on top of the world."

I squealed with delight, then clapped both hands over my mouth.

Chuckling, Jonesy sauntered from the room.

Our plan to butter up Jonesy was officially a success. Where was Reno? I couldn't wait to fill him in. As of right now, I was spying for Marcus, Allsop, and Jonesy.

Holy shit. I was a freaking triple agent.

THIRTY-FIVE

Finn

If she was here, Mama would call me a slugabed and a loafer. Sleeping in till eight thirty? The best part of the day was gone, she'd say. Bear took after Mama. Nothing made him happier than being up and about well before the sun peeked over the horizon. Me? I grew up on a ranch. I'd made my peace with rolling out of bed at five in the morning. But if I had my druthers, every once in a while I'd laze in the sack till noon.

Last night, worries about Georgia held sleep at bay. When I finally drifted off, bad dreams punctuated my rest. I'd jerk awake, my heart pounding in time with the *tick-tick-tick* of the windup alarm clock. Close to morning I fell into a deep sleep and stayed under till I woke a little after eight o'clock. I lay in the warm bed, thinking my thoughts, until my bladder made an urgent case that I really needed to roust myself.

I crawled out of bed, stretched, then pulled aside the curtain. Overnight, the clouds had scuttled away, taking the rain and the gloomy sky with them. Morning broke clear and bright. Below me, Ripper paced the parking lot, a cup of steaming coffee in his hands.

I lit the alcohol stove. While the water came to a boil, I threw on my clothes and boots. We had a few good Starbucks instant coffee packets left, but I wanted to save those for Georgia. The jar of dollar store instant coffee would do fine for me. I filled a mug, then headed down to the parking lot.

"Hold this." I handed Ripper my coffee and took care of business before sidling up next to my friend and reclaiming my cup.

"Morning," he grunted.

"Morning," I grunted back. "What's on for today?"

"Havoc, Justin, and I tested the soldiers and identified some natural shooters. We're taking a dozen of them north of town this morning and training them for distance shooting."

I recalled my crash course in Sniper 101. "How to calm your heartbeat and breath. How to time the shot. How to use the scope. How to compensate for wind and gravity and distance." I recited the lessons I'd learned from Ripper. "I remember it all, brother."

"We have Uncle Bobby to thank for the rifles," Ripper said. "Early on in the pandemic, he got his hands on two dozen sniper rifles and a shit ton of ammo."

"Must have been nice to be a millionaire with connections," I muttered.

Ripper grinned. "At least the man ended up on the right side of the fight."

We raised our mugs, both saluting Uncle Bobby's about-face.

"I promised to introduce Ever to Lorelei today," I said. "I thought I'd ask Kenzie if she wants to walk over there with us."

"Good." Ripper took a sip of coffee. "The doc said Mac should exercise every day. And it'd be nice for her to make friends in town."

"We could time it so you could meet us at Lorelei's after your rifle practice," I suggested. "Then you could walk home with Kenzie."

"You figure out what's going on with Lorelei yet?"

"Nope. I asked if she was okay, and she said everything is fine."

"You want me to meet her, don't you? To see if I think she's hiding anything?"

I shrugged. "Can you be finished with rifle practice and meet us there at two?"

His lips quirked. He saw right through me. "Sure." He pointed up to the second-floor landing. "Speaking of Lorelei, did you see the paper tacked to your door?"

Paper? I looked. Sure enough, a white piece of paper was stuck on the door to Georgia's room. "I was in a hurry to get downstairs. I missed it."

"Thought so." He rubbed his chin. "Justin spent the night at Lorelei's place. Early this morning, he left notes on your door, my door, and Rachel's. Lorelei invited us all over for dinner. She has a new recipe for stroganoff she wants to try. Guess she invited Havoc, too."

"You don't want to miss dinner at Lorelei's," I said. "She's a great cook."

"Mac and I will be there."

I gave Ripper the address of Lorelei's apartment, then went upstairs and confirmed plans with Kenzie and Mrs. B. They planned to take Ever to the library this morning. We'd meet up at noon and eat lunch together at the cafeteria. Mrs. B. would go back to the motel for a rest while I took Kenzie and Ever to meet Lorelei.

I grabbed a packet of peanuts from Georgia's room and hiked over to the warehouse for a two-hour shift. A little before noon, I walked back to the motel. We headed for the cafeteria.

As soon as we got inside the door, Anton Milewski spotted us from a few tables away. He stood up, smoothed his gray hair back from his brow, wiped a finger over a bushy eyebrow, and straightened his tie. *His tie.* Anton was wearing a dress shirt and a tie. He waved. "Cressida, come sit with me."

A flirtatious smile curved Mrs. B.'s pink lips. She turned to Kenzie. "Don't wait up, dearest."

Kenzie's jaw dropped. "Wait. What?" She turned to me. "We bumped into Uncle Bobby and Anton at the library this morning. Mrs. B. and Anton must have made a lunch date then."

And here I thought Mrs. B. was going back to her room after lunch for a nice nap. The old lady was full of surprises. "I bet they met at poker night, and the two of them must have hit it off."

"I bet you're right." Kenzie stared into the middle distance, clearly flummoxed by this turn of events. "She has to be ten years older than him. I didn't see this coming."

I shrugged. "So Mrs. B.'s a cougar. Good for her."

"Who's Cressida?" Ever tugged on Kenzie's hand. "And why is Mrs. B. a cougar?"

Ever's questions broke the spell. Kenzie laughed. "Cressida is Mrs. B.'s first name." She shot me a look that clearly said I was on my own explaining the cougar comment.

Me and my big mouth. I really stepped in it. "Sometimes older folks like to date younger folks. People used to call an older woman who dated a younger man a cougar."

"What did they call older men who liked to date younger women?" Ever asked.

"Men," Kenzie said dryly.

Ever chewed her lip, looking confused.

I ruffled her hair. "You know what? I goofed and said the wrong thing. I think it's real nice that Mrs. B. has made a new friend."

"Me, too." Ever turned her attention to the people sliding their trays along the cafeteria line. "The last time we were here, they had pudding. Do you think they'll have pudding today?"

"Let's go see." Kenzie led the way.

We picked up trays and joined the line. Hildy—Allsop's former housekeeper—worked behind the counter. She smiled and waved, too busy to talk. The servers dished up macaroni and cheese. No pudding. Ever consoled herself by sliding macaroni tubes over the tines of her fork and pulling them off with her teeth one at a time. A little before one, we finished eating, said goodbye to Mrs. B., and headed toward Lorelei's.

We knocked and waited a good two minutes for Lorelei to answer. She cracked open the door and peeked out through the slit.

"Finn, I totally forgot that you were coming today." She opened the door, glancing over our heads into the parking lot.

I craned my neck and looked behind us, but the lot and street were empty. Was Lorelei expecting a visit from her mystery man? How did that make sense after she told me she was crazy about Justin?

Lorelei stepped back. "Please come in."

Never one to hang back or act shy, Ever stuck out her hand. "Hi. I'm Ever van der Linden."

A genuine smile touched Lorelei's lips. "It's nice to meet you, Ever. I'm Lorelei."

Ever pointed at Kenzie. "And this is Kenzie. She and Ripper are going to have a baby in June."

"Hi, Kenzie. Congratulations. Have a seat."

"Where?" Ever frowned.

Clothes were strewn across the love seat and chairs.

"Sorry about the mess." Lorelei swept the clothes into her arms and tossed them onto the small dining room table. "The rain barrel is full, and I thought I'd take advantage of the water and do some laundry."

"That's smart." Kenzie sat on the edge of the chair. "I was afraid we'd have to go down to the river and beat our clothes against a rock."

"We have rain barrels connected to the gutters of most buildings in town," I told her. "Folks can haul their damp clothes to the high school gym. We set up a few old-fashioned hand-crank wringers there. And we've got clotheslines stretched from one side of the gym to the other."

"Primitive, but it works," Lorelei said.

"That's what counts," Kenzie agreed.

Ever bounced excitedly on the love seat. "Finn said you're a teacher."

"That's right." Lorelei turned her attention to the little girl. "I used to teach kindergarten."

"Did you like teaching little kids?"

"I loved teaching." Lorelei's eyes filled with tears. She glanced out the window and swallowed. "I loved my students. I'd do anything for them."

"I like school," Ever said, oblivious to Lorelei's odd mood.

"What was your favorite subject?" Lorelei asked.

"Language arts and science. I studied outer space. Nyx and I made a cool paper-mache mobile of the solar system. We hung it up in the baby's room."

"That's nice." Lorelei sounded distracted.

"Yep. Do you have any games?"

"Um… checkers and Rummikub."

Ever's eyes danced. "I love Rummikub."

Lorelei fetched the box from the bookshelf. The four of us sat on the floor around the coffee table. For the next half hour, we played a spirited round of the game. Ever whooped with triumph when she won.

I glanced at my watch. 1:50 p.m. "You have a lot to do, Lorelei, what with laundry and fixing dinner. Ripper is supposed to meet us here in ten minutes. We'll be out of your hair soon."

"I had fun." Ever threw her arms around Lorelei's neck.

Lorelei returned the girl's hug, her eyes flooding with tears once again.

Kenzie and I exchanged a glance. Something was definitely up with Lorelei.

"Are you all right?" Kenzie leaned forward, concern darkening her gray eyes.

Shaking her head numbly, Lorelei didn't answer.

"Lorelei?" I chimed in.

Somebody pounded on the door.

Kenzie hopped up. "Ripper must be a few minutes early. I'll get it." She threw open the door. The middle-aged blond man I'd spied in conversation with Lorelei stood outside.

Lorelei's hand fluttered to her chest, and a blush crawled up her cheeks. "This isn't a good time, Leonard. I have company."

Could the woman look more guilty?

"So I see." Uninvited, Leonard stepped inside and shut the door. His gaze swept over the living room, taking in the pile of clothes on the dining room table.

For the first time, I noticed the suitcase sitting inside the kitchen doorway.

"You packing to go somewhere, Lorelei?" Leonard asked.

I took exception to the man's tone. I stood and faced him. "What's your business here?"

He ignored me, focusing instead on the flustered kindergarten teacher. "I said, are you packing to go somewhere, Lorelei?"

"I… I…" she stumbled over her words.

"Answer the damned question," he gritted out.

Enough was enough. No matter what was going on between the two of them, he had no right to talk to her like that.

I took a step forward. "Time to go, fella."

Smirking, he pulled a pistol from the pocket of his jacket. Between one heartbeat and the next, he hauled Kenzie against his chest and jammed the gun into her throat.

The color drained from Kenzie's face. Her shaking hands wrapped over her belly.

Why hadn't I carried my damned gun?

Ever clasped her hands around her head. Her shoulders hunched and she curled up into a ball. She squeezed her eyes shut and rocked back and forth, a child retreating from terror. If she couldn't see it, if she couldn't hear it, it wasn't real.

Ever started humming "Mary Had a Little Lamb," and everything inside me went cold. No way in hell would I allow this bastard to hurt my little sweet pea. Or Kenzie.

Raising both hands into the air, I took a step forward, positioning myself between Ever and the man with a gun.

"There's no need for anybody to get hurt." I kept my voice easy while my mind scrambled for solutions.

If I lunged, he'd squeeze off a shot and kill Kenzie before I reached him. Best thing to do was to get him talking, to buy time. If he got comfortable, he might lower the gun or look away, creating an opening for me to spring.

And Ripper was only minutes away. This joker wouldn't stand a chance against the badass biker, especially if Ripper caught him holding a gun against his pregnant wife. If Ripper and I worked together, we'd find a way out of this mess.

I forced calm into my voice and pretended I was one of those hostage negotiators from TV. "What do you want? What's it going to take for us to end this peacefully?"

He snorted and tilted his head at a white-faced Lorelei. "What do I want? I want that stupid bitch to do as she's told and complete her mission, but it looks like she was planning to run away."

Her mission? The friendly, sweet-faced kindergarten teacher had a mission? She worked for Allsop?

My eyes cut to Lorelei. Tears streamed down her face, but she didn't deny his accusations.

"She fucked up the bomb." Leonard ground the muzzle into Kenzie's neck. "It was supposed to go off during a meeting, not when the room was empty." He shot a glare at Lorelei. "I guess you didn't want to kill your new boyfriend, did you?"

Jesus Christ. Lorelei planted the C-4? How? Then it hit me. She carried it in when she brought leftover lasagna to Marcus and Rachel at HQ. Who would have suspected Justin's girlfriend of smuggling high explosives in her pink thermal carrier?

Lorelei drew in a shuddering breath and raised her hands in a placating gesture. "Listen, Leonard. The smartest thing for us to do is to get out of town. Tell the sentries we're sick of the curfew and regulations. They'll let us go."

Leonard scoffed.

"We can tie these people up and lock them in the bathroom. By the time they get free, we'll be long gone. You're a good man. You don't want to hurt a child and a pregnant woman. Let's just go. Please."

His eyes narrowed. "You got rope?"

Relief crossed Lorelei's face, as if she actually believed he might go along with her plan. "I've got twine in the kitchen."

I didn't. I didn't believe for one second that he would tie us up and leave us alive. The fucker was trying to neutralize me as a threat. To use a gullible Lorelei to do his dirty work.

"Okay," he growled. "Go get it. Bind his wrists, nice and tight."

Lorelei scurried to the small kitchen, returning thirty seconds later with a roll of sturdy twine and a small pair of scissors.

I glanced out the window. No sign of Ripper.

"Hold out your wrists, Finn."

What would happen if I refused? Would Leonard start shooting?

I extended my arms. Lorelei's body blocked his view. I held my wrists six inches apart and prayed to God she'd understand what I was trying to do.

Her back to the gunman, Lorelei lifted her eyes to mine. She blinked both eyes hard.

Relief flooded my veins. She got it and she was aiming to help.

She wrapped a length of twine several times around my wide-spread wrists, looped one strand around the middle twice—so that it would look snug—then finished it off with a bow.

"Lemme see," Leonard demanded.

I pressed my wrists together and held up my hands. He grunted with satisfaction.

"Let's all head to the bathroom," he suggested in a deceptively mild voice. Where no doubt he planned to shoot us all. He wouldn't leave any witnesses alive. He shoved Kenzie, who stumbled forward, the gun still poking her neck.

Lorelei pulled Ever to her feet. The little girl plastered herself to my side, her arms locked around my waist. I'd have to shuffle to walk. If I tried to pounce at Leonard, I'd fall headlong over Ever.

I cut my gaze to Lorelei, who gave a small smile. Funny to find myself working in tandem with a bomber and spy, but I knew in my gut that the woman who loved her students would do whatever it took to protect a child.

She gently detached Ever from me, then hoisted the girl up into her arms. Ever buried her face in Lorelei's neck and wrapped her legs around the teacher's waist.

I threw a glance toward the patio door at the back of the apartment. If worse came to worst, while I wrestled with Leonard, Lorelei could carry Ever to safety.

Understanding flashed across her face. She tipped her head. Yeah. She'd do it.

A weight lifted off my heart. Now to figure out how to save Kenzie.

My gaze darted to the window once again. Ripper strode across the parking lot and approached Lorelei's door. I had to keep Leonard's eyes away from the glass.

I staggered and pretended to trip. "Whoa," I cried in a loud voice, calling attention to myself. I threw my bound wrists up into the air, like I was contorting myself to regain my balance. With any luck, Ripper would see that my hands were tied.

"Move your ass," Leonard growled, pointing the gun in my direction.

The door flew open. Leonard whirled, forcing Kenzie to turn with him. He jabbed the gun under her chin. She twisted her head to one side, panting.

Ripper loomed in the open doorway, larger than life. For a split second, fury rode his features. A veil dropped. A cold, dispassionate mask slid into place. My friend disappeared, subsumed into the entity he called *The Ripper.*

And The Ripper spelled death.

THIRTY-SIX

Georgia

"Jonesy cornered me last night." Reno kept his voice low while he poured himself a cup of coffee. "Asked me if I was happy working for Mr. Allsop."

"I'm not surprised." I polished the stove top, scrubbing at invisible spots while we conversed. "When he got back to Boise, Jonesy expected Allsop to welcome him like the Second Coming. To have recognized that he's indispensable and to reward him with more power. Instead, it's business as usual."

Reno leaned against the counter. "Thwarted ambition can get ugly."

"So what did you say to Jonesy?" I asked.

"I told him that my loyalty lies with him. He told me that I'm to consider myself his new second-in-command." Reno took another cup of coffee, sighed, and pointed at the cup. "This is good."

"It ought to be. I ground the beans for this pot ten minutes ago. Organic beans from Sumatra."

"How come the bad guys get to live large?" Reno wondered aloud.

"That's easy," I said. "Bad guys don't share the good stuff with others."

"Ain't that the truth."

"Jonesy asked me to spy on Allsop for him," I said. "He came right out and said that he deserves to be in charge."

"Jonesy is planning a coup." Reno smiled with satisfaction.

"Yep. That part of the mission is coming together nicely. Have you heard anything about plans to attack Valhalla?"

"Not one damned word." Reno scowled. "It's gotta be a priority for both Allsop and Jonesy. There's no way I can come right out and ask Jonesy, not without tipping my hand."

Footsteps sounded in the hall. I turned back to buffing the stove. Winnie walked into the kitchen. She frowned. "I gave you the day off, Carrie. Why are you working?"

I smiled. "I slept in for a couple of hours but decided that I don't want to spend the day loafing in my room. I thought I'd make myself useful."

"A day off is a day off. Why don't you go on a walk, get some fresh air?" Winnie suggested.

"I have an idea." Reno spoke up. "Jonesy wants me to go downtown this morning. I'm scoping out a defensive perimeter for Mr. Allsop's big birthday celebration in front of the capitol building. Carrie is new in town. How about she comes with me? Sees the sights?"

"That's a wonderful idea." Winnie smiled her approval. She turned to me. "No arguments. You're getting out of the house. Go get your coat, young lady."

"Yes, ma'am." I dashed to my room and slipped on a jacket, then followed Reno outside.

We climbed into a black SUV with the words Allsop Corporation emblazoned on the doors. As we pulled out of the long driveway, I sighed, a heavy weight lifting from my shoulders.

"Wears on you, doesn't it?" Reno shot me a sideways glance. "Watching every word. Always being vigilant."

I reached over and squeezed his arm. "It helps having a friend around."

"It does," he agreed. "We're going to get through this, you know. We're agents of chaos. We'll sow discord and have our enemies turning on each other like rabid dogs."

Laughter erupted from my throat. "I don't know about you, but being an agent of chaos is a stretch for me. I was always a good girl."

Reno grinned. "Being an agent of chaos comes naturally to me. Just ask Olivia."

"Olivia's a sweetheart," I said.

"Better than I deserve."

I studied his profile. "Why did you agree to come on this mission? You have so much to lose."

"No more than you." His brow furrowed. "I guess I have a lot to make up for. You know the story. How I got my patch. Ripper almost had my head when he found out."

Yeah, I knew the story. "And he forgave you, but it sounds like you haven't forgiven yourself."

He lifted a shoulder. "I've made peace with what I did. But I still feel like I owe the universe one, if you know what I mean."

I made a face. "I don't think the universe works that way. I don't believe there's a mysterious scale of justice, weighing right and wrong, trying to keep things in balance. If there were, Allsop wouldn't have the power he does, or his capacity to do harm."

Reno gave a noncommittal grunt. After a moment, he asked, "How about you? Why are you here risking your life on this mission when you could be safe in Pendleton with Finn?"

Longing pulled at me. I missed my man something fierce. And kissing up to Jonesy—the man who tortured Finn—made me sick to my stomach. I shook myself. I couldn't afford to think about Finn. Not now.

"I'm a soldier. Allsop poses a threat to everything I vowed to protect. I have a duty that I can't ignore."

"I respect that."

We followed Warm Springs Avenue toward downtown.

The first time we drove past a yellow poster with black lettering, I ignored it. As we got closer to downtown, more and more posters sprouted up, dandelion yellow and as thick as weeds. They appeared on at least one window on every block and on most of the light poles.

"Can we stop for a sec?" I asked Reno.

"Sure." He pulled the SUV to the curb.

I hopped out and walked over to a poster.

Across the top, large block letters spelled out *Allsop Day Celebration* and the date. Graphics of fireworks surrounded the words. Below that, *Join us at 1 p.m. for the First Annual Celebration of Allsop Day.* Then, *Attendance Mandatory for all Citizens.* Followed by, *Chips for Next Month's Rations will be Distributed to Those Who Attend.*

Jesus. That was one way to get people to put in an appearance at the big birthday bash. No-shows would starve during the next month.

"Unbelievable," I muttered, walking back to the SUV. Unbelievable, but not entirely surprising. The world couldn't be rid of Allsop quickly enough. Of course, if anything, Jonesy was worse, but in the inevitable chaos that followed Allsop's assassination, Havoc could make his move.

Sliding onto the passenger seat, I met Reno's eyes. "Ration chips? Really?"

"Yep." He threw the vehicle into gear and pulled back onto the roadway. "That's how we roll around here."

From downtown, we headed a few blocks north to the state capitol building, a sprawling neoclassical complex. Reno parked next to the main entrance plaza, in front of a replica of the Liberty Bell.

I climbed a handful of stairs and walked up to the symbol of freedom. "Proclaim liberty throughout all the land and unto all the inhabitants thereof." I read aloud the words inscribed on the bell, then turned to Reno. "Those words are the antithesis of everything Allsop stands for."

"Makes you wonder why he wants to hold his Allsop Day celebration here, doesn't it?" Reno replied. "The words might give folks ideas."

"It's a grand, theatrical setting. That would appeal to a man like Allsop." I paused and turned to my friend. "I haven't heard any of the details. Just how big is this shindig supposed to be?"

"Big. He's bringing his top folks in from Bend, Spokane, and Coeur d'Alene. And get this. He's trying to find enough musicians to put together a band. So far he's found a tuba player and a trombonist."

"Don't tell me." I lifted a hand. "He's going to have his soldiers march past the viewing stage doing the goosestep, like some tin-pot dictator? Is he going to have a tank roll by, too? Have an airplane do a flyover?"

"I wouldn't put it past him." Reno smirked.

"Allsop Day," I repeated, marveling at the man's ego. "What a grandiose, stupid waste of resources."

"The pageantry appeals to him," Reno said. "He's going to give a speech, accept accolades from his minions. Then after the executions, they'll probably serve cake and punch."

I wheeled on Reno. "Did you say executions?"

"Yeah." His expression grew grim. "Jonesy said they plan to set up gallows in the plaza and hang enemies of the state as part of the festivities."

"Jesus." Nausea clogged my throat. "Public hangings as part of a birthday party?"

"That's right. Allsop's been capturing Nampa Boys and holding them for the spectacle."

I sat down hard on the cold stone step.

David. Ethan.

Damn.

THIRTY-SEVEN

Finn

"You so much as twitch and I'll pull the trigger," Leonard told Ripper.

Outnumbered, his cover blown, Leonard had only one card to play. Kenzie.

Behind Leonard's back, I caught Ripper's eye and held my wrists apart, showing him that I wasn't as incapacitated as I appeared. Ripper dipped his chin. Leonard would think that Ripper was acknowledging his threat. I knew it was directed at me. Whatever went down, we'd do together. I'd follow Ripper's lead. His wife and his baby's lives hung in the balance. As a former Ranger, his combat experience far exceeded my own.

Ripper raised both hands in the air. "Nobody needs to die today."

"You armed?" Spittle flew from Leonard's mouth. Allsop's man had enough sense to be rattled by the big biker.

"Yeah, my Colt's in the shoulder holster under my cut."

Leonard shifted his weight from one foot to the other. He dug the gun barrel into Kenzie's neck. She gasped. Ripper's eyes flicked her way.

"Take it easy." Ripper's voice was mild, but only a fool could miss the menace behind the words.

Sweat dotted Leonard's brow. If I were in a standoff with a Janissary, I'd be shitting bricks too. "You try anything and I'll take her down with me."

Ripper didn't move a muscle. "You're the boss."

"Damned right I am," Leonard said.

I held my breath, my gaze locked on the gun pressed against Kenzie's neck. Ripper was fast, but would he dare draw his weapon if all Leonard had to do was squeeze the trigger?

Ever whimpered and Leonard glanced at Lorelei, his partner in crime. "Put the kid down. Get over here and take his gun."

Lorelei hesitated.

"Now," he barked.

Lorelei shuffled across the room, lifted Ripper's cut and gingerly pulled his Colt 1911 from the holster. She held the butt between her thumb and forefinger, frowning at it like it was a rattlesnake. So much for my hope that she'd turn the weapon on Leonard. If I had to guess, Lorelei had no idea how to disengage the safety, least of all aim and fire.

The situation was going downhill fast. Pulling on the ends of the bow, I unraveled the twine and freed my wrists. I doubled the twine over and stretched it between my hands. If I could get it around Leonard's neck...

"What do you want me to do with the gun?" Lorelei's voice quavered.

"You're next door to useless." He angled his head toward the small dining alcove. "Put it on the table, out of their reach."

She nodded numbly and stumbled toward the table. Leonard shook his head in disgust.

"Hey, asshole."

Leonard turned his eyes toward Ripper, who slowly lowered his hands and took a step forward. The murderous expression on Ripper's face would make any sane man piss himself. Leonard swung his gun toward the unarmed biker.

Ripper gave me the opening I needed.

I sprang at Leonard, throwing my arms over his head and yanking the twine hard against his gullet. His back arched. His hands clawed at the twine biting into his throat. Kenzie staggered away. Leonard's eyes bugged out. His face turned purple. I held on, no mercy in me, squeezing the life out of the bastard who'd threatened to kill Kenzie and who terrorized Ever.

I was dimly aware of Kenzie falling into Ripper's arms. Of Lorelei burying her face in her hands and sinking onto the floor. Of the door opening and Justin rushing inside. Ever screamed and the sound pierced my homicidal rage. My hands stilled. I turned my eyes toward the girl. Ever stared at me, white-faced and google-eyed.

What the fuck was I doing? I couldn't strangle a man to death in front of Ever. I couldn't be the boogeyman who haunted my little sweet pea's nightmares. I dropped the twine.

Leonard slumped against me, gasping for air, but clearly alive. I gently lowered his limp form to the floor.

"The bad man is going to be all right," I told Ever. "See, he's breathing and he's awake. But we got him and he'll never hurt anybody again."

"You promise?" she asked.

"Yeah, I promise."

"Okay."

Ripper flipped Leonard onto his stomach. "Hand me the twine."

I did. Ripper secured Leonard's hands behind his back. He cut another length of twine and tied his ankles together too. He stood and returned to Kenzie's side.

Justin dropped down onto the floor next to Lorelei. "Are you hurt, sweetheart?"

Lorelei shook her head, misery stamped across her features. Justin had no idea that his so-called girlfriend was a spy working in collusion with our enemy. Her face crumpled.

"Lorelei, baby, it's all right." Justin threw an arm across her shoulders. "It's over. You're safe."

Lorelei sobbed, her shoulders shaking.

Justin a was good man. He didn't deserve this. What would he do when he discovered that Lorelei had betrayed him? That she'd bombed our headquarters?

Sick at heart, I looked away from Justin and toward my other friends.

Ripper's hands glided over Kenzie's face and throat. He tilted her head to one side, gently touching the red spot where the gun had dug into her neck. His expression darkened.

"I'm okay," Kenzie said quietly.

Her assurance wasn't good enough for him. His hands skimmed down her body. He splayed his fingers across her belly, and he stilled, as if trying to commune with his unborn child.

"We're both okay," Kenzie assured him.

Ripper pressed a kiss to Kenzie's forehead, then turned his gaze to the man tied up on the floor.

"We need him alive." Justin's voice was low and urgent.

A muscle jumped in Ripper's jaw. Conflicting impulses flickered across his face. Vengeance warred with reason. Nobody could blame Ripper for craving blood, for wanting to gut the bastard who'd threatened to kill his wife.

I understood his wrath. I'd come close to killing Leonard myself. Thank God I'd come to my senses. A dead Leonard could tell no tales.

"Ripper." I gripped his arm.

His gaze slid to my hand, then he lifted his eyes to my face, his expression glacial.

I resisted the instinctive urge to pull my hand away from danger, the way I'd jerk my fingers back from a hot burner. "Havoc will want to interrogate Allsop's spy," I reminded him.

"I won't tell you shit," Leonard gasped out.

"I can make the fucker talk." Ripper's flat, dispassionate voice raised goose bumps across my shoulders. Sometimes I forgot that my friend had been the enforcer for an outlaw motorcycle club. I liked and respected him, but his moral code was different from mine. He'd never followed the rules of civilized society.

"Ripper." Kenzie angled her head toward Ever, who watched the exchange with wide, unblinking eyes.

Ripper looked at Ever. His expression softened. He nodded to his wife.

My chest squeezed tight. The little girl was sucking her thumb like a toddler. Shit.

Three steps brought me to Ever's side. "Come here, sweet pea," I said, praying she wasn't afraid of me now.

Without a word, she lifted her arms. Relief filled my veins.

I picked the child up. She clung to me like a monkey. "I got you. You're safe."

Ever was a tough, resilient kid. She'd bounced back from losing her family and her home to the pandemic. She'd settled into life at the ranch with a new family. We'd brought her to Pendleton to keep her safe from the threat of violence. Instead of dodging danger, I'd delivered her to a gun-toting enemy. Shit. Shit. Shit.

Whatever it took, I vowed. I'd do whatever it took to help her recover. I knew something about healing from trauma, didn't I? It wouldn't happen overnight, but Ever would get past this.

Lorelei lifted a tear-stained face. "I'll tell you everything I know."

Justin reared back, frowning in confusion. "Everything you know about what? What are you talking about?"

For a moment, nobody said a word.

"Lorelei is working with me, you dumb fuck." Leonard sucked in a breath and swallowed before continuing. "Looks like she pulled the wool over your eyes with her sweet and innocent act."

Justin's face went blank. "Lorelei?"

"It's true," she choked out. "I'm sorry." Her mouth fell open, like she wanted to explain herself, to offer some justification for what she'd done. She snapped her mouth shut. I've never seen a person look more defeated or more hopeless.

Lorelei's betrayal staggered Justin. Homicidal impulses rode Ripper hard. Neither man was thinking clearly. I had to step up.

"The downtown jail is empty," I said. "We need to put the prisoners in lockdown and inform Havoc about what happened."

"I'm not leaving Mac alone right now." The statement cost the biker. It was obvious that he desperately wanted to be present for the interrogation, but Kenzie came first. As she should.

"Lorelei, you have a car outside, don't you?" I asked.

She nodded wordlessly.

"We'll put Leonard in the trunk, nice and cozy, then Justin and I will drive the prisoners to the jail. Once they're locked up tight, Justin can go get Marcus and Rachel." I turned to Ripper. "Lorelei is willing to talk. We'll start with her. You'll get your chance to talk with Leonard later."

"Sounds good. You up to walking back to the motel, darlin'?" Ripper asked Kenzie.

"Yes. My knees have stopped shaking. I can walk."

Ripper crossed to my side and touched Ever's cheek. "Hey, kiddo. You're coming back to the motel with me and Mac. You wanna walk or do you want me to carry you?"

I expected Ever to stay quiet, to continue to stare blankly off into space. Ripper's either-or question roused her from her stupor.

"I'm not a baby." Her chin jutted out stubbornly. "I want to walk."

"All right. Let's get going." He held out a big hand. Thick silver rings glinted on his fingers, skulls and a Janissary head. Ever let go of my neck and slid to the floor. She slipped her small hand into Ripper's.

"Somebody should go to Uncle Bobby and Anton's place, to tell Mrs. B. what's going on," Kenzie suggested.

"I want Mrs. B.," Ever said. "And Fitzwilliam."

"We'll ask Marcus to send somebody to pick up Mrs. B.," I assured the girl. I hugged her goodbye. "See you in a while."

Ripper, Kenzie, and Ever departed.

Leonard was trussed up like a turkey. He wasn't going anywhere. I doubted that Lorelei would give us any trouble, but there was no point in taking a chance. She'd fooled us all before. I cut a length of twine.

This was on me. No way I'd ask Justin to shackle the woman. "Stand up," I ordered.

Lorelei wobbled to her feet.

"Turn around."

She put her back to me and held out her wrists. I bound them together. I glanced at Justin. "You ready?"

"Yeah." He was still looking shell-shocked.

"Keep an eye on Leonard while I put Lorelei in the car." I snagged her car keys from a bowl on the coffee table and led her outside.

"It's the white sedan." She pointed with her chin.

I helped Lorelei into a rear passenger seat, fastened the seat belt around her, then jogged back to the apartment. Justin and I carried Leonard to the back of the car.

"The trunk? Seriously?" he demanded.

"Do I need to gag you?" I demanded. We shoved him inside and slammed the trunk shut.

Nobody spoke during the short ride to the downtown police station. When I parked the car, Lorelei broke the silence.

"Justin… I… I never meant—"

"No." He cut her off. "No more lies."

She pressed her lips together and held her tongue.

I ran inside. Even when the cells were empty, the front desk was manned twenty-four-seen. "You have handcuffs?" I asked the soldier behind the desk.

"Yes, sir."

"I need two pairs."

He tossed the metal cuffs.

"Thanks."

Back at the car, I helped Lorelei climb out, then cut the twine binding her wrists and replaced it with a pair of police cuffs. Once inside the station, I hustled her past the front desk and down the hall to the interrogation room.

Without a protest, Lorelei sat down at the table. She held still while I threaded her shackles through the handcuff rings. "I want to cooperate, you know. I need your help."

My eyes snapped up to meet hers. "You planted a bomb. You got a funny way of asking for help."

"I—"

I raised a hand. "Save it for Havoc and Rachel."

I strode from the room. Justin and I hauled Leonard from the trunk. After cuffing his hands behind his back, we cut off the twine securing his arms and legs. He shuffled inside. The guard unlocked the door to the cellblock. We put Leonard into the first cell, the one formerly occupied by Jonesy.

His gaze traveled around the small cubical, over the metal cot, the nonfunctioning sink and toilet, before landing on the lidded five-gallon bucket in the corner.

"I need to piss," he said.

I pointed at the bucket. "Help yourself."

"With my hands tied behind my back?"

"You'll manage. Or not."

Mama would be ashamed of me for such pettiness. After the bastard held a gun on Kenzie and terrorized Ever, I didn't have it in me to care.

As one of Havoc's lieutenants, Justin outranked me. Ignoring that inconvenient fact, I kept command of the situation, at least for now. I tossed him the car keys.

"Go get Havoc and Rachel. Get somebody to bring Mrs. B. back to the motel."

"You don't want to come along?" He was still too stunned to take offense.

"If there's a third spy in town, there's a slim chance they'll try to rescue their buddies before we bring more soldiers in to fortify the station."

"Good thinking." He paused. "You're not carrying a weapon?"

I winced. "Ever keeps asking if she can hold my gun, so I've gotten out of the habit of wearing it when I'm spending time with her. I won't make that mistake again."

"I don't think that girl is going to want to touch a gun anytime soon," Justin said.

My lips pressed together in a bitter line. "Bet you're right."

"Here." Justin handed me his pistol. "You should be armed. Just in case."

"Thanks."

We stepped back into the lobby and locked the door to the cellblock. I sat down on the bench and set the pistol next to me. Justin ran to the car.

"What's going on?" the soldier asked.

"I don't have the authority to tell."

I leaned my head against the wall and shut my eyes, enjoying the first moment of peace since this debacle began. Thank God Justin had the sense not to tell his girlfriend that Georgia was away on a mission to Boise. Thank God Lorelei believed Georgia was visiting Valhalla. If Lorelei knew and she passed the information on to Leonard…

We dodged a bullet there.

A bullet. The image of Leonard jabbing a gun into Kenzie's throat popped into my mind.

How the hell had a simple visit to a friendly kindergarten teacher devolved into a near catastrophe? A friendly kindergarten teacher. I huffed out a breath. We'd all misjudged Lorelei, taken her at face value, bought her act. But was it an act? When Leonard pulled out a gun, Lorelei hadn't hesitated to help.

A car door slammed and I opened my eyes.

Marcus Havoc marched up the sidewalk, Rachel at his side, scampering to keep up with his long strides. Justin trailed behind, still wearing the baffled expression of a man who can't believe his world has fallen apart.

Throwing open the door, Marcus looked me up and down. "You're all right?"

"Not a scratch. Kenzie is shook up and Ever was scared shitless, but no physical harm."

Fury blazed in Havoc's eyes. His mouth twisted and he ran a hand down his face. Guilt—unearned guilt—branded his face. Kenzie and Ever were under his protection, and he'd failed them.

Rachel touched his arm. "Take a breath, boss."

Hands on hips, he stared down at the floor, visibly composing himself. When he lifted his head, the stoic commander once again held sway. "Lorelei is in the interrogation room?"

"Yes, sir," I said. "She said that she's eager to cooperate and that she needs our help."

"Do you believe her?"

"I dunno. When Leonard ordered her to tie me up, she only pretended to bind my wrists. She was ready to rabbit Ever away to safety. I didn't misread her intention. I trust my gut on that one. So…" I lifted my shoulders. "Will the real Lorelei please stand up."

"We'll get to the bottom of it," Rachel said.

"Rachel and I will conduct the interrogation," Havoc stated. "You can watch from the observation room if you want."

"Damn straight I want to watch," Justin put in.

Justin and I stood near the one-way glass in the observation room while Marcus and Rachel took chairs opposite Lorelei.

"Finn says you're willing to cooperate," Marcus said.

Lorelei gave a jerky nod. "I'll tell you whatever you want to know."

"Let's start with the basics. Are you really a kindergarten teacher from Meridian, Idaho?" Rachel asked. "Or was that some bullshit lie?"

"No, I really am… or was… a kindergarten teacher for the West Ada school district. I had twenty-four students in my class when the flu struck last spring."

Rachel leaned back in her chair and swung her red sneakers up onto the table. "You want to explain how a woman who spent her days teaching five-year-olds ended up planting C-4 explosive in Marcus Havoc's headquarters?"

Lorelei wove her fingers together, like she was a child saying her evening prayers. "When the flu killed everybody around me, I figured it was just a matter of time before it got me, too. I waited. It didn't happen. I went out looking to see if any of my friends survived. They hadn't." She swallowed. "Then I went to check on my students. I found Izzy."

"Izzy was one of your students?" Havoc asked.

"No. Her little brother, Caden, was in my class. Izzy is seven. Her mom and Caden died at the beginning of the pandemic. For a couple of weeks, it was just Izzy and her dad. They went around their neighborhood and cleaned out the cupboards of neighbors who had died. Filled jugs of water…" Her voice trailed off.

"What happened next?" Havoc asked.

"Izzy said her daddy woke up with a headache and fever. He sat her down and talked to her about rules for staying safe. Keep the doors locked and be careful with the flashlight at night. Be wary of strangers. Don't eat a can of food that you've left open overnight. Then he told her he had to go away. He said that she needed to take care of herself for a while. If he got better, he'd come back. If he didn't come back within ten days, she should lay low until she found somebody she could trust."

"The flu mania," Rachel suggested. "He was afraid he'd get the flu mania and become violent. He went away to make sure he couldn't hurt her. To either recover or die alone."

"That was my thought too," Lorelei agreed.

Hearing the story, my heart ached for both the little girl who was left behind and for the father who had no choice but to go away. He protected his child the only way he knew how, but dear lord, it must have torn his soul in two.

"So dad died and Izzy was by herself," Marcus prompted.

"Until one day, I pounded on their front door and called out for Caden. Izzy knew I wasn't a stranger—not if I knew Caden's name—so she opened the door. And that was that." She lifted her shoulders. "Izzy became the center of my world. Taking care of her, keeping her safe, the most important thing."

"A touching story." Rachel tilted her head to the side. "If it's true and not another one of your bullshit lies."

"It's true," Lorelei insisted. "I don't want to hide anything from you. Lying to you—lying to Justin—has been eating me alive."

At the mention of his name, Justin stiffened.

"Still doesn't explain what you're doing in Pendleton," Havoc growled.

"Well, the Nampa Boys eventually found us. They'd turned an old skating rink into a community center, a place where people could get supplies, see a nurse, and hang out with other survivors. Izzy and I were at the skating rink when Allsop's men attacked it. They killed a lot of people, took all of our supplies, but they kept Izzy and me alive."

"That much is true." Justin spoke for the first time. "When Havoc and I went to Boise to rescue Finn, we stopped in Meridian to talk to the leader of the Nampa Boys. We went to the skating rink and saw that it had been hit. Shelves were empty. Walls riddled with bullet holes. Bloodstains everywhere."

Havoc leaned over and spoke in Rachel's ear, probably relaying the same story.

"Eventually, I met with a man named Jonesy." Lorelei shuddered. "He scared the crap out of me. He said if I wanted to make sure that nothing bad happened to Izzy, I'd do exactly as he said." She dropped her head down to her clenched hands, then straightened up in the chair. "God help me, but I said yes. I sold my soul to keep Izzy safe. I had no idea how hard it would be to deceive good people. To deceive Justin."

"What was your assignment?" Havoc asked.

"Allsop knew that the Nampa Boys were going to evacuate civilians to Pendleton."

Justin jerked, clearly startled. "That was supposed to be a top secret operation."

"He knew about the evacuation?" Rachel sounded stunned.

"Jonesy told me that if Marcus Havoc wanted to feed hundreds of worthless mouths, he was welcome to them."

"The bastard," Rachel sputtered.

"My assignment was to join the evacuation," Lorelei continued. "They let me see Izzy before I left. She was living with a woman in Meridian, in an apartment complex that housed a group of Allsop's soldiers."

"What happened next?" Havoc asked.

"Leonard was already in position in Pendleton. I was to take orders from him. Allsop wanted me to get close to one of your top people. Leonard had seen the poster asking for people to volunteer for the school committee. The committee was a perfect way to meet Justin."

"God damn it. I'm such a chump," Justin muttered, shaking his head in disbelief.

"So you cozied up to Justin," Rachel bit out, not trying to hide her anger at this betrayal of her friend. "Trying to get him to talk about our operations."

"He never did." Lorelei sprang to Justin's defense. "He's too smart and too conscientious to blab, even to his girlfriend."

Justin folded his arms over his chest.

Havoc tapped a pen on the table. "Tell us about the bomb."

"Allsop wanted to kill you and your lieutenants. Leonard smuggled the C-4 into town. He showed me how to set the set the detonator and ordered me to hide it in your conference room." Her gaze turned from Havoc to Rachel, her expression beseeching. "I didn't want to do it. I didn't want to hurt anybody."

"You're telling us that you fucked up on purpose?" Rachel asked.

Lorelei hung her head, then lifted her eyes. "I pretended that I didn't know that the meeting had been postponed. I set the C-4 to go off when the room was empty."

"Why were you packing to leave town today?" Havoc asked.

Lorelei squeezed her eyes shut. Her words came out in a rush. "I met with Leonard yesterday. He ordered me to invite you all over for dinner tonight and to poison your food. He gave me a highly lethal toxin to use that can't be tasted in food or drink."

"Well… shit." Rachel flopped back in her chair.

My blood chilled. If Lorelei had followed through, Kenzie… the baby… Ripper… we'd all have died tonight.

Lorelei wagged her head back and forth. "I… I couldn't do it. I could never hurt any of you. I could never hurt Justin."

Justin sucked in a deep breath and laid a hand on the glass.

"So I decided to get out of town. To drive back to Boise and to try to get to Izzy before Allsop found out that I turned on him. I thought I might be able to grab her and run."

Justin wheeled around and stomped out of the observation room. A second later, the door to the interrogation room flew open. He stalked toward Lorelei and dropped down on his haunches next to her.

"I don't expect—" she started.

"Was any of it real?" He cut her off. "You and me. Was it all an act?"

Her hands tugged against the cuffs, as if her first instinct was to reach out to him. She sighed, her expression resolute, but without one lick of hope. "It was real. I don't expect you to believe me—or to forgive me even if you do—but I want you to know that it was real. You're a good man, Justin Mrachek. Don't ever doubt yourself. Falling in love with you was the easiest thing I've ever done. And lying to you was the hardest."

Justin lifted his chin. "If you loved me, why didn't you trust me enough to tell me that you were being blackmailed by Allsop? Why didn't you ask for help?"

Lorelei blinked back tears. Her lips trembled. "I was afraid. Afraid that Allsop would find out. Afraid that he'd hurt Izzy. Afraid that you'd hate me. Fear froze me in place, until it was too late and I had no choice but to run… I'm sorry. I truly am."

Justin's jaw worked as he pondered her words. After a long moment, he stood. His gaze cut to Havoc and Rachel. Without another word, he strode from the room. I thought he'd come back into the observation room. Instead, he kept right on walking, his footsteps echoing down the hall.

Despite my anger, pity for Lorelei stirred in my heart.

What were we going to do with Allsop's spy?

THIRTY-EIGHT

Georgia

"Winnie tells me that you and Reno went to the capitol yesterday."

I was searching the pantry shelves for another jar of thyme. Elliot Allsop's sonorous voice caught me unawares. I hammed it up, gasping as my hand flew to my chest, and lurching backward.

Clad—as always—in an elegant suit, Allsop's trim figure blocked the narrow door to the pantry. "I startled you," he said. "I apologize."

I gave a weak laugh and wiped my palms on my apron. "No, I'm sorry, Mr. Allsop. I was daydreaming. What can I do for you, sir?"

"You accompanied Reno to the capitol yesterday?" he asked again.

"Yes, sir." I frowned. "Winnie suggested I go with him to see the town. We weren't… fraternizing." I deliberately stumbled over the big word. "We're just friendly acquaintances."

He waved a dismissive hand. "I've no concerns about fraternization. I'm simply curious. During your outing, did Reno say anything that might suggest he has second thoughts about shifting his loyalty from Robert Banyon to me?"

"No." I jerked my head from side to side. "In fact, Reno's the exact opposite of a disgruntled employee. He loves it here. You should have heard him raving about the good coffee and the nice food."

"Very good." Allsop inclined his head. "Keep me apprised of any change in his attitude. And do let me know if you overhear any complaints from any of the other men."

"Will do," I said brightly.

Without another word, Allsop pivoted and walked away.

The soldier I frequently saw stationed outside the war room jogged into the kitchen.

"What can we get for you?" Winnie looked up and smiled at the young man.

Mr. Allsop had requested coq au vin for dinner. Winnie was busy cutting up a chicken. An empty bowl, a bottle of red wine, a jigger of brandy, and a can of chicken stock sat on the counter next to the cutting board.

"Mr. Jonesy asked for coffee in the war room," the young man said.

Winnie held up hands coated with raw chicken juices and glanced at the coffee maker.

"I'll bring them the coffee," I offered. "You need to get the chicken in the marinade."

"That would be a help. Thanks," Winnie said.

I ground beans and poured water into the coffee maker. While the coffee brewed, I set up the tray.

"I've never made coq au vin with dehydrated onions and mushrooms." Winnie sounded skeptical. "I hope it'll taste all right."

"It'll be great," I assured her. "Can you save some for us?"

She winked. "Always."

I picked up the tray and headed downstairs. The friendly soldier held open the door to the war room.

Jonesy glanced up from the conference table and beamed at me. I repressed a shudder. His phony Mr. Nice Guy act creeped me out.

"Carrie, I was hoping you'd be the one to bring the coffee." His eyes cut to the soldier. "Shut the door."

"Yes, sir." The young man closed the door, leaving me alone with Jonesy and Reno.

"Serve the coffee then take a seat." Jonesy gestured toward a chair next to Reno, who sat across from him. I poured coffee for the men, then sat down. Jonesy took one sip, then leaned back in his chair. He steepled his hands together and studied me. "You and Reno went down to the capitol plaza yesterday to check out the site of the Allsop Day extravaganza."

It was a statement, not a question. "That's right."

"What did you think?" he asked.

About the plaza? About the planned celebration? About the promised executions? I didn't know where Jonesy was going with this, so I played it safe. "It looks like a nice place to hold a fancy party."

"It is. A lot of powerful folks will be coming to town for the celebration, men I'd very much like to talk to. Men I hand selected for their jobs and who owe me. And it's a perfect excuse to send for my nephew in Bend. He and his pretty little girlfriend can come to town for the party and stick around for a while. He's loyal to his Uncle Jonesy, not too bright, but a good fellow to have at my side during these turbulent times."

I cut my eyes toward Reno, whose bland expression revealed nothing.

"Reno assures me that the two of you are on the same page," Jonesy added. "That you're both Team Jonesy, like you said the other day."

"That's right. We are. If it wasn't for you, we'd still be doing drudge work in Pendleton, living in freezing quarters and eating canned beans."

"And bending the knee to that sanctimonious prick, Havoc," Reno growled.

Jonesy cackled, delighted. "I asked you to keep your ear to the ground, pretty girl. You hear anything interesting?"

"I have." I leaned forward and dropped my voice to a conspiratorial whisper. "Mr. Allsop asked me to spy on you for him." I piled on, fanning Jonesy's paranoia. "He wants me to report back if I overhear you saying anything that sounds even slightly disloyal. To tell him who you're hanging out with."

"Well isn't that interesting," Jonesy drawled. "The old boy can sense the change in the wind. I'll be extra careful not to stir up his suspicions, at least not for the next little while, not until I'm ready to make my move."

"You got a timetable, sir?" Reno asked.

"I have two big things coming up." Jonesy's lips curved up in a smile so menacing that my lungs froze. "First off, I'll shoot Allsop on the steps of the capitol, right in the middle of the celebration. Let everybody see that he's gone, and I'm in charge."

"And number two?" Reno asked.

"A couple days after the celebration, I'm going to take a squad of soldiers to a ranch in Oregon. A place called Valhalla. We'll go in loaded for bear. Bazookas. Automatic rifles. Grenades. Shit, if it wasn't so far, I'd bring a tank. We'll kill everybody on site. Burn the ranch to the ground. Salt the fucking earth so nothing and nobody can ever live there again."

"That sounds personal, boss," Reno said.

"It is. The fuckers there got the drop on me and carted me off to Pendleton. I owe them. Mr. Allsop would've approved of the mission. The fuck-weasel who killed his son is hiding out there." He snorted. "I'll be doing Elliot Allsop a favor postmortem."

Reno gave a low whistle. "Hope you'll let me in on the fun."

"We'll see, son. We'll see."

THIRTY-NINE

Finn

"It's an extraction." Marcus jabbed a finger at me. "You'll retrieve the child, then turn around and come back to Pendleton."

"Yeah, I got it." I resisted the urge to roll my eyes. I'm not military and Marcus was my friend. Despite that, even I knew better than to make a face when a commanding officer gave an order.

"Seriously." Rachel piled on. "Meridian is only ten miles from Boise. Allsop's people operate in Meridian, but it's not crawling with them the way Boise is. You're on Allsop's Most Wanted list. Under no circumstances are you to enter the Boise city limits."

How many times would they tell me? Did they think I'd risk the operation and myself by sneaking into Boise on the off chance of catching a glimpse of Georgia? How dumb and desperate did they think I was?

I couldn't resist. "Yes, Mom."

Rachel smacked my arm. "I mean it. Stay the hell out of Boise."

"We will." Ripper slipped extra magazines into the ammo pouch on his shoulder harness. "We'll grab the kid and go."

The black Allsop SUV—the one we purloined from Jonesy—was pulled up next to the entrance to headquarters with a tank full of gas. We stowed two five-gallon cans of gasoline in the back of the vehicle. Snacks, water, a pillow, and a blanket awaited Izzy on the back seat.

Ripper and I wore gray T-shirts and jeans, the easy-to-replicate uniform of Allsop's soldiers. He left his Janissary cut in Kenzie's care. Dressed in Allsop's colors, driving an official SUV, we weren't likely to be challenged when we drove into enemy territory. Lorelei gave us the address of the apartment where Izzy was living. We'd knock on the door, say a doctor wanted to see the girl, hustle her into the van, then hit the road.

And Bob's your uncle, as Mrs. B. liked to say. With any luck, we'd be back home in Pendleton within twelve hours, the girl safely in tow.

After we finished interrogating Leonard and planning Izzy's rescue, I spent the evening with Ever and Mrs. B. We ate dinner together. Back at the motel, we played a few rounds of Old Maid and Crazy Eights. While Mrs. B. did a crossword puzzle, Ever and I snuggled down under a pile of quilts. I read *Harriet the Spy* aloud until she finally nodded off.

At the crack of dawn, Kenzie, Ripper, and I walked to the city hall complex. We left Mrs. B. and Ever sound asleep in my old room at the motel. While Ripper and I got last-minute instructions, Kenzie waited for Ripper in the lobby, unwilling to let him leave without a final goodbye.

"Be careful." A worried frown creased Rachel's brow.

I hugged my friend. "Don't worry. We won't do anything stupid. We'll be back before you know it."

I shook hands with Havoc, then followed Ripper to the lobby.

Kenzie tilted up her cheek for a quick kiss from me. "Stay safe." She smiled, but her lips trembled.

Ripper pulled Kenzie into his arms. She tucked her head under his chin, and they held on to each other, rocking back and forth to some rhythm only the two of them could sense. I walked outside, giving them space to finish their goodbyes in private.

Walking up to the black SUV triggered all sorts of unwanted memories. How many times had I driven around Boise in one of these blamed vehicles? An Allsop SUV meant nothing good. Nervous folk skittered out of the way when they saw us coming. I never thought to ride in one again, but here I was.

"You're doing God's work, dear boy." That's what Mrs. B. told me when I explained where we were going. That knowledge took the sting out of driving around in this accursed contraption.

I slid behind the wheel. A few minutes later, Ripper jumped into the front passenger's seat. I turned the key and we headed toward the freeway.

"I'm surprised Kenzie let you come on the rescue," I said.

Ripper turned to me, a single eyebrow raised. "Let me come?"

Yeah, I could have phrased that better. "Not that you need permission," I hastened to add.

His teeth flashed white. "Just jerking your chain, man." He sobered. "Listen, after yesterday, if Mac asked me not to come on the rescue, I would've stayed in Pendleton. She comes first."

Curiosity got the best of me. "So what happened? How did you talk her into it?"

"I didn't." He settled his wide shoulders back against the seat cushion. "After you told us about Lorelei and the little girl, Mac cried. Pregnancy hormones have made her more sentimental, especially about kids. She said that hearing about Izzy reminded her of Ever, orphaned and dependent on the goodwill of strangers."

"Izzy put me in mind of Ever too," I admitted, waving at the sentries manning the freeway entrance. "I lay awake last night thinking about what would have happened to our girl if she ended up in the wrong hands."

"Same here. Mac told me that I need to bring Izzy to safety. She said I have the expertise and the skills to pull off the rescue. Said she was confident that I'd come back to her safe and sound. So I found Havoc and told him I wanted to go to Meridian."

"Good for her." I tossed him a smile. "Still, it must be hard for Kenzie to watch you go off on a mission."

Ripper twisted his wedding band around his finger. "Yeah, it is, but you can count on my woman to do what she thinks is right."

Those words reminded me of somebody I knew. Out of the blue, fear for Georgia constricted my lungs. Shit. I white-knuckled the steering wheel.

Ripper shot me a concerned look. "Georgia?"

"Yeah." I gulped in a breath. "I know she's smart. I know she's trained. But Jonesy is a cunning bastard. If he figures out what she's doing—" I paused, then started again. "He enjoys hurting people. He gets off on inflicting pain."

"I get it, brother. If Jonesy got his mitts on Mac, I'd scorch the earth to get her back safe. But like you said, Georgia knows what she's doing. You gotta shout down that voice in your head that tells you she's in trouble. Breathe through the fear. If it gets the best of you, don't keep it bottled up. Talk to a friend. Talk to me."

"That's the most sentences I've ever heard you string together at one time," I said. "How'd you get to be so smart?"

Ripper grinned. "Life."

We followed I-84 east toward Boise. Four hours after we departed Pendleton, we exited the freeway and made our way toward Settlers Park in Meridian. The apartment complex where Izzy lived was nearby. I pulled up in front of the building and cut the engine.

Allsop men expect everybody to eat shit and do as they're told. I slapped on my game face. We strutted up the front walk, large and in charge. I kept my head on the swivel and my eyes peeled, looking for signs of trouble, but the place was quiet. Nobody answered when I pounded on the door to apartment 4-B.

"Don't mean there's nobody home," Ripper said. "I'll go around back and look through the patio door."

He took only one step before the door to 4-C cracked open. A blond woman who looked to be in her thirties peered through the opening. "If you're looking for Angie, she's out."

The stranger was either one of the civilians who opted not to flee, or she was somehow in cahoots with Allsop's regime.

"Good afternoon, ma'am." I offered the insincere smile of an Allsop hatchet man, the kind of fellow who deployed perfect manners right up until the moment when politeness died and brutality began.

"Sir." Her head jerked like a puppet on a string, and her fingers clutched at the collar of her blue sweater.

I scared the woman, and didn't that make me feel like an asshole.

"We're looking for Izzy," Ripper said.

"Oh." Surprise and worry skipped across her features. "Um… The rain finally stopped, so Angie took Izzy to the park." She pointed up the road.

"We appreciate your cooperation, ma'am." I tipped my head.

Ripper and I jogged back to the SUV. I felt eyes on me and looked back over my shoulder. A man stood in the window of apartment 4-C, a two-way radio pressed to his ear.

"Ripper." I jerked my head toward the window.

"I see."

We hopped into the SUV and drove toward Settlers Park. I brought the vehicle to a halt next to a playground. Cigarette in hand, a woman sat on a metal bench, a dozen yards from a dark-haired little girl who scrambled up the ladder of a play structure. The woman watched us approach, her expression wary.

"Angie?" Ripper rumbled.

She flicked ash off her cigarette. "Yeah?"

"We're here to pick up Izzy," I said.

The woman stared at me blankly.

"For her appointment." I waited a beat, then huffed out a deep sigh, like I had no patience for dealing with a dimwit. "With the doctor."

She frowned. "Nobody told me anything about a doctor appointment."

"Not the first time somebody got their wires crossed." Ripper shook his head in disgust. "We're here now, and we don't want to keep the doc waiting."

"Okay." She stubbed out her cigarette and stood. "Izzy, get your ass over here. We're going to the doctor."

We? No, *we* weren't going anywhere.

Izzy slid down a yellow slide, then scampered toward us. She stopped a few feet away, her cheeks as pink as her coat in the chilly early afternoon. "I don't want to go to the doctor again."

"Listen, brat, you'll do as you're told," Angie snapped.

Ripper tilted his head. I followed his eyes. In the distance, two men wearing telltale gray shirts walked across the basketball court, heading straight toward us.

Angie looked toward the men. "Tommy?"

Shit. The man with the radio must have called Tommy. Was he Angie's man?

"Time to go," Ripper said in a low voice.

The men picked up the pace. Two more Allsop men wound between the picnic tables working their way toward us.

"What's going on?" Angie asked.

I dropped on my haunches next to Izzy. "Your friend Lorelei sent us to take you away from the bad people."

Hope dawned in the girl's eyes. "Lorelei?"

"That's right, kiddo." I hopped up.

"What the fuck is going on?" Angie's voice was shrill. She grabbed the sleeve of my jacket, her sparkly fingernails latching onto my arm.

The four men bearing down on us pulled out guns. A shot rang out as one of them fired into the sky.

Izzy clamped her hands over her ears and screamed.

No way. No way was I going to allow another little girl to be traumatized by violence. Nor would I let anything keep Ripper from getting back to Kenzie.

With my free hand, I dug into my pocket and tossed Ripper the keys to the SUV.

"Take Izzy and go," I shouted.

"The fuck I will." Ripper drew his Colt, took aim, and dropped one of the men.

Angie leaped onto my back, beating me about the head with her fists and screeching like a banshee. I whirled around, trying to dislodge her, but the woman locked her legs around my waist and clung to me like a burr.

Izzy screamed. Ripper cursed.

A bullet flew past me, narrowly missing Ripper's head. With Angie on my back, I lurched from side to side. Ripper couldn't get off a clean shot.

"Go," I roared.

Ripper scooped Izzy into his arms and bolted for the SUV. One of the strangers took aim at my friend. Didn't the bastard care if he risked hitting a child?

I threw myself sideways into the path of the bullet. Felt a punch to my upper arm, followed by sizzling heat. Jerking my head, I glanced down. Just below my shoulder, the sleeve of my jacket had split open. Tufts of down filling—stained red by my blood—poked out of the slit.

Shock knocked me off balance. I stumbled, then recovered, swinging my head to look for Ripper.

The SUV peeled out of the parking lot. Ripper and Izzy got away. The air whooshed out of my lungs. Relief staggered me. No matter what, the biker would keep the child safe.

At the sight of my blood, Angie totally lost her shit. She clawed at my face, shrieking louder than ever.

The first of the three men skidded to a stop and hauled her off my back. He grabbed her upper arms and shook her like a rag doll.

She stopped screaming, and in the sudden silence, my pulse pounded in my ears.

A sob burst out of Angie. "Tommy. They took Izzy. They took our baby. You have to get her back."

Tommy pivoted toward me. I wobbled, my legs going weak. Bracing my hands on my knees, I looked up just in time to see Tommy's fist flying at my face.

Darkness.

FORTY

Georgia

The whirr of the machine almost drowned out the sound of the front door banging open. Almost, but not quite. I looked up from vacuuming the Persian rug in the living room.

A grim-faced soldier marched into the foyer. Behind him, two soldiers frog-marched a prisoner through the door. With a snarl, one of the men shoved their captive. His hands were bound behind his back. He staggered, righted himself, then snapped his spine straight.

I blinked, unbelieving. My heart stuttered and dropped to my stomach.

Oh sweet Jesus. Finn.

What on earth was Finn doing in Boise?

I gaped. From temple to chin, bruises mottled his face. His lip was split wide open. An angry red gash—as if someone had clawed him—cut across one cheek. Below his shoulder, blood seeped through the sleeve of his coat. The fabric was torn and the down filling spattered ruby-red.

A knife wound, maybe.

Or a bullet.

Heartsick, with a trembling hand, I turned off the vacuum. It took a supreme effort of will, but I wiped the horror from my face.

There was no point in pretending I didn't recognize Finn. Back in Pendleton, he'd berated me in front of Jonesy. All part of our act. Surprise was an acceptable reaction to his sudden appearance. Anguish and fear were not.

I followed the men into the kitchen and pointed a finger at Finn. "I know him." Accusation filled my startled voice. "He works for Marcus Havoc."

"Well, duh," the first soldier—the one who led the way into the house—scoffed.

Finn smirked and spat a mouthful of blood onto the clean kitchen floor. He fixed contemptuous eyes on me. "Look at you, sweetheart. Working in the big house. Guess it pays to turn traitor."

My stomach clenched. The man I loved was playing along, preserving my cover, trying to protect me, even now, when he couldn't protect himself. And there wasn't a damned thing I could do to return the favor. At least not yet.

Don't you dare go weak at the knees. I gripped the edge of the counter, steadying myself.

"Is Jonesy here?" the soldier asked me.

Oh my God. Jonesy. Finn's personal demon, the man who'd delighted in hurting him.

"Jonesy and Mr. Allsop are downstairs in the war room." My lips felt cold and stiff.

"Go get him," the man barked.

I jerked. "Yes, sir."

My gaze darted to Finn. His chin jutted defiantly into the air. No fear showed on his face, only calm resolve.

Our eyes met. In a fraction of a second, a million unspoken words passed between us. Thank God I'd opened my heart to him. Thank God I hadn't waited for some mythical safety, a safety we might never find. If that sliver of time together in Pendleton was all we ever had, it was still a gift from an often cruel universe. A blessing.

He knew I loved him. I knew he loved me. Whatever happened, we were good.

Tearing my gaze away, I dashed from the kitchen.

The friendly young sentry assigned to guard the war room frowned as I ran up to him. "What's wrong?"

"I need to talk to Jonesy."

"Okay." He opened the door and I stepped inside. Jonesy, Reno, and Mr. Allsop swung their eyes to me.

I pressed a hand to my chest. "I apologize for the interruption."

"What is it, my dear?" Mr. Allsop asked.

"Finn Rasmussen. Your men captured him."

Mr. Allsop raised one manicured brow and rose to his feet. "Did they, indeed?"

Jonesy slapped the table, a grin spreading across his face. "Oh, happy day."

On his lips, the words were a gross perversion of the old hymn.

"He's upstairs in the kitchen." Each word I spoke heaped coals of fire on my head, made me complicit in whatever happened to the man I loved.

"Excellent." Allsop smiled. "Thank you, Carrie, for delivering the news."

"My pleasure, sir."

The men walked briskly from the room. Reno's hand brushed over mine as he passed, a reassuring touch from a friend. I trailed behind them up the stairs and to the kitchen.

Allsop paused in the arched opening to the room, his fingers steepled together over his chest, satisfaction writ large across his patrician face. Jonesy stood next to his employer. His weight shifted from one foot to the other. He stared at Finn with avid eyes. It was clear that Jonesy was dying to speak, but he held back, probably out of deference to his boss.

"Finn Rasmussen." Allsop inclined his head. "After your narrow escape from execution, you're the very last man I expected to see again in Boise. How desperate must Havoc be that he sent *you* to beard the lion in his den?"

"The lion's den?" Finn rolled his eyes. "Now that's a highfalutin name for this joint. A lion is supposed to be the king of the beasts, isn't he? You folks are more like a pack of jackals."

Jonesy's smile was all teeth. "Show respect to your betters, son."

Finn answered the reproach with a scornful snort.

Allsop raised a hand, silencing the men. He turned to the soldiers. "How did you come upon him?"

The first soldier snapped to attention. "I'm Tommy. My girlfriend Angie and I have been taking care of a little girl for Mr. Jonesy. An hour ago, two men showed up, driving an Allsop SUV, claiming they needed to take Izzy to a doctor appointment. A neighbor radioed to give me a heads-up." He spread his hands. "First I heard of a doctor's appointment, so I took some men and headed to the park to make sure everything was on the up-and-up."

Allsop waved an impatient hand. "And then?"

"We spooked the men. Angie overhead this guy"—he pointed to Finn—"tell Izzy that Lorelei sent them to take her away from the bad people. Angie tried to stop them, but the other man got away with Izzy."

"He got away with the child. How regrettable." Allsop glanced at Jonesy. "It would appear that Lorelei betrayed us."

"It sure does look that way," Jonesy agreed.

"Which suggests that she has apprised Havoc of her assignment in Pendleton."

"Yes, sir," Jonesy agreed.

Allsop sighed, then tilted his head, a thoughtful expression on his face. "Unfortunate, but not altogether a tragedy."

"Sir?" Jonesy looked puzzled.

"My birthday celebration. Allsop Day. Finn Rasmussen is the crown jewel of traitors. I can think of few things more gratifying than featuring Rasmussen as the centerpiece of the festivities."

Jonesy's eyes sparkled. "He's the big cheese, all right. The Nampa Boys are nothing compared to him. We'll string him up with the other traitors in the grand finale."

The eagerness in Jonesy's eyes chilled me to the bone.

"Yes." Allsop shot Jonesy a sharp look. "That means I'll want him alive and on his feet for the execution. You can rough him up a bit." Allsop's eyes skated to Finn, taking in the bruises and bloody arm. "A bit more, that is. But otherwise you're to leave him alone. Lock him up with the others to await execution."

Jonesy's jaw tightened. "Yes, sir. I understand."

"Mr. Allsop." Reno pointed at Finn's arm. "Looks like somebody winged him. If we want him alive and kicking for the execution, we should clean and dress the wound. I'd hate to see an infection take him first and spoil your fun."

"I suppose you're right," Allsop said.

"I took a first aid class at the Red Cross." I spoke up, only slightly twisting the truth. Advanced first aid—controlling bleeding, cleaning wounds, hooking up an IV, CPR—were skills I mastered during basic training.

"Very well. Go ahead. There's a kit under the bathroom sink in the hall."

Heart thumping, I ran down the hall and retrieved a duffel bag labeled First Aid. Back in the kitchen, I turned to Finn. "Sit down on a stool."

Allsop brushed his palms together, as if washing his hands of the situation. "Reno, after Carrie finishes cleaning his wound, I want you and these good men to take Rasmussen to the penitentiary and lock him up with the other condemned prisoners."

"Yes, sir." Reno smiled. "My pleasure."

"Excuse me, Mr. Allsop." Tommy spoke up.

"Yes?"

Tommy cleared his throat. "I heard there's a bounty for the men who capture Finn Rasmussen."

"Why, yes, how remiss of me to forget. Jonesy, allow each of these men to select a bottle of alcohol from my private stock. Double their meat rations for the next month. Each man may choose either a carton of cigarettes or a box of chocolates from the luxury warehouse." He offered Tommy a shark's smile, all teeth and utterly lacking in warmth. "Angie would like that, wouldn't she? Candy or cigarettes to console her for the loss of the child."

"Yes, sir." Tommy shuffled his feet. "Thank you, sir."

"Jonesy, with me."

Jonesy's mouth twisted as he bit back the protest I saw glittering in his eyes. Too bad. No doubt at some point Jonesy would be free to rough Finn up *a bit*—as Allsop promised—but that time wasn't now.

With three of Allsop's soldiers in the room, Finn and I couldn't speak freely. He perched on a counter stool.

"Can you take off the cuffs so I can get his coat off?" I asked the first soldier.

"No can do. Push the coat off his shoulder, then cut off his sleeve."

"You're the boss."

I unzipped Finn's jacket, then shoved the coat off his shoulders.

He affected an air of indifference when I examined the furrow left in his skin by the bullet.

Fragments of cloth and tiny white feathers were stuck in the wound. If it hurt when I cleaned out the injury and dabbed it with antiseptic, he gave no indication of it, but I suppressed a wince.

I took my time bandaging it. Did my touch give him any comfort? His blank expression gave nothing away, but I felt a small tremor when I laid my hand on his shoulder. I allowed my fingers to linger on his skin.

I love you. If mental telepathy were real, if touch could convey sentiment, Finn knew what he meant to me, and that I'd do whatever it took to save him.

"We're all done here," I said too soon for my liking. I turned to Reno. "Do you guys want lunch before you go to the prison?"

If I fed the soldiers, I'd pretend to assume that I could give something to Finn to eat, too. They'd feed him in the prison. They wouldn't want him too weak to walk to the gallows, but I'd bet good money that he'd still go hungry and thirsty.

I widened my eyes at my friend. *Get with the program. Say yes.*

"Nah." Reno said. "But if you're free, I'd like to have dinner with you tonight." He smiled flirtatiously.

One of the soldiers elbowed another and snickered. "Smooth," he crooned.

"Are you asking me on a date?" I asked slowly, playing dumb.

"Yeah, I am."

I stared at my friend. "Um…"

"C'mon," he urged. "We'll drive around the city. Find a nice place to park and watch the sun go down." He waggled his brows suggestively, hamming it up for the soldiers. "You can bring the first aid kit along. If Mr. Allsop gives you any grief, tell him we're going to check on the prisoner's wound. Make sure it isn't showing signs of infection, you know." He winked, as if we'd be pulling a fast one on the boss, managing a date under the pretext of keeping his prize prisoner healthy.

"Okay," I said. "Why not? It's a date."

He shot a look of triumph at the soldiers. The Janissary had scored. One of the men raised a hand and high-fived Reno.

"Now that that's settled, let's get this bastard into lockup." Reno strutted from the room. I tugged Finn's jacket up over his shoulders.

He stood. "Thanks for cleaning my wound."

I swallowed. "You're welcome."

A soldier grabbed Finn's arm and shoved him toward the front hallway. I watched the soldiers escort Finn out of the house.

As soon as the front door closed behind them, I stumbled over to the counter stool Finn had vacated. I touched a leather cushion that still held a hint of warmth from my man's body.

"Finn," I whispered.

FORTY-ONE

Ripper

I dumped the kid onto the front passenger seat, then ran to the driver's side of the SUV. Rage rode me hard. My jaw clenched. Red spots rioted in front of my eyes. Fantasies of murder and mayhem filled my brain.

Always prided myself on my ability to keep a cool head under any circumstance, but an Allsop fucker took a shot at me when I was carrying a child. A child. My callous persona up and fled, leaving me half-blind with fury. Maybe Mac's pregnancy—the prospect of becoming a father—was making me soft, especially where kids were concerned?

Shit. I couldn't afford that.

"Put on your seat belt," I barked, slamming the driver's door shut. The engine turned over. I hit the gas and careened out of the parking lot, then checked over my shoulder for signs of pursuit.

Nothing. Guess the bastards were busy taking down Finn, and didn't that knowledge just bite? I'd left a brother behind in enemy hands while I beat a retreat to safety.

"Fuck." I pounded my fist on the steering wheel.

The kid gave me the stink eye. "That's a naughty word."

I cut my eyes toward her. She shrunk back against the seat looking scared. Of me.

Fuck. Groaning inwardly, I bit back the word this time. I held my breath for a count of ten, then blasted the air from my lungs.

"Sorry, kid. My bad. Seat belt," I reminded her, my voice gentler this time.

"Okay." Her small fingers worked the buckle. "Lorelei really sent you?"

"Yeah. I'm taking you to Pendleton. You'll see Lorelei there."

Lorelei was locked up at the police station, but I bet Havoc would let the girl see her.

I raced south to I-84. Once I hit the freeway, I floored it, eager to put as much distance as possible between us and the Allsop pricks. The speedometer topped one hundred miles per hour.

The kid frowned, watching me with judgment in her eyes. I sighed. Least she wasn't crying hysterically, which I'd half expected under the circumstances.

"You gotta problem?" I asked.

"You're driving too fast, mister."

Really? She was busting my balls over breaking the speed limit?

"Ripper," I corrected her.

"What?"

"Name's Ripper."

Silence. Then after a minute, "Are you pulling my leg?"

"About what?"

"Your name. Is it really Ripper?"

"Yeah." What was the kid's problem?

"Your mom and dad named you Ripper?" she persisted.

I shifted my weight. She had me there. "Not exactly. My… uh… friends call me Ripper. My folks named me Alejandro."

"Ah-ha!" she cried, looking as proud as a detective who cracked a case. "That was my grandpa's name, too. It's a good name, not dumb like Ripper. I'm going to call you Alejandro." She settled back in her seat, grinning. "We got anything to eat, Alejandro?"

That was that. Subject closed, as far as the kid was concerned.

"Yeah." I cocked a thumb. "Peanuts and pudding cups in the back."

"Pudding? Chocolate?" She craned her neck, unbuckled her seat belt, and started to scramble over the console.

"Hey." I used my don't-fuck-with-me voice. "Keep your seat belt on."

She flounced back onto her seat and jutted out her chin. "How come you get to speed and use bad words, but I have to keep my seat belt on?"

Jesus Christ, this was gonna be a long trip.

"Soon as we get past Caldwell, I'll stop the SUV. You can climb in the back. Got a pillow and blanket there. Snacks and water, too. You might wanna take a nap, kid."

Even I heard the hope in my voice.

She snorted. "Do I look like a baby?"

Hope died and I grunted a protest.

"My name is Izzy. Call me that instead of kid. It's friendlier."

A sigh escaped my lungs.

"Do you know any songs from kids' movies?" Izzy asked. "I know lots. I can teach you."

Yeah, it was gonna be a long fucking trip.

Four hours later, I pulled onto the exit to downtown Pendleton. The sentries waved me past. I drove to the city hall, parked, and jumped out. Havoc, Justin and Rachel stood outside waiting for us.

"What happened?" Havoc demanded as I slid open the passenger door and offered Izzy a hand.

"Four of Allsop's men showed up. Fired on us. I grabbed the kid and ran to the SUV."

"Finn?" Havoc's question felt like an indictment.

"Last I saw, he was on his feet with a crazy woman latched onto his back. The Allsop men were on him before he could get away."

"He's alive?"

"Far as I know, yes." I met Havoc's eyes. "I'm going back for him."

"Ripper!" I swung my head and looked toward the street. Mac scurried across the parking lot, a huge smile on her face.

I ran to her and swept her into my arms. "Told you I'd be back, darlin'."

She clung to me, laughing through happy tears. After a moment, she looked past my shoulder toward our friends. "Where's Finn?"

"Alive, but in Allsop's hands."

"No," she breathed, horror etched onto her pretty face.

I gripped her shoulders. "We'll get him back. Don't you worry. But there's something you can do for me."

"Anything."

"See that little girl over there?" I pointed to the child who stood watching us, her hands shoved into the pockets of her pink jacket. "That's Izzy. You think she could spend the day with you and Ever and Mrs. B.?"

"Of course. Ever would love the company."

"I'll introduce you." I took Mac's hand and led her toward the kid. "Izzy, this is my wife. Most people call her Kenzie."

Curiosity made the girl's brown eyes sparkle. "What do you call her, Alejandro?"

Kenzie's eyebrows shot up. Nobody called me by that name, not since my old neighbor Harry passed from the flu back in May. My old lady would want to know why Izzy did. That was a story for later.

"I call her Mac."

Mac smiled at the girl and held out her hand. "My real name is Mackenzie. You can decide which nickname you want to use, Mac or Kenzie."

"Okay. I'll think about it."

"You do that, kid," I said. "Listen, I gotta talk to the major. You're going back to the motel room with Mac."

"What about Lorelei? You said I could see Lorelei."

"Later."

Izzy made an unhappy face, then took Mac's hand. "Alejandro doesn't know any of the words to 'Let It Go.' Do you?"

Mac shot me a big smile, then wheeled around and headed back to the motel with Izzy.

I turned to Havoc and his lieutenants. "What about Finn?"

"Inside." Havoc wheeled around and led the way to the conference room. Rachel took her usual spot, sitting cross-legged on the table. Havoc, Justin, and I dropped into chairs.

I explained in detail what went down during Izzy's rescue.

"Finn is a prize," Rachel said. "Allsop won't kill him immediately. He'll want to make a big to-do out of it."

"You were there during Leonard's interrogation. You heard about the Allsop Day celebration and the mass execution." Justin said, sneering at the mention of the bogus holiday. "He'll want Finn's death to be part of the spectacle. That gives us some time to make a plan."

"Gives us three days." Havoc tapped a walnut against the tabletop. "We don't know where Finn is being held, probably somewhere in the old penitentiary, but we know where he'll be on Allsop Day. On the plaza in front of the capitol building, awaiting execution."

"Finn, David, and any other Nampa Boys they've ferreted out." I caught the walnut Havoc tossed me. "All our friends in one place."

"And all of our biggest enemies." Rachel's face hardened. "Leonard told us that Allsop ordered all of his top people to come to Boise for the celebration. All the bigwigs from Bend, Spokane, and Coeur d'Alene will be on the plaza for Allsop Day."

"Any way you look at it, the Allsop Day celebration is a tempting target." Justin followed Havoc's lead and swung his boots up onto the table. "There's a good chance Reno and Georgia will be there, too. Jonesy will want to keep them close."

My mind raced. "Wouldn't be surprised if Jonesy wasn't planning to make his move on Allsop Day, too," I said. "Reno and Georgia are in his ear, encouraging him to snatch power from Allsop. Could be Jonesy has allies among the bigwigs attending the celebration. Or maybe he just plans to off all of Allsop's top people in one go."

"Whatever Jonesy has planned, as long as all of Allsop's men are in the same place at the same time, it works for us." Havoc looked around the table, his gaze moving from Rachel, to Justin, to me. "We rescue our people and take out Allsop and his top brass. Decapitate the leadership and end the war."

"Just like what Allsop planned to do to us with the C-4." Rachel smiled grimly.

"How about I head over to Meridian and meet up with the surviving Nampa Boys?" Justin asked. "They need to be part of the plan."

"Agreed," Havoc said.

"Bear needs to know Allsop is holding his brother," I said. "He'll want in on the action. Kyle, too. 'Specially if this is our big move against Allsop."

"You think they'll leave Valhalla?" Justin asked.

"There's too much for Allsop and Jonesy to do getting ready for the celebration. Doubt they'll attack Valhalla before Allsop Day," I said. "When I go to Valhalla to talk to Bear and Kyle, I'll bring a couple of extra men to help defend the place while they're gone. Just in case."

Havoc slapped the table. "We've got the bare bones of a plan. Ripper, you'll head out to Valhalla in the morning. Once Bear and Kyle are here, we'll work out the details."

"Izzy wants to see Lorelei. Kid needs to know we're on the up and up." I looked at Justin. How was the man handling Lorelei's betrayal? Had he forgiven her—because of the blackmail—or were they done?

"I'll take her over to the police station," Rachel offered, clambering off the table. "They can visit in the interrogation room."

We had three days and a shitload of preparations to make before we engaged the enemy. In a handful of days, we could achieve a decisive victory over Allsop. End his reign of terror. Set our little corner of the world on the right course.

In three days we could win this fucking war. Or it could all go to hell.

FORTY-TWO

Finn

In my wildest dreams, I never thought I'd see this place again: Cell House 5, the execution site for the Old Idaho State Penitentiary. Yet here I was, shuffling once again toward the boxy, butt-ugly building that housed Death Row.

A year ago, I would have laughed my ass off at the notion of being condemned to death for a second time—not to mention a first—but apparently history liked to repeat itself.

Last time I left this place I had to be carried out over Havoc's shoulder, unconscious and beat to a bloody pulp. If all went according to Allsop's plan, this time I'd be walking out under my own steam, heading to a public execution, the grand finale to the celebration of Allsop Day.

Allsop Day. Un-fucking-real.

Tommy led the way across the prison grounds. The two other soldiers flanked me. Reno marched behind, his presence at my back a comfort. Tommy nodded to the guard stationed outside Cell House 5. We walked single file through the narrow entry door, then jogged up a flight of stairs to the second-floor landing.

I glanced around familiar, depressing surroundings, at the dingy white walls, the concrete floor with its chipped red paint, the gray metal doors leading to Death Row and the Witness Room.

"Here you go," Tommy said cheerfully. He shoved me through the open door into Death Row.

With my hands cuffed behind my back, I fought to regain my balance. Pissed off, I whirled on the man.

Tommy's grin grew wider. He shifted his weight, telegraphing his intentions.

I tightened my abdominal muscles, but the blow knocked the air out of me, and I staggered backward a step.

"For Angie," he spat.

If my arms were free, I'd clean the floor with this chump.

Reno's hand descended on Tommy's shoulder. "Take it easy. Boss wants him on his feet for the execution, remember?"

Tommy sneered at me, disappointment stamped across his features. "Guess it's your lucky day."

I looked Tommy up and down. "Right," I drawled, derision heavy in my voice. "Otherwise I'd be quaking in my boots."

Tommy tried to take a step toward me, but Reno held him back. "Cool your jets, man. He'll get what he has coming."

"Yeah, he will," Tommy agreed.

We weren't alone inside the cellblock. Allsop must have learned his lesson after my escape. He'd doubled the guards stationed inside Death Row. Two men sat on folding chairs facing the four cells, a small table holding bottles of water and a pile of girly magazines between them.

Five faces peered out at us from behind the bars. I recognized David, the leader of the Nampa Boys, from the photo Allsop's man had shown us at the meeting in Meacham. The other guys were probably Nampa Boys, too. One of them looked like he couldn't have been more than twelve or thirteen.

A kid. Allsop planned to execute a kid. Shit.

David had a cell to himself, number three. The other prisoners were split between cells one and two. Each room held only one bunk, suspended from the wall by metal brackets. The prisoners either had to sleep in shifts or get real cozy on the narrow cots. The facilities consisted of nothing more than a bucket with a lid.

"Put Rasmussen in number four," Tommy ordered a guard.

Like David, I scored a cell all to myself. Guess it paid to be a "big cheese."

A guard unlocked the door. I stepped inside. He released my hands from the cuffs. I massaged my aching wrists.

Whenever things went wrong, Mama used to say to look for the silver lining. My hands were free. And last time I'd been held in cell number three. The walls there were painted a sickly mint green, a color I'd come to associate with pain and nausea. The dirty white walls in cell number four triggered no such associations. As a form of consolation, it didn't amount to much, but I'd take whatever I could get.

"See you later." Tommy taunted me from the other side of the bars.

I lifted my chin. "You can count on it, dumbass."

Without another word, Reno and the three soldiers exited Death Row, leaving me alone with the guards and other prisoners. I looked around my cell. Besides the defunct toilet and sink, the room held only a cot, a small wooden stool, and what looked like a blue bath mat on the floor.

"Finn Rasmussen?" David called out.

"Yep. That's me."

"Shit, man, I'm sorry we had to meet like this."

"Me, too."

A guard looked up from his magazine. "No talking."

I dropped down onto the bunk. Silence pressed in around me, and the reality of the situation seeped into my bones. After months of freedom, after my nightmares had finally begun to recede, I was back in the hands of the boogeyman. I touched a raised welt on my chest. The same ugly welt Georgia touched when she first saw my scars. The same welt she kissed the first time we made love.

C'mon, man. Time to muster up some gumption.

Each time death had come for me, I'd cheated the grim reaper. I survived the Wilcox Brigade's attack on the ranch. Came down with the killer flu and got over it. Grazed by bullets twice. Already escaped Death Row once.

Hope to hell I hadn't used up my share of good luck.

If I died three days from now, what would Georgia do? We'd just found each other, and now all of that might be ripped away. I wouldn't leave her like that.

Fear could cripple a man, shut down his capacity for rational thought, for making plans. No point in pretending the terror wasn't real. I shivered, allowing the dread to slither through me. Yeah, I felt it, but you know what? Fear would never paralyze me. I was its master, not vice versa. I wouldn't allow it to cripple me. I'd stay strong for Georgia.

Think, dammit.

Ripper and Izzy got away. The little girl was safe. Havoc knew I was in Allsop's hands. Georgia and Reno's covers hadn't been compromised. The Allsop Day execution spectacle was still three days away. Plenty could happen between now and then.

I scrubbed my hands over my face. Who was I kidding? The situation was bleak.

I lay back on the mattress and started to fold my arms under my head. Ouch. The bullet wound stung when I raised my arm. I wiggled around until I found a comfortable position, then settled back to think my thoughts.

"Georgia is safe." I mouthed the words, not daring to say her name out loud. And as long as Georgia was safe, I could face anything.

Something landed on my bunk. My eyes flew open and I jerked awake. A bottle of water and a package of fig cookies lay on the blanket. Dinner was served.

It wasn't yet full dark. The frosted-glass windows on the cellblock's exterior wall allowed fading sunlight to spill across Death Row. Time had to be close to sunset, maybe a little shy of six p.m.

Sitting up, I ripped open the cookies and chowed down. When I was ten, eating cookies for supper would have been a dream come true. As an adult, not so much, but calories were calories. I downed half the bottle of water and saved the rest for later.

To pass the time, I lowered myself onto the blue bath mat and did a hundred crunches, followed by a hundred pushups. I ran a range of possible scenarios over in my mind, my imagination running wild.

I'd fake a heart attack and jump the guards when they opened the door. Or Reno would slip me a key to the cell. The Nampa Boys and I would break out of Death Row and flee town. Or Havoc and my friends would ride to the rescue once again. My logical brain shot down each far-fetched possibility.

So where did that leave me? I wouldn't give up. Where there's life there's hope and all, but I needed a worst-case scenario option.

If I had to die, how did I want it to go down? The absolute last thing I wanted was to shuffle obediently up to the gallows in front of the capitol building, to allow Allsop's men to hang me. I wouldn't be a passive participant in his ridiculous celebration. His self-satisfied smirk wouldn't be the last thing I saw before I went home to Jesus.

No. Worse comes to worst, I'd go down fighting. Bide my time. Find my moment. Make a break for freedom. If I failed, I'd force the guards to kill me, depriving Allsop of his spectacle. As a plan, it sucked, but having a plan helped put my mind at ease.

Georgia's beautiful face rose up in my mind, but I blinked it away. If I thought of her now, I might not go through with it.

Back at Valhalla, Sunny had tried to teach me how to meditate. I got twitchy and my mind wandered, so I'd given up after a couple of days. Now, with nothing to lose, I gave it another shot. A little inner peace would do me good right now.

Sitting up straight on the bath mat, I crossed my legs and rested my hands on my knees. What was the chant Sunny taught me? Oh, yeah. Sa Ta Na Ma. I whispered the syllables, touching the tip of each finger in turn against the pad of my thumb. Was it working? Not sure, but after a few minutes, I felt a tingle between my eyebrows.

Muffled voices and footsteps reached my ears. My eyes snapped open. Georgia and Reno walked into Death Row. Reno carried the Red Cross duffel. Georgia held a lunch-sized brown paper bag. At the sight of the woman I loved, my heart clunked. Only God knew if I'd ever lay eyes on her again.

"Hi." Her lips turned up and she gifted the guards with one of her beautiful smiles.

I committed that smile to memory, planting the image deep inside my heart, where I could retrieve it when I drew my final breath.

"I brought you chocolate chip cookies, still warm from the oven," she said.

The men's faces lit up. They hopped to their feet and grabbed the bag from her.

"Boss wants us to check Rasmussen's injury." Reno held up the first aid kit.

"Go ahead." The guard spoke from around a mouthful of cookie. Crumbs shot into the air.

Didn't his mama teach him not to talk with his mouth full?

The guard handed Reno the key.

Reno and Georgia paused outside my cell. "Go stand against the back wall," he ordered.

I obliged, raising both hands in the air like a good little prisoner. Reno unlocked the door and they stepped inside.

"No funny business," he growled. "You got three armed men with eyes on you."

"Sit down on the bed," Georgia ordered.

I obeyed. She sat next me, positioning herself between me and the guards. She unzipped the duffel bag and pulled out two small handguns. I took them from her and slid them under my pillow, nodding my thanks. Nicely done. The weapons tipped the odds in our favor. I'd slip one to David if I got the chance.

"Let's see your wound."

"Yes, ma'am."

I longed to pull her into my arms, to kiss her, to tell her that my heart belonged to her. Instead, I played my part and she played hers. She gave orders and I complied, holding out my arm so she could remove the dressing.

Not a single affectionate word passed between us, but the love in her eyes and the gentleness of her fingers against my skin warmed me through and through. All too soon she had to go.

She finished bandaging my injury and stood up.

"All done."

She followed Reno out of the cell. He locked the door. They exchanged a few words with the guards, then walked out of Death Row.

Outside the door, out of sight of Allsop's men, Georgia turned. Our eyes locked. I kept my expression blank—in case the guards were looking—but she pressed her hand to her heart.

"I love you." She mouthed the words, then lifted her fingers to her lips and blew me a kiss.

I laid my fingers over my heart, capturing the sentiment.

A guard looked my way. I pretended to scratch my chest, a moment of pure poetry reduced to a run-of-the-mill itch.

I lay back down on the cot, the weapons lumpy under my thin pillow. Resolve flooded my veins. If it came down to it, I'd go down fighting. But I wouldn't give up. I wouldn't meekly wait for death. No. I had too much to live for. Somehow, someway, I'd get out of this mess. Georgia and I were getting our happy ever after.

FORTY-THREE

Georgia

Winnie was a nervous wreck. Our friendly neighborhood dictator ordered her to bake a birthday cake for his Allsop Day celebration that was—and I quote—"Worthy of the hallowed occasion." His men found several sixteen-inch cake pans in the warehouse's kitchenware section and brought them to an overwrought Winnie.

Winnie stood in the middle of the kitchen, her forehead pinched with worry. "I've never baked a cake this big. What if it isn't done in the middle? What if it cracks? What if I break it flipping it over?"

I had little patience with Winnie's hand-wringing. On the scale of things that mattered, Allsop's damned birthday cake ranked in negative numbers. The man I loved had an order of execution hanging over his head. That thought crowded everything else out of my thoughts. Compared to Finn's death sentence, the stupid cake was a nonstarter.

"It'll be fine," I assured her.

"No." Winnie shook her head emphatically, and her voice took on a panicky note. "It can't be simply fine. It has to be perfect. Mr. Allsop said so."

My impatience evaporated. The prospect of making a mistake, of disappointing Allsop, genuinely frightened her. What I saw as an annoying obsession with a trivial task, she saw as a big deal. Maybe she knew more than I did about the risks of displeasing her master.

Sympathy tempered my next words. "It'll be okay. I'll help you. We got this."

How hard could it be to bake and decorate a big-ass cake?

She bobbed her head, gratitude erasing the lines on her brow. "We'll bake and decorate the cake tomorrow. It should still be fresh the next day."

Jonesy sauntered into the kitchen, Reno on his heels. He touched one of the giant cake pans. "Getting ready for the big day, I see," he said pleasantly enough.

Truth be told, a pleasant and cheerful Jonesy was as alarming as an ill-tempered one.

"Yes, sir," Winnie said. "For Mr. Allsop's birthday celebration. He wants a Black Forest cake."

"That's nice." Jonesy tapped Winnie's nose. Her polite smile stayed in place, but her shoulders tightened. "My birthday is coming up," he continued. "I'd like a nice coconut cake with custard filling."

"I'll remember that," Winnie promised.

"See that you do." *There* was the threat, delivered with a smile, but still a warning nonetheless. Jonesy glanced at me. "Reno and I are going to go sit on the balcony. Could you bring us two mugs of coffee?"

"Of course."

He asked me to bring the coffee, not Winnie. He probably wanted to talk. The Allsop Day celebration was in two days. VIPs were filtering into Boise. The five guest suites in the mansion were already occupied by out-of-town visitors.

Foregoing the silver coffee service, I carried two mugs of steaming hot coffee to the balcony, where Reno and Jonesy sat on plush outdoor chairs.

"Pull up a seat," Jonesy told me.

Willing my hands not to shake, I passed the coffee to the pair. I dragged a chair across the stone floor and sat between the men.

Sitting this close to the man who tortured Finn made my stomach turn.

"I approached two of my colleagues, and they're in," Jonesy said without preamble. "Each one's bringing an armed contingent of men to the capitol building for the celebration. Ain't that handy?" He laughed, rubbing his hands together. "My nephew and his girlfriend will be coming in from Bend. Noah's been waiting for my summons, recruiting a few reliable men to our side."

"You're the number two man in Boise," Reno said. "Have you talked to any of the men working under you here?"

"No. When I was locked up in Pendleton, Mr. Allsop promoted a couple of men. I'm not entirely sure they're still likely candidates for Team Jonesy. They're smart fellows, though. I'll be standing at Allsop's side on the dais. If I kill him in front of everybody—backed up by squads of armed men—the Boise fellows will fall in line."

"It sounds like you thought of everything," I said. Good God, his absolute indifference to the prospect of committing murder chilled me.

"Why, thank you, honey. I believe I have. Reno will be with me on the dais with orders to shoot if anybody tries to interfere. I do need you to continue to do your part. Listen in when Allsop is entertaining his guests. You might overhear something useful or notice if the boss is acting suspicious."

"I'll do whatever I can to help," I said.

"I knew I could count on you, Carrie."

"And afterwards?" I asked, a hopeful expression on my face.

"Afterwards, if you play your cards right, you'll be living like a queen." He winked, a lascivious glint in his eyes that turned my blood to sludge.

I pulled my lips back in a facsimile of a smile. "I'd like that."

Jonesy spread his hands, a magnanimous gesture that encompassed all three of us. "Reno will be my number two man. We'll all live high on the hog."

Reno whooped and clapped his hands together. "Yes, we will."

Jonesy settled back in his chair. "How about some more coffee, pretty girl?"

"Yes, sir." I took the men's cups and jogged into the kitchen.

Not for one moment did I buy Jonesy's promises about our rosy future living in the lap of luxury. Reno and I were nothing more than a means to an end, useful tools in his plan to usurp power from Allsop. If his coup succeeded, he wouldn't share real power with anybody. According to the profile I'd compiled on him, the bastard wasn't wired for it.

He might keep Reno around. What dictator wouldn't want a scary Janissary to sic on his enemies? But if he caught a whiff of disloyalty or ambition, Reno would be a goner.

And me? From the little side-glances I'd caught, from the way he sometimes licked his lips when he looked at me, Jonesy wanted sex. He wasn't smitten. As far as I could tell, he didn't particularly like me—or rather Carrie—as a person. I was nothing more than an itch he wanted to scratch, at least once.

And once was one too many times for me.

I brought more coffee to the men. With a wave of his hand, Jonesy dismissed me. I retreated back to the kitchen, where Winnie was planning tonight's dinner party. Fine china, crystal, and sterling silver adorned a table set for twelve. Allsop's top men from Bend, Spokane, and Coeur d'Alene would join him at the table, as well as Jonesy, Jonesy's nephew, Noah, and Noah's girlfriend.

Preparations for the fancy dinner had Winnie in a tizzy.

"What can I do to help?" I asked.

Winnie glanced around the kitchen. Her gaze settled on bags of vegetables piled on the counter. "I have a mountain of potatoes and carrots that need peeling."

"I'm on it." I grabbed a scrap bucket from the pantry and pulled a stool up to the counter.

Peeling vegetables was mindless work. I only half listened as Winnie muttered under her breath, listing ingredients and tasks she needed to perform. My hands kept busy while my mind raced.

Fear for Finn clawed at me. My man was living his nightmare, back at the mercy of the man who'd tortured him. I had to save him. I just had to.

I'd helped rescue Finn from Death Row once before, but Allsop had learned his lesson and increased security at the prison. Last time I'd gone in with a team of trained soldiers. If we attempted another jailbreak, it would be just Reno and me. The odds weren't in our favor. A prison break had to be a last-ditch option.

Marcus knew of Finn's capture. Could he devise a plan and intervene in time to save Finn and the Nampa Boys? If anybody could pull off such a daunting task, it was Marcus.

Finn had a gun, thank God.

My brain scrambled for solutions. The afternoon crawled by, filled with mundane tasks that left me too much time to think. At six o'clock, Winnie sent me to freshen up. I put on a clean gray dress and a starched white apron.

"We'll be serving cocktails in the living room at six thirty." Winnie checked her watch. "The last of the guests arrived fifteen minutes ago. It was Jonesy's nephew from Bend. Jonesy looked fit to be tied."

"Why?"

"Apparently, Jonesy expected him and his girlfriend to arrive in the early afternoon. They rolled up the driveway hours late, driving a red Corvette and dressed to the nines." She dropped her voice to a whisper. "I heard they were laughing like hyenas and weren't a bit apologetic about showing up late. Jonesy isn't happy."

A flashy car and fancy clothes. What would Jonesy think of his nephew's conspicuous consumption? I bet he wouldn't like it, not when his uniform was jeans and a tee.

The prospect of an unhappy Jonesy gave me chills, especially when Finn was locked up in a cell, too vulnerable despite the guns hidden under his pillow.

Voices drifted our way from the living room. It was time to get this show on the road.

"Shall I plate the hors d'oeuvres?" I asked.

"You do the hors d'oeuvres. I'll do the drinks." Winnie gestured toward two silver serving trays holding a dozen empty cut-glass tumblers, the short kind. Old-fashioned glasses, my father called them.

"What drink are we serving?"

Winnie made a face. "Negronis. I don't like the bitter taste, but Mr. Allsop loves them."

While Winnie poured the drinks, I filled a platter with bacon-wrapped water chestnuts, Allsop's favorite appetizer.

Winnie held out her hands. "Wait here. I'll serve the cocktails, then when I come back, we'll carry the hors d'oeuvres into the living room."

I fidgeted while I waited, wiping my palms on my apron, psyching myself up to play the part of a gracious and polite server. I couldn't allow my fears for Finn to bleed through my deferential mask.

"Suck it up," I whispered, straightening my spine.

Winnie bustled back into the kitchen. She picked up one of the silver trays; I took the other. Chin held high, a pleasant expression plastered on my face, I sashayed toward the living room and swept my gaze over the room.

Wearing an impeccable black suit, Mr. Allsop stood next to the massive marble fireplace. Nobody could doubt that he was the lord and master of the estate. His erect posture and haughty demeanor conveyed as much.

Men and women—his top administrators—sat on sofas and chairs. Like Allsop, they were dressed to impress. The black sequins on a woman's cocktail dress winked in the firelight and drew my eye. Talk about a blast from the past. Unreal.

Jonesy occupied one end of a sofa, his hands folded innocently on his lap. He sat in flat-lipped silence. His face gave little away, but irritation flickered in his eyes. Was it because he was the only man dressed in casual clothes, a stark reminder of his lowly status? Or maybe it was his nephew's behavior?

Giggles punctuated the low hum of conversation. My eyes traced the source. A young man sprawled in a leather club chair. That had to be Noah. A young woman with long, glossy dark hair perched on his lap. She'd twisted sideways, her mouth pressed against his ear. Shoulders shaking with laughter, she whispered to him. Her short skirt had ridden up, exposing miles of thigh. Noah spread his fingers across her bare leg.

Allsop cleared his throat, a sound of displeasure that brought all conversation to a halt. The young woman stilled, then swung her head around to face the room, a pretty pout on her face.

"What?" she demanded, her voice petulant.

Oh dear God. My spine went rigid. My fingers strangled the edge of the silver tray. I swallowed back a gasp.

Morgan?

Noah's girlfriend was Morgan, the flirtatious minx who'd thrown herself at Bear during our mission in Prineville. When the eighteen-year-old discovered that Bear was in love with Nyx, she pitched a fit and spun a web of lies that led to near disaster. At the end, Morgan stole the keys to Uncle Bobby's castle and defected to Allsop's men in Bend, where she'd hooked up with Jonesy's nephew. She'd landed on her feet, hadn't she?

Had she seen my face? I dropped my gaze to the Persian rug. Servants were invisible to some people. Maybe she hadn't noticed me. Maybe she wouldn't look past the unfamiliar short brown hair. I held my breath.

Please, God—

Winnie cleared her throat. I lifted my eyes and she tilted her head toward the guests seated on the sofa.

Right. I was supposed to be serving the water chestnuts. Slapping a pleasant expression on my face, I walked over to the sofa and held out the tray to the partygoers. I worked my way toward the chair where Morgan and Noah sat. With each step closer to the pair, my pulse ratcheted up.

Play it cool.

Holding my breath, I extended the silver tray to Noah and Morgan.

Jonesy's nephew scooped up five of the hors d'oeuvres. "Bacon. Awesome." He held one up to Morgan's lips. "Try one, babe."

Making a face, she batted his hand away. "Not now."

With a shrug, Noah popped the chestnut into his mouth. "Awesome," he repeated, chewing happily.

I straightened, clutching at the tray.

Morgan looked me square in the face. Her blue eyes danced with malicious glee, glee and the glittery silver shadow that covered her lids. "Mr. Allsop, I was just telling Noah that your house is almost as nice as Uncle Bobby's."

My heart sank. The little twit recognized me. Why else would she mention Banyon's imitation castle, the place where we'd met?

Allsop overlooked the insulting comparison. "What's your name again?"

"Morgan," she smiled coyly, clearly thrilled to be the center of attention.

"You knew Robert Banyon?" Allsop asked.

Morgan bobbed her head. "Uncle Bobby was my best friend's father. He let me live at the castle after my parents died from the flu."

Morgan simpered, her eyes locked on mine. She lived for this shit. Stirring up trouble was the girl's stock-in-trade. The question wasn't *if* she'd rat me out, but *when*.

What could I do? If I dropped the tray and bolted, one of the guards would stop me. I could shut her up by smashing the tray over her head, but assaulting one of Allsop's guests would land me in a world of hurt.

Shit.

"Jonesy, were you aware of Morgan's relationship with Robert Banyon?" Allsop demanded.

Behind me, Jonesy cleared his throat. "No, sir. I was not." It was a reluctant concession from a man who hated to admit any failure.

Morgan frowned and jutted out her lower lip, as if sensing that the conversation was veering off track. "I'm on your side, Mr. Allsop. I brought Uncle Bobby's keys to your men in Bend."

"Fascinating," Allsop drawled. "You betrayed your best friend's father? The man who offered you a home after your parents died?"

Panic widened Morgan's eyes. I guess it hadn't occurred to her that Allsop would have a problem with disloyalty. Her gaze swung frantically from Allsop to me.

Oh, crap. Here it comes.

I took a step back.

"I know her." Morgan hopped off Noah's lap and strutted toward me. She jabbed a finger into my chest. "Her hair is different, but it's definitely her."

"Definitely who?" Jonesy asked, his voice eager.

"Georgia. I met her back in Prineville when Uncle Bobby hired that group of Janissaries. You know, Bear, Ripper, and Finn. She's Finn's girlfriend."

"Finn Rasmussen's girlfriend?" Astonishment colored Allsop's voice.

"That's right." Morgan nodded her head so vigorously that her long hair flew around her face.

"And Janissaries?" Allsop repeated.

"Yeah. They were friends with Reno. That's why Uncle Bobby hired them."

My heart sank. Dammit. Morgan had implicated both Reno and me, and Reno had no clue that we'd been outed.

Where was he? I glanced into the foyer. A pair of armed guards flanked the front door. Soldiers patrolled the entire estate. If an unsuspecting Reno came back to the house, they'd arrest him the minute he showed his face.

Jonesy jumped to his feet. "Should I take her for interrogation, boss?" He stepped toward me, reaching for my elbow.

"No." Allsop raised a hand, rejecting his henchman's suggestion.

Did Jonesy hope to hustle me out of the room before I could speak up? No way would I leave him free to strike out against Finn and me. If he was still in charge, we might "accidentally" die during interrogation.

"Give it up, Jonesy," I said. "He's on to our plan to oust him from power."

"Liar," Jonesy spat. "The bitch is lying through her teeth, boss. There was no plan to oust you from power."

Allsop laughed softly. "Perhaps. Although evidence suggests that you're either a traitor or hopelessly incompetent. In either case, you're of no further use to me."

The sentries stepped into the living room. Could they possibly be Jonesy's men? My gaze darted between Jonesy and the soldiers. If he gave the order, would they start shooting? Or were they loyal to Allsop?

Allsop pulled a small pistol from a holster on his waistband. The sentries followed suit, pointing their guns at Jonesy. They were Allsop's men.

Guests weren't allowed to carry inside the house, but as the head of security, Jonesy was armed. Armed, but surrounded and outgunned. Would he draw?

"Uncle Jonesy?" Noah rose unsteadily to his feet. "Are we in trouble?"

"Shut up," Morgan hissed, rushing to Noah's side and clutching at his arm. With wide eyes, she turned to Allsop. "Not me and Noah. We're not part of any plot against you."

"Don't worry, my dear, I'll sort out the truth." He pointed at one of the sentries. "Take Jonesy's weapon. Call for more soldiers. Escort Jonesy, his nephew and guest, and Georgia to Death Row."

FORTY-FOUR

Finn

Footsteps sounded from the stairwell, and a flashlight beam sliced across the gloom. The guards lowered their girly magazines and stood up, hands on the butts of their guns. I got to my feet and looked toward the door to the cellblock.

I'd hoped that under the pretext of checking my wound, Georgia and Reno might visit today, but they hadn't showed. Allsop was probably keeping them busy preparing for his birthday bash the day after tomorrow. Maybe my friends got away for a visit this evening.

Two soldiers marched into the room, Georgia on their heels. Gratitude shot through me. Every minute spent with Georgia was a gift, every word—no matter how mundane—a blessing. I pressed my lips together, hiding my pleasure.

Georgia stumbled, shoved from behind by a third soldier. She righted herself, struggling for balance. What the hell? Her shoulders were pulled back, her wrists bound behind her at her waist. Sweet Jesus. She'd been found out.

My stomach clenched into tight coils. Fear burned a trail to my heart. I knew exactly what the Allsop organization did to spies.

Jonesy appeared in the doorway, a bruise purpling his cheekbone, his arms pinioned behind his back too. A man and young woman followed close behind him. A fourth soldier brought up the rear. The young couple craned their necks, glancing around Death Row with shocked and frightened eyes.

Wait. I looked again. I'd never forget that girl's face. That was Morgan, the teenager who'd made such a pest of herself chasing Bear in Prineville.

"Four more for the gallows," the first soldier declared.

Morgan stomped her feet. "Not me. I didn't do anything wrong."

"Shut the fuck up," Jonesy growled. Handcuffed and bruised, he still gave off a powerful sense of menace.

Morgan quieted down, sniffling against her boyfriend's shoulder.

"We're already crowded. Where are we going to put them all?" The Death Row guard scratched his head. Sighing, he pointed at cell #3. "Put Jonesy in there with the leader of the Nampa Boys."

One of the soldiers from the house pointed at Morgan. "Stick her in with Jonesy. Her sniveling will drive him nuts."

"What? No! I want to be with Noah," Morgan shrieked, stomping her feet again.

"What'd I tell you?" The soldier smirked.

The guard shook his head. "Okay. Jonesy and the girl in #3. Her boyfriend in #1. And throw the last one in with Rasmussen."

"She's Rasmussen's girlfriend," the soldier from the house said.

Shit. I held my breath. If I shared a cell with Georgia, I'd die to protect her. I stood stock-still, scared that anything I said or did might make the guard decide against putting Georgia in with me.

The guard lifted both shoulders. "What the hell. Put Romeo and Juliet in together."

The guards shuffled the prisoners around. Finally, they cut the zip ties binding Georgia's hands and shoved her into my cell. The Death Row guards and the soldiers huddled together, gossiping about Jonesy's fall from grace.

From across the cell, Georgia and I faced each other, our eyes locked. I jerked my head, encouraging her to stay back a few feet. I didn't want to reach for her in front of so many witnesses. I wouldn't put it past them to separate us out of spite.

After five minutes, the soldiers exited the cellblock, leaving behind our two guards.

The guards were lazy fellows. They rarely stirred from their seats. They passed their time thumbing through magazines or leaning back and dozing against the wall. Now that the excitement had passed, they dropped down once again onto their rickety folding chairs and picked up their magazines.

I sat down on the edge of the cot. Georgia took a seat next to me. Leaning her head against my shoulder, she threaded her fingers through mine.

In the next cell over, Morgan started to sob. Within thirty seconds, the sound ratcheted up to a wail.

"Stop with the caterwauling, or I'll give you something real to cry about," Jonesy threatened the girl. Her squawks subsided, simmering down to an occasional blubber and sniff.

"What happened?" I whispered in Georgia's ear.

"Morgan hooked up with Jonesy's nephew in Bend." I had to strain my ears to catch her words. She quietly explained how Morgan had outed her to Allsop as my girlfriend. "I didn't want Jonesy on the loose, so I told Allsop he was planning a coup. He really was. He was going to assassinate Allsop on the dais in front of everybody during the Allsop Day celebration."

"So Jonesy is just as screwed as we are," I murmured. "Guess there's some satisfaction in that."

"I'm so sorry that you're here." Georgia's fingers tightened on mine. "You were supposed to be safe in Pendleton. You were supposed to go home to Valhalla and build a good life when this is all over."

"You think I want that without you?" I slid an arm across her shoulders and pulled her to my side. "If you got killed—well, shit—I'd find a way to keep going. I'd work the ranch and stand with my family against all comers. But I'd be a hollowed-out shell of a man."

"Finn." The word shook out on a sigh.

"God saw fit for you and me to face this together," I continued, my voice scarcely more than a breath. "If I had my druthers, that's exactly what I'd choose. You and me, angel, together till the very end."

Her throat worked. She swallowed hard, then cut her eyes toward the pillow where I'd hidden the guns. "We'll fight."

"Yes, we will. And if there's a way to survive, we'll find it."

Georgia nodded and squeezed my hand. Neither one of us were quitters. The situation was bleak. The odds were against us, but we'd give it our all. I closed my eyes, offering a silent thanks to my mama and daddy, who'd taught me to cowboy up and deal with whatever difficulties life threw my way.

Georgia and I leaned against each other, silent, as the other folks on Death Row settled down around us. Morgan ceased her whimpering. After hissing out a reprimand or two, Jonesy fell quiet. If Noah had a lick of sense, he'd continue to keep his mouth shut around his irate uncle. The Nampa Boys called out to each other, quieting only when a guard ordered them to pipe down.

A guard lit a cigarette, the tip glowing red in the low light cast by their lantern. He angled back his head, blowing smoke rings. When he eventually stubbed out the cigarette, he crossed his arms over his chest, closed his eyes, and leaned back against the wall. The other guard flipped through the pages of his magazine. His eyes grew heavy, and his head fell forward as he joined his companion in sleep.

It would be easy to pull out the guns and kill them while they dozed, like shooting fish in a barrel. But then what? We'd still be locked in our cells. The guards stationed at the outside door would come running. I wouldn't squander my only advantage taking out two inconsequential men.

Georgia touched my cheek. "Hey," she whispered.

I shifted my weight, turning toward her. The mattress groaned. Would the sound wake the guards? I froze for a count of ten. They slept on. I tangled my fingers in her hair and lowered my mouth to hers. Our lips met in a silent kiss.

My mind flashed back to when I was seventeen, making out with my girlfriend in front of the living room TV while her parents slept in the next room. Desire makes a man—or teenage boy—take chances. Back then I risked an ass-whooping from an outraged father for the sake of a blowjob.

What would I risk now? My mouth hovered over Georgia's. We both were breathing hard. My cock punched against the heavy denim of my jeans. "Do you want to—"

"Yes." Her lips moved under mine. "I want you inside me, Finn."

Maybe for the last time. She didn't have to say the words. We were both thinking them.

I nodded, then slowly—so very slowly—eased my weight up off the creaky mattress. I took Georgia's hand and carefully pulled her to her feet. The bed squeaked. Dammit. I winced, frustration stealing the air from my lungs.

Georgia glanced at the guards, then flashed a thumbs-up. "Still asleep," she mouthed the words.

Lust rumbled through my blood, an overpowering compulsion to bury myself balls deep inside the woman I loved. The only thing stronger than that urge was my need to keep her safe, to protect her from harm whenever and however I could. No way would we put on a show for the guards. I wouldn't subject her to the sniggering scrutiny of Allsop's soldiers.

I cocked my head toward the back wall, a space as far into the shadows as we could retreat. She nodded.

On silent feet, scarcely daring to breathe, we edged to the back of the cell. Once there, I maneuvered her against the cement wall, putting my back to the guards. If they woke and turned a light on us, they'd see my bare ass, not Georgia's.

Georgia reached for the zipper of my jeans, freed my cock, and wrapped her hand around the shaft. Her thumb swiped over the head, spreading liquid across the tip. I almost groaned but remembered just in time that silence ruled the night.

Sucking in a slow, appreciative breath, I fingered the frilly white apron she wore over her housekeeping dress. The fancy apron tickled my imagination. In my mind's eye, I saw Georgia dressed as a French maid, sashaying around a room, waving an ostrich feather duster. If we survived Allsop Day, I'd make that fantasy come true.

Georgia's eyes glinted in the near dark, and a corner of her mouth tipped up. "Perv," she teased, the word barely audible.

I gripped her throat with one hand and shut her mouth with a kiss, a kiss that transformed from playful to feverish. My mouth claimed hers. Awareness of time and place and circumstance melted away.

The only thing that existed was the here and now. The sweet taste of Georgia's lips. The tiny moan she suppressed. The thrum of her pulse beneath my fingertips. The lust clawing through every inch of my body. Every touch, taste, and sound an indelible brand on my memory, on my soul.

Georgia jerked her head away, gasping. Tears brimmed in her eyes. "Finn." Her lips silently formed my name.

I caught her face between my hands. "No. Stay in the here and now, angel." My voice was low and urgent. "Don't waste this time. It's a gift."

Her eyelids fluttered and her chest heaved as she pulled herself together. "Okay."

I slipped my hands under the hem of her dress and shimmied the skirt up her thighs, all the way to her waist. She shoved her panties down her legs and kicked them aside. My fingers touched her slick, wet heat.

Biting back a groan, I clamped my hands around her thighs and hoisted her up, settling her against my groin. She wrapped her legs around my waist and arched her hips, dragging her heated pussy against my dick.

God, I'd give anything for the chance to do this right. To prolong our lovemaking. To linger over every touch. To drive Georgia half-mad with pleasure. But time and privacy were commodities we did not possess. If we survived, I'd never take them for granted again.

"Ready?" I murmured against her mouth.

"Yes," she breathed. With a sense of urgency that matched my own, she captured my lower lip between her teeth. She clutched at me, her fingernails stabbing into my shoulders.

My hands shook. I pressed the head of my cock against her slit. Swallowing Georgia's small whimper, I drove home, then stilled, catching my breath.

Her thighs tightened around my waist, and she rolled her hips, silently imploring me to move.

Cradling her skull with one hand, I slowly withdrew. She moaned, the sound a whisper-soft protest. I thrust back in. Sweet heat surrounded my cock on every side. Buried to the hilt inside her body, I was as close to heaven on earth as I could come. Every hypersensitive nerve in my body jangled.

Seconds ticked by, each one bringing us closer to the inevitable moment when the guards woke up and opened their eyes. I shut down that knowledge and focused instead on Georgia.

Yanking my lower lip free, I dropped kisses on her upturned face, across her cheeks and eyelids. When a small sound of pleasure slipped from her lips, I claimed her mouth, silencing her moans.

I couldn't pound into my woman, not when she was pressed against a cement wall, not when the slap of flesh against flesh might awaken the guards. Instead, I found a smooth rhythm, arching my hips and going deep with each thrust.

Georgia snaked her arms around my neck. Her teeth latched on to my uninjured shoulder. She panted against my skin. A deep shuddering took hold in her core, one that made my own insides quiver.

My heartbeat banged inside my head like a drumbeat. A tingling took hold in my balls. With every thrust that tingling grew stronger. My muscles tensed, my arms and legs going numb.

With a small strangled cry, Georgia threw back her head. Glazed eyes fixed on mine. Her pussy clamped and spasmed. I swear to God, her eyes rolled back in her head.

The ripples from her orgasm pushed me to the very edge. My mind blanked. The champagne cork popped. My cock pulsed and surged as pleasure almost drove me to my knees.

Breathing hard, I gazed into her face. Lips swollen from my kisses, eyelids heavy with the best kind of exhaustion. No woman had every looked more beautiful.

"I love you." She mouthed the words.

I might die the day after tomorrow, but tonight, I felt like the luckiest man in the world.

FORTY-FIVE

Ripper

Arms crossed over my chest, I leaned against the red minivan. Shouldn't be more than another minute or two before Havoc finished giving orders to the two soldiers who were riding with me to Valhalla.

Behind the wheel of the black Allsop SUV, Justin had taken off for Boise five minutes ago. He'd meet up with remnants of the Nampa Boys, coordinate plans for the attack, then return to Pendleton this evening.

I glanced across the street at the motel room where I'd left Mac sleeping like the dead. Pregnancy made her horny as hell. Kept my old lady up half the night satisfying that particular itch. When I kissed her goodbye this morning, her eyes fluttered open, then with a grunt, she fell back asleep.

Mrs. B. liked to quote a Bible verse, something to do with not worrying about tomorrow because each day has enough trouble of its own. Saw some sense in that advice. I wouldn't get tied up in knots over the upcoming battle. No matter what the future held, I'd be back with Mac tonight.

Izzy was sleeping over with Ever. Last night—after an acquaintance of only a few hours—the pair had declared themselves "best friends forever." Ever invited Izzy to visit the ranch, promising they could ride horses and feed chickens. It'd be good for Ever to have somebody close to her age around, but with two hard-core chatterboxes in the house, I'd have to hide out in the barn to find a moment's peace.

A big bad Janissary hiding from two little girls. God damn, I was going soft. Instead of pissing me off, the thought brought a smile to my face.

The two soldiers walked toward the mom mobile.

I erased my grin and stood up straight. Their eyes took in my cut. Their step faltered and their jaws snapped shut. Yeah. The reaction didn't surprise me. Solid-citizen types usually took one look at the cut and peeled off in the opposite direction.

Jerked my chin at the back of the minivan. "Get in."

Without a word, they threw their backpacks into the cargo space, then climbed into the second row of seats. Neither one offered to ride shotgun.

Fine by me if the cut intimidated them. Hoped they kept their mouths shut for a while. Wanted to drive without listening to constant yammering. The silence held as we headed out of town, and lasted for a good hour before the men loosened up.

I kept my foot heavy on the gas. We pulled up to the ranch gate before noon. The sight of the timber crossbeam and the iron letters spelling out Valhalla hit me like an unexpected punch to the gut.

Never before been sentimental about a place. Home was where I laid my head and stowed my shit. But now, Valhalla was home. Its sprawling house, barnyard, and pastures, the place where Mac and I would raise our kid. Where we'd grow old, surrounded by good people. I'd never forget my Janissary brothers, but Kyle, Sahdev, Bear, and Finn were my brothers now. Levi and Topher too. I got everything that mattered. I was luckier than I deserved.

Just gotta get through the next two days. Kill Allsop and Jonesy. Bring Finn and Georgia home safe.

Easy-peasy, like Ever would say.

Levi jogged to the gate and let us in. He hopped into the empty front passenger seat and rode back to the house with us. Kyle and Sahdev stood on the porch.

I climbed out of the van and approached my friends.

Kyle took a step toward me. "What happened? Why are you here?"

Holding up my palm, I silenced his questions. "Gotta talk to Bear first. Where is he?"

"Bear's in the tractor shed," Sahdev answered.

I tipped my head at the two soldiers who stood at the side of the minivan. "They'll be staying for a few days. Can one of you show 'em around?"

"I'd be happy to." Sahdev exchanged a worried glance with Kyle.

I strode to the open-sided building and found Bear tinkering with the rotary mower. He looked up and frowned as I approached.

No easy way to upend a man's world. I wouldn't insult my friend by sugarcoating the bad news. "Allsop has Finn. Plans to execute him in two days."

Bear straightened to his full height, his knuckles white around the wrench he gripped. He shook his head, like he had water in his ears and couldn't hear right.

"What did you say?"

"Finn and I went to Idaho to rescue a little girl. Operation went sideways. I got away with the kid. Allsop's men took Finn."

Bear blinked, his expression blank with shock, then confusion flooded his face. "You left Finn behind?"

"Yeah, I did."

Far as I was concerned, abandoning Finn was a clear-cut dereliction of duty. Nothing I could say would make it right—justify it in my eyes—so I offered no explanation. If Bear wanted to take a swing at me, I'd let him.

He set the wrench on a workbench, then turned to me. "What happened?"

I spilled the whole sorry story. By the time I was done, Bear was reeling.

"We're going after Finn," I assured him. "Havoc reached out to the surviving Nampa Boys. We're gonna strike day after tomorrow, during the Allsop Day celebrations in front of the capitol building. This pans out right, we'll get our people out and put Allsop down once and for all."

Bear didn't hesitate. "I'm coming with you."

"That's why I'm here. Figured you and Kyle would want in on the action."

"Shit." Dismay screwed up his features. He shoved a hand through his hair. "Jonesy and the ranch."

"Not likely that Allsop can spare the men to attack Valhalla. Not till his damned party is over. But to play it safe, Havoc sent two soldiers to cover for you and Kyle."

Tension pounded off the man. "All right. Give me ten minutes to pack a bag and talk to Nyx."

"You got it, brother."

We strode back to the house. Kyle, Sunny, Nyx, and Sean Darragh—the Marine—waited for us on the porch. Bear filled them in on the situation.

"Finn is my friend and Boise is my hometown. I'm going." Kyle turned to Sunny. "But you're not. You've learned how to shoot—you'd defend your friends—but you're not ready to go into battle."

Nothing but the truth there, and Sunny knew it. "You're right."

When she heard that Finn had been taken prisoner, Nyx's horrified gasp cut me to the quick. Instead of laying blame, she threw her arms around me. "You bring Finn home and be careful. I don't want to lose any of you."

I returned her hug. "Don't you worry, Nyx. We got each other's backs. I promise."

Bear looked at Nyx. "You want to come to Pendleton with me?"

Nyx hesitated, then wagged her head back and forth. "I can't believe I'm saying this, but no. If there's even a small chance that Valhalla will be attacked, a Rasmussen should be here to defend the place. With you and Finn gone, I'm the closest thing to a Rasmussen you've got."

"Far as I'm concerned, you *are* a Rasmussen." Bear snaked an arm around Nyx's waist and hauled her close. "In fact, if you said yes and we had a minister, I'd marry you today."

Nyx's blue eyes sparkled. She lifted her chin. "If *you* said yes and we had a minister, I'd marry you today, too."

This from the woman who a few months ago wanted nothing more than no-strings-attached sex. Too bad Mac wasn't here. She'd eat up this hearts and flowers, happy ever after shit.

"That's so romantic." Sunny pressed a hand to her chest. No surprise there. The woman was a sentimental sweetheart.

"Hey." Kyle took her elbows and turned her to face him. "I love you, sunshine. Nothing would make me prouder or happier than to be your husband."

Sunny's lower lip trembled. "And I'd love to be your wife."

Good God. Nothing like the prospect of a life-or-death battle to turn people into romantic saps. I glanced at the front door, half expecting Hannah and Levi to sail outside and pledge their undying love, too.

"Um..." Sean Darragh spoke up. "Sorry to interrupt, but do you guys know that Ryan is an ordained minister?"

"Who's Ryan?" Bear asked.

"One of the soldiers Havoc sent to defend the ranch," Sean said. "Outstanding guy."

Bear cocked a brow. "What do you think, sugar? You want to ask Ryan to marry us before I leave for Pendleton? Without a license it might not be strictly legal, but we'd be married in the eyes of God."

"Let's do it, cowboy."

"Sunny? Do you want to get married before I go to Pendleton?" Kyle asked.

"Oh, I'm coming to Pendleton with you." Sunny's voice and expression left no room for compromise or debate. "I get why Nyx is staying at Valhalla, but I'm going to be at your side until the very last moment. And once you all leave for Boise, I'm going to sit with my girls—Kenzie, Ever, and Mrs. B.—and we'll wait together for you to come back."

"Good. I'm glad you're coming with me. But how about it? Will you marry me first?"

Sunny threw her arms around his neck. "Of course I'll marry you."

"I'll go get Ryan," Sean offered. He wheeled around and jogged across the yard toward the outbuildings.

"This gotta be fast," I reminded them, feeling like a wedding day Scrooge.

Nyx took charge, pointing at Bear, Kyle, and Sunny. "You guys have five minutes to pack." Hand on the doorknob, she turned to me. "Ripper, can you ring the dinner bell?"

"On it." I grabbed the striker and beat on the cast-iron bell that dangled from the porch roof. Sahdev ran over from the direction of the barn. I told him what was up.

"Do you want me to come with you to Boise?"

The doc was a healer first and a fighter second, but he could handle himself in battle. Saved my ass when we took the ranch back from the Nazis.

"I'd have you at my back any day, but it's your call, brother."

Sahdev's brows pulled together while he thought about it. "On the off chance that the Allsops do attack the ranch, I should be here to treat the wounded."

I clapped him on the shoulder. "We're leaving Valhalla in good hands."

Sean and the other soldiers jogged toward the porch. I motioned for them to follow us inside.

Nyx, Hannah, and Levi had shoved the leather sofas to the perimeter of the front room, creating a big open space in the middle. Sean introduced Nyx to a middle-aged soldier who had to be Ryan.

Nyx took an old, leather-bound book down from a shelf. She held it out to the minister. "The Rasmussen Bible. Can you hold it during the ceremony? And then afterwards, we'll sign it?" She shot me a quick look. "Sorry, Ripper. It'll just take a minute."

No way I'd complain if my friends took an extra minute to uphold a family tradition. "Not a problem."

Bear, Kyle, and Sunny ran into the front hall, dumped their backpacks by the door, then walked over to Nyx and the minister.

Holding the Bible in both hands, Ryan got the show on the road. He lined Bear and Nyx and Kyle and Sunny up in front him, while the rest of us ranged out behind the brides and grooms.

Ryan cleared his throat. "Dearly beloved—" He cut himself off. "There's no time for that. We're going to skip right to the vows. Bear and Nyx: Do you swear that you will stand by each other in plenty and want, in sickness and in heath, in failure and triumph? When one of you stumbles, will you promise to restore the other? Will you share all things? Will you serve each other and your fellow humanity?"

Bear and Nyx exchanged a smile. "We will."

Ryan repeated the vows for Kyle and Sunny.

Kyle jumped the gun, dropping a quick kiss on Sunny's mouth. "We will."

An image popped into my mind. A sweltering summer day. Sitting with Mac on the porch swing. Sliding the diamond band onto her ring finger. Promising to love, honor, and protect her. A two-minute exchange of vows that left me a changed man. More at peace within myself. Bone-deep happy. Certain of my way forward. Ready to face whatever fucked-up shit the universe threw my way.

"It is my honor and joy to declare you married. And you may now seal your marriage with a kiss."

Everybody in the room whooped.

I swallowed.

What's a hard-ass like me doing with a lump in his throat?

The minister laid the Bible on the table. Bear and Nyx added their names and the date to a list of Rasmussen brides and grooms that stretched back to the 1800s.

Bear held out the pen to Kyle and Sunny. "You sign, too. You're family."

Sunny leaned against her new husband. What had to be happy tears flooded her eyes. "Did you hear that? We're family."

Bear put the Bible back on the shelf, took Nyx's hand, and pulled her toward the hall. He paused and looked over his shoulder. "I need fifteen minutes to say goodbye to my wife."

Fifteen minutes. Not much of a honeymoon.

We loaded the packs into the back of the minivan. After a few final words with Sahdev and the others, we waited by the front door for Bear.

"Do you think Mrs. B. and Ever will forgive us for getting married without them?" Sunny asked. "Ever was counting on being a flower girl at our wedding."

"Of course they will." Kyle rubbed a hand up and down her back, soothing away her concerns. "They'll understand why we did it."

I snorted. Who was he kidding? "Mrs. B. might, but Ever's gonna be pissed." The kid would pout for a minute, but she loved Kyle and Sunny. She'd get over it.

Bear strode into the hall. He spoke to our friends, clapping Sahdev, Levi, and Topher on the back before joining us by the door. He looked at us each in turn, then stuck out his hand, his fingers curled into a ball. I held out my own. After a few seconds, Kyle and Sunny raised theirs. Our hands met in a four-way fist bump.

"It's time," Bear said. "Let's end this."

FORTY-SIX

Georgia

Bright afternoon sunlight streamed through the window and over the twelve armed soldiers who stood at attention outside our cells. A dozen gun-toting men to escort ten prisoners from Death Row to the gallows? Allsop wasn't taking any chances, was he?

Talk about overkill.

Overkill. I winced. A truly unfortunate choice of words.

Ten condemned prisoners awaited death, not eleven. Allsop's men would be scouring the city for Reno. If they'd found him, they would've dragged him to Death Row, another prize for the gallows. All day yesterday, I waited for any sign that my friend had been taken prisoner—the clang of a metal door, the shuffling of feet—but nothing. That meant one of two things—either Reno had evaded capture, or he died resisting arrest.

Please, God, let Reno be okay.

Four men stepped toward the cells, keys in hand.

I clutched at Finn's arms, my heart thumping, deliberately pushing away panic. This might be the last time we touched. The last time we kissed. The last time we exchanged words in private.

Be in the moment.

Finn cupped my face and his blue eyes bore into mine. "I love you, angel. Now and forever."

I jerked my head, my chest so tight I could barely breathe. "I love you too."

The guard stepped close and I threw my arms around Finn. I buried my face in his throat and slowly drew in a breath, memorizing his scent.

My fingers touched the handgun he wore tucked into his waistband, under his coat. My gun was hidden under my gloves, deep inside the front pocket of my jacket. Thank God the soldiers had allowed me to snag the coat on my way out of the mansion.

"One at a time. Out." The guard grabbed Finn's shoulder, then shoved him toward the open cell door.

One Allsop man held a gun on Finn, the other bound his wrists behind his back with a zip tie. They'd searched us for weapons before locking us into the cells. It didn't occur to them to search us again on our way out, a stroke of luck undermined by the simple fact that Finn couldn't reach his pistol.

Dammit.

Waving a gun, the guard ordered me to step outside the cell. I complied. They hadn't searched Finn; they probably wouldn't search me, not unless I looked anxious or squirrelly. I banished concern from my face, managing to look little more than stoic when they tied my hands behind my back. Like Finn, I still had my gun, even though it was inaccessible.

Once all ten of us prisoners were out of our cells and cuffed, the twelve soldiers marched us down the stairs and out of the building. Each prisoner had a personal guard at their elbow. I followed behind Finn, keeping my gaze on his broad back. I felt Jonesy's eyes on me as we marched through the old penitentiary complex and out through the main entrance.

I stumbled to a stop. A bright-yellow school bus idled next to the door. Riding to your execution in a school bus felt all kinds of wrong. Finn turned his head and met my eyes, arching one thick brow.

The soldiers hustled us onto the bus. We sat two to a seat, a prisoner and their guard. I slid awkwardly onto the bench seat in front of Finn. Turning around, I tossed him a small reassuring smile.

I'm okay, that smile was meant to convey. I'm hanging in there.

Hanging in there. Shit. Another unfortunate choice of words. Gallows humor at its best.

I glanced to my right, where Ethan perched next to a burly guard. The boy pressed his lips together in a flat line, clearly trying not to cry. Morgan—two seats in front of him—made no such effort. She rocked back and forth, blubbering without restraint. Jonesy dropped heavily onto the padded seat in front of me, his expression murderous.

The distinctive hiss and squeal of a school bus door closing, another familiar, incongruous blast from the past, made me jerk. The bus lurched into gear, and the driver headed toward downtown. The unforgiving seats jostled us, prisoners and guards alike.

It would be easy to stare out the window in a daze, to let my mind wander back to happier times, to allow the minutes to slip by as death grew nearer and nearer. Nope. Daydreaming was a luxury I couldn't afford.

Outnumbered and outgunned, our wrists secured with zip ties, there wasn't a damned thing we could do while riding in the bus. What happened once we got off the bus, that was another matter.

Twisting around on the seat, I locked eyes with Finn. Circumstances were dire, but as long as my heart beat and my lungs drew in air, I'd be searching for a way to survive, to claim my happy ever after with the man I loved. He dipped his head, his steely gaze radiating the same resolve.

We turned right at the old Pioneer Cemetery, then left onto Jefferson Street, the road that ran directly in front of the capitol. As we approached our destination, I spied orange plastic barriers blocking the street in front of the neoclassical building. The bus made a right turn, then parked on the side of the capitol complex.

"Everybody out," the driver barked. The folding door opened with another hiss and squeal.

One by one, we exited the school bus. Our personal guards followed each of us out the door.

"Line up," the driver shouted.

I fell into place behind Jonesy and in front of Finn.

"March," he ordered.

Trudging along the sidewalk, we made our way toward the front of the building. Our sorry cavalcade rounded the corner onto Jefferson Street, and the capitol grounds came into view.

A solid line of Allsop's soldiers faced the street. The wall of armed men separated the dignitaries gathered on the steps of the capitol from the crowd that filled the street and park in front of the building.

I'd studied crowd risk analysis and knew how to estimate the size of a gathering. Close to five hundred surly people were packed together in front of the capitol. None of them looked happy to be there. You don't win people's hearts and minds by threatening to withhold their food rations.

A speaker's podium had been erected in front of the replica Liberty Bell. Elliot Allsop, resplendent in a black suit and red tie, stood behind the lectern.

Two soldiers flanked him, their eyes scanning the crowd and surrounding buildings, probably looking for shooters. Every gun in the city had been confiscated, but caution ruled the day.

Behind Allsop, suit-clad functionaries occupied prominent places on the wide stone steps. A huge white banner proclaiming the *First Annual Allsop Day* hung on the front of the building.

"Good citizens of Boise." Allsop's voice crackled through what had to be a battery-powered public-address speaker system. "Please welcome our guests of honor." He turned and threw an insincere smile at our line of prisoners, then lifted his hands and clapped.

People in the crowd murmured and shuffled their feet, clearly unsure of what to make of Allsop's call for applause. A spattering broke out. Allsop waved his arms, encouraging more. The applause grew louder.

What an asshole.

As if drawn by a magnet, my gaze moved past Allsop and his flunkies to the grassy area on the far side of the capitol steps. When Reno and I visited the site, three ornamental trees had filled the space.

The trees had been chopped down and gallows erected in their place. Ten nooses dangled from the crossbeam.

I gulped and stumbled to a halt. Shit just got real.

The wooden platform stood close to fifteen feet off the ground. The height wasn't simply for optics—so the crowd would have a good view of the executions—although I'm certain Allsop wanted the executions to put the fear of God into Boise's citizens. No, the long drop would ensure that our necks snapped when we plunged through the trapdoors.

"Move it, bitch." My guard poked the barrel of his gun into my back, prodding me forward.

Behind me, Finn growled.

I had a sudden vision of him lowering his head and charging the soldier who threatened me. No. I wouldn't let my man throw away his life on a chivalrous gesture.

"I'm all right," I called over my shoulder, briefly meeting eyes that sparked with fury.

I picked up the pace, walking briskly toward the damned gallows. Despite my training and my determination to fight back, I didn't see an opening. With my hands zip tied behind my back, a gun aimed at me, my options were limited.

The guard shoved me, and I stumbled on the steps to the platform, coming down hard on my knees. I bounced back up, ignoring the pain that shot through my joints.

We lined up in front of the ten nooses, Jonesy on my left, Finn on my right. How quickly would the guards slip the nooses over our heads?

Before all of the seconds ticked away, before it was too late, I moved toward the man who held my heart. Finn stepped sideways. We bumped shoulders, our old greeting, then he dropped his forehead onto mine. A gust of wind carried his scent to my nostrils. I held my breath, a lump in my throat.

The guards wrenched us apart.

I glanced down at the trapdoor that still supported my weight, then at the grim-faced soldier standing at the end of the platform. His hand rested on the lever that would release the hatch.

My guard slid the noose over my head, adjusting it so that the hangman's knot lay beneath my left ear. Old army regulations required the knot to be placed below the ear, an act of mercy, bringing a quick death when the rope snapped taut.

The ten soldiers clomped away, leaving us alone with the executioner.

Jonesy cursed a blue streak. Morgan wailed. Ethan trembled and David murmured quiet words to the boy.

Jesus. This was really happening?

I swung my eyes to Finn. Instead of casting a final, loving look my way, he tipped his head at the crowd. I frowned in confusion. He did it again.

What did he want me to see?

I raked my gaze over the assemblage, then paused. There. In the third row of spectators, a tall man, with his jacket's hood pulled up over his head. The man lifted his chin, and bright-blue eyes met mine.

Bear.

Behind him and to his right, another familiar face half-hidden beneath a hood.

Kyle.

Like a phoenix rising from the ashes, hope surged through my veins.

FORTY-SEVEN

Ripper

"No fucking way."

Havoc's exact words when I told him it'd be smart for him to sit this one out. Our plan of attack was solid, but shit goes sideways during a battle. No plan survives contact with the enemy and all. Losing Havoc wouldn't end the resistance, but it would be a major setback. The risk-to-benefit ratio didn't justify his participation.

He shrugged off my arguments.

Didn't blame the man. Nothing would have held me back, either.

Which meant that Justin and Rachel had to stay behind in Pendleton, ready to step up if Havoc died. Calling Justin unhappy about it was the understatement of the year. Of the century. The man wanted payback for what Allsop did to Lorelei—what he did to everybody—but orders were orders.

Twenty soldiers left Pendleton this morning. Havoc, Bear, Kyle, and I rode in the black Allsop SUV. We approached Boise from the north, took out the guards at the roadblock, and left two of our men in their place.

Our spies reported that Allsop had around two hundred soldiers in Boise. Maybe half of them would be assigned to security and crowd control at the capitol. We dodged the patrols and approached the downtown.

Havoc was too smart to put all of his assets into play. He held five men in reserve, ready to call up if needed. Another five men were stationed along likely escape routes from the capitol, in case any bigwigs tried to flee on foot. Bear, Kyle, and a handful of our best soldiers joined the remaining Nampa Boys in the crowd.

Havoc and I set up sniper positions overlooking the capitol. I was close, less than a hundred yards away, on the roof of the post office. Havoc stationed himself farther out, on the roof of an insurance company, as far out of harm's way as his conscience would allow.

Now all we had to do was wait for the signal.

A large crowd assembled in front of the podium. Standing with linked arms—like old-world riot police—a line of soldiers faced the throng. Allsop's voice rang through the tinny speakers.

"Good citizens of Boise. Please welcome our guests of honor."

Half-hearted applause as a line of prisoners trooped past the podium.

Did a double take.

What the fuck?

Hands bound behind her back, Georgia stumbled along the sidewalk with the other condemned prisoners. Shit. Her cover had been blown.

How about Reno? I eyeballed the line, searching for my fellow Janissary. No sign of him, but I spied Finn, Jonesy, and that troublemaking twit Morgan. What the hell was she doing in Boise? Something big had gone down in the past couple of days. Just bet Morgan played a major part in the fiasco.

The prisoners made their way toward the gallows. Guards jostled them up the steps and secured the nooses around their necks. The soldiers beat a retreat back down the stairs, leaving the hangman the only Allsop man still on the platform.

I scoped on my target, the fucker with his hand on the lever, waiting to release the trapdoors.

Cocking my head, I listened for the signal for Havoc and me to take our shots. Seconds ticked by. Frustration bit at me, but I kept my shoulders loose and my breathing easy.

A shrill whistle pierced the air.

Before the sound subsided, I shot the hangman, pulled back the bolt, and chambered a new round.

Pop. Pop. Pop. Pop. Pop. I dropped the soldiers in front of the gallows, clearing a path for Bear and Kyle to rush the platform.

Confusion took hold.

The crowd stampeded in every direction, a few unlucky souls trampled underfoot. Our soldiers and the Nampa Boys took advantage of the confusion, working their way through the crowd toward the line of soldiers.

Allsop men came in two flavors. Ruthless maniacs, like Jonesy, were the minority. Most of his men were too scared and intimidated by their boss to do anything without a direct order. He'd told them to hold the line against the crowd, and that's what they did.

He hadn't ordered them to shoot into the crowd. Yet.

I spared a glance at the podium, hoping to see Allsop's crumpled body.

Nope. Allsop's two bodyguards were hustling him off the stage. Dammit. Bet the asshole wore a bulletproof vest under his fancy suit, and Havoc shot center mass. One of the bodyguards went down. Allsop dove behind the line of soldiers, out of sight.

Bodies littered the capitol steps. Havoc's agents in Bend, Spokane, and Coeur d'Alene had sent Polaroid photos of Allsop's top people. One after another, Havoc picked them off.

Allsop's top supporters eliminated. Check.

I cut my eyes to the gallows.

Finn and our friends freed from the damned nooses. Check.

Pop. Pop. Pop.

Havoc kept up his relentless barrage. An Allsop soldier shot into the crowd. A few seconds later, Havoc brought him down with a head shot. The line of soldiers started to break apart. Men scrambled for cover.

Their last-minute salvation spurred David and the Nampa Boys into a fit of bloody vengeance against the men who almost killed them. They grabbed weapons from the downed guards and went after the others.

Chaos reigned.

Allsop still lived.
I touched the Colt 1911 in my shoulder holster.
Not for long, motherfucker.
I ran toward the melee.

FORTY-EIGHT

Finn

The rope bit into my neck, not so deep that it restricted my breathing, but hard enough that the scratchy fibers were sure to leave behind an angry rash. I had trouble drawing in air. Panic danced along the edges of my consciousness.

The reaction was probably more psychological than physical. Knowing that the trapdoor could give way any second, and that I'd drop to my death, colored a man's perceptions.

Still, when all hell broke loose—when the shots rang out and the hangman fell over dead—when my brother rushed onto the scaffold, my overriding thought wasn't of getting myself free.

"Georgia first," I choked out.

Without a word, Bear turned to Georgia and hacked at the rope attaching her neck to the crossbeam overhead. Only when the rope frayed and tore apart did he turn back to me. He made short work of cutting me down, then he sliced through the zip ties binding our wrists.

Gasping, I loosened the noose and yanked it off my neck. I sucked in a deep breath. Air never tasted so sweet.

Free at last, Georgia and I lurched toward each other. She buried her face in my chest, her breath hitching. So close. We'd come so damned close to losing everything. We clutched at each other, swaying, for a good minute before Georgia pulled away.

"We aren't done here." Her voice was steady. From her expression, the soldier was in ascendance, and she was dead set on seeing this through.

"You're right." I glanced around the platform.

Kyle stood on the steps, gun raised, ready to shoot any of Allsop's men who tried to interfere with the rescue. Not that they were likely to. Sniper fire dropped the soldiers where they stood arm in arm facing the crowd. The descent from order to chaos happened so quickly that I'm sure everybody's heads were reeling.

Bear freed David, Ethan, and the other Nampa Boys.

Their fingers worked the knots on their nooses. Once free, David pointed at Ethan. "You stay here. The rest of you, with me."

Murder in their eyes, they vaulted down the steps. Kyle made way for the stampeding teenagers. They snatched up weapons from the downed soldiers. Like bloodhounds off the leash, they took off in pursuit of the others.

Shit.

"Do me next," Morgan cried.

Knife in hand, Bear stepped up to her. He hesitated.

Couldn't blame the man. The little troublemaker almost got Nyx killed. Shoot, she almost got Georgia killed, too, ratting her out to Allsop. Wherever she went, Morgan stirred up a hornet's nest.

With her wild eyes, tearstained face, and smudged makeup, Morgan looked downright pathetic. The wrinkled, grubby cocktail dress she wore probably cost $5000 before the pandemic. She tottered on ridiculously high heels.

The girl was a greedy, shallow, conniving little bitch.

But did she deserve to die for her crimes?

I sighed. No. No she didn't.

Morgan stamped her foot. "Come on, Bear. Cut me down."

He tapped the blade against his palm. "I cut you down, then what?"

Bet he was wondering what mischief she'd get up to next. Morgan had a gift for coming up roses. If he showed her mercy, would he live to regret it?

She misunderstood his question. Tossing her dark hair, she smiled coquettishly at him. "Let me go and I'll make it worth your while, big guy."

Jesus Christ, the ego on the woman. Had she forgotten that Bear shot down all of her unsubtle come-ons during our mission in Prineville?

My brother's face wore the expression of a man who'd stepped barefoot on cat puke.

"The very last thing I want is for you to make it *worth my while*," he drawled.

"Then what do you want?" She pouted.

"I cut you down and let you go, you do what you do best. Look out for number one. In this case, that means you get out of town and never look back. If I see your face again, you'll be sorry."

"We'll do it." The young man strung up next to Morgan spoke up, his voice shrill and reedy. "We'll leave town. Head south. You'll never see us again, I promise."

Looks like Morgan propositioned Bear under her boyfriend's nose. I couldn't pretend to be surprised.

Georgia pointed at the guy. "That's Jonesy's nephew, Noah. He was helping him stage a coup against Allsop."

"Is that so?" Bear raised a brow.

"I... I was just along for the ride," Noah blustered. "I was never the brains of the operation. Ask my uncle."

"Worthless piece of shit," Jonesy snarled.

Georgia rolled her eyes. "Between them, Morgan and Noah don't have two brain cells to rub together. If we let them go, they'll be lucky to survive a month on their own."

Bear considered her words, his lower lip jutting out. "Well, all right. Just remember, gone means gone. You'll stay the hell out of the new free state."

"Yes, sir." Noah bobbed his head. "We surely will."

Bear sliced their ropes and freed their arms. Hand in hand, the pair skedaddled. I hoped to God this was the last time I ever laid eyes on Morgan.

A familiar face pushed through the agitated crowd. I elbowed Georgia and pointed to the man climbing the scaffold stairs.

"Reno." Georgia's face lit up with happiness, and she rushed over to hug her fellow spy. "I thought for sure Allsop would arrest you when you got back to the house."

"He would've, except Winnie snuck out of the house and waited at the bottom of the driveway to give me a head's-up. Jonesy had sent me to Idaho Falls, and I got back after midnight."

"Thank God for Winnie." Georgia pressed a hand to her chest.

"I hid out in an empty building till this morning. Once I was sure Allsop and his guards had left for the damned celebration, I went back to the mansion. They'd left only a skeleton crew. I got the jump on them. Then Winnie helped me move all the weapons and ammo from the armory into the back of an SUV." He paused, regret etched across his features. "I didn't think I could stop the executions by myself, but I could deprive Allsop of his armory."

"You did good," I said.

"Where's Winnie?" Georgia asked.

"In the SUV, hoping for a ride to Pendleton."

"Now that the reunion is over, how about me?" Jonesy's voice was surprisingly friendly. "You going to cut me down, too, son?"

Bear jabbed the knife under Jonesy's chin, his expression flinty. "You think I'd free the man who tortured my little brother?"

Jonesy's defiant grin deflated. He shrugged. "Seeing how you're in a forgiving mood, I figured it was worth a try."

I met the eyes of the sadist who'd burned me. "If I were you, I wouldn't look for forgiveness. You got a lot of sins to atone for."

Jonesy hadn't lost his bluster, but with his arms bound and a noose around his neck, he looked diminished. Nothing like the boogeyman who'd haunted my nightmares. I doubt he'd ever bedevil my dreams again.

"Leave him there," Georgia said. "Let Havoc decide what to do with him."

I turned my gaze to the podium, where only a few minutes ago Allsop was gloating over his successes. His henchmen sprawled on the capitol's stone steps, felled by sniper fire. But the top man himself, where was he? I looked over the remnants of the crowd.

Ripper ran toward the podium. He caught my eye and pointed to the side of the building. "Allsop," he shouted.

"Bear, can you and Kyle and Reno watch Jonesy?" Georgia asked.

"Of course."

Kyle stepped aside as Georgia led the way down the stairs. "Good luck," he called.

Dashing after Ripper, we rounded the capitol building. Three shots rang out. A man—not Ripper thank God—stumbled and fell to the pavement in the middle of State Street. We cautiously drew close. I recognized the guy. Allsop's bodyguard. He must've taken a shot at Ripper, who put him down.

An office building surrounded by trees and overgrown grass lay straight ahead. Through a break in the trees, I saw Allsop running across the knee-high grass with Ripper hot on his heels.

Georgia and I hit the grass, then skidded to a stop.

Allsop backed up to a tree, both of his arms raised in the air. "I surrender."

Ripper cocked his head to one side, studying the dethroned dictator like he was a particularly interesting variety of bug.

"I'm… I'm unarmed," Allsop sputtered.

"Yeah?" Ripper sounded unimpressed.

It occurred to me that my friend might haul off and shoot the asshole where he stood. Much as I sympathized with the impulse, we were the good guys. We had to do better than that.

I laid a hand on Ripper's arm.

He shook me off.

"We should take him to Havoc," Georgia said quietly.

The biker's expressionless eyes remained locked on his quarry. "You think?"

The deadpan response unnerved Allsop. "Surely you… you… wouldn't kill... an unarmed man," he stammered.

Ripper raised one powerful shoulder. "Wouldn't I?"

Allsop stumbled backward. A dark stain spread over the crotch of his pants. Liquid dribbled down his leg and pooled by his polished shoes.

Good God, the aristocratic bastard actually pissed himself.

Allsop's hand scrabbled wildly at his pocket.

I reached for my weapon. By the time my fingers closed over the grip, Ripper had fired.

A fountain of blood erupted from the base of Allsop's neck. He toppled over, pressing a fluttering hand to his throat.

Ripper calmly walked over and shot again, right in the middle of Allsop's forehead.

He glanced over his shoulder at me. "Insurance shot."

My daddy's voice echoed in my mind: *Every good hunter knows you have to make sure the deer is dead. You have to deliver the insurance shot, son.*

Was Ripper a good hunter?

Had he deliberately goaded his quarry into reaching for his weapon, justifying the kill? If he had, I almost didn't want to know.

Georgia bent over, picked up a small pistol, and held it up. "He had a gun."

My heart kicked against my chest, relief making me weak. I braced my hands on my knees and sent a silent thank you to heaven. My conscience would've had a hard time reconciling the notion of a friend shooting an unarmed man, even a monster like Allsop.

"His people need to see he's dead." Ripper hoisted Allsop's body over his shoulder and started back toward the front of the capitol.

Georgia took my hand. We silently followed behind Ripper.

Havoc and Reno stood in front of the Liberty Bell, surrounded by his soldiers and the Nampa Boys. They stopped talking and watched us approach.

"Fucker drew on us." Ripper slung the corpse onto the ground.

Havoc nudged the body with his boot. "Good riddance to bad rubbish."

"Amen." David spat on the ground.

"We gotta cut the head off the snake." Ripper fixed his eyes on the scaffold. "Jonesy needs to die."

"Yeah, you're right." Havoc crossed his arms over his chest. "He's too dangerous to leave alive. And he deserves to pay for his crimes."

"He's strung up and ready to go," Ripper said. "All we have to do is pull the lever."

Havoc met my eyes. "Finn. It's personal for you. You want to do the honors?"

I stepped backward. "The fact that it's personal for me is precisely why I shouldn't do the honors. An execution is about justice, not vengeance. At least it should be."

"You're a better man than I am," Ripper told me, then he turned to Havoc. "I got no problem doing it."

"Let me," David urged. "Payback is sweet."

"No." Havoc's head sliced left, then right. "Finn's right. This needs to be about justice, not getting even. This is on me."

He wheeled around and strode toward the gallows, Ripper at his side. After a beat—I had absolutely no desire to watch—Georgia and I followed. Reno, our soldiers, the Nampa Boys, and a couple dozen citizens assembled at the base of the scaffold. Bear and Kyle joined us. Havoc spoke quietly to Jonesy. My brother clamped a hand on my shoulder.

"Shit," Kyle muttered. "If anybody deserves to die, it's Jonesy… but an execution..."

"Yeah," I agreed. "Shit."

Georgia grabbed my hand. "It's hard, but the world will be better off without him. His death is the only way to make sure he never hurts anybody else the way… the way he hurt you."

Her voice trembled on the final words.

"You want a blindfold?" Havoc asked Jonesy.

"A blindfold?" Jonesy scoffed. "Hell, no. I'm no pussy." He leered down at Georgia. "Although I wouldn't mind a kiss from the pretty girl, a condemned man's last wish, you know."

Georgia's spine snapped straight. "The pretty girl?" Her mouth twisted. "You think you're smart—a master manipulator—but it looks like you haven't figured it out yet. *I* played *you.* You're the clueless chump I manipulated. And now you're going to die knowing that you were outsmarted by a *pretty girl.*"

"It was worth a shot." Jonesy blew her a kiss.

"Any final words?"

"You bet." Jonesy gaze swept over the folks gathered to witness his death. "Fuck you all." He glanced at Havoc. "I said my piece. Now do it."

I sucked in a breath, refusing to look away. Georgia took my hand, her fingers locking around mine.

Havoc pulled the lever. The trapdoor sprung open. Jonesy plummeted through the opening. The rope snapped taut. His body spun in a counterclockwise motion for five or six turns, his head canted at an unnatural angle.

I swallowed the bile rising in my gorge, then closed my eyes.

"The war's over," Havoc called. "Now the rebuilding begins."

FORTY-NINE

Georgia

The next few hours passed in a blur of activity.

Allsop and Jonesy were dead, their corpses suspended from the gibbet for all to see, a ghoulish, but necessary display in a world without television or the internet. Marcus snapped a dozen Polaroids of the bodies, proof of death that our soldiers could show people in outlying areas.

Marcus, Finn, and I took a contingent of soldiers to the downtown hotel that served as barracks for the bulk of Allsop's men. I'd worked undercover as a housekeeper there during the early days of the occupation, at the same time that Finn had infiltrated Allsop's inner circle.

Two spies who didn't know of each other's existence. And now we were the center of each other's worlds.

"It's a done deal." Marcus slapped a photo of Allsop's body down in front of Captain Mataraci, the commander of the installation.

A bold assertion, part truth and part bluff. Allsop's surviving soldiers outnumbered our forces, but the deaths of their leader and his top people took the wind out of their sails. Allsop's brutal regime was a cult of personality. Without the leader to hold the reins, I doubted it could survive. Many of his surviving men looked relieved when informed of his death. They shrugged and turned over their weapons.

Captain Mataraci saw the writing on the wall and surrendered.

Havoc took a hard line with our allies, the Nampa Boys.

"You'll have a part to play in rebuilding Boise. You've earned a place at the table, but the time for vengeance is over," he sternly told David and the Nampa Boys.

"We can live with that." David extended a hand to Havoc.

After parting ways with the Nampa Boys, Finn, Bear, Ripper, Reno, Kyle, and I huddled together with Marcus.

"I've stationed soldiers to guard the warehouses," Havoc said. "They're filled to the rafters with essential supplies. We won't allow looting."

Finn nodded. "I've seen the warehouses. Allsop hoarded everything: food, medicine, booze. His personal warehouse is stuffed with luxury goods. You'll probably want to share the contents with other communities."

"Exactly."

Ripper caught Havoc's eye. "Now that Allsop's finished, we wanna get back to our family. They're waiting to hear if we're alive or dead."

Havoc scrubbed a weary hand over his jaw. "Yeah. I was hoping some of you might decide to stay in Pendleton."

"Nope." Bear answered for the group. "Valhalla is home, at least for most of us."

I glanced at Finn. He smiled, his eyes gleaming. Slinging an arm across my shoulders, he pulled me to his side. He dropped a kiss on my temple, then his lips found my ear.

"Valhalla *is* home, isn't it angel?" he whispered.

I nodded, so happy I could burst. After months of fear and uncertainty, our future was full of promise. I'd build a life with the man I loved, surrounded by good friends, by family.

"Olivia and I will be staying in Pendleton. Although—" Reno shot a smile at Ripper. "We will want to visit the ranch."

Ripper dipped his head. "Anytime, brother."

"I'll be glad to have you," Marcus told Reno. "We have a lot to do in the coming months. We'll reach out to survivors in the cities that Allsop's forces occupied—Bend, Spokane, Coeur d'Alene—and let them know he's gone. Justin will take charge in Boise, at least temporarily."

"My hometown will be in good hands," Kyle said with satisfaction. "Sunny will be happy to hear it."

"Gonna take a while to put together a new state," Ripper rumbled. "To determine the borders. To get survivors to buy in. No matter what you do, you won't please everybody."

"It'll be a challenge," Havoc conceded. "Baker City, Walla Walla, the Tri-Cities, folks there are already on board. We'll spread the word. Hold town hall meetings across the region. Reaffirm the Constitution. Eventually, we'll hold elections and reestablish the three branches of government."

"Whew." Finn blew out a breath. "Is that all? And don't forget, you'll want to restore electricity and water, too."

"Right. Build a new state and bring back the power grid." Havoc groaned. "You sure you guys don't want to stay and help?"

"You need us, we'll come," Bear said. "But we plan to do our bit by making Valhalla the premier cattle-raising operation in the Pacific Northwest Republic."

"Feeding folks is a worthy cause." Havoc smiled. "Maybe when things settle down, I'll visit the ranch myself."

"And bring Sara." I batted my eyes at Marcus. Would he confirm what we all suspected, that the doctor and soldier were falling in love?

Havoc's lips quirked. He saw right through me. "I'll ask her. In fact, a ranch might be a nice place for a honeymoon."

Finn whooped and pounded Marcus on the back.

Bear grinned. "A nice place for a honeymoon or even a marriage ceremony. We had two weddings there the day before yesterday."

Finn and I whirled to face his brother. "What weddings?"

"Didn't I tell you? Nyx and I, and Kyle and Sunny got hitched."

Finn's jaw dropped. "You got married and I missed it?"

"You, Ever, Mrs. B., and Kenzie all missed it." Bear winced. "I suspect come spring we'll all be renewing our vows."

I stood on my tip-toes and kissed Bear on the cheek. "Congratulations."

"Thank you, little sister."

Bear called me sister. My heart swelled. I dashed happy tears from my eyes, then kissed Kyle, too.

"We're heading back to Pendleton." Ripper brought the subject back to our departure. "What do you want us to tell your people?"

"Tell them exactly what happened here. Ask Justin to bring two dozen soldiers to Boise, to keep the peace during the transition."

"Will do."

Dark had fallen by the time Finn, Bear, Ripper, Reno, Kyle, and I took off for Pendleton. Reno and Kyle rode with Winnie in the SUV loaded with weapons from Allsop's armory. The rest of us piled into another SUV.

The sight of two Allsop vehicles approaching the freeway exit to Pendleton caused quite a stir. Armed soldiers surrounded our SUVs. It made sense. If the confrontation in Boise had gone the other way, we might well have been enemy soldiers. Our people were right to be cautious.

Rachel, Justin, Thanh, and Sara were all at headquarters, waiting for news of the battle. When we pulled up in front of the city hall complex, they rushed outside to greet us.

"I'll fill you all in tomorrow morning," Reno called to our waiting friends. "For now, I'm gonna go home to Olivia."

"And I'm off to find Sunny." Kyle waved to the group.

Without a word, Ripper took off for the motel and his reunion with Kenzie.

Finn and I woke up this morning with the threat of execution hanging over our heads. And now we ended the day safely back in Pendleton with our friends. Tired, emotionally spent, my legs trembling, I climbed out of the back seat, clinging to Finn's hand.

I met the eyes of the man I loved. "We did it. We survived to live another day."

"Better than that." Finn's smile warmed me down to my toes. "We survived to love another day."

"I'm so damned happy to see you." Rachel threw her arms around my neck, then took my hand and pulled me toward the door to city hall. "Tell me everything that happened since you left town."

We trooped to our new meeting room and took seats around the conference table. For the next hour, we spelled out exactly what had gone down since Reno and I fled Pendleton with Jonesy. Finn chimed in with his own details about his capture and incarceration.

Rachel paled and pressed her hand over her mouth when we described standing on the scaffold with nooses around our necks, then cheered when we told her both Allsop and Jonesy were dead.

The conversation wound down.

Rachel tapped my shoulder. "Come help me fetch a bottle of tequila from my office. We'll all do shots before we say goodnight."

Shots would knock me on my ass.

Come to think of it, that didn't seem like a bad thing. I walked with Rachel to her office. She pulled a bottle of tequila from her bottom drawer.

"You really okay, girlfriend?" Concern puckered her brows.

"Yeah, I am." I made a face. "You couldn't pay me to relive the past few days, but I'm getting my happy ever after, so I have no complaints." Happy ever after. A question occurred to me. "How is Justin doing with the whole Lorelei spying for Allsop thing? Do you think he'll ever forgive her?"

Rachel threw her hands in the air. "Honestly, I don't know. He won't talk about it or visit her in jail. He was falling in love with her. She didn't tell him she was being blackmailed." Rachel shrugged helplessly. "I don't know what the future holds for them."

So no happy ever afters all around, at least not yet.

I yawned, exhaustion smacking me upside the head. "Let's get back to the conference room and have our shots, then I really need to sleep."

We rejoined the others, downed our tequila, then Finn, Bear, and I retired to the motel. Bear had the key to an empty room on the ground floor. On the second floor, a lantern was lit in Ripper and Kenzie's room. Finn and I knocked on the door and quietly made plans to caravan back to Valhalla in the morning.

A light came on in Mrs. B. and Ever's room. The door opened and Mrs. B. stepped outside. Smiling, she patted Finn's cheeks. "Thank goodness you're back in one piece. I've been beside myself with worry."

"It was rough going for a while, but at the end, we all made it through fine."

"Bloody but unbowed," she murmured, turning to hug me.

Finn's eyebrows squished together. "Ma'am?"

She waved a hand. "A line from a favorite old poem."

"We'll be heading home bright and early tomorrow morning," he told her.

"Wonderful news." She hesitated. "May I ask a favor?"

"Of course."

"I can't leave town without saying goodbye to a dear friend."

Anton Milewski. She was talking about Anton Milewski.

Finn figured it out, too. "You know, if you want to invite Anton to the ranch—for a visit or something else—you'd be welcome to. He's a fine man, and we all want you to be happy."

"Thank you, dear boy."

Our conversation roused the kids.

"They're back?" Ever scrambled through the open door and flung herself on Finn. "Did you miss me?"

"More than peanut butter misses jelly," he said, swinging her around. "More than a dog misses his bone."

Ever giggled. "More than Fitzwilliam misses Hector? More than Mrs. B. misses Jaffa cakes?"

"Yep. That much and more."

"Izzy," Ever called. "Come say hi to Finn and Georgia."

A dark-haired little girl peeked out from behind Mrs. B. "Hi."

"Hiya, kiddo. Looks like you and my little sweet pea have become good friends."

"Best friends," Izzy agreed.

Ever tugged on Finn's coat sleeve. "If I'm your little sweet pea, what can Izzy be?"

"Hmmm… that's a good question." Finn cocked his head, then snapped his fingers and pointed at Izzy. "I know. How about my little marigold?"

Both girls giggled.

"Off to bed with you both." Mrs. B. clapped her hands.

"Good night, sweet pea. Good night, marigold," Finn said. "You need your sleep because we're leaving early in the morning for Valhalla."

"Izzy, too?" Ever asked, wide-eyed.

"Izzy, too." Finn glanced at me, then spoke in a low voice. "While you were with Rachel, I asked Havoc how the little girl was doing. He said Ever and Izzy are inseparable, so I offered to take her to Valhalla with us, at least until things are settled with Lorelei. Or maybe forever."

My heart turned over in my chest. Every day I found something new to love about this man. This kind, heroic, thoughtful man.

"We'll see you in the morning." I smiled at Mrs. B. and the girls, then laid a hand on Finn's chest. "But now, I want to fall asleep in your arms."

His eyes sparkled. "There's nothing I'd like better."

We were too tired to warm our hot-water bottles. Body heat would have to suffice to keep us warm. We stripped out of our jackets and clothes. Teeth chattering, we climbed under the covers. Finn spooned me, pressing his muscular chest against my back.

With a happy sigh, I snuggled against my man. My eyes were heavy, my body limp. I summoned just enough energy to speak. "Query: What's your favorite place in the whole wide world?"

Finn's arm tightened around my waist. His hand slid up over my ribs and cupped my breast. The bristles on his chin tickled my shoulder, and I wriggled against him. His cock stirred.

"That's easy, angel." His low, sexy voice was drowsy and content. "Now and forever, my favorite place is by your side."

FIFTY

Finn

A Few Weeks Later

I walked into the front room, and an echo of the past—a bittersweet mix of memory and nostalgia—knocked me off my stride.

Sunny and Nyx had spread a plastic tablecloth over the coffee table, just like my mama used to do when we decorated Christmas cookies. But now, instead of cookies, frosting, and sprinkles, the table was covered with construction paper, glue sticks, colored markers, and tubes of glitter. Instead of two towheaded little boys sitting on the floor spreading icing on cookies, two little girls bent over their homemade valentines.

The thread of continuity linking the past to the present jerked tight.

"You got glitter on your nose, sweet pea," I observed.

Ever tossed me a lopsided smile. Her new canine tooth had finally made an appearance, although it had a ways to go before it filled in the gap. "Izzy got glitter *up* her nose. That's worse. She sneezed three times."

"You okay, marigold?" I asked.

I'd figured out pretty quickly that when I called one of the girls by her nickname, I'd better call the other by hers, or somebody's nose got out of joint. Whether taking turns picking a story for bedtime, or comparing the size of their slices of pie, both girls were obsessed with things being fair.

Izzy wrinkled up her face. "Yeah. It was only a little bit, and I blew all the glitter out."

"I'm going to ask Sahdev to stick a scope up her nose to check out the glitter situation," Nyx said. She and Sunny were sitting on the floor across from the girls, supervising the valentine-making operation.

Izzy held up a folded piece of pink construction paper. On the front, she had drawn a figure of a tall, shaggy-haired man wearing a black vest. In his arms, he held a fluffy tan-and-white cat with big blue eyes. At least a dozen red hearts were scattered across the front of the card.

"It's for Alejandro," she said.

To Ripper's bemusement, the little girl had adopted him as her "favoritest grown-up in the whole wide world."

"Ripper will love it." Sunny smiled at the little girl.

"You did a good job." I admired the card. "Looks like you girls will be ready for the Valentine's Day celebration tonight."

"We will," Ever said. "Kenzie and Ripper are making heart-shaped pizzas. And Hannah and Levi are baking cupcakes with pink frosting."

"Nice."

"And Bear found your great-grandpa's windup gramophone in the attic and a bunch of old record albums." Ever bounced up and down in excitement. "He said we can have a dance party tonight."

Great-Grandpa had collected a whole passel of 1940s swing music records. When I was a kid, my father sometimes hauled the old gramophone down from the attic. He'd push the couch against the wall, roll up the carpet in the front room, then the four of us would dance to Benny Goodman and Artie Shaw and Count Basie. Mama and Daddy had taken swing dance lessons and liked to "cut a rug" to the old music. Bear and I danced with energy, but no attempt at style. We stomped our feet, twirled around, and waved our arms over our heads, hooting and hollering to the music. What we lacked in finesse we made up for with unbridled gusto. A Rasmussen Rumpus, that's what my folks called our dance parties. It warmed my heart to think of reviving the family tradition.

"Bear said he found another cool surprise in the attic, but he won't tell us what it is until tonight," Izzy added, pouting.

Nyx looked up from her drawing. "It'll be worth the wait, kiddo."

"How come you know about the surprise and we don't?" Ever demanded.

"Because a smart man doesn't keep secrets from his wife," Nyx said.

Ever narrowed her eyes, then swung her gaze to me. I saw the wheels turning in her head and guessed what was coming. "Are you and Georgia ever going to get married?"

I had absolutely no doubt that I'd spend the rest of my life loving Georgia, or that she felt the same way. But marriage? We hadn't talked much about it, choosing to savor each step along our journey from friendship to true love. Most likely we'd get to marriage by and by, but there was no need to hurry.

"Tell you what, sweet pea. If Georgia and I decide to get married, we'll let you know first thing."

"And me, too?" Izzy asked.

"You bet, marigold."

That promise placated the girls, who went back to their valentine-making.

"You know where Georgia is?" I asked Sunny.

"She's at the bunkhouse making soap with Jenn."

"I'll head on over there."

When we got back to Valhalla a few weeks ago, Sean Darragh, the former Marine, asked if he and his girlfriend Jenn—another soldier sent to defend the ranch—could stay at Valhalla. They turned the old bunkhouse into their private quarters.

Both possessed practical skills. Sean was one smart son of a bitch. He'd been a combat engineer in the Corps. He brought the same energy and can-do attitude to working on the ranch.

Before the pandemic, Jenn had an Etsy shop where she sold homemade soap. Soap was essential for keeping clean and staving off infections in the post-pandemic world. Beef tallow and wood ash, that's all you needed to make it. Valhalla had both. In a barter economy, soap was good as gold.

I walked across the yard, past the big barn, the tractor shed, and the machine shop to the bunkhouse. Ripper asked that Kenzie and the little girls not be exposed to fumes from the lye, so Jenn confined her soap making to the bunkhouse. The door and windows stood open, allowing fresh air into the place.

"Knock, knock," I called, stepping across the threshold. Georgia and Jenn looked up from the big stainless steel pot of lye and beef fat simmering on top of the woodstove. They'd tied western bandanas over their noses and mouths, and wore goggles and rubber gloves. I pointed to their red paisley bandanas. "You two look like bandits about to rob a stagecoach."

"Hey, baby." The corners of Georgia's eyes crinkled, so I knew she was smiling underneath her neckerchief. "We're almost ready to add dried lavender to the batter, then we'll pour the soap into the molds."

I crossed the room and peered into the pot. The soap batter looked like thick oatmeal. "Yum."

Georgia bumped her shoulder against mine. I brushed newly blond hair back from her forehead and dropped a kiss on her temple. Nyx had helped her bleach the brown dye from her hair, then they applied a color close to her natural blond. The brown hair had been pretty, but Georgia said it reminded her of Jonesy, and she wanted to get back to her old self.

I think we were all ready to let go of Jonesy and Allsop and get on with our lives.

"I can finish up if you want to go with Finn," Jenn offered, not pausing as she stirred the soap mixture.

Georgia shook her head. "No, thanks. I like to see projects through to the end. Besides, I wouldn't leave you to clean up the mess by yourself."

That was my cue. "I'm going to get out of your way. I'll see you ladies at supper."

I hugged Georgia goodbye, waved at Jenn, then went looking for my brother. On a hunch, I checked the stables and found Bear inside the tack room, applying leather conditioner to a saddle.

He tilted his head toward the workbench. "You can wipe down the buckles and metal fittings."

"Sure thing." I picked up a dry cloth and started polishing the metal. Never chatty, Bear was content to keep his mouth shut and work in silence. Ten minutes of quiet was as much as I could take. "I missed this," I said. "Working side by side with you on the ranch."

Bear grunted his agreement.

Smiling to myself, I tried again. "Reminds me of the old days before the pandemic, you and me, cleaning out the stable, taking care of the tack."

Bear raised a brow. "Glad you feel that way. When we're done here, you can help me muck out the stalls and put down fresh bedding."

"Be happy to," I said.

Bear's eyebrow shot back up. My big brother knew that forking out manure and urine-soaked straw was one of my least favorite chores. "You would, huh?"

"Yep." I paused and shoved a hand through my hair. "After everything that happened in Boise—after coming *this* close to losing it all—I'll never complain about shoveling shit again."

Bear set down his rag. "We came waaay too close to losing you, brother. And more than once."

"The flu. The Wilcox Brigade. Allsop. Jonesy. I survived 'em all. I feel like the luckiest cuss who ever lived."

"A walking, talking miracle," Bear agreed.

I flashed a grin. "And now I have Georgia, and you have Nyx. Life is good, brother."

"Amen to that."

I spent the next couple of hours working alongside Bear. We stopped in time to get cleaned up for supper and the Valentine's Day party.

Seventeen souls gathered around the long trestle table in the dining room. Eighteen, if you counted Ripper and Kenzie's baby.

We'd found kits for making mozzarella cheese when we cleared out the farm store. Levi and Topher decided to add cheese making to their repertoire of useful skills, so we had fresh mozzarella for our pizza, not the freeze-dried stuff. Fresh cheese. Sometimes the littlest things brought the greatest pleasure.

After a dinner of heart-shaped pizza and pink cupcakes, we all headed to the front room. Bear and I scooted the couches out of the way and rolled up the rug, creating a dance floor in the middle of the room.

"What's the surprise?" Ever asked, eyeing the old trunk Bear had hauled down from the attic.

Bear lifted the lid and stepped back. "Ta-da." With a flourish, he gestured at the contents of the trunk.

Ever and Izzy rushed over and peered inside. Ever squealed.

"Fancy hats! Are they for playing dress up?" Izzy asked.

"Great-Grandma had a weakness for fancy hats," Bear said. "She wore one to church every Sunday."

"After Grandma passed, Mama put them away in the attic," I added. "Mama never liked dressy clothes, but she said the hats were too pretty to throw out."

Ever took out a lavender one covered with silk pansies and plopped it on her head. Izzy tried on a straw hat with lacquered cherries, apples, and bananas circling the brim.

"Come pick out a hat, everybody," Ever called.

Folks gathered around the trunk. Nyx laid claim to a green velvet hat shaped like a turban. Mrs. B. chose a satin one covered with pink rosebuds. Georgia selected an elegant black one with a wide brim and a single swooping feather.

"You look beautiful." I ducked under the brim and kissed her.

Ever skipped across the room, carrying a yellow hat studded with rhinestones and sporting a jaunty bow with a daisy in the middle. "Try it on," she ordered, holding it out to me.

"You think that's going to fit on my fat noggin?" I asked.

Ever giggled, nodding.

"Well, all right." I slapped it on my head and fastened it to my hair with the little combs build into the side of the hat. It was a mite small, but with the combs, it wasn't going anywhere. "What do you think?" I asked, preening.

"I like it. Will you wear it while we dance?"

"You bet I will." I clapped my hands. "Everybody on your feet for a Rasmussen Rumpus."

"A what?" Kenzie asked, laughing. A cobalt-blue velvet hat dotted with pearls perched atop her glossy hair.

"A Rasmussen Rumpus," I repeated. "A happy dance. A wild cavort. You don't need to know any fancy steps. Just kick up your heels and have fun."

Bear cranked the old gramophone and set the needle on the record. The rollicking chords of the "Chattanooga Choo Choo" filled the room. Bear bowed and extended a hand to Nyx, who curtsied and joined him on the dance floor.

Kenzie laid a hand on her belly. "Okay, sprout. Ready for your first wild cavort?" She shot a glance at Ripper, who looked like he'd rather be anywhere else. "You going to dance with me, Mr. Solis?"

Ripper's expression softened. He inclined his head. The black leather beanie he wore—probably the most sedate hat in Great-Grandma's collection—slid down his dark hair. He caught it before it hit the floor, then tossed the beanie onto a couch.

He held out a hand to his wife. "My pleasure, Mrs. Solis."

We all took to the dance floor. Ever, Izzy, and Topher stomped and clapped their hands over their heads. Sahdev led Mrs. B. in an incongruous sort of waltz. Hannah and Levi performed some form of the Charleston. The rest of us twirled, bopped, and hoofed it from one side of the room to the other. Even Hector joined in the fun, throwing back his head and bouncing on his front paws. Only Fitzwilliam was a spoilsport. Tail held high, he stalked from the room as if offended by the undignified commotion.

Bear played record after record. We danced until we wore ourselves out. After we finished, Ever and Izzy distributed handmade valentines to everybody. We all oohed and aahed over the girls' handiwork. Ripper solemnly promised Izzy that her valentine would go in a place of honor on his dresser.

Afterwards, Bear and I restored order to the front room. Topher and Levi wandered off to the kitchen to look for leftover cupcakes. Nyx and Jenn insisted on taking a turn cleaning up after supper. Ripper escorted a yawning Kenzie to bed. With a "Goodnight, dear ones," Mrs. B. retired to her room. Lured by the promise of an extra-long story time, Ever and Izzy followed Sunny to their bedroom. Sahdev and Hannah set up the Parcheesi board and cajoled Kyle and Sean into joining their game.

"Gonna go pay my respects to the folks before I hit the hay," Bear said. "You want to come?"

I often joined him during his nightly visits to the Rasmussen cemetery. We'd sit together on the marble bench under the branches of a crabapple tree next to our parents' grave. With so many people now calling Valhalla home, this was our quiet time, when we'd talk brother-to-brother. We'd reminisce about the old days, before the deadly flu virus shattered the world. We'd laugh over family stories.

Strategize about how best to run the ranch. Share our joys and our woes, our hopes for the future.

I was raised to count my blessings. The fact that I had a brother who was alive and well—a near-miracle in the post-pandemic world—was a piece of good fortune that nearly brought me to my knees with gratitude.

"Not tonight," I said. "I want to give Georgia her valentine. How about you and I have coffee early tomorrow morning instead?"

"It's a plan." Bear clasped my shoulder. "Goodnight, brother."

"'Night."

I held out a hand to Georgia. "Got a surprise for you."

"I have one for you, too." She rolled her eyes. "A little one, that is."

"Now you got me curious." I snagged a solar lantern from the hall table. Side by side, we walked toward our bedroom. Once inside, I shut the door and set the lantern on the dresser.

Our room reflected the coming together of our lives. Georgia's Christmas quilt covered a Rasmussen brass bed. We'd brought her green area rugs and Rossetti prints from Pendleton. My maple dresser and bookcase stood against the walls. Our books and mementos mingled together on the shelves. By a stroke of luck, Nyx had found the missing photograph of Bear and me standing behind bars in the Pendleton Underground jail. That photo now sat atop the dresser, right next to the one of Georgia wearing her Little League uniform.

I sat on the edge of the mattress and patted the spot next to me. Eyes sparkling with curiosity, Georgia sat down.

"Can I go first?" she asked.

"Of course you can."

Sucking in a breath, she dug in the pocket of her sky-blue hoodie, then held out a clenched fist.

"What you got there?" I asked.

She squirmed, appearing slightly abashed. "The more I think about it, the more I realize that this is a dumb present."

"Whatever it is, I bet I'll love it."

"Okay." She dragged out the word, then opened up her hand. In the middle of her palm sat a red lump made of yarn.

"Huh." I rubbed my chin, my mind scrambling to figure out what I was looking at so I could be appropriately impressed with my gift.

Georgia groaned. "Mrs. B. helped me make it."

I picked up the mysterious lump. As I examined it—a crocheted circle with loops on either side—its function dawned on me. My lips twitched. I placed the red circle over my nose, then slid the yarn loops over my ears, securing it in place.

"You crocheted me a nose cozy," I exclaimed.

"My first project. It's a little wonky—"

I shook my head. "It's perfect. I love it."

"I crocheted one for me, too, so we can match."

"Thank you." Sliding my hand around her nape, I hauled her close and pressed my mouth against hers. My tongue traced the seam of her lips, then delved inside. I tasted the sweet strawberry jam from the cupcake frosting. With a moan, I deepened the kiss.

Georgia yanked her head away. She slipped the yarn loops from around my ears and tossed the nose cozy aside. "I'm glad you like it, but a red nose isn't exactly conducive to romance."

"What? You never had a clown fetish?"

She batted my shoulder, laughing. "No. I've never had a thing for clowns, but cowboys… now that's a different story."

"Lucky me." I reached for her again.

"Hold on." She raised a hand. "You said something about a surprise."

"That's right." I opened the drawer to the nightstand, took out a folded piece of heavy art paper, and handed it to Georgia.

She held it up to the light, admiring the image on the front of the card. A golden-haired angel—wings outstretched—held a red heart in her cupped hands. "Finn," Georgia breathed. "It's beautiful."

"I asked Nyx to draw an angel on your valentine."

Squinting, Georgia studied the image, then raised her eyes to meet mine. "She… she looks like me."

I nodded. "The first time I saw you, I thought you were an angel, remember?"

Her lips parted, like she wanted to speak, but no words came. She swallowed, the muscles in her throat working. Tears glistened in her eyes.

"And later on, after all the burns on my chest have healed, Nyx is going to tattoo this angel over my heart. You're part of me, Georgia. As long as I draw breath, I'll cherish you and hold you close."

The tears brimming in her eyes slipped down her cheeks. Her lips trembled. "I love you, Finn Rasmussen."

I smiled. "Love you, too, angel. Now and till the end of time."

EPILOGUE

Ripper

June

After a cool and rainy spring, summer arrived with a vengeance. Did I say arrived? No. The fucker kicked down our door and made itself at home. Day after day, bright sun and blistering heat.

Mac didn't complain, but I overheard her warn Sunny never to be nine months pregnant in the middle of a heat wave. She was sweating in places she didn't know she could sweat, she said. By nine o'clock most nights, she'd conked out, her swollen feet propped up on a pile of pillows.

Mrs. B. wilted in the hot weather too. She'd toddle out to the porch swing and spend hours swaying back and forth. Hector often kept her company, sleeping at her feet. Fitzwilliam opted to stay inside, sprawled belly-up on the hearth, soaking up the chill from the flat stones. Tells you everything you need to know about the difference between dogs and cats, doesn't it?

Anton Milewski kept Mrs. B. company too.

Six weeks after we returned to Valhalla, the retired teacher drove up to the gate, a suitcase and three boxes of books in tow. Said he'd advised Havoc on setting up the new state, then followed his heart to Valhalla. He dropped down on one creaky knee and asked "his beloved Cressida" to marry him.

Mac and Georgia swooned. Sunny welled up. Ever and Izzy asked to be flower girls. A few days later, Kyle and Finn walked Mrs. B. down the aisle. Well, actually, they escorted her across the front room to the big stone fireplace, where her smiling groom waited for her. We didn't have a minister, but Sahdev conducted the ceremony, and that was that. Another happy ending.

Ever asked if we should start calling her Mrs. M., but the old lady said she was sticking with Birdwhistle. Mrs. B. it was.

Anton didn't mind the summer heat, but he fussed over Mrs. B., bringing her water and swishing a fan to cool her down.

Hannah and Sunny devised handheld fans made out of folded paper and Popsicle sticks. The two little girls painted designs on them. Pink flowers for Mrs. B. A smiling man in the moon for Mac. Purple stars for Nyx. Yellow daisies for Sunny. Horses for Bear and Finn. What passed for a motorcycle on the one the girls solemnly presented to me.

The vegetable garden grew like gangbusters. Sahdev, Nyx, and Levi were out there early every morning, hauling water and tending to the plants. Reminded me of Miles's garden back in Portland. My friend would carry bucket after bucket of water to his carrots and beans and tomatoes. He'd fuss over the vegetables like they were old friends, give 'em pep talks, cajole them to grow.

Hell. Was that just one year ago?

Bear and Finn called the hot weather a good thing. Cows gotta eat come winter, and after the spring calving season, the herd was growing. The hot and dry weather was perfect for cutting, raking, and baling hay. Last month, we planted corn. We'd harvest it in August, chopping up the green plants for winter silage for the cows.

Ripper Solis, farmer. My Janissary brothers would bust a gut laughing. Shit, I hardly believed it myself. Never imagined I'd spend my days toiling on a ranch, but I don't mind hard physical labor. A man does whatever is necessary, that's how I was raised. And I loved the way my woman's eyes sparkled when I stripped off my shirt, all hot and sweaty, and flexed muscles sore from a hard day's work.

Working toward a common goal in the company of good friends, it wasn't a bad life. Kyle, Sahdev, Levi, Bear, Finn, Topher, they were my new brothers. Sean Darragh, too.

In the middle of the afternoon, on a sweltering day in late June, Finn and I stood on the platform built onto the top of the windmill, tightening a loose blade. In this heat, we gotta keep the water pump working at maximum efficiency.

Somebody banged on the cast-iron dinner bell.

Finn shot me a look. "It's too early for supper. Maybe somebody's at the gate?"

I cocked my head, listening.

The bell clanged again.

On a hunch, I climbed down the ladder and jogged toward the house. Finn followed me.

"Ripper." Georgia's voice carried across the yard. "Ripper, Kenzie needs you."

Mac needed me. That could mean only one thing. The baby was coming.

My step hitched, and I almost tripped. I was gonna be a father. Not the first time I realized that, of course, but the first time it hit home that it was happening *now*. The baby was no longer an abstract thing. It was coming. Today.

Don't let me fuck this up. Closest thing to a prayer I've said in eons.

Finn caught up with me. We raced around the tractor shed and past the big barn. Soon as we got within view of the porch, Georgia and Sunny waved.

"Kenzie's in labor," Georgia said.

I nodded, rushed past the women into the house, then stopped short. I expected to find Mac propped up in our bed, assuming the woman-about-to-give-birth position I've seen on TV. Instead, she sat in the rocking chair by the fireplace, her bare feet pushing against the floor, setting the chair in motion.

"Hey." She tossed me a smile.

I crossed to her side and crouched down. "What are you doing, darlin'?" Maybe the rocking somehow sped up the birthing process?

"Rocking."

Not a helpful response. I tried again. "Shouldn't you lie down?"

"No. Not yet." Damp tendrils of hair stuck to her forehead. She lifted her long hair away from her neck and fanned herself with her hand. "I wish it wasn't so hot."

"Lemme help." One of those paper fans sat on the coffee table. I snatched it up, dropped down onto the ottoman, and fanned Mac's overheated face.

She closed her eyes, tilted her head back, and let out a happy sigh. "That's nice. Thank you, baby."

"First time mothers typically are in labor for at least twelve hours." Sahdev came up behind me. "At this stage, the contractions are mild and irregular. Kenzie can go for a walk, putter around the house, even try to nap between the contractions."

"All right." Damn, but I was out of my element.

Finn, Georgia, and Sunny huddled together at the side of the room. "Can we do anything to help?" Sunny asked hesitantly.

Mac opened her eyes. "Thanks, Sunny, but I just want to spend time with Ripper right now—" She gasped and her mouth formed an O.

"A contraction?" I guessed.

"Yes. You want to feel?"

I laid my hand on the baby bump. Beneath my fingers, her belly felt tight and hard, then it relaxed.

"This is really happening." I heard the wonder in my voice.

"There's no going back now," Mac said with a grin, then she settled in the chair.

Never before in my life had I felt so helpless. I couldn't take command of the situation. Couldn't bend it to my will. All I could do was see it through till the end. Let Mac know that I got her back and that I'll stay at her side no matter what.

"What can I do?" I asked.

"Just be with me, okay?"

"Okay."

It was a promise I intended to keep. Now and for the rest of our lives.

Mac dozed off and on in the rocking chair. Good thing she got some rest while she could because her labor took twenty-two hours.

I read aloud to her. Massaged her back. Told stories about my childhood adventures. We walked up and down the long hall in the guest wing of the ranch. When a contraction hit, she'd dig her fingernails into my arm and lean against a wall while she breathed through the pain.

Childbirth ain't for pussies.

It got rough near the end. Her legs cramped and she felt nauseated. Fatigue and pain left Mac as limp as a wrung-out rag.

I made sure my face revealed nothing of my inner panic. Why the fuck was this taking so long? What if something went wrong? What if she hemorrhaged? What if she needed a C-section?

Nothing went wrong.

I sat behind Mac on the bed, supporting her back and murmuring words of encouragement while she pushed. Sahdev caught the baby, checked its airway, then clamped and cut the umbilical cord.

"It's a boy," Sahdev said. He lifted the baby onto Mac's bare belly and covered him with a blanket.

"It's a boy," Mac repeated, laughing. She touched the mop of dark hair that covered his head. "Look at him, Ripper." Her voice held a mixture of awe and pride. "He's so beautiful."

I stared at my son in disbelief, marveling at this little miracle we created.

"He's perfect," I said. Tears prickled the back of my eyes. I kissed my son's mother, the woman who held my heart, my old lady, my wife.

Sahdev wrapped the baby in the blanket and held him out to me. "Kenzie and I need a few more minutes here. There's a group of people waiting in the front room who are dying to meet our new arrival."

"Thank you, Sahdev. Thanks for everything, brother."

I took my son in my arms.

Mac and I picked out baby names months ago. After some debate, we decided that if the baby was a girl, we'd call her Clarissa, after my mother. For a boy, there was no need to weigh our options. Only one name would do.

"Hello, Miles Dunwitty Solis."

Don't know how well newborn babies can see, but I swear to God, my son looked right at me. Pewter-gray eyes, the same color as his mama's—the same color as the first Miles Dunwitty—solemnly studied me.

"I'm your daddy and that pretty woman over there is your mama. Someday, we'll tell you all about the man we named you after. Her cousin. My friend. One of the finest men who ever lived."

Miles blinked. A spit bubble popped between his lips.

For the second time in my life, I fell head over heels in love.

I kissed Mac again, then carefully carried Miles up the hall to the living room, where everybody waited for their first look at the baby. They crowded around, a sea of eager faces.

I angled my arm so they could see him. "Meet Miles."

Kyle drew in a sharp breath. Sunny took his hand. Kyle knew and loved the first Miles. "Hey, little dude." His voice shook. "I'm happy to meet you."

Everybody fussed and exclaimed over the baby.

"Can I hold him?" Ever asked.

"Soon, but not today," I said.

Bear lifted the old Bible down from its shelf. "Miles is the first baby of the post-pandemic generation." He glanced at Nyx. "Although he won't be the last, will he, sugar?"

Nyx batted his arm and widened her eyes. "Not now. Today is about Kenzie and Ripper and baby Miles."

Despite Nyx's protests, the cat was officially out of the bag. Finn fist-pumped the air. Georgia hugged Nyx. Everybody offered their congratulations.

Couldn't wait to tell Mac that Miles would have a friend close to his age on the ranch.

"We need to add Miles's name to the family Bible." Bear opened the leather volume.

With one hand, I held my son against my chest. With the other, I signed his name and birth date on the page, right under the signatures that marked Mrs. B. and Anton's marriage.

"With all the weddings and births, we'll be filling this up fast," I said.

"Life goes on." Finn smiled and hauled Georgia to his side.

I pulled back the blanket and touched the baby's palm. His fingers closed around mine. I wiggled my finger, but Miles held on tight. Tenacious. Resolute. Just like the best of humanity.

I lifted my eyes to my smiling friends, then looked again at my son. Gratitude and resolve filled my heart.

I have it all. At last. And I'm gonna keep it.

Thank you for reading *Requiem*. I hope you enjoyed it. If you have the time and inclination, please visit the site where you purchased it and leave a brief review.

Want more Susanna Strom?

Sign up for Susanna's newsletter for book news, sales announcements, and exclusive content. When you subscribe, you'll receive a free short story set in the World Fallen world. http://eepurl.com/h6WRRb

Join my readers group: https://www.facebook.com/groups/1572291033136914

Follow me on Facebook: https://www.facebook.com/susannastromauthor

Follow me on TikTok: https://www.tiktok.com/@susannastrom

Follow me on Instagram: https://www.instagram.com/susannastrom.author

ACKNOWLEDGMENTS

I'm grateful to the many people who offered support and assistance while I wrote *Requiem.*

Many thanks to my brilliant developmental editor, Christina Trevaskis, aka the Book Matchmaker. Tina brings decades of experience and expertise to our collaboration. With endless enthusiasm, she teaches me to craft better stories and encourages me to believe in myself.

A big thank you to my writing BFF, the very talented author Raven Dark. Raven is my go-to person for brainstorming, advice, and the occasional pep talk.

Brittany Meyer-Strom and Sharon Shook are a proofreading dream team. They tackle the process of hunting for typos and errors as if it were a treasure hunt. When they find an especially boneheaded mistake—Ripped instead of Ripper—good-natured ribbing ensues. Their skill and diligence have spared me much embarrassment.

Author Michael Aspen, of The Writing Guys Podcast fame, is one of the wisest and most generous people I've met during my writing journey. He's a fount of knowledge with a gift for breaking complex subjects down into manageable bits of information. He's patient, humble, and kind. I'm grateful for his friendship. Check out his podcast: https://anchor.fm/writing-guys

My writing mojo needed a tune-up when I started working on *Requiem*. Once again, I turned to author and Better Faster Academy coach, Milana Jacks. Milana reminded me of the importance of consistency and helped put my writing back on track.

A special thank you to Brooke Armstrong, Executive Director of the Pendleton Underground Tours. I called Brooke and asked permission to set a scene in my upcoming novel in the Pendleton Underground. She graciously took the time to give me a step-by-step description of the tour. If you'd like to follow in Finn and Georgia's footsteps, check out the Pendleton Underground Tours the next time you visit the city.

The wonderful Lori Jackson designed the cover for *Requiem* with an image from the fabulous Wander Aguiar.

Thanks to Imogen Keeper, H.R. Savage, and Jessica Gomez—all exceptionally talented authors of post-apocalyptic romance—for their advice, encouragement and support.

And finally, a big thank you to my husband, John Hoefer, who always encourages me to follow my dreams. I couldn't ask for a better, more supportive partner.